Being her employer, Gio had always been careful to keep his low-key arousal to himself, but everything about their relationship was changing, becoming far more personal.

"If I agree to those terms, will I have your solemn promise that you will never tell anyone about...?" She dropped her gaze to her thickening waistline.

"I can promise that." He held out his hand.

"Do we have an agreement?" he prodded. "Are you thinking about extorting more for the signing bonus first?"

"Don't be ridiculous. You're already being very generous. Thank you."

He snorted. "I'm not generous, Molly. Merely willing to pay the price required to get what I want."

Bound by a Surrogate Baby

Two couples. One baby. A billion-dollar scandal!

When secretary Molly agrees to be the surrogate for her best friend, heiress Sasha, she's giving her the greatest gift of all.

But what started as a simple act of kindness soon turns complicated when pregnant Molly gets promoted by her gorgeous Italian boss—to his convenient fiancée!

Don't miss Molly and Gio's story in
The Baby His Secretary Carries

Available now!

When Molly goes into early labor, it's time for Sasha to become a mother to her tiny son while finally facing the still-sizzling passion between her and her estranged husband!

Enjoy Sasha and Rafael's story

Coming soon!

Dani Collins

THE BABY HIS SECRETARY CARRIES

HARLEQUIN
PRESENTS

HARLEQUIN®
PRESENTS™

Recycling programs
for this product may
not exist in your area.

ISBN-13: 978-1-335-59318-4

The Baby His Secretary Carries

Copyright © 2024 by Dani Collins

For questions and comments about the quality of this book, please contact us at CustomerService@Harlequin.com.

Harlequin Enterprises ULC
22 Adelaide St. West, 41st Floor
Toronto, Ontario M5H 4E3, Canada
www.Harlequin.com

Printed in U.S.A.

Canadian **Dani Collins** knew in high school that she wanted to write romance for a living. Twenty-five years later, after marrying her high school sweetheart, having two kids with him, working at several generic office jobs and submitting countless manuscripts, she got The Call. Her first Harlequin novel won the Reviewers' Choice Award for Best First in Series from *RT Book Reviews*. She now works in her own office, writing romance.

Books by Dani Collins

Harlequin Presents

One Snowbound New Year's Night
Innocent in Her Enemy's Bed
Awakened on Her Royal Wedding Night

Four Weddings and a Baby

Cinderella's Secret Baby
Wedding Night with the Wrong Billionaire
A Convenient Ring to Claim Her
A Baby to Make Her His Bride

Jet-Set Billionaires

Cinderella for the Miami Playboy

The Secret Sisters

Married for One Reason Only
Manhattan's Most Scandalous Reunion

Visit the Author Profile page
at Harlequin.com for more titles.

For you, Dear Reader, for your endless love of dramatic, glamorous, passionate romance. I hope you find all of those things in this one.

PROLOGUE

MOLLY BROOKS WAS already hyperaware of her sale-rack blouse, cotton culottes and discount sandals when she stepped off the elevator onto an upper deck of the *Alexandra*. She hadn't had time to shop and had had to make do with what was in her closet, not that she owned clothing that belonged in this setting, anyway.

The superyacht was gliding past Cyprus as though barely touching the water, but she was thrown off balance when someone in a crisp white uniform asked sharply, "Are you supposed to be here?"

No. Definitely not.

Her immediate supervisor, Valentina, had twisted her knee while skiing yesterday. Molly had been on a plane within the hour and was strictly here as a gofer so Valentina could stay in her stateroom and keep her leg elevated.

"I'm bringing this to my employer, Georgio Casella." She nodded at the leather portfolio she held with the freshly printed document inside it. "For his review and signature."

"Why isn't he doing it electronically?" the man asked with a scowl.

Because it was a court document detailing the theft of proprietary information, not that it was any of his business.

"I'm not privy to his reasons." Molly channeled Valentina's polite smile and cool tone. "Perhaps you'd like to ask him when you show me where to find him?"

With a grumble, he led her through an opulent lounge, where emerald cushions accented ivory sofas placed to view the wall of windows overlooking the sea. A crystal chandelier sparkled and the fresh flowers on an end table perfumed the air as they passed.

They moved into a darker room with tinted windows and a curved cherrywood bar. Colorful bottles were arranged behind it and glasses dangled above. The stools were low-backed and upholstered in black leather. Highboy chairs and drink tables were arranged near the windows and the doors opened onto—

He was in the freaking *pool*.

Please don't keelhaul me, she pleaded silently as she looked into the mirrored finish of Gio's unforgiving sunglasses.

If she hadn't felt his attention zone in on her like a raptor swooping for a bunny, she would have thought he was asleep. He didn't even lift his head. He sat low with his arms splayed along the edge of the free-form pool. The water cut across his tanned, muscled chest, right in the middle of his brown nipples.

Don't look!

Molly jerked her gaze back to his sunglasses, hoping he hadn't seen her ogle him. She didn't mean to, but the man absolutely fascinated her, leaving her mouth dry every time she had to talk to him. Thankfully, that wasn't often. Valentina was his executive assistant and Molly was Valentina's support. Until this trip, she had never seen him outside the London office and he was only there on and off, as he traveled constantly, usually with Valentina by his side.

Today, he had a topless woman next to him. She lowered her sunglasses to give Molly a look that asked, *What on earth has the cat dragged in?*

Oh, God.

Gio was a guest aboard this yacht. He wouldn't like her embarrassing him or jeopardizing the deal he was working out with the yacht's owner, Rafael Zamos.

She sent a wavering, apologetic smile to the handful of people here with him: the other couple in the pool, also mostly naked, the two men at the bar, one with his shirt hanging open over his barely there swimsuit, and the two women lying topless on nearby loungers.

"I—" Her throat closed and her heart stalled as she recognized…Sasha?

She looked so different! Her burnt caramel hair was tinted a bright blond. Her face and figure were elegant and lean, not rounded by youth and pregnancy. She wore pink gloss on her lips, eyelash extensions and diamonds in her ears.

She also wore a look of horror as she yanked her filmy cover-up across her naked breasts.

"What are you doing here?" Sasha—or Mrs. Alexandra Zamos, Molly was realizing through the rushing sound filling her ears—sounded livid.

All the blood in Molly's body drained into her sandals. A plummeting sensation assaulted her gut. She genuinely thought she might faint.

"What's wrong, Alexandra? Is the help supposed to stay belowstairs?" Gio's topless paramour was laughing at Molly, though, not her friend. "You're such a snob."

"Molly is my assistant's assistant," Gio said crisply. Now his head came up. "What do you need, Molly?"

"Valentina, um…" Molly cleared her throat, trying to recover from seeing her adopted sister's mother for the first time in eleven years.

She should have done her homework! Her coworkers had been green with envy that she was leaving the blustery November streets of London to spend a week aboard the Zamos yacht, but Molly hadn't bothered looking up photos or gossip about the owners. She had used her time on the flight to Athens to study the deal the men were negotiating. It had been made clear to her that she was expected to stay on the crew level. If anyone would rub elbows with Gio's vaunted peers, it would be Valentina, exactly as it always was.

And how could Molly ever imagine she would bump into Sasha like this? She had known Sasha's family was wealthy, but not *this* wealthy.

"Valentina finished the, um…" She waved the portfolio, mind splintered, voice still jammed. "She said you wanted to sign it as soon as it was ready."

She hoped Gio attributed her raging blush to the mortification of finding them all like this, rather than the anguish that she was dragging Alexandra's painful past into what seemed to be the happily-ever-after she very much deserved. Would she tell Gio to fire her? No. She wouldn't do that to her. Would she?

"Your executive assistant has an assistant?" the man behind the bar drawled as he poured from a silver shaker into martini glasses. "No wonder it was so difficult to get hold of you to extend this invitation."

He must be Rafael Zamos, the yacht's owner and Sasha's husband. Molly couldn't make that detail work in her head, but she pushed aside her utter astonishment, even though she was highly curious about him. He was very easy on the eyes, with dark hair and a tanned, powerful chest, but she made herself look away.

She glanced once at the ashen face that Alexandra was smothering with big sunglasses and a floppy hat, and pulled herself together. Betray *nothing*.

"I'm very sorry I've interrupted your..." Orgy? "Shall I leave this?"

She forced herself to meet the glint in Gio's sunglasses again when she actually wanted to sprint to the bowels of the ship.

"No. Valentina is right. I want to keep that moving." He turned and set his hands on the ledge, propelling himself upward, seemingly without effort. One foot touched the ledge and he was standing before the water had fully sluiced off him.

How dare he? Now he was nothing but swarthy skin, sculpted muscle and neatly trimmed body hair. He had the lean physique of a swimmer with broad shoulders and long limbs. His narrow hips wore a slash of black that barely contained whatever cockatiel he was smuggling. Not that she was looking!

"Sir." The purser hurried forward with a towel.

Gio—he was always Gio in her head, even though she'd never called him anything but Mr. Casella—took the towel in a laconic reach of his arm and wrapped it around his hips. He rolled his wrist to invite Molly closer.

With her heart pounding, she picked her way past Sasha's painted toenails and opened the leather portfolio.

She felt everyone's gaze pinned on them as he read the top page, then swiped his fingertips on the towel before he lifted the second page.

Rafael began dishing out martinis, briefly distracting everyone's attention.

"Thank you, my love," Sasha said, then took a hefty gulp of hers. Her hand seemed unsteady. Did Rafael's gaze linger on his wife an extra second, noticing that?

The yearning to talk to her old friend was so strong, it was like a scream trapped in Molly's throat. Her hands felt sweaty and all her muscles were threatening to twitch violently, purely to discharge the tension trapped within her.

"Pen?"

Gio had finished reading. She stared at her own reflection in his sunglasses, wishing she could see his eyes, but also glad that she couldn't. His mother's Icelandic blood was crystal-clear in his blue eyes and they often felt as though they pierced into her soul. His eyes always mesmerized her, being such a contrast to the rest of him, which was a reflection of his father's Italian heritage.

She shakily fished into the pocket of her culottes.

"Calm down," Gio said in an undertone that only she could hear. "I'm not angry that you're here."

He had noticed how rattled she was. As much as she loved her job, however, getting fired right now was the least of her worries. She was terrified of exposing Sasha when she had promised so sincerely and solemnly that she would never, ever reveal her secret.

Gio took the pen she offered and grasped the edge of the portfolio. His cool fingertips grazed the overheated skin of her own hand.

What fresh hell was this?

She stayed very still while he applied the weight of his signature, holding her breath until she could bolt.

"You can get this to the mainland for me?" he asked Rafael as he returned the pen to her. "I'd like it in London by morning."

"Of course." Rafael nodded at the man in the white uniform, who continued to stand by, waiting to escort the riffraff back where she belonged.

"Again, I'm very sorry," Molly said to the gathering, closing the folder and doing her best to hide behind it. "I'll stay below from now on."

"I was just surprised," Sasha said in a defensive tone. She adjusted the fall of her bathing suit cover so it was level across the top of her thigh. "I like to know who is on board, including any staff our guests bring along."

"You thought we had a stowaway?" Rafael was sipping his martini, once again watching his wife with a narrow-eyed, inscrutable expression.

"What exactly do you do for Gio?" Sasha asked without answering her husband.

"As Mr. Casella said, I report to his executive assistant, Valentina. I help her with emails and correspondence, assist with reporting and presentations. I also run personal errands to free her time, so she can be more accessible to Mr. Casella. She suffered an injury so I came along at the last minute to be her legs. That's probably why you didn't see my name on the passenger list."

"I didn't see 'Legs,' either," Sasha said, prompting a few dry chuckles. She turned a pout upward to her husband. "Much as it pains me to admit it, I think you may be right, darling. I need my own assistant. Either that or you should hire an assistant for Tino, so little things like sending me an updated passenger list doesn't fall through the cracks."

"Happy wife, happy life. I'll have Tino call an agency today."

"I'll reach out to him myself once I know exactly what I want. Tell me a little more...Molly, is it?" Sasha didn't give her a chance to reply. "Never mind." She flicked her hand. "We don't need to discuss that here. Come by my stateroom tomorrow. Have breakfast with me," she offered with a pleasant smile. "You can tell me about your duties so I can hire exactly the right person. Would you mind, Gio?"

"If you're planning to poach her, then yes. I mind very much." He threw off his towel and levered himself back into the pool. "I'm sure Valentina would, too." He took little notice of the woman who drifted closer, bare breasts practically grazing his rib cage as he stretched out his arms again. "Molly may make her own choice, of course."

Was that a threat? She shot a look of alarm toward the water, but he didn't sound worried.

"Come by at ten," Sasha said. "The men will be in their meetings. Everyone else will still be sleeping. Won't you, dolls?"

"Oh, I expect to be up all night and needing my beauty sleep, yes," the woman in the pool purred as she slithered even closer to Gio.

Ugh. Molly did her best not to think about that and smiled weakly at Sasha. She didn't know if she should be relieved that she would be able to speak privately with her, or filled with dread. Should she call her mother? Pack her bag and prepare to find her way back to New York?

"I'll see you tomorrow," she said and quickly made her escape.

CHAPTER ONE

Eight months later...

"MOLLY. MY OFFICE."

Molly jolted as she came back from the powder room to find Gio standing in the doorway between her office and Valentina's.

How did the man get more compelling each time she saw him? He wore one of his tailored suits. This one was a dark gray pinstripe, but he'd removed the jacket.

She was a sucker for any man wearing a vest and tie over a crisp white shirt, but when he wore it, she was dazzled. Maybe it was the way his icy blue eyes glittered and the way his jaw gleamed from a fresh shave. Maybe it was the fact he wore his hair in a more rakish style these days, still short at the sides, but a little longer on top, giving him a lean, hawkish look that was intolerably sexy.

Not that she wanted to notice, but she was a woman with a pulse, wasn't she?

"Let me get my tablet." She rubbed her clammy palms against her hips, nervous because today was the day she was asking Valentina for a medical leave. They had a meeting with Gio in the diary. Afterward, she planned on talking to Valentina privately.

"You don't need it." He waved for her to move through Valentina's sumptuous office ahead of him. Valentina's office was empty, the lights not turned on yet.

Strange.

Gio's office was a massive, airy space in relaxing earth tones. There was a comfortable lounge area where an oxblood sofa and matching chairs faced a view of London's skyline. A discreet nook held a bar and a kitchenette to service the small table for dining or hosting a one-on-one meeting. Nothing so crass as a whiteboard existed in here. That was saved for the boardroom down the hall, beyond the carved, double doors.

She reflexively moved to stand in front of the chair she used when she and Valentina met with him in here.

"I understood you were coming in at ten for our meeting. Is Valentina on her way?"

"Valentina isn't coming." After shutting the door to Valentina's office, he moved to close the double doors as well. The click seemed overly loud and ominous.

"No?" Molly's stomach gave a dip and roll that warned her she might not be fully past the morning sickness after all. Her lungs compressed as she waited for him to circle his marble-topped mahogany desk and take his seat.

This was already a very nerve-racking day. Now she was also hyperaware that she was alone with him.

Despite a crush on her boss that she was certain she

had not hidden well, Gio had never once acknowledged it or acted with any hint of impropriety. Nevertheless, his masculine energy radiated toward her like a heat wave. She couldn't seem to ignore it. She needed Valentina's buffering presence—especially when she caught his gaze flickering over her light gray pants and pale pink blouse when he nodded at her to sit.

She had made great strides with her wardrobe and hair, given her generous salary and Valentina's sophisticated example, but she still felt like a bumpkin from New Jersey, always obvious in her awe. She didn't feel she had anything close to equal footing with this man, which was glaringly obvious to her so it must have been to him.

"I hope Valentina's all right?" The last time her boss had failed to come into the office had been while she was still recovering from her knee injury.

"She's perfectly fine." He leaned back in his chair. "She wanted to be here for this, but I sent her to New York last night. She's taking over as executive director of R and D."

"What?" There she went, sounding like an uncouth hayseed. "I mean, that's fantastic for her. Wow. I had no idea she was even interested in taking a position like that."

Molly was genuinely pleased for her mentor while also experiencing immediate panic. Had Valentina not wanted to bring Molly along?

What does this mean for me?

Her brain took another sharp swerve. What did it mean for the *baby*?

Her hand started to reflexively cover her unsettled stomach, but she caught it with her other hand, resisting the urge while her mind continued to stumble and race.

"This promotion has been in the works for some time, but we kept it between us. She needs to clean house on arrival. Aggressively." His eyebrows went up with the significance of that.

Heads will roll.

She blinked. She was often privy to confidential information, but never like this, where he was not only sharing the actions that would be taken, but also his view of it. She felt as though she was being invited into the inner circle. It was flattering, if disconcerting.

"You'll draft the announcement, with her input," he continued. "Once I approve it, you can send it out. There will be several releases as we restructure. Brace yourself for some busy days."

"Of course, but…" She barely stopped herself from stumbling into an *um…* "Sensitive press releases usually happen at Valentina's level. They should include the name of her replacement as a contact. Has that been decided?"

"You tell me, Molly." He tapped the keyboard beneath the monitor on his desk. The screen flickered to life. "Valentina assured me you are the best person to take her place. I agree. All of your reviews are excellent." He angled the screen so she could see the column of nines and tens in the matrix she and Valentina had filled out two months ago.

"Wait." Molly almost fell out of her chair. She genuinely wanted to lean forward and dangle her head between her knees, but clung to the arms instead.

"I encourage promotion from within. You know that."

"Yes, but..." That's how Molly had come to London, by applying for an internal posting while she'd been assisting in the marketing department in the New York office. She had a business degree with a focus on marketing and analytics, but she had never expected her PR position to lead to a top-floor job here, let alone *this*.

"I'm not ready to work for the president and CEO." The *owner*.

Even as she blurted out her protest, she could hear Valentina chiding her in that very same review.

"Confidence inspires confidence," Valentina had insisted. "Believe in yourself, Molly.

"Valentina deliberately increased your responsibilities after this review, ensuring you could seamlessly take over for her."

"Because there was a mandate for every department to have a succession plan. For emergencies," she blurted. A lovely young woman named Yu had jobshadowed Molly for a week, to ensure she could cover Molly's desk in a pinch.

That pinch was supposed to happen three weeks from now, when Molly went on medical leave.

"R and D is leaking like the *Titanic*," Gio said starkly. "Not just money, but information. I consider that an emergency. Valentina has been dispatched to right that ship. I need a qualified assistant. You are qualified."

He waved at the screen. "Welcome to your new title of executive assistant."

"But—" She once again stopped herself from covering her belly. Her stomach was churning with a load of gravel. "I was…" She crushed her own fingers as she clenched her hands in her lap. She couldn't announce her pregnancy. She'd signed a nondisclosure agreement committing to hiding it.

Hiding it was becoming an issue, however. Two days ago, a coworker had had the temerity to ask if the salad she was eating was an attempt to drop the weight she was gaining.

"I have a thyroid condition," Molly had lied coldly.

She had hoped to speak to Valentina after the twelve-week scan and be on leave by now, but Valentina had been traveling with Gio. Molly had just rounded fourteen weeks and even though her bump wasn't pronounced, everything about her was becoming rounder, from face to breasts to tummy to backside.

Offering three weeks' notice as they entered July seemed more than fair. Things usually slowed down in summer. She could finish training Yu and not be missed too badly.

She had thought.

Gio was watching her with raised eyebrows, awaiting whatever words she was trying to find.

She couldn't take this job without disclosing that she didn't intend to be here.

"May I have a few days to think about this?" She needed to ask Sasha— Well, she couldn't explain her predicament to her, could she? Everything that happened in this office was strictly confidential. What the heck was she going to do?

"I know you've been taking meetings with headhunters, Molly," Gio said with a jaded blink.

"What?" It truly felt as though the room was spinning, she was so disoriented by this conversation. "What makes you think that?"

"Valentina said you've booked personal time during work hours lately. Afternoons here and there. I respect that." He shrugged it off. "Everyone should test the waters now and again to find out what they're worth. Now you're better prepared for this meeting."

She really wasn't. A bubble of hysterical laughter was trapped in her throat because those meetings had been about engaging her for something far more personal than "assistant."

"Of course, now I'm also prepared," he said dryly as he tapped a few more keys. "If I must compete for your loyalty, I'll bring more to the table. This is the salary I'd like to offer with a signing bonus if you commit to at least two years. You'll hire your own assistant, of course. Valentina said you seemed to like Yu, but she pulled a handful of other résumés she thought might be a good addition to this floor. You'll have an allowance for wardrobe, since you'll accompany me constantly. Also, a company expense account and use of a car service. I think you'll find I've been very generous, but by all means, let's negotiate. No one is irreplaceable, but I'd rather not replace you. Not when we're so comfortable with each other."

Comfortable? That was the last thing she felt around him!

Dear Lord, those numbers on the screen were positively blinding.

Why did he have to offer her dream job *now*? She had not only agreed to be a surrogate for Sasha, but she was also three months pregnant with the couple's baby!

She couldn't take this job. Not only was it demanding as hell, but she also couldn't become visibly pregnant, take a few weeks off, then come back without a baby. There would be a *lot* of questions.

The thought of refusing made her want to cry, though.

"This is a lot to take in," she managed to say in a cracked voice. "I won't leave you in the lurch now that Valentina is gone, I swear. But I'd like a few days to give more thought to all of this."

He sat back, tongue sliding across his teeth behind his closed lips as he used his laser vision to x-ray her insides. Could he see the baby?

For some reason she blushed and dropped her gaze, feeling transparent in other ways. Could he see how deep her crush went?

"Are you romantically involved with someone?" If there was gruff dismay in his tone, it was work-related, she knew that, but his question made her nerves go taut.

"No." Her throat was hot. She watched her own fingers torture themselves. Dating was a nonstarter. She compared everyone to him, but she couldn't help pointing out, "Not that you're allowed to ask that."

"I was asking as a friend." His tone was heavy with

irony. "I understand why you want time, Molly. That's another reason I know you're right for this job. You're not impulsive. You manage a crisis with a cool head and not a lot of hand-wringing. Typically." His gaze penetrated the marble desktop as though he knew she was knitting an invisible scarf in her lap.

She could have laughed uproariously at his judgment of her. He should have been in that stateroom with Sasha eight months ago, when a mere hour after reuniting with her friend, she had declared, "I'll do it. I'll be your surrogate."

She had no regrets. None. But she hadn't thought she would inconvenience Valentina with her absence. An assistant to an assistant was an easy job to cover. Executive assistant to a man like Gio required near twenty-four-seven accessibility. Travel at a moment's notice. He needed to be comfortable granting access to his most personal details—which woman required flowers after staying over, for instance.

A potent silence grew between them as she searched for some way to explain her reluctance. Dare she explain that her recent meetings were medical in nature? That's what she had been planning to tell Valentina. She had a note from a doctor and everything.

The burble of an incoming call had him glancing at the screen and hitting a button.

"Valentina," he said crisply. "Molly is here with me and she's being modest, trying to persuade me that she's not qualified."

"Gio, I'm so sorry." Valentina's cultured, boarding-school accent had never sounded so pained. "Ilario called me. He didn't know that I've been sent to— It's your grandfather. He's very ill and refuses to see a doctor. Would you like me to meet you in Genoa or…?"

As Molly watched the color drain from Gio's swarthy complexion, her heart was nearly pulled from her chest. It was well known that he was estranged from his parents. His grandfather had raised him and the pair were very close.

She snapped into the reliable assistant she had trained so scrupulously to become.

"I'm here, Valentina. I'll arrange everything and go with him. It sounds like you have your hands full, but please keep your line open. I'd like to know I can call with any questions that might arise."

"Absolutely. Thank you, Molly. Keep me posted."

"I will." Molly stood and reached across to hit the button that ended the call. "I'll have the jet readied."

"Signor." Ilario was the *maggiordomo* here in Gio's grandfather's Portofino villa. He had worked for the family since Ottorino's marriage sixty years ago.

"He's in his room?" Gio asked.

"Sì."

"Have the doctor come. I'll go up and persuade him to let him in."

"Grazie." Ilario flicked his gaze to Molly.

Gio had hold of her arm again. He kept doing it and didn't mean to. She wasn't his date. She wasn't wearing five-inch heels and an evening gown. She didn't need a supportive hand as she climbed in and out of his jet or his car.

Nevertheless, he had offered assistance every single time.

She was so damn warm, though. He felt encased in ice. His frozen fingers kept seeking out the warmth that seeped through the sleeve of her silk blouse, trying to thaw blood that had slowed and thickened with dread.

He *hated* this sensation, so he was seeking the most immediate and efficient means of melting it away: touching her.

"I'm Molly." She offered Ilario the sunny smile that Gio had felt like a strike of lightning through his center the first time he'd met her. That extreme reaction was the reason he had kept her firmly in the role of employee, enjoying the heat of being near her, but staunchly avoiding stepping into the fire.

"Valentina is tied up," she continued, notably *not* introducing herself as Valentina's successor, which annoyed him. "She told me you usually have a room set aside for her. Perhaps you could direct me to it and I'll keep myself out of the way?"

"No." Gio firmed his hold on her arm. "Let me see him so I know what I'm dealing with. Then you and I have things to discuss."

He might have dropped everything to come straight here, but he had also dropped a proverbial bomb on the New York office by sending Valentina there. He'd descended into a bleak place on receiving this difficult news about his grandfather. His mind had become fully occupied by the ways he'd have to reassemble his life if it shattered.

The demands of his position waited for no one,

though. Molly had been fielding calls the whole flight, rising to the challenge, he had dimly noted with satisfaction. She maintained an air of smooth aplomb, calming the most hysterical voices while keeping a force field of untouchability around him, providing him the space and privacy to process whatever was about to happen with his grandfather.

She was also being ridiculously accommodating, murmuring things like "If that's what you prefer." She slid her hand into his, as though he was a damn child needing a sense of security.

He knew better. There was no such thing as "security," but he accepted the interlacing of her fingers. There was a sick knot in his gut that grew bigger and thornier as he drew her up the wide staircase and along the black-and-white checkerboard tiles of the upper hall.

"Gio?" Her voice was small, but it was the first time she'd ever called him by his first name. That startled him enough to halt him in his tracks.

He tried not to notice his female employees in any way beyond the skills they brought to their positions, but he had always been aware of Molly. She was a natural beauty with a pale peach skin tone and big brown eyes. In the year she'd been working under Valentina—who was an example of the Swiss boarding school she'd attended, full of heiresses and aristocracy—Molly had begun making the most of her own attributes. Her rich brunette hair was in a smooth twist, her makeup had been freshened on the plane and her slacks had a chic flare over her wedged heels.

Lately, she had put on a few pounds. They added a

voluptuous softness to her already very feminine figure, making it harder than ever for him to keep his eyes off her.

"You're hurting my hand." She wiggled her grip in his.

He swore and released her, then pinched the bridge of his nose, realizing that a terrific pounding sensation had lodged behind his eyes.

"It's okay. I understand," she murmured. Now she was petting his sleeve. "This is a difficult thing to face. If you want me to come in with you—"

"I do." He would swear that he wasn't a dependent person. He didn't allow himself to be. He removed people from his sphere before they had the chance to cut him out. It was a lesson he had learned very early. Too early.

Perhaps that was what was at play here. He was irritated that she hadn't leaped to swear allegiance to him this morning. He was keeping her where he could see her until he understood exactly which way she would jump.

Why? When Valentina had asked to be promoted and leave his day-to-day world, he had made it happen without a single qualm. "Everyone is replaceable," he had told Molly this morning, and he'd meant it.

This isn't about Molly, he chided himself. This was about the inevitable loss of his grandfather. Death could be delayed, but not escaped. No one lived forever.

He took a deep breath and looked to the door into his grandfather's private suite, dreading what awaited him.

Molly's warm hand tucked itself into his again. She

covered the backs of his knuckles and gave him a patient look. How had he never noticed those gold flecks in her dark brown eyes? Her skin looked so downy, he wanted to cup her cheek and run his thumb along her wide bottom lip. Maybe his tongue.

Her lashes flared wider, as though she sensed his carnal thoughts.

He yanked his attention back to the door, away from a weak attempt at self-distraction.

Taking greater care this time, he clasped her hand then quietly opened the door, drawing her through the sitting room to the bedroom, where his grandfather was lying in his wide bed.

Gio had occasionally come in here as a child, but couldn't remember being here as an adult. It looked the same, though. Ottorino's bride had redecorated the entire villa when they'd married and Nonno hadn't changed a thing in the decades since. He'd never remarried and never had more children beyond the son his true love had given him.

The sheers were drawn so the view of the sea was blurred. Muted light fell on his grandfather's pale, aged face.

"Nonno," Gio said gently as he stood beside the bed.

Ottorino was eighty and wore his pajamas, but his iron-gray hair was neatly combed, his jaw shaved. He blinked his eyes open. His dark brown irises were immediately alert.

"You're here," he said in raspy Italian. "That's good. Who's this? Not a nurse."

"No, this is Molly. My…" He still had her hand in

his. She hadn't yet agreed to the job so it seemed a misnomer to say "My assistant," but that's what he called her.

"Oh?" His grandfather seemed to perk up, drawing some significance from Gio's brief hesitation. His gaze slid to their linked hands.

Gio released her.

"What does the doctor say?" Gio asked.

"It doesn't matter what he says. If it's my time, it's my time." Nonno's fingers lifted off his chest. "I only wish you were married with a son, Gio. Then I could die in peace." His eyebrows inched into a wrinkled line. "A daughter even. *Someone* to carry on this legacy we've built. Why did we bother, if not for your children?"

"I know, Nonno." Guilt stabbed at Gio, along with old anger. He had tried to fulfill his grandfather's wish three years ago, but after spending a fortune on a lavish wedding, his fiancée had chosen to run off at the last minute with her childhood sweetheart, leaving Gio with the bill and the humiliation of being left at the altar.

He hadn't bothered with a serious relationship since.

There was a quiet knock on the sitting-room door.

"Not the doctor." Nonno rallied into sounding cross.

"Your legacy includes creating a stubborn man in your own image. What did you think I would do?" Gio asked. "Let's see what he says. Won't you feel foolish if I've come all this way and you only need more fiber in your diet?"

"You're not funny." Nonno had a stare like a basilisk, but his mouth twitched. "Let's see if I have time to plan my own funeral, then."

"I'll step out," Molly said quietly. "It was very nice to meet you Signor Casella," she added in decent Italian. "I hope you feel better soon."

"Otto," his grandfather corrected. "Don't go far. You brighten up the place."

"I'll be here as long as Gio needs me," she said with a reassuring smile. She walked away through the sitting room.

"Assistente?" Nonno pried gruffly.

Gio ignored that and turned to greet the doctor Molly let in on her way out.

CHAPTER TWO

NAUSEA STRUCK HARD. Molly had no choice but to seek out the nearest powder room.

She would love to believe this was food poisoning. She doubted it was even morning sickness. It was stress, pure and simple.

What a day! And it was only midafternoon.

As Gio had predicted, her phone had exploded once Valentina began composting the bad apples in New York. Panic had spread like a plague from the lowest receptionist to the board of directors. Everyone wanted to speak to Gio, to know if they, too, were going to lose their jobs. Molly had drafted the announcement, but Gio had been so withdrawn, she hadn't asked him to approve it.

All she had managed to do was put lids on fires with cryptic phrases like "An announcement is forthcoming" and "Leave that with me."

She usually thrived on days like this. She loved the challenge in this job, which made the new role, and her inability to embrace it, all the more frustrating.

That conflict had her moaning in suffering as much as this awful dry retching.

"Molly?" Gio knocked sharply on the door. "Are you sick, too?"

"What? Oh, God." She flushed the toilet and lurched to her feet, then splashed water on her face and rinsed her mouth. Her mascara was smudged from her watering eyes and her cheeks were splotchy.

Wonderful. Not that she expected him to see her as desirable, but she didn't want him to be outright repulsed.

She dabbed herself back to presentable and yanked open the door, practically walking straight into Gio. He stood in the doorway, frowning with concern.

"Should I get the doctor?" was his baffled question.

"No. I'm fine," she insisted. "What did the doctor say about your grandfather?"

"Could be a virus that's got into his heart. Nonno has accepted IV fluids, but still refuses to go to hospital. He doesn't want major interventions." He raked his hand through his hair. "He lost my grandmother after fifteen years of marriage and says it's been too long without her."

"Oh." She covered her chest where her heart turned over in sympathy.

"I can't force him to accept treatment, but…" He wanted to. That's what she took from the tortured way he looked toward his grandfather's suite.

"I'm so sorry, Gio." Empathy overwhelmed her. These last hours had been so difficult to watch and now he was facing possibly his grandfather's last hours. It was unbearable.

She reacted on instinct, the way she would to anyone in such blatant pain. She closed her arms around his waist, trying to offer what little consolation she could.

He turned to iron, making her realize she was grossly overstepping their boundaries, but as she started to pull back in embarrassment, his arms clamped around her, squashing her to his front with a hard hug.

This was supposed to be comfort, but she found herself closing her eyes, absorbing the feel of him. This was what it would be like to be with him in a different role. To be someone he cared about who touched him all the time. To know intimately the beat of his heart against her cheek and the precise degree of heat that radiated through his crisp shirt, warming her torso. To draw in the fragrance of cedar and spice, and recognize it as his and hers and home.

She had an urge to run her hands all over his back and tilt up her mouth to his, one that was almost impossible to resist.

He released her abruptly, then muttered, "That wasn't appropriate."

"I know, I'm sorr—"

He flicked his hand, dismissing the hug as inconsequential. Which made her heart pang.

He seemed to have pulled a cloak over himself, one that made him impossible to read. He nodded jerkily toward the powder room. "What was that, if not illness?"

"Nerves," she insisted and pushed her hands into

her pockets to keep from stacking them protectively over her belly.

"Why? Not this job? You've stepped up exactly as I expected you would. It's done," he said with finality. His expression was hard, his vivid blue eyes piercing into her. "If you want more money, say so, but quit being coy and let's move on to addressing the day's business."

The air in her lungs turned to fire and evaporated, making her voice a thin squeak as she said, "I can't take it."

She hated to refuse when she knew he needed her right now. She paced down the checkered tiles of the hall. How apropos. She felt as though she was in a real-life chess match, watching all the careful, strategic moves she had planned being thwarted. She'd been racking her brain all morning, trying to figure out new options.

"What is the issue?" He folded his arms, very much the imposing boss who intimidated the hell out of her. "Spell it out for me."

Working for him was the chance of a lifetime, but it was also too much. *He* was too much. Even without this other secret she was carrying, she would struggle to hide her attraction. It was bound to become as obvious as her pregnancy if she worked closely with him, the way Valentina always had.

On the other hand, if she left, she would regret it forever. Professionally, it amounted to walking away from her career. Yes, in roughly six months she'd be able to return to it, but she wouldn't have *this* job, not if she turned him down now. On a personal level, she would lose the chance to know this extraordinary man a little better.

A maid bustled past with a tray, heading toward his grandfather's room.

Gio tossed an impatient look at the interruption, then clasped Molly's elbow the way he had been doing since leaving the London office. He steered her into a bedroom of masculine colors with a sitting area, a desk beneath a tall window and doors that opened onto a balcony overlooking the sea.

At any other time in her life, she would be charmed beyond measure by a room like this, but— She flung around in time to see him closing the door.

"This is my room. No one will bother us." He crossed his arms again. "Now speak freely," he demanded.

I'm not at liberty to!

She had to tell him something, though. She licked her lips and said haltingly, "The appointments that Valentina saw in my calendar were medical. I don't want to discuss it, but I anticipate needing time off—"

He swore sharply. "You're *pregnant*?"

"Wh-why would you say something like that?" Molly asked. Her hand grappled the air before clasping onto the back of the chair by the desk.

"It's the only conclusion that makes sense." His ears rang as though he'd taken an uppercut to the jaw. But, yes, this explained both her reluctance to accept a job that most people would kill for and the retching he'd just overheard. "Don't deny it. Guilt just landed on your face like a cream pie."

Her hand tightened on the chair and her color seemed to drain away. For one second, he thought she might faint, but she looked toward the window and her spine straightened.

He might pass out—his shock was that profound. Why? People were entitled to a private life. Even his employees, he thought ironically, but how? *Who?*

"You said you aren't seeing anyone."

"I'm not." Her voice was firmer than he'd ever heard it. "I don't want to talk about this. My personal health is not my employer's concern."

She shifted to face the door to the balcony, leaving it closed, but staring out. Her silhouette was the figure he had involuntarily memorized—average in height, narrow shoulders, a deliciously round ass. She was definitely plumper than a few months ago, though.

He ran his hand down his face, trying to assimilate this development with the rest of what had happened today.

"Valentina doesn't know." Would she have told him if she had? She was very loyal, but also very ethical. She wouldn't betray anyone's medical status without their permission.

"No one knows." Molly twisted around, voice taking on a note of warning. "It's common for people to keep things under wraps for the first trimester, in case it doesn't work out as planned."

If she was concerned about miscarriage, she obviously wanted this pregnancy. His mind filled with wild thoughts he wasn't entitled to have, but who the *hell*

was this man who'd made love to her, but wasn't involved with her?

"Does the *father* know?"

Her mouth tightened. "None of this is information I
am required to share with you."

"I'm not threatening your employment, Molly. I'm
trying to preserve it." Wasn't that obvious? "If you need
a mat leave, fine. Tell me what we're working with.
We'll find a way around it. I don't see how this prevents
you from becoming my assistant."

Assistente? His grandfather's skepticism rang in his
ears, then his plea. *I only wish you were married with
a son, Gio. Then I could die in peace.*

"This is a very private matter that is not up for discussion." She stubbornly folded her arms. "I was about
to ask Valentina for a six-month leave, starting three
weeks from now. Provided I have no health complications, I can offer that to you. I'll support whoever you
pick to take over for Valentina—"

"*Three weeks?* How far along are you?"

"*Three,*" she said firmly, ignoring his question. She
pointed at her middle. "Everything about this topic is
firmly off-limits. It's as classified as any company information that you have ever sent across my desk. I
mean that, Gio. Tell *no one.*"

He'd never seen her like this, with her chin up and
her eyes sparkling with battle. It was hot. She was.

Shut up, libido.

Don't go far... Nonno's voice echoed in his head. *You
brighten up the place.*

Could she brighten up an old man's final days?

"Three weeks," he repeated, swiveling the puzzle pieces in his head, trying to make them fit. "I'm not prying—" he was definitely prying "—but I need to know whether the baby's father will be annoyed at your devoting every minute of the next three weeks to me."

She clung to her elbows, shoulders hunched. After pursing her lips and seeming to debate her words, she finally gave a small, pained frown of concession.

"The father and I are not involved. Not in the way you're suggesting."

Good.

"I was intending to work until the twenty-first," she continued, looking to her toes. "I can give you that without any reaction from him."

"Does he plan to support you and the baby? Is that why you're refusing my offer?"

"Three weeks and this topic is off-limits." She drew a circle above her navel. "Those are my terms."

"Three weeks in which I will continue to sweeten *my* terms in order to persuade you to stay. You'll immediately take everything I offered you this morning." He kept speaking even though she opened her mouth to interrupt him. "You'll take the full signing bonus. I'll double it each time you double the timeline of your commitment."

"You don't mean—"

"I'll double it if you agree to stay another three weeks, double it again if you stay for twelve."

"That won't happen," she cried. "I'm not playing hardball, Gio. This is the reality of my situation."

"We see it differently." He shrugged. "You'll need

more than one assistant because I am now your sole priority." Why did he like that thought so much? "We'll stay here and work out of the Genoa office. I understand you may have physical limitations, but outside of that, you're mine in whatever role I need."

Her eyes widened. A soft blush came into her cheeks.

He usually did his best to ignore that, too. A lot of women betrayed an awareness of him. He was rich, well-dressed, intelligent and kept himself fit. He never let female attention go to his head, though. With Molly, however, he always felt when she was watching him and he damn well liked it.

Being her employer, he'd always been careful to keep his low-key arousal to himself. There were enough mermaids in the sea that he didn't have to fish where he worked. In fact, his latent interest in her had been his only reservation in bringing her on as his executive assistant. He'd been confident he could keep his hands to himself, and still was, but everything about their relationship was changing, becoming far more personal than he had expected.

Which didn't matter. He could handle that, too.

He believed, until she bit the edge of her lip in a way that tightened his gut.

"If I agree to those terms, will I have your solemn promise that you will never, ever tell anyone about…?" She dropped her gaze to her thickening waistline.

"I can promise that." He didn't like it, but he could and would. He held out his hand.

She swallowed and searched his expression.

Was she waiting for him to clarify that he wouldn't

cross any lines? Because he was about to wipe his feet on those lines and blur them into oblivion.

"Do we have an agreement?" he prodded. "Are you thinking about extorting more for the signing bonus first?"

"Don't be ridiculous." Predictably, she hurried forward to shake his hand, horrified by the implication she might be greedy. "You're already being very generous. Thank you."

He snorted. "I'm not generous, Molly. I'm merely willing to pay the price required to get what I want."

"What do you mean?" She tried to withdraw her hand, but he held on to it.

"I mean we're going to tell my grandfather that you're my fiancée."

CHAPTER THREE

MOLLY WAS STUNNED SPEECHLESS.

Gio's eyebrows went up, daring her to protest when her handshake of agreement was still withering in his hand.

The profound silence made the growl of her stomach all the louder and more cringeworthy.

"Let's have lunch." Gio dropped her hand and went to the door. "Then we'll give Nonno our happy news."

"Mr. Casella—"

"Oh, no, Molly." He did his thing where he used one glance to impale her like a barbed hook. "No take-backs. I accepted your terms. You accepted mine."

He opened the door, letting all the pent-up energy in this room flow out into the hall.

"You tricked me. You know you did." She walked through the door to escape the intimacy of his bedroom.

"Consider it a lesson in reading the fine print. Lunch on the terrace, please," he said in Italian to the first maid he saw.

Numbly, Molly accompanied him, too hungry to

stage a mutinous walkout. All she could think was *I need to tell Sasha that he knows about the baby.*

"Where did my bag go?" she asked the young woman who poured them a cool glass of something that smelled of orange peel and nutmeg.

"We have a lot to cover, don't we? Let's get Valentina's announcement out of the way. What other business can't wait?"

Her laptop bag arrived and they worked while putting away a refreshing green-bean salad followed by a pasta course of pesto over gnocchi brightened with cherry tomatoes and yellow zucchini. A light cake with ricotta icing was their dessert.

By then, Molly was fully intoxicated by good food and the thrill of working directly with Gio, responding to his dynamic decision-making in real time. It was like dancing, but a really sexy tango, where she had to match every beat, count and step.

When Gio rose to speak to the doctor, who was on his way out, Molly finally caught a breath. She drew out her personal phone and sent Sasha a text, asking to set up a call.

It was tagged "read" immediately and three dots appeared.

"You have two phones?" Gio asked.

Molly jolted and almost dropped it.

"I didn't hear you come back," she said with a shaky smile. She clicked off the screen and set it face down on the table so only the bright floral phone case was showing. "It's for my sister, mostly. She knows I'm busy and in a different time zone, but she sends me things constantly. I love it, but I can't have that on my work phone. I would spend all day clearing notifications from her so I could see what's actually on my plate."

"I don't know much about your family. Do you have other siblings?" He retook his chair and nodded for coffee. "Where does everyone live?"

He wasn't really interested. He thought he should know these things because he wanted her to pretend to be his fiancée.

Molly had pushed that ruse to the back of her mind while they ate because it created such a disconcerting shiver in her chest.

"What did the doctor say about your grandfather?" she asked as a dodge against replying.

"Nothing good." His tone was very somber.

"I'm so sorry." She looked to her hands in her lap, thinking about how much his grandfather seemed to mean to him and how defeated the old man had sounded at not knowing who would steward the family empire after Gio.

"I want his last days to be happy ones, Molly," Gio said quietly.

"I know." It sounded as though Ottorino only *had* a few days. Where was the harm in a white lie? In a bit of hand-holding to comfort both of them?

The harm would be in the way it would feed into Molly's already thick catalog of fantasies, but she could bear it. It wasn't as though Gio was leading her on. She knew exactly what he expected of her and it was purely a pantomime for his ailing grandfather.

"It would only be him, right? That we would pre-

tend for?" She lifted her lashes. "We would keep it inside that room?"

Would they kiss? She veered her gaze from his stern
mouth. Surely, that wouldn't happen.

"Sì."

"The promise you made me." She looked down
again, so he understood she meant her pregnancy. "It
includes him."

"I know." He nodded.

Her phone pinged, making her jolt at the possibility it was from Sasha, but even as she turned it over, it
pinged three more times in rapid succession.

"See?" she said wryly. "Cat video, dance video. 'Can
you do my homework for me?'" She showed him the
gif with a man on his knees, hands clenched in a plea,
with the word *Pleeeze* pulsing over it.

"How old is she?" His eyebrows drew together with
curiosity.

"Eleven. And this is such a dilemma." Molly pon-
dered her response. "If I text back, I run the risk of her
teacher realizing she's texting in class. She'll lose her
phone for the day, which is a suitable consequence. On
the other hand, I like her to know I'm here for her as
much as possible." She spoke aloud as she replied, "'I'm
in a meeting. Say you forgot it in the library, then do it
while you're there.'"

"Not bad."

She shrugged and set aside the phone again.

"That's quite an age difference. You're twenty-five?"

"Six." She debated briefly, then told him what she
told anyone if the topic of her much younger sister came

up. "My mother wasn't planning to have more children. She and my father divorced when I was six, mostly because Mom's career as a midwife was so demanding. After that, I gave up on getting the little sister I wanted, but a situation came up where a young mother was looking to place her child in a private adoption. Libby joined Mom and me and she's been an absolute joy and blessing in every way."

So much so that Molly had wanted to help Sasha in the most reciprocal way she could.

Her melancholy must have reflected on her face because Gio said, "It must be hard to be so far away from her."

"It is. The age gap puts us in different life stages, too. I homeschooled for the rest of high school, then went to a local college, so I could live at home as long as possible. But when I finished my degree, I was ready to start my life. I wanted to live on my own and build a career. Mom was always adamant that she didn't adopt Libby so I could raise her. She's been nothing but supportive of my ambitions and encouraged me to put in for the transfer to London when I mentioned it. I honestly didn't think I'd get it, let alone wind up here."

In his family home in Genoa, about to pretend she was his fiancée.

"Ah. Now I understand." He nodded. "You want to go back to New York so you're with your family when—"

"Gio." She gave him her sternest look.

"Off-limits." He lifted his hands. "But we can look at working out of New York."

"You're relentless, aren't you?"

"I consider it one of my strengths, yes."

Her phone pinged again. She glanced and saw Sasha had responded.

Can't talk right now. Getting ready for a thing.

Molly didn't take offense at what seemed like a dismissal. For many reasons, Sasha and Rafael were being very secretive about having a baby by surrogate. If there were stylists and others milling about, Sasha wouldn't be able to talk freely.

"Everything all right?" Gio asked.

"Mmm-hmm." *Note to self: keep your thoughts off your face around him.* She clicked off her phone and dropped it into her bag.

"Good." He rose. "Let's go tell my grandfather."

Otto's color was still poor and he had an IV taped to the hand that rested on his chest.

"She's back." He weakly lifted his other hand.

Molly hurried forward to cradle his cool, stiff fingers in both of her own.

"Ah, *sei caldo,*" he said of her warm hands. "Why have I never met you before?"

"I work in the London office." She glanced at Gio for guidance.

"But you're American?" He switched to English.

"Molly started in our New York office a few years ago." Gio's heavy hands arrived on her shoulders, provoking an acute, prickling awareness from the fine hairs on the back of her neck, down her spine.

Every cell in her body switched its polarity to align toward him. Her stomach muscles tensed and her breasts tingled. Her cheeks stung with a blush she fought to reveal, but she was certain Otto read her reaction to Gio like a neon sign.

"For the last year, she's been working under Valentina. I dispatched Valentina to New York, to deal with that issue we've been chasing there," he said in an aside.

"Bene, bene," Otto said distractedly, his sharp gaze moving from Molly's pink cheeks to the way Gio's hands lightly massaged her upper arms.

"I wasn't entirely honest with you earlier, Nonno," Gio continued.

"I can see that. *Assistente?*" he scoffed.

Molly was reacting so helplessly to Gio's caresses on her arms, she used her free hand to cover his, stilling his touch.

He immediately brought her into the cage of his body, folding one arm over hers while sliding the other around her stomach. He pulled her into the wall of his chest and settled her backside against his pelvis.

Heat flooded through her, melting her bones like wax. She found herself leaning into him, blushing hard while helplessly trying to hide her profound reaction and certain she was failing. She stared at the hand she still held so Ottorino wouldn't see directly into her soul.

"This is happening faster than we expected." The rumble of Gio's voice vibrated from his chest into her back. "But I've asked Molly to marry me and she has agreed. I wanted you to know, to put your mind at ease."

"This is good news." The old man gave a long, shaky sigh. Tears came into his eyes. The cool hand in Molly's shifted to turn hers over. "But no ring? Fetch Nonna's from the safe, Gio."

Gio's whole body jolted and she heard his breath catch.

His reaction was so visceral, her heart lurched and her veins stung with alarm.

"Oh, I—" *Couldn't.* Molly's instinctive protest was cut off by Gio's light squeeze of warning before he gently released her.

"I would be honored, Nonno. Thank you."

Gio walked away, leaving Molly feeling chilled despite the fact the room was being kept as toasty as a sauna for Otto.

Gio moved to a large black-and-white photo of a couple in wedding regalia from the 1800s. He swung it back on its hidden hinge, revealing a wall safe.

"The ring belonged to my grandmother," Otto told her. "Then my mother wore it, then my Theresa." His shaking fingers were moving restlessly on hers. "It will be good to see it on you."

What about Gio's mother? she wondered, but Gio was bringing a velvet box toward her. His gaze locked to hers, some hidden meaning sparking behind his eyes as he approached. It was a message that urged her to keep looking at him. *Stay with me.*

He went down on one knee!

"Oh!" she blurted, slapping both her hands over her mouth.

"Molly Brooks, will you marry me?" He offered the

ring, which she could barely see because her eyes welled with tears. Her throat closed and her mouth couldn't form any words. Why? This wasn't even real!

Otto chuckled. "Give him your hand, *carina*."

She offered her right hand. *No, silly.* Her left. It was visibly shaking, which made her feel so horribly obvious.

This isn't real. It isn't real.

Gio slid the ring onto her finger—it fit beautifully, as though it was meant for her. He kissed her knuckles.

She had the wildest thought that she wanted to tell her mother she was engaged. She wanted to tell Libby. *Sasha.*

She really was going to cry. Why were all her dreams coming true at the worst possible time?

Gio rose, bringing her hand upward so he held it between them. His expression was impossible to read because her eyes were too full of mist. She looked at their joined hands, dying of embarrassment.

"I feel so foolish." What must he think of her acting this way?

"You're perfect." He sounded tender as he gently cradled her face, tilting up her mouth before setting the lightest of kisses on her lips.

Perhaps he only meant it to be that chaste performance for his grandfather, but as he drew back a hairbreadth, her lips clung to his. It was the hug all over again. She was instigating something she shouldn't have, but feelings were brimming out of her. Everything in her wanted to hold on to this moment. To make it real.

Her vision hazed over even more. Her bloodstream was hot and fizzing. Her weight tipped forward ever so slightly while she lifted against him, inviting a firmer kiss.

His nostrils flared. There was a flash behind his eyes like sheet lightning, then his mouth sealed to hers. He angled his head, parting her lips without effort, then plundered in a way that sent a shock wave into her belly.

She had never been kissed like this. Not just the rough-gentle expertise that threw her so off balance she had to cling to his shoulders. No, the greater difference was the way her whole body reacted, as though she'd plunged into a fire that burned away the rest of the world, promising to leave her forged into something new.

But even as her cells and synapses were calibrating to his, he was pulling back. She heard Otto give another dry chuckle.

It had only been a few seconds, but she'd been bronzed and changed, and no longer made of one element, but two. She held particles of Gio within herself and they made her feel radiant.

"*Now* you have given me something to live for," Otto said in his paper-thin voice. "Call the ambulance, Gio. The hospital can keep me alive long enough to see you married."

Hours later, Gio exhaled a mountain of tension as they entered his apartment in Genoa. It was located closer to both the office and the hospital, so it made sense to sleep here instead of the villa.

The transfer to the hospital had been taxing on Nonno, but he was accepting oxygen and some antiviral medication. He had even sipped a little soup.

While ensuring his grandfather was settled, Gio had overheard Molly speaking to a boutique. She had arrived without luggage and was making the whole thing sound a lot more complicated than it needed to be. He'd asked her to let him speak to them.

"You have her sizes? *Bene.*" He'd mentioned a generous budget. "She needs everything, top to toe, every type of occasion, for several weeks. If you don't have it, call around to one of your competitors. Whatever she doesn't use will be returned within the month." His name had been enough to guarantee their fullest cooperation. He'd given them the delivery address and had handed her back the phone. "Learn to delegate."

They'd taken him at his word and, judging by the parcels and bags lined up along the wall, had spent every last euro of the amount he'd mentioned.

The rest of their afternoon and evening had been spent working late at the Genoa office.

"Do you want something?" He went to the bar.

"You have no idea." She sounded exhausted and was staring at the parcels as though they were a fresh mountain to climb.

Pregnant, he recalled. He kept forgetting that incredibly significant detail, probably because he didn't want to believe it. It was not only inconvenient on a professional front, but it also bothered him at a deeper level. Who was this man she had slept with? Why wasn't he fighting for the right to be in her life and his child's life? *I would.*

Gio knocked back the Scotch he'd poured, trying to erase that errant thought. Trying not to remember a kiss that had shaken his foundation.

Emotions had been running high. That's all it had been.

The whole episode had been surreal, from the way his hands had found their way around Molly's delicious figure to the way she had melted into him.

Through a haze of unexpectedly sharp arousal, he'd heard Nonno offer the ring he had refused to give to Gio's father, for Gio's mother, and had neglected to offer to Gio for his own engagement four years ago.

It had made his willingness for Molly to wear it seem doubly impactful. It meant Nonno truly expected to die.

That, too, Gio was refusing to believe. The hospital had assured him a mere thirty minutes ago that his grandfather was sleeping, his fever under control and his color good. They would call him immediately if there was any change.

Molly had removed the ring so she wouldn't start rumors at work. He touched his shirt pocket to ensure the ring was still there, immediately feeling the weight of responsibility it entailed. He had always known he had a duty to marry and make children, but he was ambivalent about it. What if he turned out to be as feckless as his own parents? What if he broke his child? What if he failed his grandfather as gravely as his own father had failed both of them?

Molly seemed more than ready to become a parent.

She was fiercely protective of her pregnancy, was off coffee and alcohol and had taken a few minutes in the afternoon to insist they pause for a healthy snack.

Had he pushed her too hard? It had already been a demanding situation before his grandfather's illness and he had asked a lot of her today.

"Which room is mine?" She gathered a number of bags by their handles and glanced down the hall.

"What are you doing? Put those down."

"They're not heavy."

"Your new assistant will put those away. Why is Nelo not here?" After weeding the applicants down to three, each with specific strengths, Molly had suggested utilizing all of them as a cohesive support team. They each happened to live in the cities where Casella Corporation had offices so they would have feet on the ground in New York, London and Genoa, which appealed to Gio.

"I sent him home."

"Why?"

"Because you said we were finished working for the night."

"*We* are. How many times did you pick up the phone at four a.m. to order breakfast for me and Valentina while we were traveling?"

"I don't know." She shrugged. "Dozens?"

"*Every* time. Otherwise, you wouldn't have kept that job. You wouldn't have this one. Call Nelo and tell him to make us a dinner reservation, then get his tail over here to put this away. If he gives you any excuse, he's not the right man for the job."

Molly glared a belligerent look at him, then let the bags fall to the floor.

"Do we have to go out?" she asked crossly. "If I'm off the clock, I'd rather have a bath and go to bed."

Pregnant, damn it.

He rubbed the stubble that was coming in on his jaw.

Now he was picturing her naked, skin shiny and coated with trailing bubbles. She wasn't even in the tub yet and he knew the image would persist for weeks.

"Fine. But don't you dare call in that dinner order yourself."

To her credit, she didn't roll her eyes, though he had a feeling she wanted to.

She didn't apologize when she reached Nelo, either. She politely said that she had thought they were done for the night, but explained, "This is a very demanding role and things will continue to surface unexpectedly. I hope you're prepared for that?... Oh?...I'm pleased to hear it. Dedication is rewarded over time, so do keep that attitude. We need a meal delivered. Something light for me with lots of vegetables, please. You might as well organize breakfast while you're at it and plan to be here bright and early to put some things away for me."

"Better," Gio said when she hung up.

Her eyebrows went up in a small commentary at his arrogant remark, but she only asked, "Which room does Valentina use?"

"She doesn't. We usually stay at the villa. I only keep this as convenience for late evenings or if I have a—" Date.

In those cases, if a woman stayed over, she didn't

use the spare room. Gio didn't even know if his guest room had a bed in it, let alone whether it was made up.

Molly chewed the corner of her mouth, not meeting his gaze.

He led her down the hall. This was in a heritage building on the waterfront, but the interior had been completely redesigned and modernized into a his-and-hers pair of bedrooms joined by a shared bath.

Molly barely glanced at the rose-and-ivory decor in the second bedroom, seeming both uncertain and done in.

It was hitting him that she had been more than his professional support today. She'd been an emotional one and had even gone the extra mile, allowing him to hug her for comfort and kiss her for his grandfather's sake.

A fresh burst of carnal hunger struck his belly and rang behind his fly. In the same way that he had walked in here craving a strong drink, he longed to lose himself in sex.

Judging by the way they reacted to each other, sex with Molly would be all-consuming and deeply gratifying, but it couldn't happen. She was his employee, blurry as that distinction had become, and she was pregnant with another man's child.

A hard fist clenched inside him, a resistance. No. There were too many complicating factors to consider an affair with her, but he couldn't help envying the father of her baby, for knowing how it felt to make love to her.

Why wasn't that man in her life, though? Gio was grateful he was out of the way, but he had no respect for him. As someone who'd suffered parental neglect, he instinctually loathed a man who would leave a woman and their child to fend for themselves.

His thoughts were so frustrating and contradictory, he escaped them by moving into the bathroom to start the tub. He closed the door into his own bedroom, then decisively locked it, as though the action would lock her out of his mind.

He hesitated, though. What if something happened?

Nonsense. She was a grown adult. She wasn't going to drown in a thirty-minute bath.

And she was only his assistant. Why the hell was he in so many knots over her?

Concern. It was simple, human concern. Physically, she was in a vulnerable state and, much as he was not behaving like the best employer in the world, he valued the health of his employees.

"Listen," he said as he came back into her bedroom. "You know that my personality is to push until my strength gives out. I expect you to recognize your own limitations and tell me when you're reaching capacity."

"You mean that?"

"I said it."

"Okay." She nodded. "Then let me be very clear. I can't marry you. I won't. That's a hard limit." She had brought a few bags into the bedroom and dumped one onto the bed, spilling a powder-blue nightgown onto the bedspread.

Ignore it, he demanded of his inner barbarian, but he instantly had a vivid fantasy of her nipples lifting that fine silk while the gathers cupped her full breasts and scalloped lace fell around her thighs.

"I want your grandfather to recover, and if he does… This can't go any further, Gio. It shouldn't have gone this far." She shook moisturizer from another bag.

She might be right, but… "He's in the hospital accepting treatment. I won't apologize for my tactics in getting him there."

Including the kiss? She shot him a mutinous look, making him certain that's what she was wondering.

Despite his resolve to keep her from penetrating any deeper under his skin, he wound up holding her gaze, refusing to express regret over their moment of passion. It had been mutual. Her hand had been in his hair, urging him to kiss her harder.

Heat pooled in his groin at the memory.

She blushed and looked away, rolling her lips inward. Her very soft, luscious lips.

Once again, he was accosted by the most lascivious of fantasies, one where he kissed more than her mouth. He pushed silk upward to expose her curves and secrets, and tasted all of her, from that thumping artery in her throat to the humid heat between her thighs.

Both yearning and persecution flashed across her expression before she looked away. Her shoulders were heavy and her mouth tilted down at the edges, warning him that this day had taken more out of her than was comfortable on his conscience.

"I appreciate everything you did today, Molly." He was trying to drag this back to a professional relationship, but the way her bottomless brown eyes swept back to his, wary and soft, had him biting back a groan of hunger. "I asked a lot of you. You rose to the challenge, which is why I want to keep you on."

Was that disappointment that glinted in her eyes? A sting of rebuff that scorched her cheeks? If it was, she hid it very quickly behind a bland smile.

"This is you pushing for me to agree to a longer tenure?" She moved to the door to the hall, signaling that she expected him to leave.

"No." He came to stand in the doorway. "I'm reminding you that the company rewards dedication over time, so—"

"Oh, shut up." She sputtered into laughter, which was his goal in throwing her own words at her. "Three weeks, Gio. Minus today. Hard limit."

It *was* hard. And sharp. He wasn't used to being denied anything he wanted. Who knew it was such a diamond-tipped arrow? It penetrated his breastbone, vibrating there as he walked out and she closed the door behind him.

Molly dozed in the tub, then ate what had been delivered while she was catching up on her personal banking. After that, she slept like a log, waking feeling infinitely better.

The only awkward moment was when she almost walked in on Gio in the shower, hearing the water at the last second.

She bit back a groan as she pictured him running a cloth over his swarthy skin.

Okay, she *had* to shake this off. Yesterday had been

an aberration of a day. She might have to pretend to be his betrothed when they were with his grandfather, but she was his executive assistant and she took her position seriously.

Thankfully, she had washed her hair after her bath last night, so she didn't need a shower now. She used the powder room off the kitchen to wash her face, then did her makeup and put her hair up in its simple twist before she dressed in one of her new outfits.

Gio had been ridiculously generous, forcing more than a handful of work outfits on her. There were cocktail dresses and casual wear, swimsuits and lingerie. It was pure bribery and an effective tactic for making her feel beholden to him.

There were a few skirts in the deliveries that she immediately set aside to return. She disliked wearing skirts to work. Valentina had once advised her to dress well, but comfortably. "You're not effective in your job if you're worrying about a wardrobe malfunction," she'd said.

That tacit permission to wear trousers had changed her life. She kept the style feminine, but her work clothes ran the gamut, from three-piece suits that were nipped and tucked to accentuate her figure, to crepe Bermuda shorts with a matching wine-colored jacket.

Today, she chose a pair of houndstooth capris and paired them with a flouncy green silk top that bloused over a stretchy band that hugged her hips, neatly disguising the thickening of her waist.

When Nelo arrived with breakfast, Molly showed him what needed to be done, then sat down to eat with

Gio. He looked and smelled fantastic, freshly shaved and wearing his suit, seemingly engrossed in whatever was happening on his tablet.

"Valentina is asking for a conference call today," she said, determined to remind both of them this was a working relationship. "I told her we're visiting the hospital on our way to the office."

"They said he's showing some improvement. It should be a short visit to cheer him up." He offered the ring. "Before we head into the office."

"Oh, um." She glanced down the hall to ensure Nelo didn't see, then put it on her finger, aware that Gio watched it go on. "That's good to hear, that he's improving."

"It is." He returned his attention to his tablet.

Molly checked her personal phone, but didn't have anything from Sasha yet. She sent a few silly memes to Libby. Then rose with the phone, taking it to the window.

"Do you mind if I send a photo of the view to my mother? I'd like her to know I'm working in Italy for the next while. She knows I can't say much about what I do, but I'd like her to know where I am."

"Fine," he said absently.

She took the photo, sending it with a text.

My view for the next while. I'll call later today to explain.

She would love to bring her mother and sister here to see it for themselves. She could easily afford it with her new salary, but Libby didn't know she was pregnant and likely never would. Her mother did. Sasha had fond memories of Patricia and had agreed that her discretion, advice and support would be invaluable to Molly as her pregnancy progressed.

With a wistful sigh, she walked back to the table.

"That's disturbing," Gio murmured.

"What is?" She curled one leg beneath her as she retook her seat.

She expected him to mention a conflict or disaster somewhere. Perhaps an unexpected plunge in market numbers.

"Do you remember the Zamos couple? You were with us on their yacht last year, when we began putting together a partnership agreement with their container division in Athens. We were actually due to finalize that next week."

Molly knew that, but *were*?

"I—I remember them," she said hesitantly, weirdly feeling as though the walls were both closing in and disappearing. Her ears were filling with water. "Why?"

"They've been in a terrible car crash."

"What?"

Gio thought Molly was leaning down for the phone she dropped and only realized at the last second that she was fainting. He barely reacted in time to catch her, saving her slumping body from crashing onto the floor. Her chair fell over with a clatter and he must have shouted something because Nelo came running.

"Signore?"

"Call the doorman. There's a doctor in this building. See if he can come. If not, an ambulance." Gio's knees were throbbing from the way he had plunged to the floor to catch her. Molly was a rag doll in his arms, but even as Nelo was snapping out instructions and Gio was still gathering her to pick her up, her eyelids began to flutter.

He got her onto the sofa, only then realizing how hard his heart was pounding. What the *hell*?

"The doctor is coming. I have first aid," Nelo said. "Please, let me do an assessment?"

Gio left Nelo taking her pulse while he opened the door to the doctor. As he showed him into the lounge, Molly was brushing Nelo away, trying to sit up.

"I'm fine. I was light-headed from moving too fast." She was still white as a ghost. The way she covered her mouth suggested she was fighting not to throw up.

"If you're finished here, Nelo, head into the office. I don't need to tell you this doesn't leave this room."

"Understood." Nelo nodded. He sent one worried glance backward and left.

Molly was hollow-eyed as she had her blood pressure taken, but didn't seem inclined to share her condition with the doctor even when the man asked point-blank, "Is there a possibility of pregnancy?"

"I'll follow up with my own physician on that," she said firmly and shot Gio a glance that warned any word out of him would be grounds for her to walk.

The father must not know of her pregnancy. It was the only explanation for her secrecy. Who was he? Someone abusive? *Married?*

That started to make sense.

"I'm very sorry to have inconvenienced you," she said. Her voice was still shaky, but she was giving the doctor a firm brush-off. "Could we offer you coffee or croissants for your trouble?"

"No, thank you." The doctor sent a puzzled look to Gio, then cautioned her to have her iron levels checked. He accepted promised tickets to the opera as compensation for his house call.

Gio showed him out, then came back to find Molly had walked herself to the table and was texting someone.

"What are you doing? Sit down," he ordered. "And why the *hell* didn't you tell him you're pregnant?"

"I'm texting my physician right now, giving her my vitals. She'll tell me if she thinks it's serious."

"It *is* serious," he insisted. She was still pale. He came across to right her chair and pointed at it. "Sit."

"I don't want to talk about this right now." She set aside her phone, hand shaking, but did lower into the chair. She glanced at her half-eaten breakfast as though it was a bowl of worms. "Your grandfather is expecting us. We have a full day at the office."

"Molly, you have to tell me what is going on. Is he married?" That didn't fit with the type of person he thought her to be, but perhaps she hadn't known. Lots of people lied about that sort of thing.

Her mouth quivered. Tears came into her eyes. For one moment, she looked at him in a way that sent surprisingly deep claws into his heart.

"Are you afraid of him?" He braced himself for that answer because he didn't expect to react well if she was.

"What? No. I told you that topic is off-limits." She leaped to her feet, almost sending the chair flying again.

He caught at her, holding her still.

"Don't move so fast. Do you want to faint again?"

She seemed made of twisted iron, there was so much tension in her. She kept her head down, refusing to look at him, but her hand curled into his sleeve, almost as though she was hanging on for dear life.

"You *are* frightened." He sensed it in a primal way, at a level that made all his body hair stand on end in reaction.

"Not of him. Of—" She cut off her choked words. Suddenly she was made of something delicate. Strands of brittle frost. She was quivering like a leaf encased in ice. Anything could break her.

"What, then?" he demanded, trying to gentle his gruff voice.

She gave one sniff and crumpled into him. Clung.

He had woken this morning uneasy with how much of his inner life he'd allowed her to see yesterday. He hadn't just introduced her to his grandfather, he'd *kissed* her in front of the old man. They were pretending an engagement and she was sleeping in his home. More than that, she was in his thoughts, provoking sexual infatuation and very deep *concern*.

Now he had his hands on her again, reflexively trying to soothe away her trembles. Trying to absorb the emotions that had her in their grip while ignoring his own. He was furious, though. Furious with the man who had left her fainting and shaking, worrying for a baby on her own.

"If he's married or a criminal… I won't judge. I swear. But I can't help you unless you tell me."

She drew in a jagged breath and stepped away from him.

"I promised myself I'd be more professional today."

He barked out a laugh since "professional" had been thrown out of the car miles ago.

"You're the one who muddied the waters." She flinched and hugged herself, shoulders tense and defensive. "I know this is an illusion." She gestured at the ring she wore. "But…" Her brow pleated and she turned her gaze to the windows.

"What?" he prompted, experiencing a strange teetering sensation in his chest.

When she didn't say anything, he gently touched her chin, wanting to see what was going on behind her troubled expression.

She pulled away and blinked her red eyes, increasing the smudges around them.

"Come on, Gio." She swiped impatiently under her eyes. "You have to know every single, heterosexual woman in the company has a crush on you. Plus half the married ones and probably all the gay men."

"Do *you*?" He was a bastard for making her say it. He knew she was attracted to him. He'd always known. It was one of those things he actively ignored, but he wanted to hear it.

"Yes," she choked out. Her eyes brightened with tears of mortification. "Now we're hugging and kissing every five minutes…" She flung out a hand in an expression of how wretched she felt. "I want to help you

with your grandfather, I do. But I'm also a person and I'm not a sophisticated one. I don't date a lot or have casual relationships."

He lifted his eyebrows, dying to ask how she'd wound up alone and pregnant.

"Don't lead me on." Everything from her voice to her body language reflected how excruciating she found this, revealing her attraction and begging him not to exploit it.

He wanted to exploit it. This attraction was mutual. Close to irresistible, which was difficult enough to acknowledge privately, so he veered from admitting it aloud. He would be a cad for doing so when she had explicitly asked him not to lead her on. She wasn't a woman he could date casually to see where it led. He had to be explicit about his intentions.

"I don't accost my employees with unwanted attention. Or wanted," he said with an ironic curl of his lip. "Workplace romances makes for messy headlines."

Her gaze flashed up to his. Her lashes quivered unsteadily as she searched his eyes. Humiliation stained her cheekbones.

He looked away, not wanting her to read how his fantasies were flaring to life at the knowledge she reciprocated his interest. She would see how he wanted her. And *where*. The bath. The sofa. His desk. A flood of heat accompanied the reel of places and ways in which he wanted to make love to her.

In the charged silence, he heard her swallow.

Then there was a buzz from the table. Her personal phone.

She hurried across and picked it up, shoulders falling in what seemed to be disappointment. Expecting someone else? A sensation like breaking glass struck inside his ears.

"My physician wants me to get some blood work," she said stiffly. "I'll ask at the hospital where it would be best to have that done. Let me fix my makeup and we can go."

CHAPTER FOUR

SASHA AND RAFAEL had been side-struck while driving home from a gala, Molly learned as she surreptitiously scrolled the news on their way to see Otto. Rafael had broken bones and was in surgery. Sasha was still unconscious. Their driver was also listed as critical. They were in a hospital in Rome and all were expected to recover.

She grasped onto that. *Expected to recover.*

She wished she could go to Rome. So near and yet so far.

Gio's driver parked, so she put away her phone and dragged on an outward cloak of composure, but she felt as though she was walking through gelatin.

It was absolutely no shock to her that she'd fainted. She had made a life-altering decision when she had offered to become Sasha's surrogate, but her life kept turning and shaking out into new patterns faster than she could adjust to them.

Valentina was no longer her boss. That job was now Molly's, but she couldn't keep it. She was in Italy. Gio's grandfather thought they were engaged. The parents of the baby she was carrying were gravely injured.

She had accidentally thrown herself into her boss's arms, twice, and he had basically told her to put it away.

Which was exactly what he ought to say, but she was horribly disappointed and feeling rebuffed.

It ought to be the last thing she was turning over in her mind, but it colored all the rest in bleak shadows. It made her inevitable departure from her job and *him* all the more urgent.

Why had she opened herself up that way, revealing her attraction? She could have just shut up and moved on, but no, she'd had to spell out for him that she was having trouble remembering this engagement wasn't real.

In some ways it felt very real, though. She had come dangerously close to blurting out everything to Gio when he had offered to help her. He had seemed genuinely concerned, but he was only being decent. Indulgent, perhaps, since he wanted her to stick out this job and keep pretending they were engaged.

For a few seconds, however, she had been tempted to spill her guts and lean on the man who was posing as her partner in life. Her person.

That's not what he was, though. And there was nothing Gio could do to help her. Nothing she could do. There were contingencies in place. The surrogacy agreement had covered many scenarios, including the loss of both parents before the baby's birth. In that case, Molly had agreed to raise the baby herself, so it could inherit the fortune to which it was entitled.

Such an easy thing to say at the time, believing it would never happen, yet here she was, fearful it might.

No. Sasha and Rafael would recover. They had to. While they did, the very best thing she could do for them was keep their baby healthy.

She wanted to cry, though. She wanted to go to them. To Sasha. She wanted her mother to be here and tell her everything would be fine—even though her mother was a realist who would definitely never make that sort of false promise.

Molly was so wrapped up in her own thoughts, she was barely aware that they were walking into Otto's suite. It was tastefully decorated, looking more like a hotel than a hospital room. Only his IV and the oxygen tube under his nose indicated he was receiving care.

Gio swore and came up short as another couple straightened from hovering over the bed.

"What are you doing here?" She'd never heard his voice so ugly and cold. His hand on her elbow tightened.

"My father is dying. Where else would I be?" the middle-aged man said.

"You wish that was true, but it's not." Gio sounded so hostile, Molly instinctually grasped at his sleeve, subconsciously holding him back from attacking them. "There's nothing for you to gain here. *Leave.*"

Were they really his parents? The only thing Molly knew of them was that they were occasionally linked to scandals, like a politician turning up in the wrong bed or a party being busted for rampant drug use. Each time something like that had happened, Valentina would slip away with Gio for a few days. Sometimes there was an announcement that would distance Gio and the Casella Corporation. More often, their chaos was simply swept from the headlines and forgotten.

Curious, she studied the pair, thinking they looked much older than their years. They were dressed well, or rather their clothes were expensive, but worn sloppily. Neither was paunchy, but they both had faces that were well-lined. Not merely sun-weathered or full of laugh lines, but showing miles and miles of a dissolute life. His father's eyes were sunken, his skin sallow. His mother was probably a natural blonde, given her Icelandic heritage, but her blue eyes were glassy and her hair looked overprocessed and brittle.

When she came forward to try to embrace and kiss her son, Gio recoiled, not allowing her to touch him.

She gave an amused sniff and turned a smile on Molly that was both patronizing and ingratiating.

"Hello. I'm Fridrika, Gio's mother." She held out her hand. "This is my husband, Ambrose. And you are?"

"Molly," Gio answered for her, voice blunt as a hammer. He stopped Molly from lifting her hand to shake, bringing both her hands to his lips while holding his mother's gaze. "My fiancée."

Fridrika's wild-eyed gaze pinned itself to the ring. She raked in a breath.

"You gave her the ring?" She shot a look to Otto, who was watching from the bed, looking weary.

"No!" Ambrose came across and made to grab at Molly's hand himself, but Gio angled his body between them and brushed away his father's reaching hand.

"If I had thought you would have the gall to show

your faces here, I would have told the hospital staff to refuse your entry," Gio said grimly. "Leave or I'll have Security escort you out."

"He's my *father*," Ambrose insisted. He was shaking, gaze pinned on Molly as though she was some multi-headed monster that had arrived to nip at him.

"When it's convenient," Gio shot back.

"It's convenient for you that I'm *your* father, isn't it? You think you can take all of this without a fight from me?" Ambrose waved his arm. "Think again."

"How much do you want? Hmm? Leave without a fuss and I'm more likely to be generous. Molly, go see that Nonno isn't upset by this while I walk them out." He gave her a small nudge in the middle of her back then jerked his head at the door.

The older couple wore disgruntled expressions, but shuffled out, glancing back once. Gio pulled the door firmly closed behind him.

Molly swayed under this fresh shock. It must be equally upsetting for Otto.

"Do you know that I've actually led a very quiet and boring life until the last few days?" She picked up his hand to warm it between her own. "At one point, I thought I might become a librarian because I was so content seeing the world through books, rather than with my own eyes."

He smiled faintly. "Tell me more."

"To help you sleep?" she teased. She told him about her first jobs babysitting, then her work in a bistro, where she had exploded the shop's popularity with social media. "Everyone said I had a flare for marketing so I started my degree in that field. Then I discovered *statistics*."

"Now I will sleep." He closed his eyes.

She chuckled and told him about her entry position in the Casella Corporation and the small successes that had allowed her to advance to London and work for Valentina.

"That was hard, leaving my mother and sister."

"No father?"

"He moved to California after their divorce. I still see him sometimes, but I'm much closer to my mother and sister. They're still in New Jersey. Not the exciting part of the state, either," she confided with mock glumness. "It's a rural town in the hills. Very beautiful, though, especially in the fall. I like to take my sister walking..."

She had first discovered those trails with Sasha. Her friend's dire condition rushed back with such force Molly began to choke up.

"I'm so sorry." She released Otto's hand and gathered a couple of tissues, trying to stem her tears before she smudged her makeup *again*. "I had some upsetting news about a childhood friend today. It keeps hitting me."

"Oh?" he prompted with concern.

"I..." She shouldn't talk about Sasha, she knew that, but her anguish was so great, she had to spill out something of what was going on inside her. "She was the closest friend I've ever had. Even though I was so envious of her when I met her that I was downright rude."

She still chuckled at the memory of Sasha, when she'd asked, "What is wrong with you? Your life is perfect. Gawd!"

"Her life looked very glamorous from the outside, but she had a lot of heartache." Molly blinked back tears, remembering quiet walks in the woods and playing board games. "I was at that age when you're in a hurry to grow up. She made me realize how lucky I was to have my simple life and the last pieces of childhood."

Sasha had been the sister she always wanted, then her baby had become that cherished sister.

"She sounds wise."

"And generous. She gave me more than I could possibly tell you." She swallowed. "We were so close for a short time, then I didn't see her for years. I thought she'd forgotten me." Sasha had probably tried. It had been a very dark period in her life. "I understood. Her world is very different from mine, but when I did see her, it was as though we picked up where we left off."

She couldn't help smiling as she remembered the huge hug she had received the moment she had stepped into Sasha's stateroom on the *Alexandra*. The mood between them had turned melancholy when Sasha burst into tears, then refused to hear about Libby. That had hurt, a lot, but Molly had seen the agony in her friend's eyes. It was too painful for Sasha to go back to that time. Molly had to respect that, especially when she learned that Sasha's life had become a fresh level of torture, trying to conceive and having that dream not work out.

"What can I do to help?" Otto asked.

"Nothing. There's nothing I can do, either." Sasha's parents were there. They didn't know about Libby or that Molly was carrying Sasha's second baby. Molly couldn't be seen at her side and risk revealing that. "But it helped me to talk about her. Thank you for that. I was feeling as though I was being held under water. Now I've finally caught a breath. Please don't tell Gio about this. He already has a lot to worry about—"

Gio strode back in looking like a pressure cooker emanating steam from its seams. His dial was definitely hovering at the red line.

"I have arrangements to make," he said flatly. "How are you, Nonno?"

"Better than you, I suspect." His voice was weak, but his gaze was sharp as he took in his grandson's simmering mood. His expression softened when he asked Molly, "When can you come back so we can talk more?"

"Why don't we bring dinner?" she suggested.

"I'd like that. Maybe a little wine, too." He winked. "Can I have a moment with Gio?"

"Of course." She faltered briefly, worried Otto would reveal something of what she'd just told him, but he gave her a reassuring smile so she went to inquire about the blood work.

"Keep this one," Nonno said after Gio had caught him up on how he planned to deal with his father.

"Molly?" Gio's fuse was already short, so Nonno's remark burned right against his skin. "I would have kept the last one. She chose to leave."

"You chose a woman you didn't love and expected her to be satisfied with wearing your name and spending your money. I could see it would never work. That's why I didn't give her Nonna's ring. Molly is different. She has a big heart. You can trust her with your own. Get her pregnant. Do whatever you have to do, but *keep her.*"

Good news, Nonno. She's already pregnant.

Gio pinched the bridge of his nose.

"Se insisti," he vowed, because what else could he say when his grandfather's eyelids were drooping so heavily. He was exhausted after being attacked by his own son, demanding he change his will. "Rest up. We'll be back soon."

The hospital staff had instructions to call Gio with any changes—or the names of any visitors—so he left Nonno drifting to sleep, found Molly and took her to the office.

"Here," Molly said in the car, surreptitiously offering him the ring she had removed and glancing at the driver, who had earbuds inserted to give them privacy.

"Wear it."

"Gio—"

"My parents will have the news of our engagement across the Italian Riviera by lunch. Draft a formal announcement as soon as we're in the office. I need this leverage against them. They see an opportunity because Nonno is ill, but anyone who is anyone understands the significance of you wearing the family ring. *I* am Ottorino's heir. Not my father."

"This wasn't our deal," she hissed, but pushed the ring back onto her finger. She faced forward, mouth tight, eyes shining with distress.

You can trust her with your heart.

Not if she had one foot out the door. On the other

hand, Gio was not looking forward to another well-publicized breakup.

Keep this one.

He had promised his grandfather he would, but there was a knot of resistance within him. He knew he needed to marry, that he needed an heir. Otherwise, if something happened to him, his parents really would have a chance to swoop in and destroy everything he and his grandfather had built. But what was he supposed to do? Marry his secretary and claim her baby as his? It was ludicrous. Hell, until yesterday, they hadn't spoken two words about anything that wasn't work-related.

But that kiss...

Stop it.

"We have a lot to cover this morning," he said with more snap than he intended, making her stiffen. "I want to revisit the closing dates on the Athens deal. I'm not signing anything until I know that Zamos is in the clear." He began rattling off the rest of his priorities, pleased when she efficiently began delegating to Nelo, directing him to push tasks onto his counterparts in London and New York.

By the time they were striding into his office, the aroma of fresh coffee was in the air, a tray of biscotti was being delivered and Gio's desk phone was ringing.

"Signor Donatelli," Nelo said of the call, hovering with his tablet.

"Bene." Gio picked up the receiver and said, "Vittorio." Gio waved for Molly to shoo everyone from the room. "No, you stay in here, Molly."

"Buongiorno," Vittorio Donatelli said in Gio's ear.

"I saw the report that your grandfather is in hospital. I'm so sorry, Gio. I hope he recovers quickly."

"So do I. And I'm pressed for time so I'll get to the point. I need an arrangement like the last for my parents. Double the amount, but in order to access it, they must relinquish all claim to the Casella estate and corporation. Is that something you can arrange or shall I get my own lawyers onto it?"

"I'll have a draft by end of day that your lawyers can look over."

"Perfetto. And thank you for excusing my brevity. It's been a difficult two days."

"I understand. Will we see you Saturday at our anniversary party?"

"I expected I would be in New York so I sent regrets." He shot a look at Molly. She had seated herself on the sofa and was concentrating on her tablet. Milan was less than an hour away by helicopter. "But if Nonno is well enough, yes. I'll bring my fiancée."

Molly lifted her head, eyes flaring with outrage.

"My grapevine is failing me," Vittorio said. "By 'grapevine,' I mean my wife. I had no idea you were engaged. Congratulations."

"For once you have a jump on Gwyn. It will be announced later today."

"Ah. I'm flattered to be one of the first to know and I shall be smug as hell when I pass your happy news along to her. I won't keep you. We'll speak later today on the other matter."

"Grazie." Gio hung up and asked, "How is the announcement coming along?"

"Of our engagement? I put Nelo on it, didn't I?"

She sounded very facetious, so he asked, "Did you?"

"No! He would have spat his coffee across the office. Gio, think about this." She set aside her tablet and folded her hands in her lap. "You are my boss. A surprise notice that you are engaged to a midlevel employee—"

"You weren't my direct report until yesterday."

"It still looks terrible."

"Am I the first man to find his wife at the office? This isn't an affair. I'm marrying you. It's *romantic*," he said through his teeth.

She made a choked noise and reached for her tablet again, then stated firmly, "We are not marrying."

"But you're writing the announcement?" Rather than ask her to forward it to him so he could read it on his own screen, he walked over to settle next to her. She stiffened again, perhaps out of umbrage, but there was also a delicious crackle in the air between them.

I'm asking you not to lead me on.

He wasn't trying to, but this attraction was positively magnetic.

He heard his grandfather again. *Keep this one.* He had to stop himself from leaning closer to her, touching her.

He made himself focus on what she was writing. She kept it brief, calling it a "surprise engagement" to forestall anyone making a mountain of that. She stated that his new fiancée was not his direct report and "recently gave notice of her decision to leave Casella."

That part rankled.

"What about a photo?" she asked.

"We don't have time for a formal sitting." He picked up her phone with the floral case, since it was right there, and touched the camera icon. "Look happy, would you? You're going to break the screen."

"Gio." She made him lower the phone and angled to face him. "I know that you got as far as a church once before."

"This is nothing like that," he said flatly.

"It's exactly like that. I'm not going to marry you. And I don't want to be the person who causes you another embarrassment."

Then don't be. The words were right there on his tongue, but it was only his sense of obligation to his grandfather prodding him to say that.

"Look." He set aside the phone and rose to pace off his restlessness. "I've always known I had a duty to marry and produce the next generation. I put my engagement together like any other merger and acquisition. She was beautiful and charming, well-connected and her family needed the money." He had thought that would buy her steadfastness. That's all he had really cared about. "When it fell apart, I was annoyed that I had put time into something that didn't work out, but I was not humiliated. My parents do things that are ten times worse. I've learned not to care how other people's actions reflect on me."

"I'm so sorry you had to see them today, Gio. Do you want to tell me—"

"No," he said flatly. "I never want to talk about them so don't bother asking."

She pursed her mouth into a circumspect pout. "So

you weren't in love with your fiancée? Your heart wasn't broken when the wedding was called off?"

"No," he said with a choke of jaded laughter.

"Then why haven't you found someone else since?" Her lashes came up and it felt very much like she picked up a curtain and peered inside him.

"Fine," he muttered. "I was stung by it."

Rejection was something that landed in a very deep place when he experienced it. That's why he took steps to avoid caring too deeply about anyone. That's why he hadn't pursued someone new.

There was also that other piece. The part where he hadn't been interested in anyone except a woman who was off-limits. There had been a certain comfort in that situation, where he saw Molly intermittently. He could hear her laughter down the hall or watch her ass leave a room, but he couldn't pursue her and therefore didn't risk a rebuff.

"I don't *care* if this ends in three weeks." That was a lie. It would grate like sandpaper. "But this engagement has become about more than easing my grandfather's mind. It signals that I am securing the Casella legacy. Our engagement solves a lot of problems for me."

"How nice for you. It creates an infinite number for me," she said tartly.

"But you'll go along with it," he pressed.

Her gaze cast about the room as though looking for some other solution. When it landed on her personal phone, her brow pleated.

"For nineteen days," she conceded.

A thousand questions leaped to his lips, the top one being "Who is he?" But he quelled them, coming back to sit next to her and picking up her phone again.

"Put your hand on my face. I want the ring to be visible. No, come closer or it will look ridiculous." He scooped his arm around her and pulled her snug against his side. "Better." Much better. She was a lovely armful of soft curves that melted into him.

"Don't take so many! I don't have time to delete a thousand useless photos."

"Kiss my cheek." He kept clicking as he extended his arm higher, trying different angles.

"No more kissing." Her fingertips were against his jaw, but one extended to cover his lips.

Her touch was lovely. The startling caress amplified his craving for her. He turned his head to look at her and found her expression admonishing, yet filled with yearning.

Don't lead me on.

"For the camera," he said in a voice that emanated from the bottom of his chest. He dipped his head closer, allowing his lips to hover near hers, and clicked blindly.

She closed her eyes and said his name in such a helpless tone that he lowered his arm, dropping the phone between them.

He should have moved away, but he stayed right there, waiting for her lashes to flutter and lift. Her eyes were filled with more than longing. He read *hunger* and it made his whole body brick up.

Her gaze softened and her head tilted. Her hand on his cheek flexed, urging him closer.

A primitive noise left him, one that was possessive and carnal. He wrapped both his arms around her, taking the kiss she offered. Claiming it. It was the kiss he'd wanted for a year or more. Ever since Valentina had introduced her new assistant and Molly had nervously licked her lips while her cheeks turned pink.

She tasted of anise and tea and capitulation. Her hand slid around his neck and her mouth opened to his, drawing him into a long, dark tunnel of sensuality. He filled his hands with her curves, greedy for the flare of her hips and the small of her back and the swell of her breast.

A sobbing noise resounded in her throat, but she wasn't pulling away. She was pressing closer. Her knee bumped his.

He hooked his hand behind her leg and pulled her astride his thighs as he sat back on the sofa, dragging her to straddle his lap.

She gasped in surprise, drawing back to blink in startlement, but when he cupped her beautiful ass and slouched so she was pressed more intimately against his unmistakable arousal, her eyes hazed with lust. She dove her fingers into his hair and bent her head to kiss him with aggressive abandon.

He drank her unbridled desire straight, wanting the blindness it offered. Wanting to roll her beneath him and discover the full depth of her passion while proving to both of them that he was the only man who mattered to her.

That wasn't true, though. Maybe she didn't want to reveal the father of her baby, but that unnamed man was still a part of her life. A big part, if she was willing to draw such firm boundaries around that incredibly intimate connection.

What the hell were they even doing?

Gio dropped his head back, breaking their kiss.

They were both breathing heavily. She licked her lips and looked at him with such dazed longing he wanted to bottle it. Her hands were still cradling his jaw, but she self-consciously dropped them to her thighs. Remorse crept in around her mouth and eyes.

He fished for the phone, where it had fallen to the cushions.

"Don't you dare!" She stole the phone and clambered off him. "You're kind of a monster, do you know that?"

"I just wanted to see if we got anything we can use." He didn't usually ignore elephants or unwise kisses, but he was trying to break the mood so he wouldn't touch her again. His palms were burning with the imprint of her curves.

He watched as she swiped through the photos he'd taken before they kissed.

"That one," he said.

It was candid and tender. The ring was visible and they were looking into each other's eyes. The naked hunger she had revealed was already coloring her expression.

"That's too… This one," she insisted. Her eyes were closed and it was poorly framed.

As she flicked between the two, her phone pinged with a text.

Mom: I have some difficult news. Call me as soon as you can.

That was a douse of cold water. Gio swore with concern.

"That's—" She lurched to her feet.

"Stop getting up so fast," he ordered, still not over the way she'd crumpled to the floor this morning.

"I think I know what this is about, but I need to call her."

"She's a midwife, isn't she? Tell her you fainted. I want her number in case anything else happens to you."

Molly sighed with tested patience.

"I'm sending the announcement and the photo you like to Nelo, asking him to release it. All right?" She tapped and he heard the whoosh. "You and I are officially engaged. Happy? Now keep your nose out of my personal life."

She walked into the adjacent office that had been Valentina's and shut the door.

CHAPTER FIVE

HER MOTHER WAS as upset about Sasha's crash as Molly was.

Along with her busy midwife practice, Patricia Brooks had always done volunteer hours in a teen clinic. That's where she had met a troubled, pregnant sixteen-year-old. Sasha wanted to have the baby and place it for adoption, but she was hiding her pregnancy from her parents and the much older, married father. She needed somewhere safe to stay.

Patricia had a duty to report abuse, but Sasha had threatened to run away if Patricia involved the authorities. Talking to the teen, all Patricia could see was her own daughter, about to turn that age. She couldn't ignore Sasha's plight so she had brought her home. She gave her the care she needed through her pregnancy, hired lawyers and a counsellor who specialized in adoption, and personally caught Libby the day she was born.

Sasha stayed to nurse her daughter for almost two weeks, but as much as she seemed bonded to her baby, she insisted she had to leave without her.

By then, none of them could imagine Libby going to

strangers. Patricia had adopted her. She made it clear to Sasha that she considered it an open adoption. Sasha could come at any time to see her daughter and be part of her life, but Sasha was adamant they never reveal she was Libby's mother. *This never happened.*

Given their close ties to Sasha, Patricia had understood Molly's willingness to surrogate for her. She was being as supportive as possible, but she worried, especially now that Sasha had been hurt.

"What does this mean for you?" she asked.

"I'm not sure," Molly replied. "The news reports say her parents are with her so I can't go see for myself. It sounds like she has a concussion, but they expect her and Rafael to make a full recovery. I'm sure Sasha will reach out to me as soon as she's able. In the meantime, I've been promoted and I'm in Italy right now."

"That's closer to Sasha, at least."

"Yes, but there's one more thing I have to tell you." Ironically, this was the hardest to say. "I'm engaged."

"To *who*?"

Ten minutes later, Molly walked back into Gio's office, probably looking as though she'd been run over by a truck because that's how she felt.

"Is your sister all right?" Gio frowned with concern.

"Yes. That was about a friend. I, um, warned Mom about the engagement. I told her it's not real."

His eyebrows shot up.

"I will lie to the entire world for you, Gio, even to my baby sister, but I will not lie to my mother." She and her mother had agreed it was best to let Libby believe it since she tended to overshare, especially when she was excited.

"Did you tell her you fainted this morning?" He narrowed his eyes.

"Yes. And while I was talking to her, my physician texted. She sent a requisition for blood work to a lab here in Genoa. I told Mom I'd make sure the results are shared with her."

"Get that taken care of, then." He jerked his chin toward the door.

"We have that conference call with Valentina," Molly reminded him. "Oh, I know," she said with mock discovery. "I'll send Nelo."

Gio didn't offer so much as a twitch of amusement. "That joke is wearing thin. Take Nelo, so I know someone is with you if you faint in the street. I'll handle Valentina."

Molly gathered her bag and hurried out because she needed a break from his nonstop lightning storm of commands.

She used the time in the car to personally send her "engagement" photo to her sister. Libby lost her preadolescent mind and rang through while she and Nelo were having a quick bite at a bistro after the lab, something Nelo said Gio had insisted they do before returning to the office.

Libby demanded to see the ring and meet her fiancé.

"He's not here, but we'll call you later." That would be just punishment for Gio for getting her into this mess. Libby would ask him all sorts of probing and awkward questions. "Right now, I have to go back to the office and you have to get ready for school, but I love you. Mwah, mwah, mwah." She blew her kisses through the screen.

If she had thought Libby's reaction was over-the-top, it was nothing compared to the way all the employees stood and clapped when she and Nelo entered the reception foyer.

"Oh, God." She covered her mouth. "The announcement has hit the internal channels, I presume?" She waved and smiled and blushed so hard, she thought she might actually die.

"Yes, and I'll apologize now," Nelo said once they were inside the elevator. "You were on the phone when I asked Signor Casella whether it would be appropriate to, um…" He swallowed loudly. "It's a very special occasion for the president to become engaged," he said, as though that was some kind of apology or excuse.

"No-o-o!" she moaned in premonition, even as the elevator doors opened to reveal balloons, streamers and a crowd of employees waiting to greet her. They applauded and someone began to play a romantic tune on an accordion.

"Are you kidding me?" she cried, which was the appropriate level of shock because everyone laughed with enjoyment.

"You told me last night to be prepared for anything," Nelo said, expression somewhere between a cringe and a grin of pride.

"Well done, getting her out of the office, Nelo." Gio beckoned her to join him at a table where a cake of ivory buttercream sat. It was in the shape of two interlocking hearts and read *Congratulazioni Gio e Molly.* Delicate cherry blossoms in pale pink icing were nestled between white roses and lavender sprigs that spilled off the side.

"This is a really beautiful surprise, Gio," she said sincerely. "It's such a pity I'm going to have to kill you for it later."

That provoked another roar of laughter from the crowd, who demanded a kiss.

Please, no. But also, *yes, please.*

She wasn't finished processing that other kiss, the one that she would have allowed to turn to lovemaking if he hadn't dropped his head back against the sofa to stare at her with those arresting blue eyes of his. His hands had mapped all of her and she'd loved it.

Gio drew her into his arms and she set nervous hands on his shoulders, fearful she'd make a fool of herself. She searched his eyes. She had warned him not to lead her on, but he was making this engagement seem so perfect. So real.

It would be over in three weeks, though. Less.

Even as she reminded herself of that, she wished the end would never arrive. Her arms slid themselves behind his neck and she lifted her mouth for the touch of his. He kept it chaste, but her lips clung to his, encouraging him to linger, her body not listening to her mind.

Her chest ached with loss when they drew apart.

The swoony "O-o-oh…" from their audience brought a blush to her cheeks, but now they were back to the business of selling this engagement. A series of photos followed, first as they cut into the cake, then as they shared the first piece.

A solid hour passed as they handed out cake, accepting congratulations. Everyone was so nice and genuinely happy for them that Molly began to feel ill with guilt.

When they finally got back into Gio's office, she collapsed onto the sofa.

"I cannot believe you did that to me," she groused.

"Neither can Valentina. She wants to hear from you before she decides whether to report me to HR. She wasn't joking," he added when Molly chuckled. "She said she'd risk her job if necessary. I assured her she is not at risk for doing her job, but I did tell her this is a pretense for Nonno and my father."

"Thank you for that," she said sincerely. It had been bothering her, wondering what Valentina would think of all of this.

The rest of the day was business as usual and very busy, but she was finding her feet with Nelo and the other assistants, which helped a lot.

They had an early dinner with Otto on their way home. He was sitting up and ate a few bites of the cake Molly brought him. His spirits were high because his doctor had told him he could go home in a day or two, to finish recuperating there.

Molly was equally pleased, especially because she could see that Gio was relieved, but the talons of guilt at their subterfuge were digging ever deeper under her skin.

"I hate lying to everyone, especially your grandfather," she told Gio when they returned to his apartment that evening.

Gio yanked at his tie, then poured himself a drink and a glass of sparkling water with lime for her.

"My grandfather would rather it wasn't a lie," he stated as he brought her the glass.

"Yes, I'm aware." She had already kicked off her pumps, so she curled her legs under her as she settled into the corner of the sofa and accepted her drink. "But as fond as I'm becoming of him, that's not the sort of love I intend to marry for."

"You're a romantic?" His eyebrows went up as he settled into the chair that faced her. "I've always thought of you as pragmatic, but you do let people prey upon your emotions, don't you?"

"You, for instance?" she asked with a facetious smile.

He sipped his drink, saying nothing.

She curled herself tighter into the corner of the sofa.

"I like to help people when I can." Who didn't? "But my desire to marry for love is actually a practical choice." Why did saying that make her feel so exposed? Maybe because it sounded as though she was refusing an offer he hadn't actually made?

"How do you mean?" he asked with curiosity.

"My parents married because they accidentally got pregnant with me," she explained with a pang of her old feelings of inadequacy. "In fact, my mother went into reproductive care because she felt so betrayed by how poorly she had been educated as a teenager about her own body, then neglected as she went through a difficult pregnancy. They both loved me, but they felt trapped in their marriage. I don't blame them for divorcing, but it was hard for me. When you're the reason your parents married, you also feel like a failure when they don't stay married."

"You knew all of that when you were *six*?"

"No. At six, I only knew that Dad moved out. Then he moved far away and started a new family. I visited a few times a year, but I didn't feel like I had a place there. Eventually, it came out that they had never been in love. They had tried to make the best of an unplanned pregnancy, but were better apart. They were trying to help me understand, but I still felt like the glue that wasn't strong enough. I don't ever want to put my own child through a divorce, but more than that, I don't want my child to suffer the pressure of holding a couple to-gether."

Only two end table lamps were burning, so it wasn't easy to read his eyes, but she was certain his gaze slid down to her middle. She sealed her lips, reminding him they weren't talking about *this* baby or the fact she wasn't with its father.

"What happens in three weeks?" he asked after a long pause. "You go home?"

"No." Her thoughts flashed to the plans she'd made with Sasha to stay out of sight for the remainder of her pregnancy. Would the island villa still happen? Why weren't Rafael or Sasha texting her back?

Her uncertainty must have shown on her face.

"So stay. Continue to work until you take your mat leave."

"And let everyone, including your grandfather, be-lieve this baby is yours? No. This lie has already gone too far. I don't even know how anyone is buying this engagement. It's obvious I'm a Podunk girl who doesn't belong in your world. I'm not even someone you'd have an affair with."

"Why do you say that?"

"Would you?" Her stomach swooped. Was he joking?

His expression was inscrutable as he sipped his drink, gaze seeming to pick her apart. "Would *you*?"

She had kind of implied that she would when she'd told him not to lead her on, hadn't she?

"That's neither here nor there," she quickly said. "I'm pregnant, so it's moot."

"Is it not safe?" He cocked his head with intrigue. "I was under the impression most women could have sex while pregnant."

She was struck dumb by that, then managed to answer him. "You're not wrong, but how on earth would you know that?"

"This is Italy." He shrugged. "Most men are trying to get their wife pregnant before she's delivered the one she's carrying."

"Oh, for heaven's sake," she sputtered, but she couldn't help a moment of speculation about whether he would find her growing curves sexy.

Don't, she cautioned herself. She couldn't let herself start thinking anything was possible between them other than this fake engagement.

"Have you received your results from today's tests?" he asked, technically pushing up against the boundaries of their deal, but she could tell he was asking out of concern.

"My doctor said she would call me once she reviews them."

"Hmm." It was another thoughtful rumble. "We'll table a discussion about an affair until after you've consulted with her, then."

"Oh, is that what we'll do?" Her voice went up an octave and so did her internal temperature. "Will I have any say in that discussion?" She was trying to sound sarcastic, but it was tough to pull off, especially when he rightly pointed out—

"You brought it up. I'm the one who's being sensible and saying we should check with your doctor first. I'll have a physical, too. Better safe than sorry."

"You're unbelievable." But it had been her Freudian slip. Was she out of her tree? She absolutely could *not* sleep with her boss while pregnant with the secret baby of her dearest friend…who was married to his business associate!

"I'm going to have a bath." She couldn't handle the way he fried her brain circuits.

"Let me know if you want me to wash your hair," he called to her back, taunting, but her skin tightened with anticipation at the thought of it.

She wanted him to touch her and see her naked and do all the rest. That was the stark, shameful truth.

She flipped him the bird. What was he going to do? Fire her?

The remainder of the week was a blur of work and training her team and getting Nonno settled back in his own bed. Molly also moved back to the villa with

Gio, but Gio shrugged off her bringing more than a handful of essentials.

"Ilario has prepared the room next to mine with everything you'll need."

Indeed, the closet was completely stocked with yet another wardrobe from the same boutiques that had been raided when they had arrived. Evening wear had been added, and so many designer shoes that her mind boggled.

Molly had greater concerns than how Gio chose to spend his money, though. She found a report that Sasha had regained consciousness, but it didn't say anything else. Rafael was out of surgery and seemed to be recovering, but hundreds of other news stories had taken over, so she wasn't able to learn more than that. Her handful of texts to both of them remained unanswered.

Molly's physician, Dr. Kala Narula, reviewed Molly's blood work and saw nothing serious. She concluded what Molly suspected—she had fainted from shock.

Kala had been Sasha's fertility specialist and was equally concerned by the news about the pair. She had reached out to the hospital in Rome, but they refused to share anything more than what was released to the press. She agreed with Molly that the best thing they could do for Sasha and Rafael was continue to keep Molly's pregnancy as healthy as possible. She urged Molly to rest and eat smaller meals more often.

"And what about..." Molly almost swallowed her own tongue. "Sex?"

There was a beat of surprise, then Kala replied, "You're far enough beyond implantation and your pregnancy is not high-risk. Physically, there's no issue, but I wouldn't advise this become an experimental phase in your life."

"No." Molly's dry laugh held little humor. "That's not what I'm considering. It's someone I've known a long time and…" And she kind of wished the doctor had told her she was forbidden to have sex. Now the decision was all on her.

"I can't tell you what to do, Molly, but I would remind you that this is a distressing time. It's natural that you might be drawn to a relationship as comfort. Be aware that may be coloring your desire."

"Thanks," she murmured, even as she acknowledged that comfort was not what she was wanted from Gio.

She wanted what their kisses had promised. *Fire.*

She couldn't, though. Shouldn't. Beyond the immediate problem of her pregnancy, they really were from two different worlds. She was a smart, dedicated employee, so she didn't have imposter syndrome about her ability to do her job, but she felt the side-eye at work now that everyone knew they were engaged. They were all wondering how a midlevel employee had risen to the top and caught the boss's personal attention. None of the explanations were flattering.

On the other hand, her lack of a real future with Gio made a brief affair now, while she had the chance, seem justified. If her choice was no cake or a crumb, she wanted the crumb.

"We should leave soon," Gio said as he drained his coffee.

"Hmm? I didn't think we were going into the office

today." It was Saturday and she was still in her yoga shorts and a loose T-shirt over her sports bra, having done her stretches before joining him in the garden for breakfast.

"We have the party in Milan tonight. You need to be fitted for a gown."

"I have gowns." She'd been planning to try them on after her shower.

"Those are samples that designers send in hopes of gaining your attention," he disclosed. "This is a very high-profile party and your first event as my fiancée. You'll want something you've chosen yourself."

That *she* chose? Or he did? This was exactly what she had meant when she called herself Podunk. She didn't know how to choose an evening gown for a high-profile event. Nor did she want to be molded by him into someone he thought was good enough to be seen beside him.

"I'll check in with Nonno, to be sure he's comfortable with our being away for the night." Gio rose.

"The night?" she repeated, halting him.

"We'll stay in Milan unless he wants us to come home. Can you be ready in thirty minutes?"

She was ready in ten, seeing as the maid had already packed for her. She had a quick shower and snuck her prenatal vitamins into her bag, then went to Otto's room to say *arrivederci*.

"What color is your gown tonight?" Otto asked her.

"I don't know yet. Apparently, I'm choosing something when we get to Milan."

"The white serpent, then," Otto said to Gio and pointed to the safe.

"Otto," Molly protested.

"Call me Nonno. Yes, that's the one." He nodded at Gio to open the velvet case.

It was a snake of diamonds—literally a serpent-shaped head biting its own dangling tail. Each reticulated scale held nine diamante diamonds and the head was an eye-catching sparkle of tapered baguets. Matching earrings were fashioned to appear as though the serpent had pierced through the wearer's earlobes.

"I had that made for our fifth anniversary. Theresa loved it. She didn't enjoy big parties, but these always sparked compliments and conversation, which put her at ease."

Molly was genuinely falling in love with this caring, old-world gentleman.

"I would be honored to wear it, Nonno. What else can I tell people about it?"

He told her about the designer and why he'd chosen it and where he'd presented it to his wife and how she had reacted. His eyes were damp by the time he'd finished.

"That's enough from me," he said, patting her hand. "You go enjoy yourselves."

"This is killing me," Molly said when they were aboard Gio's helicopter.

She ought to be getting used to the luxury that his level of wealth afforded, but she was still agog at the private cabin with four armchairs arranged around a round table with drink holders set into it. The decor was slate-gray and silver, the windows huge and tinted, offering a view from ground to clouds as they lifted out of the city and traveled over green pastures and rolling hills.

"What is?" Gio prompted.

Molly was trying to be careful about not twisting the antique ring on her finger, but she constantly checked to be sure it was still there, terrified she would lose it.

"You have to tell your grandfather the truth, Gio. I like him too much to lie to him."

"Once he's fully out of the woods, I'll consider that, but not yet," he countered. "I have a clean bill of health, by the way."

"Wh-what?" She sat back into her armchair and stared across at him.

"It's information I want you to have." He was watching her through the screen of his spiky lashes. "What did *your* doctor say?"

"That my blood work was fine. I told you that," she mumbled and looked to the ground again. Was that a castle?

"You didn't ask whether—"

"Oh, my God, Gio!" A raging blush consumed her, licking her with flames of guilt and yearning and enticement.

"So you did ask." His mouth quirked with amusement. "And given that reaction, I hope to hear those words again soon."

Oh, my God, Gio? "You're not funny."

"I wasn't joking."

She ignored him for the rest of the flight. Or rather, tried to, which was impossible. Thankfully, the flight wasn't long. Very soon, they were touching down in Milan.

A drive through congested traffic ensued, then they

arrived at the hotel, where they were shown into a beautiful suite with a sitting room, a terrace and two bedrooms. One bedroom was already occupied by a team of busy bees who looked up with smiles of greeting.

"Molly, this is Ursula." Gio came up behind her as Molly stood in the bedroom doorway, too intimidated to enter. "She and her team will look after you today."

A gorgeous woman with a wide smile and shimmering gold shadow on her eyelids stopped fussing with the gowns on the rack and came toward her to shake her hand.

"It's a pleasure to meet you."

"It's nice to meet you, too." Molly was agog at the gowns, the likes of which she'd only ever seen on coverage of the red carpet at award shows.

"I need to meet with Vittorio, to finalize the arrangements for my parents." Gio squeezed her shoulders. "Once you've chosen something, Ursula will take care of alterations while you relax in the spa. Have a massage, eat, nap if you can. She'll make sure you're back here in time to have your hair and makeup done."

"You're not…going to tell me what to wear?" She turned to face him, perversely disappointed and already bereft that he was leaving her.

"You'll look beautiful in whatever you choose." It felt very natural that he dropped a light kiss on her lips. It was the sort of kiss any engaged couple might exchange when one was heading out the door, but she wound up pressing closer and settling her hands on his waist, unconsciously urging him to linger.

He drew in a small, sharp breath, then swept his

mouth across hers a few more times, more deeply, sending delicious tingles through her.

When he drew back, his blue eyes were the hot center of a flame. He trailed a caress in the curve of her throat, one that felt like a promise. Like anticipation.

"Until later." His voice had become a rasp in his throat that made her skin feel tight in the most pleasurable way.

He left and she turned into the bedroom in time to see everyone exchanging looks of raised eyebrows that said, *Ooh-la-la*.

CHAPTER SIX

THE CASELLA FORTUNE had its roots in the shipping trade and the earliest forms of cargo insurance, which had essentially been a series of gambling ventures on shipments making it to harbor. Most had, which had provided capital to a long-ago Casella son to build ships of his own. His son then married the daughter of a steel-mill owner. Together, they produced a dozen ships and almost as many children, one of whom had a passion for trains.

The locomotive enthusiast expanded the corporation into the manufacture of engines and rail cars. His brother, Otto's uncle, founded the Casella brokerage firm. Another uncle became an active buyer and distributor for the import-export arm of the company.

By the time Ottorino took over as president, the Casella Corporation was manufacturing airplane parts and owned enough farmland that they supplied and packaged their own brands of olive oil, pasta and pesto, among other goods.

Otto married the heiress to an automobile manu-facturer, a move that was decried by the press as mercenary, but Otto had genuinely loved his bride. Sadly, they only birthed one son before she passed away from an undiagnosed heart condition when Ambrose was fourteen.

Otto became a withdrawn man and his son became a troubled teen. Ambrose was expelled from his boarding school twice for drug use.

As an adult, Gio was capable of some compassion for his father's desire to self-medicate his adolescent grief. If that had been the extent of Ambrose's failings, and he had subsequently sought help along the way, they might still have a relationship.

Ambrose had only paid lip service to rehab, however, using it as a means to get on Otto's good side when it suited him. Sobriety was not something he wanted. He liked to party and travel and spend money that was handed to him. At his core, he was an entitled, narcissistic parasite of a man.

When Ambrose found a woman as superficial, debauched and manipulative as he was, he married her and they produced a son in a calculated effort to oust his own father from his position as president of Casella Corporation. While Gio had still been an infant in the arms of a series of ill-treated nannies, a small war had raged around him, one that splintered the extended family and nearly sank the company altogether.

By the time Gio was leaving for boarding school, he had seen his grandfather only twice. Otto upended the challenges from his son by paying for Gio's schooling, taking guardianship of Gio in the process.

That had worked for a time, but Ambrose regularly

reared his head, throwing out custody threats and other strong-arm tactics to squeeze more money from his father. If he had ever applied himself so diligently to actual work, he might have been an asset to the company, but all his efforts went toward ensuring he continued to enjoy a free ride.

Gio's mother was even worse. At least Ambrose was open about his financial motives. Fridrika liked to bait emotional hooks to drag people in and keep them serving her. Gio's earliest memories were thankfully blank, but later, he had fallen for her claims that she wished to know her son. He'd always been stung. Badly.

If his grandfather had not been alive to see it, Gio would have cut them off long ago, but Nonno still saw glimpses of his beloved Theresa in Ambrose. He also needed to know that her grandson, Gio, had inherited her sense of decency, even if her son had not.

Nevertheless, this latest exercise in buying them off reminded Gio that if something did happen to him, Ambrose would make every attempt to take control of the Casella Corporation. There were a handful of cousins who were excellent in their executive roles, but none as hardened by experience to deal with Ambrose as cold-bloodedly as Gio could.

Gio had always known he needed to produce an heir, but he had foolishly believed there was no urgency. With Otto's recent illness, however, Gio had to accept that even if Otto recovered, he would not live forever.

Gio had to ensure there would be strong, ethical leadership on the horizon. He needed a wife who would not only embrace motherhood, but would also understand the role her children were being raised to take on.

Molly and her protectiveness of her unborn child leaped to mind, mostly because they were already "engaged." With his grandfather improving, Gio would have to come clean about their ruse sooner than later. He hated to disappoint the old man, especially when Otto seemed so attached to Molly.

Was it really so far-fetched that he would want to marry her? She had wondered how anyone believed they were engaged and yes, they were from very different backgrounds, but he had learned from his first experience that knowing the same people and attending the same charity events didn't guarantee a happy union.

He and Molly had a far better rapport than he'd had with his fiancée. Her baby was not as big an issue as she might think. He understood firsthand that not every parent was meant to become one. Sometimes a man other than the baby's father had to step in for the good of the child, as Nonno had done for him.

Of course, he and Otto had a blood connection, but those kinship ties had been soured on both sides by the time the sullen and mistrustful Gio had been left with yet another stranger, this time a cynical and remote old man.

It had taken a long time for them to warm into the close relationship they enjoyed today, which only told Gio how important it was to bond with a baby from the beginning.

The more he thought about it, the further he went down the road of seeing marriage as a viable path for both of them. Rather than become a single mother, Molly would have a husband who could provide an excellent life for her and her child. There was a time when he had feared what type of father he might make, but he had Nonno's steady example to follow. Molly's innate warmth would counter any reticence he still possessed.

If he married Molly, he would gain a life partner whose company he enjoyed. His grandfather already adored her. That was incredibly important to him, given that Nonno had seen straight through Fridrika's external beauty to the ugliness inside her.

Then there was the animal attraction. Gio kept trying to put that aside so he could think clearly, but he kept hearing her say *You wouldn't have an affair with me. Would you?*

Hell, yes, he would. He was mindful that he was still her employer, though.

As he wrapped up the unpleasant business of forcing his father to disinherit himself, he allowed himself to replay their kiss the other day and her adorable blush today, when he'd asked what the doctor had said.

He couldn't press her into an affair if she didn't want one, but he didn't understand why she was hesitating. When they kissed, she encouraged him. She obviously wanted him as badly as he wanted her and he wanted her so badly, his blood was on fire.

By the time he had visited the barber and dressed in his tuxedo, he was downright impatient to see her again.

She was worth the wait, he decided, when she finally appeared. The sight of her knocked the breath out of him.

The top of the sleeveless gown was reminiscent of

a breastplate in pale, metallic green. The skirt was a filmy waterfall that parted over her left thigh, revealing the three silver bands that formed her five-inch heels. His gaze ate up the glimpse of her leg, the roundness of her hips and the swells of her breasts plumped beneath the serpentine necklace.

She was a goddess, one who controlled all the fey creatures of the forest.

For once, she wore her hair down. The rich brunette waves framed an expression that awaited judgment, but how could she doubt she was anything but entrancing? Her makeup was heavier than he'd ever seen her wear it, but it was playfully dramatic with greens and golds accentuating her eyes. Her bold lip made him want that particular shade of crimson smeared all over his naked body.

"You look very nice," she murmured, looking down as she adjusted Nonna's ring on her finger.

"I would have said it first, but I'm speechless."

She lifted her long, thick lashes. "Don't mock me."

"Mock?" She might as well have hit him with a sledgehammer, he was so at a loss as to what that was supposed to mean.

"I feel like a fraud, Gio."

"In what way?"

"In every way. I don't..." She looked over her shoulder toward the bedroom, where faint voices were still conversing in Italian, then came closer to him. "I don't belong here," she whispered. "I'm not one of you."

"I hesitate to say this, *cara*, because I've promised

myself I won't come on too strong tonight. But if you belong to me, then you belong."

Her lips parted and her breasts rose in a shaken breath. "But I don't."

"But you will." The embers of want in his belly flared even hotter.

He wanted her to belong to him, physically, but in other ways, too. That desire was growing into such an intense imperative, he pushed it aside for examination later.

He brought her hand to his mouth and kissed her painted nails. "Shall we go?"

Molly didn't need a wrap. The party was in the hotel ballroom on a lower floor.

As they stepped into the elevator, she crushed a tiny, emerald-green clutch in her fist, as though it contained an elixir that would save her life.

Nothing could save her from the way Gio was looking at her, though. From the moment she had walked out of the bedroom, she'd been a bundle of nerves that she would disappoint him. Ironically, it was harder to take the burn of approval that ignited his gaze. It warmed her from the inside out, scorched away her insecurities and seared away any resistance she had left.

How could she not respond to being admired by a man like him? What had begun as a crush was now a full-blown infatuation with a man who seemed to reciprocate her attraction, but hadn't outright said so. She kept trying to convince herself there was nothing between them, then he would look at her or touch her or kiss the daylights out of her and make her think *if*...

If you belong to me...

"We don't need to stay long if you'd rather not."

She had slept a full hour in the spa's serenity room. That was after she had been soaked and massaged, mani-ed and pedi-ed, fed light snacks and hydrated with citrus-infused mineral water.

He wasn't suggesting they go upstairs to rest, though. When she met his glittering gaze, she saw lust. The bottom fell out of her heart.

The doors opened and she was so disconcerted, she was glad that he took her hand to lead her into the room full of pearlescent balloons and fairy lights, with tuxedos and gowns in every color.

He was right. She was glad that she wore something that could compete with the rest of the haute couture around her. It was a full-on runway, with enough sparkling diamonds to inspire a hundred jewel-thief movies.

A beautiful couple was greeting every guest personally.

"Gio! You made it," the tall, dark and handsome man said.

"Molly, these are our hosts, Vittorio and Gwyn Donatelli."

"Oh, my God, I love your necklace. We're so delighted to meet you, Molly." Gwyn was blonde, sounded American and was also very attractive.

"Thank you for inviting me," Molly murmured as she learned the art of cheek kisses, exchanging them with Gwyn, then her husband.

"Call me Vito, *per favore*," he murmured.

"Gio, you scoundrel," Gwyn greeted. "That was a very generous donation you made to my foundation, thank you."

Molly had asked if they were supposed to bring a gift, but the party was an annual fundraiser for an organization that promoted online privacy and helped victims of revenge porn. Apparently, Gwyn had met her husband after nude photos of her had been leaked without her knowledge or consent.

"You're American, too," Gwyn said to Molly. "I still stumble over cultural differences so please call me if anything comes up or you need help finding anything. Gio has my number."

"Thank you, that's very kind." Molly hadn't expected to be greeted with such warmth, especially after her experience on Sasha's yacht.

"Let's plan to connect, anyway," Gwyn urged. "I'd love to get to know you better."

"I'd like that," she said, even as she recalled that she wasn't really marrying Gio. In another twelve days or so, she would melt into the woodwork, never to see any of these people again. Not even Gio.

A chill wind whistled through the cavern of her chest.

"We'll let you greet the rest of your guests," Gio said, branding the small of Molly's back with his hand.

"*Grazie*. But find Paolo. He wants to say hello and Lauren is eager to meet you," Vittorio said with a wink at Molly.

"I seated you with my brother and his wife, Imogen,"

Gwyn added. "She's also American and very funny. I think you'll like her."

Molly was touched they'd gone to such trouble to ensure she was comfortable and entertained. Gwyn was right, too. Imogen was very witty. She lived with her husband, Travis, in New York. They had two children, six-year-old Julian, who was precocious, and three-year-old Lilith, who was a dreamer, often getting lost in her own imagination.

"I'm quite sure that Julian is setting us up for a water-damage bill as we speak, but Paolo insisted we leave our children with their four and Gwyn's two. That's ten children in an ancestral mansion full of priceless art. Paolo organized a clown and an extra nanny, as if that'll be any help. Lion tamers, Paolo! *That's* who you call. Am I right?"

Despite her jokes, Imogen was visibly pregnant and ecstatic with it.

"I notice you're not drinking, either," Imogen said, leaning close with a cheeky side-eye.

"I don't actually drink much. Alcohol gives me a headache," Molly lied. She was dying to compare pregnancy notes. It was one of the few things she was truly missing in this process.

"So much for Gwyn's theory for your sudden engagement. Tell me more about Genoa. We visit Italy at least once a year, but we always stay with Gwyn and Vito, either here or at the lake. We really should see more of the country. I say that, but I'll have a newborn in five months so when would that even happen?" Imogen rolled her eyes at herself.

"How long are you here this trip?" Gio asked, proving that he'd been dividing his attention between their conversation and the one he was having with Travis. "We're at the villa in Portofino with my grandfather. My apartment in the city is empty."

"That's kind of you to offer, but you don't want a pair of children tearing up the place," Imogen said with a wave of her hand.

"Immy." Travis waited for her to turn her head, then looked at her with heated adoration. "I love our children with all my heart, but *I* don't want our children tearing up his place. Not if I could have you to myself for a couple of nights. Gwyn will keep the kids, I'm sure."

"That's quite the anniversary present for her, isn't it?" Imogen joked, but Travis was already walking away.

Moments later, it was settled. The pair would fly to Genoa with them in the morning and stay for two nights.

"That was nice of you to offer your apartment to Travis and Imogen," Molly said to Gio, when dinner was over and they were dancing.

"Her husband is a useful connection." He shrugged it off. "And you seem to enjoy her company. See? My world isn't so different from yours."

She stifled a wild "Ha!" since there was a small orchestra providing the music and she was waltzing for the first time since being forced to take stilted, uncomfortable lessons in middle-school PE classes. If he hadn't been so skilled at leading, she would be stumbling onto his toes.

She was fighting the urge to crane her neck at all the starlets and royalty circulating the room, but others weren't being so polite. Despite the warm welcome Gio received when he introduced her, nearly everyone here viewed her as a curiosity. She could tell.

All of that faded away, however, when the music switched to an instrumental of a modern tune, one that was sensual and had Gio drawing her closer.

As his hand rested at the small of her back and his thumb shifted in a lazy caress against the sensitized nerves there, she felt herself melting into him. Her head grew heavy and sought the firm plane at the front of his shoulder. Lingering traces of his aftershave against his throat made her feel drugged.

"Are you trying to seduce me?" She picked up her head when the song wound down and he kept his arms around her, not moving them off the dance floor.

"I hope I'm succeeding." His fingertips skimmed up her arm and across her bare shoulder, lifting a shivering wake of goose bumps. "*Mio Dio*, I want to kiss you." His gaze was so intent on her lips, they stung with anticipation.

She wanted that, too. But not here, like this. She wanted to be alone with him, where their kisses could progress to…

She dipped her head, fingers playing with the ruffle beneath his bow tie. She was very aware how short her window of time with him was. When Ursula had been fitting her, she had given Molly's midsection a curious moment of study, but the pins between her lips had kept her from asking questions with anything but her eyes.

Time was sifting like sand through her fingers. Molly had to wring out every minute that she could with him.

"It would only be for now." She peeked up at him and a small rasp entered her throat as she added, "You know that, right?"

"Let's take it one day at a time." He drew a tantalizing pattern in the hollow beneath her ear, but there was a faint curl of smugness to his lips.

Her heart pounded as they slipped out of the party without saying goodbye. In the elevator, he pressed her to the wall, caging her with his arms. She lifted her mouth in offering. His head dipped past her lips as he ducked to set a hot kiss against her neck.

A ragged groan left her, one of denial and enjoyment and agony at the delicate way he opened his mouth and sucked a damp spot against her skin. A flush of heat poured into her chest, making her breasts feel swollen. Her nipples stung.

She felt his smile against her tender skin. His teeth moved in the barest scrape of a wolf reminding his mate that he was dangerous, but would never hurt her. When his nuzzling gaze worked up to her chin, he leaned his hips into her abdomen, letting her feel that he was already hard.

"I'll be careful with you, I promise, but you'll tell me if I need to stop."

"You won't need to stop." She was pretty sure she would die if he stopped.

The doors opened and he whirled her out, then swept her down the hall, barely allowing her feet to touch the floor.

Inside the suite, all the lingering staff were gone. It was tidy and quiet, and dimly lit by a single lamp throwing golden light against the shadows.

Nerves struck and Molly brought her hands to her ear, as she started to remove her earring.

"You should take this necklace. I don't want anything to happen to these."

He shrugged off his tuxedo jacket and threw it over the back of the couch, then tugged his bow tie loose as he walked to the door into the bedroom.

As he stood there, opening his cuffs and setting fire to her with his gaze, he said, "I would love to strip you naked where you stand and have you on the floor, *bella*, but I just promised to take care with you. Come into the bedroom. I want you in my bed."

Her knees almost gave out.

Shakily, she crossed toward him, offering the one earring she had managed to remove.

He took it, then kept her hand as he drew her into the room and lazily closed the door behind her.

"I want to ask you what you like, but I don't want to hear about other lovers right now." He touched her shoulders to turn her, then his fingers searched under her hair for the clasp of the necklace. "Lift your hair."

She did, thinking she should warn him that her other lovers were as scarce as her sexual experience. It was another reason she was stealing this chance with him. No one had ever aroused her beyond idle curiosity. No one made her burn with the simple act of unclasping a necklace or lowering the zip of her dress.

"Stay just like that," he said of the way she held her

hair gathered against her crown. "You're very beautiful." His voice seemed to resonate from the depths of his chest. His hot breath stirred the fine hairs at the back of her neck and the cool links of the necklace tickled her skin as he kept hold of it while shifting his fist to her shoulder. His other hand traced down her spine, sending more of those sharp tingles into her breasts and lower. A throbbing ache settled between her thighs.

Hot, hot kisses touched every single vertebra until he was on his knees behind her, dragging the gown down into a puddle on the floor. She was braless and, a few kisses later, divested of the lace that had graced her hips.

"I have a small obsession with your ass," he informed her in that gritty, erotic voice. He set a damp kiss on one cheek. As he rose, his hand trailed its way up her inner thigh, dipping ever so briefly toward the heat at her center before lingering to fondle each of her cheeks.

Then he was turning her into his arms. His shirt and trousers abraded her skin as he pulled her close.

"You're still fully dressed and I'm…" Wearing only shoes and a hard blush. Her hand reflexively shielded her mound.

"Oh, I am very aware," he said with molten satisfaction. He brought her hands to the buttons on his shirt while his own shaped her hips and waist, and spread over the subtle curve of her belly.

She faltered in trying to release his shirt buttons, shooting a look upward, worried how he was reacting to that evidence of her pregnancy, but his gaze was eating up her naked form. He was hungrily taking her in all the way to her toes, then coming back to her anxious eyes with a dazzled gleam in his own.

"You're so beautiful," he growled before he dove his fingers into her hair and sealed his mouth to hers.

A thousand sensations accosted her—the light pull on her hair that held her captive to his ravenous kiss. The rough-sweet way he devoured her lips and tagged her tongue with his own. The sense of being overwhelmed by him, by his wide shoulders and height. The crispness of his shirt against her hand, then the hot satin and fine hairs and underlying strength when she bared his chest. His torso scorched her own as they pressed closer. His possessive arm banded her against him and waves of pleasure emanated from the way his palm drew slow circles on her backside.

She could hardly bear how good it all felt and threaded her arms beneath his shirt, clinging around his waist as she strained to deepen their kiss, rubbing her breasts against his chest as she did.

When her knee instinctively came up, he took full advantage. He trapped it against his waist with his elbow. His palm slid to the underside of her butt cheek and his long fingers began to play in the eager slickness that had welled against her folds.

"Gio," she gasped.

"I have you. I won't let you fall." He tilted her and dipped his head, capturing her nipple to lick and lave and suck until she was groaning. All the while, his touch explored and discovered the spot that made her breath catch.

She clung across his shoulders, head falling back, never imagining she could be this helpless and uninhibited.

She wasn't. Not really.

"Gio, please," she sobbed.

"You're so close, *bella*," he said, offering one more lingering stroke of his fingertip across her swollen clit before he eased her upright. "I would never drop you, I swear."

She wanted to believe that, but she knew that one day, she would walk away, and she had a very strong feeling that despite all her warnings, he would not take it well. He wasn't used to being rejected.

Rejecting him was furthest thing from her mind in this moment, though. She opened his shirt wider and dragged the tails from his waistband. Then she tried to open his belt, but her hands were shaking too badly.

"That is possibly the most erotic thing I've ever seen," he told her, but took over, yanking his pants open. "Walk to the bed for me. Let me watch."

Wanton excitement gripped her. She started toward the bed, then glanced over her shoulder as she decided to take the long route around the foot of it. She deliberately set one five-inch heel in front of the other and let her hips ticktock in a shameless way.

When she looked back at him again, he was fully naked, fully aroused. He held himself in a light grasp of two fingers and a thumb, as though any more would finish him off.

It was flagrant and so sexy, she kind of lost the plot.

"Sit down," he said as he circled around to her. "As

much as I want those shoes on my shoulders, I'd rather help you take them off."

Her legs were so weak, she sank down, then swallowed as she stared at his erection.

"Do you want me to—"

"I want *everything*, Molly." He cupped her face and tilted her gaze up to his. "The catalog of things I want to do with you will take years to accomplish. But we have time." He ran his thumb along her bottom lip. "Tonight, I just want to be inside you. Would you like me to wear a condom?" He went to his knees to remove her shoes.

"You s-said that your doctor said there were no concerns."

"I would still wear one if you want me to. I've never not worn one." His gaze flicked up to hers, steady, but there was a feral flash behind it that caused her stomach to swoop. "I want you very, very badly. I don't know how long I'll last."

"I think…without?" Was that too intimate? Too *naked*?

Her second shoe dropped away and he pressed her to the mattress as he rose, sliding her to the middle of the big bed, then covering her with every inch of his powerful body.

When she delicately took hold of his erection, he muttered a string of Italian that she didn't catch. He drew her hands above her head, stretching her out beneath him as he spread her legs wide with his iron-hard thighs and rocked to settle himself against her tender folds.

The intensity of his expression was almost too much

to take. She wanted to shut her eyes, but she couldn't seem to look away. His gaze searched over her features as though memorizing them. He kept her hands pinned with his one hand while his other made a delicate dance along her temple and cheek, then traced her bottom lip.

Incredible yearning struck. She was getting everything she wanted, and loved the way he was drawing this out, but she wanted more. She wanted *forever*. She wanted that so badly, a scorching heat accosted the backs of her eyes.

She made the most of now by opening her mouth and turning her head just a little, keeping her gaze locked to his while she sucked his finger into her mouth and blatantly caressed it with her tongue.

His inhale was a torn sound, then he released another guttural few words in Italian. After a moment, he withdrew his finger and replaced it with his mouth. It was the most carnal kiss of her life, hard and hungry and infinitely possessive. At the same time, he shifted and his touch was there, where her folds were as wet as his finger. He pressed it inside her and they both groaned.

He held her like that for long minutes, trapped in his kiss, splayed for his pleasure as he slowly, slowly brought her to the brink.

When she was arching and writhing and moaning unabashedly, he replaced his touch with the damp crest of his erection and let his full length sink into her.

That was it. She had gotten her wish. She was his. Forever. Her heart quivered inside her chest as she acknowledged that.

He released her arms then, so he could brace on his

elbow and tuck her more completely beneath him. He began slow, powerful thrusts.

"Don't close your eyes," he commanded in a rasp that made her blink her eyes open. "It's good? Does it hurt?"

"It feels so good, Gio, I can't—" She couldn't touch enough of him, couldn't take him deeply enough, couldn't sustain this height of arousal.

She couldn't bear to look him in the eye and let him see all this tortured ecstasy he was stirring within her, but she couldn't shut him out, either.

He was determined to wring every note of pleasure from the experience, thrusting in that steady, delicious way that strummed all her nerve endings and made her moan with abandon. Perspiration coated his back and his thigh was hot and tense where her foot stroked him. She was so lost to this experience that she trembled and grew feverish.

She had fooled herself into believing she could steal this time with him as though it was as inconsequential as a candy bar. This was the opposite of stealing. It was relinquishment. Even as he gave her more pleasure than she could withstand, he stole her ability to ever settle for anything less than this with anyone else. She would never be the same after this. She would be his in ways that could never be undone.

Maybe she clutched on to him tighter in those seconds because she was trying to take back the pieces of her soul that were flowing into him. She was catching and clasping before it was too late, but then it *was* too late.

With a ragged noise, he began to thrust harder. Faster. Deeper.

"Don't hold back. Let go," he commanded, and she did.

She arched in ecstasy as her orgasm swept over her in a tsunami of breathless, wild joy. He rode with her through it, continuing to thrust, unevenly now. She was dimly aware of his muscles bunching, his body jerking, then his animalistic cries joined hers.

They clung and tumbled and withstood the powerful waves for a thousand years, bodies fused. It was the most perfect moment of accord she had ever experienced with another human being.

I want this, she thought. *I want him in my life. For the rest of my life.*

But as her postclimactic euphoria receded and the final flutters left her nerve endings, a harrowing sense of darkness took its place.

CHAPTER SEVEN

SHE WAS EVERYTHING he had imagined and more. *They* were.

He had woken to her ass spooned into his lap and they'd made love that way, with her breast in his palm and her delicate shivers of release milking his. It had been exquisite.

Now she was being adorably shy, blushing bright red when he said, "Let the maid pack for you. Surely you're as hungry for breakfast as I am?"

She gave up on her attempt to arrange her new cosmetics in the too-small case she'd brought. "Do you have the necklace?"

"Yes. It's safe. I reserved a table on the rooftop terrace, since we don't have time to see the city this trip."

"That was thoughtful. Thank you." She dropped her two phones into her bag, along with a lipstick and the pill dispenser he'd noticed she used for her prenatal vitamins.

"How do you feel?" he asked when they were alone in the elevator.

She gave him another admonishing look. "Yes, Mr. Smug. I've worked up an appetite."

"I meant... No adverse effects from our activities?"

"You make it sound like we went rock climbing or some other high-risk hobby."

"I've never had time for hobbies, but I see the appeal now. I'll start *making* time."

She giggled and flashed him a knowing look that was loaded with enough sinful speculation to have him wondering if they would have time to use the bed once more before they left the hotel.

"You didn't answer my question," he pointed out as the elevator let them out.

"I'm fine. Thank you," she said pertly.

Good. Because one night would not be enough. That certainty was crystalizing inside him. He wanted more from her. More time, more commitment. More of *her*.

Did he want her as his wife, though?

He considered that question while they enjoyed a pleasant, leisurely breakfast, intermittently speaking with a few guests from last night who were also staying in the hotel.

Molly was wrong to think she didn't fit in his world. People were curious about her, but much of it was around him and his history of being jilted. They wanted to gauge whether she was in it for the long haul. She didn't talk much about herself, though. She was naturally empathetic and curious and listened intently, which built trust and charmed everyone very quickly.

As they were finishing up, Travis texted to say they

were on the way to meet them so they could drive to the helipad together.

"He sent me Imogen's contact details. Do you want that to go to your work phone or personal?"

"Personal." She had glanced over her work emails while they'd eaten, but now brought out the other phone.

It pinged with the text he sent her and she opened it to check it, then gave a few swipes as though checking for other messages. Her expression shadowed with dismay.

"What's wrong?"

"Nothing." She gave him an overbright smile. "I want to take a couple of photos for Mom."

She rose and moved to the rail while he signed their meal to the room, but he couldn't help wondering if she'd been hoping for communication from the baby's father.

The secrecy around that part of her life was really starting to irritate him. They would definitely have to dig into that before he brought up marriage.

He was pondering how he would open that topic as they walked out of the restaurant and were accosted by a woman waiting for her table.

"Gio! I heard you were here for the Donatelli anniversary party last night." She swept her talonlike nail through the fall of her raven-black hair. "I was supposed to be there, but I only arrived this morning."

He flickered through his mental contact list, coming up with… "Jacinda. It's nice to see you again." It wasn't. She reminded him of his mother. He would bet the Casella fortune that Jacinda had not received an invitation to last night's party and had arrived here this morning with the intention of running into him or some other poor sod she'd chosen to target.

"The rumors are true?" She took off her sunglasses and bit the tip of one arm as she studied Molly. "You're marrying your assistant's assistant?"

"I don't think anyone is so crude as to say that," he said with a note of warning.

"Oh." Molly jolted slightly. "We've met. I didn't recognize you with your, um, hair down."

"We weren't properly introduced last year." Jacinda swept a catty glance down Molly's flowing pants and the lace top that hugged her breasts and arms. "You've had quite the transformation yourself, haven't you?"

"We're meeting someone," Gio said flatly and set his hand against Molly's back to signal they were cutting this short.

Molly stubbornly dug in her heels, staying where she was. "I heard that Mr. and Mrs. Zamos were in a terrible car accident. I'm so sorry. I hope they're recovering?"

"Alexandra?" Jacinda dragged her attention from Gio's half embrace of Molly to Molly's penetrating gaze. "Pfft. I'd never worry about her. That woman has nine lives. They're already back in Athens."

Molly was visibly taken aback by the callousness of that response, as any decent human being would have been. Gio was.

"Excuse us," he said firmly, and escorted Molly to the elevator. He waited until they were alone inside it, then said, "You didn't have to try to be nice to her. She's not someone I cross paths with often." He couldn't think of any other reason she had made such an effort at conversation.

She didn't say anything and kept her nose forward. Was she pale?

"Molly?"

"Hmm?"

"You're upset." Of course, she was. Jacinda had been outright rude toward her.

For the barest moment, Molly's mouth quivered, then she firmed it, blinked rapidly and asked with a hint of belligerence, "Because I came face-to-face with one of your past lovers? That's none of my business."

"Is this you being possessive, Molly?" He didn't hate it. In fact, he found it heartening that she was invested enough in their relationship to be annoyed.

"No." She scowled and stubbornly kept her face forward. "I know where you slept last night. As long as we're monogamous while we're together, that's all that matters to me."

While we're together. That raised his own hackles of possessiveness.

"We all have a past that can't be changed." She folded her arms and looked to her shoes. "I'd be a hypocrite if I was upset about yours."

Like her past with the father of her baby? If he wanted her to tell him about that, he needed to earn her trust.

"Jacinda was never my lover."

She released a choked noise of disbelief. "Perhaps we have different definitions of that word. When I came out to the pool that day on the yacht, her boobs were in your face."

"I don't take something just because it's offered. I decide what I want, then I don't rest until I have it." He held her gaze, drilling the deeper meaning of his words into her.

He wanted her.

She swallowed and her lashes quivered.

Tension was creeping in around her eyes, though. A vulnerable tug pulled at the corners of her mouth, giving her a look of persecution.

Pregnant, he reminded himself. He couldn't take the high-handed, steamroller approach that was his preferred method of getting what he wanted. He eased the moment with humor instead.

"Her breasts were in *your* face, too," he reminded her. "She shows them to everyone."

After a beat, she muttered, "I felt like I'd stumbled into a nudist colony."

They were both chuckling as the doors opened, but her humor fell away very quickly.

She was still bothered by the interaction. He could tell.

"Molly—"

"We have to meet Travis and Imogen, don't we?"

"Yes," he agreed, accepting that this conversation was too important to have on the fly. He would wait until they were back at the villa, where there would be no interruptions.

He had the sense of walking up a dune of sand, though. Every footstep should have gained him ground, but it slipped away beneath his feet instead. The harder he tried to climb it, the slower his progress became.

He hated this feeling. This lack of surety. It took him back to a time when nothing in his life had been stable. When the people who were supposed to be constants in his world were only consistent in letting him down.

Marry her. Keep this one.

It wasn't his grandfather's voice this time. It was his own.

Otto was looking infinitely better when they returned. He was able to move into a chair for his meals and was in very bright spirits. He even dressed long enough to meet Travis and Imogen when they came for lunch before they flew back to Milan and their children.

"I think I'll be able to attend your wedding," Otto told Molly when he made it all the way to the terrace for breakfast the following morning. "Have you set a date?"

"Um…no." She silently pleaded for Gio to tell him.

They'd had a busy few days, fitting in playing tour guide with the other couple between the demands of work.

"I don't have much time left," Otto scolded with dark humor. He sent Gio an incisive stare that belied the fact that he was barely able to hold his espresso cup in one hand. "Plan a big reception if that suits you, but marry quickly. Before she changes her mind."

Oof. Apparently, Otto really was feeling stronger if he was throwing down gauntlets like that at his grandson.

"My mother is a midwife," Molly blurted. "It's hard

for her to get away without a lot of notice. I couldn't possibly marry without her and my sister here." Patricia actually worked through a clinic to ensure they always had coverage for expecting mothers. She had also lightened her patient load this year so she could be responsive to Molly's potential needs.

Otto brushed off that excuse with blasé confidence. "Gio will find someone to step in for her. The two of you are already going through the motions of starting a family. Take it seriously."

"Nonno!" Molly covered her blush with her hands, not surprised he knew she wasn't using the bed in the room she'd been given, but not expecting him to be so brash about mentioning it.

"Since you seem back in fighting form, we'll go to the London office for a few days." Gio transferred his hooded look to Molly. "That will give you a chance to close your apartment. We'll discuss the wedding date while we're away."

Since she actually did need to close her flat, she didn't argue.

They arrived in London later that afternoon. Nelo had flown with them on Gio's private jet and Molly had been busy arranging for Nelo's counterpart from New York, Avigail, to meet them for an all-hands meeting with their London colleague, Yu. They were gelling as a squad, but she thought it would be good for all of them, including Gio, to work together for a few days.

"If you want a team-building exercise, have them

close your apartment for you," Gio suggested after they dropped Nelo at his hotel.

"Ew. No." She had asked her neighbor to empty her refrigerator of perishables the day after she'd flown to Genoa. "I already have a moving company arranged to put everything into storage. I need to collect a few personal items, though. Maybe I'll spend the night, so I can be sure I have everything."

She could use a night away from him, to recalibrate. The more time she spent with him, the more they made love, the more she wished this could be her life. She needed to remind herself that was not only impossible, but it also wasn't something *he* wanted. They had agreed this was an affair. Temporary.

"Drop me and I'll meet you at the office in the morning."

She was dreading the office. She had left with Gio very abruptly, before her promotion to being his executive assistant was even announced. Instead of that news, she had come out as his fiancée who was leaving the company. The coworkers who had reached out with congratulations had definitely been fishing for more information.

"I'll stay with you to help," Gio said, nodding for her to give the driver her address. "There can't be much? You gave Ilario a list of everything you wanted to be waiting at the town house."

Then Gio had added to it. Some poor maid was probably unpacking boutique deliveries as they spoke.

"I can manage. You don't have to come with me." A rush of inadequacy flooded through her. Her flat was very modest. She had chosen it for its minimal maintenance and excellent location, close to the tube. It was nothing like how he lived.

He didn't say anything more, only waited patiently for her to give the driver her details so they could pull away from the hotel entrance.

Molly gave in, but her tension ratcheted up when she led Gio up the two flights to her quirky, corner unit. Inviting him to enter her personal space felt a lot like opening her diary.

It was tidy and cheerful, at least. She liked it for its abundance of natural light and a decor that was a little too colorful to be sophisticated, but it was comfy and welcoming after a long day at the office.

Gio immediately began studying the photos on the wall, then picked up the snapshots of her with Libby and her mother that rested on a shelf and the end table.

He had already met her family over video chat, but he suddenly asked, "Who is this?" in a dangerous tone.

"Is that you being possessive, Gio?" She couldn't help throwing that pithy question at him as she took the framed photograph from him.

"It damned well is," he said without hesitation.

She couldn't help being flattered that he thought she could punch so far above her weight, but he didn't have anything to worry about.

"He was a child actor in America. I guess he's still an actor since he's doing a play in the West End. Libby watches reruns of his show and thinks he's dreamy. I happened to see him at a coffee shop so I asked him for a photo. This is her birthday present."

She stowed the photo in her laptop bag, then drew an overnight bag from the closet.

"You really were planning to leave." His gaze dropped to the boxes that were labeled and stacked in the closet, filled with off-season clothing that already didn't fit her.

"I *am* leaving," she confirmed, voice not as strong as she would have liked. A sting rose under her cheeks and arrived in the back of her throat. Chagrin? She didn't want to leave, especially when Otto was talking about attending their wedding. That wasn't on her, though. Gio was the one who had made this so difficult by faking this engagement of theirs.

She threw a handful of everyday items into the small suitcase along with her supplements and the historical romance novel she'd found at a café and hadn't finished yet.

When she picked up a thick hardcover off the bookshelf, Gio said, "Another gift for your sister?"

It was an iconic title about a wizard that Molly had defaced by carving a hole in the pages. She opened it to reveal the slender yellow envelope she stored there with her birth certificate and her company ID when she wasn't working.

"I'll empty my safe-deposit box tomorrow." She put the key in her purse. "I have custodial documents for Libby, in the event something happens to Mom, along with other papers I need access to if things go sideways." Like her surrogacy agreement.

She had volunteered to carry Sasha's baby knowing that an extreme outcome could include keeping the baby and raising it herself. This baby was the heir to the

Zamos fortune, but Molly only cared about that in so far as that fortune was this baby's birthright. Between her savings and her mother's support, she could provide a good upbringing—not privileged, like Sasha's, but stable and rich in other ways.

It was still a daunting prospect. Was that what Sasha and Rafael wanted, though? Were they changing their mind about the baby? She didn't believe that, but it was hard to imagine anything else when they were ghosting her. Jacinda had shown little concern for her friend, but Molly was growing ulcers of anxiety in her stomach, wondering what was going on with the other couple.

With Sasha and Rafael top of mind, she felt compelled to be firm. "Gio, we can't keep leading Otto on. You have to tell him the truth when we get back."

"It's not that easy," he said testily. "Nonno has given me everything. Not just the wealth and position I enjoy, but everything that means anything to him." He pointed to the ring on her hand. "He saved my life when I could have died of neglect or turned out like my father. I can't bear to disappoint him."

"Neither can I, but…" She clenched her hand over the ring. The gem dug into her palm. It was an instinctual safeguarding. She was always aware of the value it carried beyond its carat or clarity. Now a pebble, hard and sharp as a diamond, arrived in her throat. "What do you mean…you could have died?"

"You've seen my parents," he muttered, scraping his hand over his hair as he tried to find a pathway in the tiny area between the coffee table and the love seat.

"They are the poster children for why people ought to need a license to procreate."

She had never seen him so agitated. Well, not since he'd received the news that his grandfather was ill.

"Gio…" She tried to move to stand in front of him, but he turned away. "You don't have to tell me what they did if you don't want to talk about it." It was obviously a painful memory. "But you *can*."

"Nothing," he said starkly, slicing his hand through the air. "They did a lot of nothing. Which didn't make much impact while I was an infant. There was usually a nanny around to feed or change me. Occasionally, one was fired for insubordination or *intoxication*, because they would get her drunk or high with them. A new one would be hired within a day or two, so I survived it."

"Are you saying…?" She started to feel ill.

"Yes. They left me crying in a room, hungry and wet. I know this because Nonno hired investigators later, when he took guardianship. They interviewed dozens of people who had worked for them in those years. Staff and others who did what they could, taking a minute to give me a bottle out of pity. No one stayed working for them long, though. They were terrible employers. They bullied and sexually harassed their staff, ordered them to do things that weren't legal."

"Otto let that happen to you? How long did it go on?" she asked with sick dread.

"My father wouldn't let him see me. He was trying to take over as head of Casella, but when I was due to leave for boarding school, my father told Nonno to pay the tuition or he wouldn't send me. Nonno did, which meant the school sent their initial report to him. That's how he learned I was underweight and well behind my peers. I lacked basic social skills and had behavior problems."

"Gio, I'm so sorry." She took another step toward him, but stopped herself when he tensed up.

"He pulled me from school and brought me to his villa, hired specialists and nutritionists. Spent all day with me, bringing me to the office so we were together constantly. My father tried to take me back, but Nonno bought him off. My parents continued to use me as a pressure point for years, threatening public custody battles until I was old enough to tell them to go to hell."

"I can't understand how anyone could be so heartless." Her heart was aching. Her throat was hot, her eyes pressured by a force of tears she was fighting to hold back.

"Because they never cared about *me*. I was conceived to be a pawn," he said bitterly. "My father thought a son would secure his place as Nonno's heir, even though he'd proven himself inadequate time and again. Nonno didn't imagine how bad it was. It took a long time before we enjoyed the relationship we have today, but eventually I learned that he would always be there for me."

Not forever, though. Time, that inexorable thief, wanted him.

"Gio." She couldn't stand it any longer. She rushed across to him and hugged her arms tightly around his waist. "I'm so sorry that happened to you. So glad that you had Nonno to turn to."

"That's why I can't bear to hurt him, Molly." He cupped the back of her head, all of him stiff, as though trying to withstand great pain. "If I had been left at boarding school, I would be as profligate as my father. Worse, likely. I had a daredevil streak in my childhood that bordered on a death wish."

She hated to hear that. Hated to think of him alone and hungry and scared, or so angry he endangered himself.

"I would stay with you for Otto's sake if I could, Gio. But I *can't*." She clenched her eyes shut, feeling the tears press through her lashes. What would he think of her if he learned this baby wasn't hers? That she didn't plan to raise it herself?

Her heart juddered in her chest.

"Would you?" He closed his fist over the low ponytail she was wearing, gently pulling so she was forced to turn her tearstained face up to his.

She tried to nod, but his hand was too heavy on her hair. Her lips trembled as she tried to find the words to explain why she couldn't, but those words were on a document in her safe-deposit box. He would never see them.

Something seemed to break in him. He covered her mouth with his own, once, hard, as though physically trying to stamp himself onto her, then softened into a tender plea that dragged an ache from her chest and a moan from her throat.

I can't, though. I can't.

This needed to stop. She couldn't continue the charade of their engagement or the affair that had no future. She knew that, but when he would have drawn back, she pressed her hand to the back of his head, urging him to keep kissing her. To singe away all the angst and terror of the future. All the anguish that would come soon enough. Just not today. Not yet.

The moment her hand started to slide his jacket off his shoulder, the mood between them altered, becoming frenzied. They hurriedly raked at each other's clothes. He tore open his shirt, then hers just as ruthlessly.

It was one of her favorites, but she didn't care. She threw it off her shoulders with her bra and grasped at his waistband, yanking his belt free.

They didn't even go to the bedroom. As he dropped to his knees and dragged her pants down her legs, he elbowed the coffee table aside. She stepped out of them and sank to her knees, too, naked, and kissed him as she jerked at his fly and freed his erection.

His breath hissed in, then he was cupping her mound. Giving her equal pleasure, sweeping his tongue against hers before dragging his mouth across her skin, pressing her onto her back.

The carpet was rough and cool, the weight of him scorching. He was so intent, she should have been alarmed, but his control was not completely gone.

"Tell me," he demanded in a rasp as he clasped her breast and ran his tongue against the pulsing artery in her throat. "Say you want this."

"Always," she moaned, writhing at the way his mouth was straying down, down, down. A flagrant suck of her nipple, a scrape of teeth against the underside of the swell. Hot breath against her ribs and a lascivious lick into her navel.

He spread her legs and she arched in agonized ecstasy as he claimed her.

They knew how to do these things to each other now. She knew he liked the feel of her hands in his hair and her thighs twitching in pleasure. He knew when she was approaching her crisis and that she was flexible enough to let him keep her legs over his arms as he rose over her. She knew it only took the tiniest bit of guiding for him to arrow into her with one slow, implacable thrust and that they both loved that moment almost more than the finale.

Almost. Because then there was this. The act.

"Say you want this forever," he demanded, pinning her there on the floor with her legs splayed over his arms while he withdrew and returned in thrusts of careful power.

It wasn't a lie. "I do," she admitted, then closed her eyes, knowing they were words that shouldn't have been uttered. They felt too much like a vow.

Her statement was the button on a detonation, one that was as physical as emotional. After a few more heated thrusts, they were both exploding, clinging and shuddering and crying out with both exaltation and defeat.

CHAPTER EIGHT

"I SHOULD HAVE taken you to the bed," Gio said with less remorse than he should have been suffering.

He had managed not to crush her in the quivering aftermath, sinking beside her and pulling her into him, but sex on the floor was a poor example of how well he intended to take care of her. His knees were stinging with a friction burn and this flat was cold enough that he dragged her mostly on top of him to keep her warm.

It wasn't like him to cast off self-discipline, but he'd been talking about things he never revisited in his own mind, let alone spoke of aloud. He'd been feeling raw and, worse, threatened by the reality of her packed boxes.

If his grandfather's illness hadn't arisen to keep her with him that day two weeks ago, she would have given notice and be out of his life after next week. Perhaps she would have come back after the baby was born, but he would have missed this time with her.

Recognizing that had filled him with an urgency he wasn't expecting, making him greedy for her. More demanding than he should have been.

"Did I hurt you?" he asked, bracing himself for her response.

"No. I would have stopped you if I didn't like it." She was tracing a tickling pattern against his pec, but she sat up beside him. Her hair was falling out of its clasp and her eyelids were still heavy, her makeup smudged and her mouth sensually swollen. "I'm going to have a quick shower."

"I'll join you."

"Ha! Good luck."

The stall was a tiny corner unit without a tub. He squeezed himself in with her purely for the entertainment of rubbing their soapy bodies together while sharing a few wet, lingering kisses.

She kept her hair out of the spray, but washed her face. Afterward, she leaned over her dresser to reapply her makeup, providing a delightful view of her backside where her T-shirt rose to reveal the lace edge of the cheekies that cut across the globes of her spectacular ass.

He wore only a towel as he waited for his body to cool. Absently, he paced her small flat, liking the way she'd decorated it. Her possessions weren't abundant or extravagant, but they were arranged tastefully. The whole was an appealing mix of plain and bright colors with soft textures and inviting warmth.

He wanted to bring up marriage and had since Milan, but he was uncharacteristically unsure, despite what she had said while they were making love a little while ago. When Molly had talked about her parents' marriage, she had said she was holding out for love as a practical choice. Surely she would see that he offered an extremely comfortable life for her and her baby, though?

The baby.

He glanced over as she straightened to sort through her palettes of cosmetics. Her T-shirt fell to rest against her baby bump, something he saw every time she was naked, but for some reason, seeing it now caused a sledgehammer of emotion to hit him. Something between longing and anticipation.

For the first time in his life, he was enthused by the idea of fatherhood. The concept had shifted from being a role he felt obliged to take on, into one that he wanted. With Molly at his side, he felt ready for the challenge.

"I can feel you staring holes through me." She shakily pumped her mascara wand before applying it to her lashes, then said in a conciliatory tone, "I promised you three weeks and I'll honor that. I don't want to make the lie worse by giving Otto a date, but if he presses the issue, we could say we're looking at August, before Libby has to return to school."

He relaxed slightly and returned to his aimless pacing, mind turning to how he would use the next week to convince her to stay for a lifetime.

His gaze snagged on the only art hanging on her walls. It was a butterfly of pins strung with colored threads against a black background. The maker had taken great care with it, but it was the type of makeshift craft one expected from a preteen summer camp.

Was this why she felt she didn't belong in his world? Because she didn't have Renaissance oils? From what he could tell, her single mother had provided her a far superior upbringing than the dismal start he'd endured. That's what made her right for him. She didn't *care* about money or material possessions. She cared about that baby she carried. About her family.

He absently glanced at the white signature, expecting to see Libby's name. Maybe Molly's.

"Who's Sasha?" he asked.

"What?" She flung around from the mirror. "Oh." Her eyes widened as she realized what he was looking at. "I've had that so long, I forgot it was there. She's, um, a friend from my high-school days."

She dropped her makeup and moved to fetch a clean towel from the bathroom.

"I thought you homeschooled?" he asked.

"I still had friends." She took the artwork off the wall and wrapped it in the towel, then set it in her suitcase. Her hands were shaking. She was avoiding his eyes.

"Are you telling me the truth, Molly?"

"Yes." She snapped a look at him that was so surprised and unwavering that he dismissed his suspicion. It still seemed like a strong response to an idle question, though.

"She must be very special to you."

"She is. Are you hungry? There's a takeaway place around the corner that does an amazing rice bowl. I probably won't get to enjoy it again for a while so…" She picked up her phone to tap into an app. "I'll say thirty minutes and we'll pick it up on the way to your town house? I'm almost finished here."

He glanced once at the suitcase, still puzzled, but she asked him about his order. Then she was gathering up her last few items and he put the odd moment out of his mind, pleased that she was coming home with him, which was all that mattered.

Molly felt like the worst person alive. Even her mother gave her a fretful look when she had a private moment to catch up with her over the tablet.

"You can't stay into August, Molly. You're already showing."

"I know, but I had to tell him something." She understood Gio better now, and saw why he felt such an allegiance to his grandfather. Her heart went out to the neglected child he'd been and she was so filled with admiration for the man he'd become.

It made her crush all the more intense.

Oh, who was she kidding? She was way past crushes and infatuation. She was falling in love with Gio. Given his childhood, he could have turned out bitter and cold, but he was a man of strength and integrity, capable of kindness and even tenderness. If she hadn't been pregnant with Sasha's baby, she would stay with him as long as he wanted her to.

But her time in his world was evaporating.

"Still no word from Sasha?" her mother asked.

"We're going to Athens tomorrow. Gio is meeting with Rafael so I know they'll be there. If I have to walk up to their front door and ring the bell, I'll see Sasha. Once I know where I stand with them, I'll know whether…"

"What?"

"Whether I'm raising this baby myself." If that happened, everything would change, but she didn't let herself consider how. She would cross that bridge when she got to it.

"Do you think Sasha is having second thoughts?" Patricia asked with deep concern.

"*I don't know.* I've texted so many times, asking them to call, to tell me what's going on. She seemed extremely sure that she wanted this baby, when we were seeing that counselor in London, before the implant." Sasha had admitted things between her and Rafael had been strained at the time, but blamed herself. She was upset about her fertility issues and not an easy partner to live with. "Perhaps her parents are there? Or her injuries are more serious than they're letting on in the press?"

"That doesn't explain why Rafael isn't replying to you."

"I know," she murmured, disturbed by that. She couldn't understand why they would give her the silent treatment when she was *carrying their baby.*

"When you see her—" Her mother *tsked* with distress. "If she seems open to it, let her know that Libby is curious about her. We would still love for her to be part of Libby's life."

"She knows, Mom." Molly had made that crystal-clear the day they'd talked on the yacht. "I'll tell her again, though. Oh, Gio's back," she said as she heard the door.

She smiled at him as he came into the sitting room.

"Would you like to say hi to Mom?" Gio popped into the frame behind Molly and her mother offered the smile of natural warmth that inspired such trust in pregnant mothers.

"Hello, Gio. Molly tells me your grandfather is improving. That's good to hear."

"He is, and he would love to meet you and Libby. Molly said you might have time before Libby goes back to school. Can I book you a flight? My treat."

Her mother was briefly taken aback, as was Molly.

"I would have to ensure my colleagues could cover for me. Let me get back to you," Patricia said, but Molly felt the pointedness in the way her gaze asked, *How long will you continue this farce?*

They ended the call a moment later.

"What was that?" Molly twisted around to ask with astonishment. "I'm only here until the twenty-first. I'm not taking that bonus you offered to double my time."

Gio moved around the end of the sofa so he faced her and pushed his hands into his pockets. He stared over her head a moment, seeming to be choosing his words, then dropped his gaze to hers.

The weight of his stare landed so hard, she instinctually braced herself.

"What's wrong?" she asked.

"Nothing. I'd like to make this engagement real."

"Real?" Molly pulse skipped so hard she heard it. "What do you mean?"

"I'm proposing marriage, Molly."

He had done that already. She actually looked at the ring she wore as if it had been made of sugar and had somehow dissolved. It was there, though.

"You don't mean… Like, have a wedding for your

grandfather's sake? Gio, I can't." And why was he torturing her this way? Did he not realize she was falling in love with him?

Or was that precisely why he was asking? Did he feel the same? She drew in a breath and held it.

"We're good together," he said in the same voice he used when he was negotiating across a boardroom table. It was the furthest thing from tender and made her throat tighten. "I'm not just talking about in bed, either. We're well-matched intellectually. We have similar values. You understand my work demands and I'm supportive of your continuing to advance your career, if that's something you want to do. I would like a family. Obviously, you do as well."

No mention of love. The swell of hope in her chest shriveled.

"My grandfather likes you and I'd like him to have the reassurance of our being married."

"Oh, your *grandfather* likes me," she said facetiously. A semihysterical laugh was trapped behind the rock that was sitting inside her chest. She began to see how he had approached his first engagement, *like any other merger and acquisition*, and felt some sympathy for the woman who hadn't been able to go through with it. "What do you feel, Gio?"

His expression grew stoic. "Liking. Respect. *Desire*," he added in a tone that held a rasp.

"That's not enough!" She rose to pace, trapped in this impossible situation and longing for escape.

"I disagree. It's a strong foundation. We're both sensible people, Molly. We'll find a way to make it work. If it doesn't, we can divorce after Nonno's gone."

"I told you how I feel about divorce." She flung around to face him. "If you're already considering it, then why bring up marriage at all?"

"Because I'm confident we'll stay married," he said with exasperation.

"You genuinely believe you want to spend the rest of your life with me? *Me?*"

"And your baby. Yes."

Her chest knotted up. The baby. Oh, God.

"Whatever is going on with the baby's father, you can tell me." He came closer and tried to take her hands.

"I can't—" She pulled her hands away. "You don't understand."

"No, I don't," he said with instant frost, withdrawing. "But I want to."

She was hurting him with her rebuff. It went beyond the fact that no one ever said no to him. They were lovers. Close. He had told her about his childhood and why it was difficult for him to trust that people would be there for him.

She didn't want to reject him, but she didn't have a choice. She shook her head, filled with despair. What if she did wind up raising this baby? Would he understand? Would he still want her? Them?

"Can we talk about this in a few days? I need some time." She needed the weekend. She needed to see Sasha and Rafael.

When she warily lifted her gaze, she saw his cheeks were hollow, his mouth tight with dismay. He nodded curtly. "Fine. We'll revisit this after we get back from Athens."

"Thank you," she said through an arid throat, doubtful that she would have a better answer for him by then.

Her stomach was in knots when they landed in Athens the next day.

Yesterday, when she had worked out details with Rafael's assistant for a meeting between him and Gio to finalize their business agreement, the assistant had tacked on a personal message to the email.

Mr. and Mrs. Zamos are hoping to see Mr. Casella and his fiancée at the art museum benefit on Saturday night. They want to congratulate them on their recent engagement.

Was it a coded message meant for her?

Molly was on pins and needles as she dressed in a one-shouldered gown of gold. Ruched silk formed the bodice. Gold leaves decorated the shoulder and the high waist. The skirt fell in narrow pleats that hid the thickening at her waist.

"Is the serpentine necklace in the safe?" she asked Gio when the stylist had finished her makeup. She wore her hair up tonight, with a few long ringlets dangling to frame her face.

His admiring gaze took her in, making her skin warm under his regard.

She was warming and softening with more than that. She was fighting an urge to agree to his proposal and fold her life into his. He might not love her, but he loved his grandfather very much. He was *capable* of love, which filled her with hope that he could love her, given time and absolute honesty.

Sadly, she couldn't give him either of those things, which was cleaving her heart in two. She felt torn every minute of the day, but especially now, when she was preparing to confront the parents of the baby she carried.

Gio removed a velvet case from the hotel safe, one that was unfamiliar and pristine.

"I bought something else for you to wear." He nodded to dismiss the stylist and opened the case.

"Brought? Or b-bought?"

"Bought. I thought you might like to wear something of your own for a change."

No-o-o.

She swallowed as he revealed a stunning necklace in yellow gold with a dozen links made of pear-shaped yellow sapphires. Each was surrounded by white diamonds. A larger sapphire, also a pear surrounded by bigger diamonds, formed the pendant. The earrings matched.

"It's too much," she said weakly.

"It's an incentive. We both know that," he said impassively.

He really wanted her to marry him, she realized with a thudding sensation behind her heart. Why, though? For those dispassionate reasons he'd given her yesterday? For his grandfather? Or was he developing feelings for her?

She couldn't bear to slight him again by refusing the necklace, so she stood still while he circled behind her and set the weight of the pendant against her throat. He clasped the chain behind her neck before he set a kiss on her nape, exactly in the spot that weakened her knees.

"Surely this is an incentive, too?" He lingered to nuzzle and inhale.

Goose bumps rose on her skin and a moan of longing throbbed in her throat.

She couldn't resist turning to kiss him. To touch and hold on to him a little longer, a little harder. She was in Athens. The last grains of their time together were falling into the bottom of the hourglass.

Since becoming lovers, they had been making love every chance they got. Each time she felt as though she lost a little piece of herself, and today, with this dark cloud looming, she felt an urgent need for one last act of intimacy.

She sank to her knees and worked to open the fly of his tuxedo pants.

"That's not what I was hoping to gain," he said in a voice that had turned gritty.

She paused in freeing him. "Is that a no?"

He swallowed. "You know I always want this."

She finished exposing his thickening flesh. A feral noise came out of him as she took him in her mouth. He grew harder against her tongue as she sucked flagrantly on his salty flavor, exploring his textures then tilting her head to take him deeper into her mouth.

His fingertips dug into her shoulder and he made a noise as though he was trying to withstand acute pain.

His other hand cupped her cheek and he pumped a few times, saying something unintelligible.

His stomach tightened. All of him did as she caressed between his thighs and closed her fist around the base of his shaft, trying to give him every bit of pleasure she could.

Just when she thought he would lose it completely, he crushed his fist around her own and carefully withdrew from her mouth. He pulled her to stand before him.

She swayed drunkenly. "Don't you want...?"

"I want *you*," he said in a rasp. "All of you."

He brought her with him as he backed toward the bed and sat on the edge.

She wanted him, too. All of him. Forever. But she could only have this, so she gathered the delicate fabric of her skirt before she straddled his thighs. When he moved her underwear aside and caressed into the slippery heat that awaited him, she closed her eyes to savor the sensations.

"Take me," he growled as he dropped onto his back.

She was aching. Not just physically aroused, but aware of a hollowness in her heart, in her soul. She needed more than pleasure. She needed the indelible connection of their bodies.

She guided herself onto him, lowering and blinking away the rush of tears that had been prompted by the starkness of the moment. By the magnitude of it.

She loved him. She loved him with everything in her and, one way or another, she was going to lose him.

His wide hands slid up her thighs to bracket her hips

beneath the skirt. He lifted his hips, urging her into moving on him.

She let her skirt spill around them and braced her hands on his shoulders while she rode the rhythm he set. The wool of his pants abraded her legs, but she embraced that discomfort in the greater frenzy of claiming him.

As the intensity of emotion and pleasure converged, she cried out what was in her heart. What couldn't be contained or denied anymore.

"I love you, Gio! I love you!"

Ecstasy shot through her like golden light, but even though he threw back his head and bared his teeth, releasing a shout of pure exaltation, he didn't say the words back to her.

Molly disappeared into the bathroom to put herself back together while Gio picked up the ringing phone.

"The car is waiting for us," he called to her, still tucking himself back into his trousers, titillated by the smudge of lipstick she'd left on him.

He moved to ensure he wasn't wearing that shade on his mouth. He was still perspiring and dull-witted from his powerful orgasm, but also off-kilter. Had she heard herself?

He wasn't sure how to take her confession. Was it an agreement to marry him?

Women had claimed to love him in the past, of course, including his mother. For Fridrika, the word *love* was a means of manipulation that had worked when he'd been young. She had used it to twist his feelings and impose a sense of obligation, which had made the words downright repulsive to him for a long time.

Not every woman was a sociopathic narcissist, however. Eventually, he had come to understand that *love* was something some people believed they were experiencing when enthusiasm and accord ran high. Hell, when he'd watched Molly's painted lips close around his aroused flesh with such erotic greed, he could have said he loved her and meant it. Context was everything.

Molly would have a definition of love that was deeper and more meaningful than his, though. She wouldn't say it to impose obligations on him, but she wouldn't say it superficially, either. She had said she wanted to marry for love, so…?

She joined him, makeup once again flawless, hair a tiny bit less polished than it had been, which was actually very sexy. The blush of orgasm still sat on her cheekbones, which was also sexy as hell. She sent a vague smile in his direction and hurried to put on the earrings that matched the pendant he'd given her.

Her hands were trembling, which distracted him from the thick tension coating the air. Was she waiting for an acknowledgement of what she'd said? Reciprocation?

"Shall we go?" Now she was looking into her clutch and moving to the door, making him realize she hadn't once met his eyes.

He'd been waiting for her to look at him so he could better read her mood, but she was opening the door herself and walking through it.

They made their way down to the lobby in weighted silence.

As the car took them the short distance to the museum, he reached across to take her hand, starting to say "thank you for earlier," but he stopped himself when he realized how ambiguous those words might sound.

Her fingers curled loosely around his, but she kept her focus out the window.

It wasn't until they walked into the gala, where Rafael Zamos and his wife were holding court, and he felt her stiffen beside him, that he realized she might be suffering nerves. Gio took his acceptance in any group of people for granted, but she was still finding her feet in his social circles. Plus, the last time she'd met this couple, Alexandra Zamos had been very condescending toward her.

"Don't worry," he murmured. "They'll be polite." They had damn well better be.

Thinking back to that day, however, Gio recalled that it was the first time he'd had to admit to himself that he had a personal interest in Molly, one that went deeper than sneaking glances at her figure. When she had appeared on deck, he'd been preoccupied with his negotiations with Rafael, irritated that lunch had turned into a swim and drinks. Precious time had been wasted and Jacinda had been circling like a shark. Despite her very pretty breasts, he'd been dead from the waist down... until Molly appeared.

She had been a wild rose among manufactured silk blossoms. Her beauty originated in the way that nature had put her together, not from any false adornments. She smelled fresh and moved fluidly, and smiled with shy warmth.

When Alexandra had been so offended that Molly had dared to show herself above her station, Gio had genuinely questioned whether he should be doing business with her husband.

That rush of hostility and protective aggression had been so ferocious, he'd almost missed that Alexandra was trying to smooth things over with Molly. She'd been clumsy about it, but she had invited Molly for breakfast and had seemed genuinely embarrassed by her own behavior. He'd left Molly to decide for herself whether she wanted to give the woman an opportunity to make up for her discourtesy.

Now, however, as they made their way toward the couple, he could feel tension coming off Molly in radioactive waves. It ignited a prickling need to guard, but he couldn't identify the threat.

Rafael spotted them and excused himself and his wife from their group. He glanced at Alexandra in a silent signal that she should accompany him as he began making his way toward them on a pair of crutches. Alexandra was frowning with tension. Her attention skimmed the room in a way that struck Gio as hunted.

Molly's grip tightened in his. Was her palm clammy?

He squeezed her hand in reassurance. Alexandra might have the arrogance of blue blood, but Rafael was the last man to portray any snobbish tendencies. He might wear a bespoke tuxedo and a Girard-Perregaux on his wrist, but he'd come from the humble roots of operating his father's marine repair business before turning it into a heavy player in marine manufacturing and technologies. Once they signed their agreement, they would expand container cargo transfers, so they would become one of the largest players in that industry. It was something Zamos needed more than Gio, but if Gio didn't leap on this partnership, someone else would, so he wanted to exploit it.

Rafael wore an even more inscrutable look than Gio was used to seeing on him, which subconsciously increased his own tension.

Gio had judged Rafael's marriage to be a practical one. Alexandra was an American heiress who had attended school in Switzerland. They taught haughtiness there, that was a fact, but she was enormously well-connected. Alexandra was capable of warmth and witticisms, but she had the conceit of exceptional beauty. Her superciliousness bordered on appearing spoiled, which Gio found off-putting, but he kept his opinions to himself.

As the couple arrived before them, Alexandra skimmed a blank, polite smile over Molly, one that dismissed her as unimportant. Her attention only landed on Gio because Rafael was tucking his crutch beneath is armpit and offering to shake his hand.

"Gio. Good to see you again. Gio was on the yacht with us late last year," Rafael told Alexandra. "And this must be your fiancée?"

"Molly, yes," Gio confirmed, disconcerted by the bland smile Alexandra offered them.

"I was on the yacht, too." Molly said, offering her

hand to Rafael while looking to Alexandra. "We met briefly. You may not remember."

"I don't," Alexandra stated flatly. She turned her gaze up to the blue balloons and silver streamers in a rude lack of interest. "I have a concussion. I can't remember a damned thing. I don't even know why I'm here. None of this means anything to me."

Her husband's expression tightened. He shot Molly a look that might have been apologetic.

Molly's eyes were swallowing her face as she stared intently at Alexandra. Her lips parted and trembled with what looked like disbelief. Horror, even.

When her glance flashed to Rafael's, something passed between them that closed a fist around Gio's heart. It was gone in the next second as their eye contact broke, leaving him to believe he'd imagined it. Molly went back to studying Alexandra.

"That must be terribly confusing. I'm so sorry," Molly said with genuine concern. "It looks like you're both still recovering from the crash. Should we sit down?"

"No. I don't like these lights. They're giving me a headache." Alexandra touched her brow and winced. "Rafael insisted on my coming so people can see I'm only half there—"

"I never said that," he bit out.

"What else are they going to think when you parade me around, explaining my brain injury like I'm a circus attraction?"

"Would you excuse us?" Rafael said tightly. "I'll see you at the office tomorrow, Gio."

As the pair moved away, Gio said, "Here I was so confident she wouldn't be rude."

"She's injured," Molly defended quickly. Her face was still white. "Why did they even come out?"

"They didn't have a choice," Gio said in grim observation. "Rafael's growth was fast and furious. His success is new enough that he's vulnerable." Buzzards would be circling, sensing his weakness. "He's making it clear that he's not going anywhere." Crutches notwithstanding.

"You mean he could lose—"

"Everything. Yes."

"That seems…impossible." Her gaze fixated on the exit long after the couple went through it.

"Business is cutthroat. You know that. Rafael might have survived the car crash, but he's a stag with a broken leg. He and his wife were a very powerful team and she still seems feisty despite her injury, but I don't know that she's capable of taking over in his place if she's suffering memory issues. They're in trouble on many fronts. It would be different if they had a baby—"

A jolt seemed to go through Molly, one that was so electric, he felt it like a shock in his hand, as though he'd grasped a live wire.

"Wh-what do you mean?" She took her hand from his and rubbed it with the other.

He was so startled by her reaction, he almost forgot what they were talking about. He gave his head a slight shake, trying to dispel the strange vibes he was picking up.

"For all our marks of civilization, humans are still pack-mentality animals. We protect what we have so our young can thrive. That's why I've become so serious about putting the pieces in place for the next generation at Casella. Until recently, I didn't appreciate how important that was because I *was* the next generation. When I took the helm, I presumed that settled things, firmly bypassing my father. I naively believed that if something did happen to me, Nonno would step in." He ran his tongue over his teeth, feeling raw as he touched on brutal reality. "But he won't always be here."

Her worried gaze searched his. "A baby can't take over, either," she pointed out faintly.

"No, but those who are invested in an heir protect what belongs to him or her. I'd name you as my successor at Casella Corporation before I'd let my father so much as walk through its front doors. I know you would safeguard every brick and pencil in the place because that's the kind of person you are, but if your own child stood to inherit? You'd be relentless."

She blinked emotively. "I'm glad you see me that way, but…"

He ignored that *but* and closed his hand on hers again, trying to impress on her why their marrying was so important to him.

"Having an heir matters, Molly. Look how exposed Rafael is without one." He nodded toward the door.

She caught her breath, and her profile seemed to grow hollow with angst.

An acquaintance approached them. They had to circulate, but Molly was so quiet and withdrawn, he insisted they leave a short time later.

CHAPTER NINE

"I'LL GO TO the meeting alone," Gio said the following morning when Molly came to the breakfast table. Given both men's demanding lives, and Rafael's recent injuries, they'd had to reschedule this signing of the final agreement for a Sunday, but that didn't mean Molly had the day off. "Go back to bed. You barely slept."

"Did I bother you last night? You should have let me go to the other bed." Molly had had a tension headache by the time they got back to their hotel. She'd been awake much of the night, trying not to toss and turn.

When Gio had asked her why she couldn't sleep, she had tried to leave, but he had spooned her. His cradling hold had been such a comfort against her angst-ridden thoughts, she had stayed in his arms, still awake, trying to make sense of the incomprehensible. Then she'd felt a faint, fluttering sensation in her middle that had made her want to cry into her pillow with a mixture of elation and misery.

Would Sasha care that this baby was beginning to make itself known with those tiny movements? She didn't even remember Molly! Neither she nor Rafael had acknowledged that Molly was carrying their baby. Did she even remember that she had given birth to Libby eleven years ago?

The idea that she had forgotten Libby broke Molly's heart. Libby would never know, but it was still tragic. Patricia would be equally upset to hear it.

It was tragic for Sasha, too. Maybe the suppression of the memory of her daughter was something her brain was doing to protect her, but it also meant she didn't remember how devastated she'd been over her recent fertility troubles. Or how she had seemed so jubilant when Molly's pregnancy had been confirmed.

"You look exhausted. That's not an insult. It's concern," Gio continued.

"It's one meeting," she mumbled, wishing she could skip it. Facing Rafael again, and pretending they didn't have a closer relationship, would be a difficult test of her acting skills. "Once I shower and put on makeup, you won't even notice how awful I look."

"I will always notice how you look and I will always be concerned if you don't look well," he assured her. "If your insomnia had anything to do with what you said to me yesterday, before we left for the museum—"

"Oh, God, please don't." She covered her face like a child, too mortified for him to continue. She had revealed her heart in the most glaring way, then had felt raw all the way to the museum, waiting for him to say something while praying he wouldn't.

That torture had been eclipsed by their encounter with Sasha and Rafael and everything Gio had said about how precarious Rafael's position was, but her mortification was still sitting under her skin like a splinter that wouldn't stop throbbing.

"Molly." Gio reached across to take her wrist, urging her to look at him while he tangled their fingers. "I hope you understand that any emotional reserve on my part is a result of my childhood. It took me a long time to accept that my grandfather genuinely cared about me. I was taught *not* to attach to people. The few who were kind to me, always left."

She clung to his hand, searching his expression for something more than concern. Tenderness. Affection. Something that would indicate that he returned her love.

"Hearing those words from you…" His expression flexed with anguish, but his eyes were burning flames. "I know you wouldn't say something like that lightly. It means a lot to me that you did."

She knew he was being sincere, but it was still a disappointing shortfall compared to what she longed for him to say. Her mouth began quivering and her eyes filled, which only made her feel transparent, increasing her agony.

Her personal phone, the one she had been carrying like a lifeline since Sasha's crash, pinged with an incoming message.

"That's early for Libby," Gio noted as she picked it up to glance at the screen.

It's R. When can we talk?

"What's wrong?" Gio asked sharply, making her realize she'd allowed her shock—and relief?—to show on her face. Finally she would have an explanation!

"Nothing. It's Mom. Late night with a client," she lied. "I will stay here while you go to the meeting," she decided, texting essentially the same thing to Rafael, asking him to come up as soon as Gio left. It took all her courage to lift her gaze and betray nothing of the way her nerves were screaming with tension. "If you don't mind."

Gio's brow furrowed as he searched her expression, but after an endless moment of silence, he nodded jerkily.

Gio left an hour later. She texted Rafael, then hurried to change from the pajamas she still wore, pulling on a pair of floral leggings and a belted shirtdress.

She clutched her roiling stomach as she waited.

The room phone rang and the concierge said, "You have a guest. Rafael Zamos?"

"Send him up, thank you."

"You got here fast," Molly said moments later, when she let Rafael in. Neither of them bothered with greetings.

"I was in my car on the street, waiting to see him leave." Rafael looked even worse than she did, wincing in pain as he came in on his crutches. He was still very handsome, wearing a suit for his meeting with Gio— the meeting for which he'd be late since he'd come to see her first.

"I don't imagine we have much time," Molly said. "Has she really lost her memory?"

"Yes. It's a bloody nightmare." He slouched on one crutch and pinched the bridge of his nose. "I hoped that when she saw you last night, something might be triggered. I should have talked to you sooner than this. I know that. It's been hell—"

"It's okay. I can imagine you've had a lot to deal with."

"Between the surgeries and painkillers, I can hardly work, let alone prepare for—" His tortured gaze struck her middle. "Forget about me. How are you? How is the baby?"

"Fine." She covered where the flutters had heartened her last night. "We're both fine. Gio knows I'm pregnant, though."

"You told him? *Why?* And why the hell are you two engaged?"

"I had morning sickness. He figured it out," she cried with exasperation. "Then I fainted when I heard you'd been in that crash. I didn't know what was going to happen to you! Gio has been going through some things. He needed me."

Did he, though? Or was she still using his grandfather's illness as an excuse to stay with a man who didn't love her?

"He doesn't know everything," she clarified. Heck, *Rafael* didn't know everything. He didn't know Sasha was Libby's birth mother. Tears of distress came into her eyes as she wondered what Sasha's memory loss meant. "Rafael, what are we going to do?"

"I don't *know.* I told her we're expecting a baby, but—"

A subtle beep was the only warning before the door was thrust open. Gio entered wearing exactly the thunderous expression that anyone might, when they walked in on what looked like brazen infidelity.

Molly's blood went cold. She hugged herself and stammered, "Wh-what are you doing back here?"

"There was a traffic snarl. My driver had to circle back. He turned the corner in time for me to see a man on crutches entering this hotel. *This* is why you refused to tell me who the father is? Because he's *married*?"

"No. Gio—" She held up a hand. "Rafael, tell him."

"No," Gio said coldly. "The only thing he has to do is go home and pack whatever he can carry because I am pulling our deal," he snapped at Rafael. "I know that knocks the legs out from under you. Think about that the next time you step out on your wife."

Rafael swore sharply and tried to speak, but Gio spoke louder.

"And *you*—" He pierced Molly with his severest look. "You could have told me the truth. I *asked* you if the father was married. I told you I wouldn't judge. Rather than be honest, you're still involved with him and sneaking behind my back to meet him? While wearing my family ring? That's unforgivable. Give it back." He held out his hand.

"I *can't* tell you the truth." She wanted to throw up as she gave the ring a tug. Her fingers were still morning-swollen. It wouldn't budge and only hurt her knuckle to wrench against it. "I'm bound by an NDA. *Tell him, Rafael.*"

Rafael's fists were clenched around the cross bars of his crutches. His features were carved from granite as he returned Gio's look of utter contempt.

"You're right. The baby she's carrying is mine," he said through gritted teeth.

Gio raked in a harsh breath, as though the words had been a knife into his lung.

"It's also *my wife's*."

Shocked confusion made Gio's dark eyebrows crash together.

"I'm their surrogate," Molly clarified, still struggling with the ring, but exhaling with relief as she finally, *finally*, was able to tell the truth. "The embryo was implanted through IVF. I've never had sex with Rafael. I told you I wasn't romantically involved with the father."

Gio looked between them with astonished disbelief.

"I would have my wife confirm all of this, but she's lost her memory," Rafael said with bitter humor. "Perhaps the word of the specialist in London will suffice?"

"Why would you agree to this?" Gio asked Molly with utter bafflement.

Here came the lie she had cooked up for Rafael's sake, to protect Sasha from having to confess she'd given birth as a teen. Even now, she couldn't reveal her true connection to Sasha.

"You know that my mom is a midwife," she said with a tremor in her voice. "I've always been very aware of the difficulties some women face with pregnancy. I was moved by their situation and…" This was so hard to dance this close to the truth, yet tell him something she knew would be hard for him to accept. "You know how close I am to Libby. My dad helped with my college fund, but he's not Libby's father. Her future is all on Mom. I want to ensure Libby has every advantage I had."

Libby already had more than Molly ever would. A trust had been set up through an intermediary that Libby would access when she was old enough, but only Molly and her mother knew about it.

"You're doing this for *money*?" Gio recoiled the way he had when his mother had tried to kiss him. "If you needed a raise, you should have said," he growled.

"It's not for *me*." Her argument was futile. She could see Gio shutting down, closing every door and window to his soul against her.

"Along with taking time away from her career, Molly is putting her body through significant stress," Rafael pointed out. "Professional athletes are paid to treat their body well and make every effort to produce a desired result. Why shouldn't she be compensated for doing the same?"

Gio released a choked noise. "You're going to carry this baby for nine months, then give it away to strangers?" He shook his head at her as though he didn't recognize her.

Not strangers. Sasha was *family*. But she couldn't say that.

This was what she had dreaded, that he would think he was seeing her through clear eyes when he had a more distorted view of her than ever.

"Pull our deal. I don't care," Rafael said grimly. "Destroy me if your ego demands it, but leave my wife alone. She hasn't done anything except try to give us a baby the only way she can."

Fresh tears sprang into Molly's eyes as she heard that. Poor Sasha. She'd been so piteous that day on the yacht. So ground down by the harsh realities of her life.

"Don't make Molly a target, either," Rafael continued in warning. "People like you, born to this kind of wealth—" He sent a disparaging look around the luxurious sitting room. "You don't understand why some of us have to do whatever the hell we can to get ahead. And even if you have nothing but disgust for her—"

A sob of anguish caught in Molly's throat at that thought. She instinctually covered the swell in her middle.

"She's carrying an innocent baby. Exposing what she's doing could impact that baby, and I promise you, if you do anything that causes harm to my child, my retribution will be swift and very final."

Gio's cheek ticked with insult.

Lethal tension was so thick in the air, Molly could hardly draw a breath.

"He wouldn't," she stated, feeling compelled to say it. "Gio would never hurt me or anyone's baby. I don't blame him for being angry, but he won't retaliate against the baby. I *know* that."

"I don't need you to defend me," Gio said with a curl of his lip.

"Let's not take chances," Rafael said, still using that stark tone. "Get your things."

Molly's heart stopped. "But—"

"You'll go to the villa with Alexandra. She needs time to get used to the idea she's going to become a mother."

"Are you saying she doesn't want this baby any-more?" Molly asked numbly.

"*I* want it," Rafael said fiercely, then scraped his hand over his face. "You need to give her a chance to…get used to the idea again." Desperation edged into his tone.

Molly's heart lurched. All she could think of was a teenaged Sasha, so determined to say goodbye to an infant she clearly loved. And later, Sasha refusing to hear about her daughter because leaving her had hurt too much for her to bear.

When Molly looked to Gio, she saw a man made of granite, but there were fissures running through him. Cracks of anger and resentment and disbelief. Beneath it all was an underpinning of acute pain.

I was taught not to attach to people. They always left.

"I told you I couldn't marry you," she said, plead-ing for his understanding. "I *told* you I couldn't stay. That this pregnancy made it impossible for us to be to-gether. I told you…" *I love you.* "I told you as much of the truth as I could."

It didn't matter. He turned his face away in rejection.

She jammed her knuckle into the butter on the table and was finally able to work the ring off her finger. She had to pick up his hand to make him accept it.

"Where's Molly?" It was Nonno's first question when Gio returned.

"Gone," Gio said flatly. "We're not marrying."

Gio was blissfully numb, still in shock, but also wearing the insulated cloak of disinterest that had al-lowed him to survive the emptiness of his early years.

She had said she loved him and he had believed it, but she had known they were on their way to see the Zamos couple when she'd said it. She had been hiding such an explosive secret at that point, he found himself replaying every single thing she'd ever said to him, uncertain what to believe anymore.

Walking in on what had looked like an affair had shocked the hell out of him. Discovering she was carrying Rafael's baby, but that the baby wasn't actually hers…? He still couldn't wrap his head around that.

All of the twists and developments left him wondering if her version of *love* was as manipulative as his mother's.

That thought sliced through his chest like an electrified knife, leaving him so disturbed, he could only think that he was glad she was gone. Glad the ruse was over.

His life was simple again. Clean, if bleak and empty.

"I lied to you," Gio admitted to his grandfather. "Molly was my assistant. Valentina's assistant, actually. I was worried about you when we arrived so I asked her to pretend we were marrying."

"I know."

Gio shot Nonno a sharp look.

His grandfather was still convalescing, not leaving home, but his color was much improved and he dressed every day. He ate well and Gio had come to him where he was seated on a bench in the garden, soaking up the late-afternoon sunshine.

"I was sick, not stupid," Nonno said with an impatient *tsk*.

"You told me to keep her."

"I meant it. Why didn't you?"

"Because—" Gio squeezed the back of his neck, forestalling his impulse to blurt out her pregnancy.

Rafael had gotten under his skin, though, warning him not to attack his injured wife or a helpless baby. *Molly* had got under his skin, sounding so confident when she had said he would never hurt her. He'd been furious in those moments of finding her with Rafael. Scorned and, yes, feeling attacked by her secrets and prevarications, and her *departure*. He'd been deeply tempted to say terrible things to her. Unforgivable things.

Agonizing fissures were still extending their way through him, breaking through his cloak of shock. His entire world had been overturned in twenty short minutes, from the moment he had caught sight of Rafael entering his hotel, when suspicions had skyrocketed inside him, to watching Molly gather a handful of things and leave.

"Because?" Nonno prompted.

"Because she's not who I thought she was. She's like *them*." His parents, he meant. "Motivated by money."

"Pah." Nonno refused to believe that. "Did she keep the ring? The necklace?"

"No." Perversely, Gio was insulted that she had not only handed him the heirloom ring, but she also hadn't taken anything he'd given her, just the modest clothes she'd been wearing. The electronics she'd shoved into her laptop bag were her own. She'd left all the jewelry and clothes, the company tablet and phone. Even her ID badge, which had felt very final.

Apparently, she would rather Rafael support her than take one thing from Gio.

"I thought she would make a good mother for our children, but she's actually very dispassionate about family." Despite his anger and sense of betrayal, he was trying to give her the benefit of the doubt. Molly had likely been moved emotionally. It was her body, her choice, but it seemed very out of character that she would carry a pregnancy for money.

That was the part that kept smacking him in the face—that he hadn't really known her or understood her circumstances or what motivated her.

Was it really as Rafael had said? Was she trying to get ahead via the only means open to her? That didn't ring true. She *had* been getting ahead. Maybe she hadn't known she was in line to be promoted to his executive assistant, but she had held a very prestigious position under Valentina and enjoyed a generous salary.

He'd been shocked at how modest her flat was, though, given how well she was paid. It was in a good neighborhood and the building itself had been upscale. She'd told him she liked to live below her means so she could send money to her mother. "I'm helping Mom pay off her mortgage since the house will come to me one day," she'd said. "Real estate is always a good investment."

"You're mistaken, Gio," Nonno chided. "She has very strong feelings around family. She's close with her mother and sister. I would swear on my life that she's in love with you."

She had said she was, but it hadn't kept her with him, had it? She had walked away with another man.

Angry words burned on his tongue. He wanted to malign her because, if she felt love, if her feelings were strong and true, he would expect her to have been honest with him. She wouldn't have walked out without a backward look.

Maybe she had looked back. He would never know because he had turned his back on her, refusing to watch her leave.

"You pushed her into the engagement," Nonno said pensively. "And I pushed marriage. I thought..." He sighed heavily. "I thought if she was tied to you, you would begin to open up to her. Women need more reassurance up front that a man's heart is available to her. A lifetime is a long time to live without love."

"I've lived without it. It's not that bad."

Such a heavy silence crashed down upon the garden, the bees seemed to stop buzzing in the flowers.

"I love you, Gio." Nonno's eyes grew damp. "I have loved you since the moment I learned you were on the way. I failed you by not letting you know that. By allowing you to believe for a long time that no one loved you. That is a cross I will bear all the rest of my days. Don't do that to Molly. Don't withhold your heart because you're angry or hurt. Don't leave her wondering and feeling that emptiness you suffered."

"She's fine," he said through his teeth. She had her mother. Her sister.

She wouldn't have the baby she was carrying, though. How did she imagine she could give it up? That was the real question that was pounding like a rusty nail behind his eyes. Her attachment to her sister and mother was indisputable. He had seen her with his own eyes looking for signs of the baby in her body—not with a critical eye, but with a tender look and a shaping touch of her hand, revealing anticipation. If he wasn't so confused by her and her motives, he would have called *that* love.

How did she think she could walk away from the baby after carrying it so close to her heart? Why would she put herself through such an agonizing ordeal?

"I'm not the one who walked out," he said. "If she wants to talk to me, she knows how to reach me."

He went into the villa and tried to put her out of his mind, but reminders cropped up over the next days and weeks. If it wasn't the cautious way people spoke to him at the Genoa office, it was a visit to New York, where he kept thinking about how near he was to her mother and sister. He had fully expected to meet them the next time he was here.

After a few hollow days in that city, where he worked nonstop, trying to shorten his trip, he found himself staring out a window. Far below, a woman pushed her baby in a stroller. How far along was Molly? Was she well? He couldn't help thinking of the morning she had fainted. He'd been so worried—

Damn it! That had been the morning he'd told her about the Zamos car crash, he realized. No wonder she had passed out with shock. What if they had died? Would that have prompted her to tell him everything? Would she still be engaged to him?

Not that he wished the Zamos couple dead. He hadn't even pulled his deal with Rafael, only left it in limbo. Rafael wasn't reaching out, either, and that suited Gio fine.

When he found himself pacing that evening, still brooding, he impulsively texted her mother.

I'd like to speak to you.

Her response came promptly.

Tomorrow would be better. Libby will be at school.

He wasn't sure why he was surprised by her willingness to see him, but he replied, I'll come to you. If this was a conversation he wanted to have over a video chat, he would have had it already.

The next morning, he drove himself into New Jersey, halfway to Pennsylvania, turned up a country road, then climbed a short, private driveway. The lawn was mowed, but the house was surrounded by encroaching woods and shrubs that could have used some aggressive pruning. The garden was in need of weeding, but it was filled with vibrant color. The house was modest and quaint, with a gable over the porch and a pot of flowers next to the front door.

"Gio." Patricia opened the door before he knocked. "Come in. I just made coffee. Have a seat." She waved at the overstuffed blue sofa that faced the television.

He stayed on his feet, glancing over the home office tucked into the corner next to the wood fireplace, then at the floor-to-ceiling bookshelves filled with both fiction and what looked like medical textbooks.

"How do you take it?" she called from the kitchen.

"Black is fine."

She came out a moment later and set his mug on the coffee table. She was an older version of Molly with silver strands in her brunette hair and a similar build encased in comfortable jeans and a T-shirt. She turned the chair from the desk to face the sofa.

"I'm going to sit and drink mine, if you don't mind," she said as she sank into the chair. "I had a late delivery last night. I've only slept a few hours."

"You should have said. I could have come at another time."

"Do you mean that?" she asked against the rim of her cup.

"No," he admitted. "Thank you for seeing me, even though it's not convenient." He was still on his feet, too restless to sit. "Is Molly well? Do you know?"

"As a rule, I take confidentiality very seriously." She lowered her mug. "But I'll put your mind at ease and say that I have no concerns around her health."

He leaped on that comment. "But you have concerns."

"She just ended a relationship that was very important to her. She's in a situation that is very complicated and makes it awkward for her to come home. I wish she was here, so I could feed her chicken soup and watch rom-coms with her, but I can't." She shrugged and sipped her coffee again.

"Your concerns don't extend to…" He was distracted,

still turning over "a relationship that was very important to her." "Do you condone what she's done? Offering to surrogate?"

"I'm also under an NDA," she said with a pained smile. "But I can tell you that I counseled Molly exactly as I would anyone considering pregnancy. We talked extensively about the risks. Ultimately, the decision was hers. As a midwife and her mother, my role is to support her however I can. This wasn't a decision she made lightly."

"I should hope not," he muttered, turning to pace again.

There were photos on the small space of wall that wasn't taken up by bookshelves. One showed Molly as an infant in Patricia's younger arms. Another showed Molly grinning widely, showing her missing front teeth. There she was winning an award at eleven or twelve, then dressed in a pretty gown for what he imagined was prom.

Here she was proudly feeding a bottle to Libby, he presumed. There she had the toddler in her lap while they read a book. There the two of them were asleep and there they were with Santa.

"How is your grandfather?" Patricia asked.

"Much better," he said absently, still studying the photos.

"Was that why you wanted to see me?" Patricia asked, tugging at his attention. "To ask whether I approve of what Molly is doing?"

"Yes." He turned in time to see her tense expression ease into an attentive smile.

"I didn't quite approve of your engagement, given the circumstances, but Molly has a big heart. She wanted to ease your grandfather's mind. It got out of hand."

"I know. I backed her into a corner. And I understand that she couldn't talk about the surrogacy. That part I can get over. What doesn't make any sense to me is *why* she's doing it. She's the least materialistic person I know, and this is not poverty." He waved at the home. It was rustic, but cozy and in good repair. The laptop on the desk was a recent model. The car outside the window wasn't sporty, but it was newish and a top brand for safety.

"She said she was doing it for Libby," he said. "To pay for college and give her a strong start like you and her father were able to give her."

Patricia's face blanked, then she looked into her mug as she sipped.

"Is it not?" Gio asked with sharp suspicion.

"It's true that I don't have the same type of college fund set up for Libby as I had for Molly. As I said, Molly has a big heart. She would absolutely want Libby to have everything and more than she has been able to enjoy."

That struck him as a prevarication, especially since she wasn't meeting his eyes, leaving him at a loss. Suspicious.

"Did Molly give birth to her?"

"Who? Libby? No!" she said with genuine shock. "Why on earth would you think that?"

"Because this doesn't make sense!" As he turned his head, he spotted a pin-and-thread craft like the one Molly had had in London. Two of them.

One was a turtle and quite clumsily done. The other was a hummingbird, made with beautiful finesse in the way the strings crossed to produce different intensities of color. The turtle was signed by Libby, the humming-bird by Molly.

Next to it hung a recent photo of the sisters. They sat on a rock overlooking a river.

The sunlight struck golden lights into Libby's dirty blond hair. At eleven, her profile was only starting to hint at the mature features she would carry into wom-anhood, but it was obvious she would be beautiful. She was caught in a moment of solemn contemplation, look-ing toward the sky, but squinting against the reflection off the water.

A sense of recognition, almost déjà vu, accosted Gio. He heard a woman's voice say *These lights are giving me a headache.*

That same voice had asked with profound shock last November, *What are you doing here?* He'd been so fo-cused on Molly that day, he hadn't heard the small, but significant inflection in Alexandra's voice, the one that had stressed, "What are *you* doing here?"

Molly had been shaking. He'd put it down to ner-vousness at being the center of attention, but the women had recognized each other. That's why Alexandra had invited Molly for breakfast. At the time, he'd dismissed it as the whim of a spoiled socialite.

As he put all of this together, the colored threads on the pin art were stretching like red yarn in a blockbuster mystery, joining to the photo of the women at the river, reaching across an ocean to connect to the butterfly he'd seen on Molly's wall.

"Who is Sasha?" He turned slowly, but felt as though the floor was falling away beneath his feet. He had detached from earth and was drifting through space.

"I beg your pardon?" Patricia went ghostly white.

"It's a sobriquet—" No, that wasn't right. He searched for the English word and couldn't find it. "Sasha is short for Alexandra, isn't it?"

My wife hasn't done anything except try to give us a baby the only way she can. Molly has a big heart.

"That's why Molly is having this baby," he said in realization. "She wants to give her sister's mother a child."

CHAPTER TEN

I͟T͟ H͟A͟D͟ B͟E͟E͟N͟ eight weeks since he'd seen her.

At first, Gio had walked through a noxious fog every day, unable to see colors or feel anything but the weight of existence.

After meeting with her mother, and learning Molly's real reason for agreeing to surrogate, things had changed. He had clarity, but that only brought the world back into focus, so everything felt sharp now. Painful. He wasn't sure why. Perhaps because, when he'd thought Molly's motivates were mercenary, he'd been able to put up a wall between himself and the things they'd shared. He'd dismissed his attraction and affection as something he'd felt for a woman who was an illusion.

Now he knew it had all been real. When she had promised to keep her friend's pregnancy a secret, she had meant it. When she told him she couldn't marry him, she had meant it.

When she had said that she loved him, she had meant it.

And then she had left.

The pain of her absence was both fresh and agonizingly familiar. No one should have this effect on him. He simply couldn't allow it. It was too debilitating.

He continued to use Genoa as his home base because his time with his grandfather was finite. He curtailed some of his travel for the same reason, but otherwise, he became the man he'd been before Molly had entered his life. He attended benefits and forced himself to at least go through the motions of taking a date with him. He had zero interest in starting a relationship of any kind with anyone, but he still had to legacy to secure.

He tried to convince himself that Molly was a chapter in his past. Not even a whole chapter. A footnote.

"*Signor*, the lawyers are asking again if we're scratching the Athens deal or…?" Nelo ventured warily.

"Enough," Gio said aloud. He refused to have that ever-present reminder hanging over him any longer. "Set up a meeting with Zamos. Tell him my last offer stands. I'm not interested in negotiating. Take it or leave it."

Two days later, Rafael came to him, walking into Gio's office without so much as a trace of a limp. He was completely alone.

"No lawyers or assistants?" Gio asked, jerking his head for Nelo to leave and shut the door so it was only the two of them.

"Legal has read through everything. We both know I need this deal to close and I don't have room to negotiate, especially given all you know about my personal business." He didn't bother to sit, staying in the middle of the room. The leather portfolio he'd brought dangled from one hand.

"I'm not extorting you," Gio snarled. "All of this was negotiated in good faith before your crash and the rest."

Gio did know things, though. Things even Rafael didn't know about his wife. It was a startling moment of comprehending exactly how much power he wielded over the other man. On the other hand, Rafael knew things Gio didn't.

Gio bit the inside of his cheek, refusing to ask… *How is she? Where is she?*

Presumably Rafael saw her every day. He wanted to hate him for that, but he couldn't seem to.

If you do anything that causes harm to my child, my retribution will be swift and very final.

Rafael was protecting his unborn child and had stood up for Molly, too. Gio couldn't help but respect him.

"Let's sign it and I'll get out of here," Rafael muttered.

Gio rose and they both sat down at the small table. Rafael opened the folder and, aside from initialing a handful of adjusted dates, they made no changes. It was completed with silence and a final flourish of their signatures.

If Rafael was relieved, he didn't show it. He ought to be relieved, considering this would take a lot of pressure off his cash flow and signal to his investors that if Gio had faith in his operations, they could, too. It also made an attack on Rafael's company an attack on Casella Corporation. Most would think twice before embarking down that road.

"She's well, by the way," Rafael said as he rose and secured the contract in the portfolio.

"I didn't ask."

"I know. I wanted to know if you were serious about her or just using her for your own purpose. Now I do." His lip curled with contempt.

"*I'm* using her?" Gio said with outrage.

"At least I care whether she's well, Gio."

I care, he wanted to shout, but his throat was too dry. He did care. Too much. If this was a taste of what it was like to be loved by her, to have had her and then to lose her, he couldn't bear a lifetime of fearing it could happen again. Better to heal this sense of having a limb amputated and be done with it.

Molly's hands had been clammy for weeks, ever since her mother had told her about Gio's visit.

"I told him Sasha's story is not mine to tell and neither is it his," her mother had stressed. "I pointed out that it's not up to him to reveal Libby's birth mother to her or anyone else, but I don't know what he'll do with what he knows."

Molly had relayed everything to Sasha.

Sasha was still dealing with headaches, real and proverbial. Her parents were pestering her and her marriage was foundering against the many rocks between her and Rafael.

Those things were to be expected, but the minute she and Molly had been left alone at this villa on a remote island south of Athens, Sasha had confided, "I didn't really lose my memory, Moll."

"Oh, my God, Sasha. *Why* are you faking amnesia?" Molly had cried.

"It got out of hand! I was trying to get my parents out of my hospital room. Out of my *life*. Then it helped me avoid dealing with how hard things had become with Rafael, but it turned into this…" She waved helplessly. "I wanted to text you, but then Rafael might have figured out I knew everything. *Please* don't tell him."

Molly groaned with mental agony.

"You know I'll always have your back, but I also know how these things snowball into something that becomes bigger than you can handle." Before you knew it, you were fathoms deep in love with the man of your dreams and he was shutting you out of his life. "The sooner you come clean to him, the sooner you can get past it."

"I know, but…" She blinked damp lashes.

Compassion overwhelmed Molly. She couldn't blame Sasha for trying to protect herself when she was genuinely suffering from crippling headaches.

"Will you tell me one thing?" Molly prodded her gently. "I need to know. Do you want this baby?"

"Yes! So much." A thicker sheen of tears came into her eyes. "But I'm really s-scared that I'll be a terrible mother."

"No. You'll be wonderful."

"You don't know that!"

"I do. I have every faith in you." Then, they had hugged it out. "But let's both have a rest. We can talk more later."

It became a time of healing for both of them.

A nurse came weekly to monitor Molly's pregnancy

and Sasha's concussion, but for the most part, it was just the two of them in the modern home built on the ruins of an ancient villa. Crumbled walls formed the garden fence and were covered by hibiscus and wisteria. Fragrant thyme and sage bloomed in the corners of the yard and bright pink bougainvillea flowered against the white walls of the house.

If they followed the path around to the back, there was a vegetable garden filled with tomatoes, peppers, eggplants and herbs. Beyond the arched gate in the wall were arid hills and barley fields, groves of fig and fruit trees, and rows and rows of grapes.

In the mornings, they wandered the olive groves and the acres of vineyards, breathing in the serene ambience and breathtaking views of the Aegean. Then they ate breakfast on the terrace by the pool and swam when the day grew hot. They had naps in the afternoon and spent the evenings reading or watching television, if Sasha's head could stand it. Sometimes they did very little at all.

It was not unlike the time Sasha had spent living with them as a teenager, when they would find silly things to amuse themselves, such as completing jigsaw puzzles or collaging a dream board while they waited for the baby to grow.

Sasha didn't want to talk about her marriage, but she did let Molly tell her about Libby. Sometimes Molly talked about Gio. Her heart was cracked in half over the way things had ended with him. She missed him constantly. She felt as though she'd lost a lifetime with him and it made her sick with regret.

Not that she blamed this baby, though. In the weeks

she'd been here, her baby bump had become pronounced and its subtle kicks put a gleam of happy tears into Sasha's eyes. Every week, after the nurse left, Sasha said, "Thank you for doing this, Molly."

Thankfully, Rafael had business in Asia for several weeks. He often asked Molly how she was feeling when he chatted with Sasha, but it was awkward for her, since she knew Sasha was lying to him about her memory loss.

At one point, Molly said to Sasha, "I might have had second thoughts about this if I'd known you two weren't in love."

"I'm in love with him," Sasha said with quick defensiveness. "He's the one who—"

She didn't finish the sentence and Molly decided it wasn't her place to judge. She knew what it was like to be in love with a man who didn't love you back. All too well.

Which was why, as she was closing in on her twenty-fifth week, when everything should have been sunshine and roses, Sasha came upon her crying on the couch.

"I thought we agreed that only one of us is allowed to cry at a time," Sasha said.

"Was it your turn? I didn't realize." Molly grabbed a few tissues and tried to mop up.

"Why are we even crying over them, anyway? Should I order a hit? I can afford it and I'm not afraid to go to jail again."

"You've never—*tsk*." Molly chuckled as she blew her nose.

"Made you laugh, though." Sasha sat down beside her and nudged her shoulder into Molly's.

They leaned on each other for a bolstering moment.

"Here's what I think we should do," Sasha proposed. "We'll hang a sign on the door that says No Boys Allowed. Then we'll stay here forever, raising our little peanut, just the two of us."

"That's very tempting," she said truthfully.

Can Libby join us? She didn't ask, though.

Sasha was making progress at her own pace. She had reconnected with their counselor in London and had said, after yesterday's chat with her, "I want Libby to know she has a sibling, but I don't know how to tell Rafael about her."

The same cheerful woman had checked in with Molly about how she was feeling about the inevitable separation after she delivered.

Molly expected it was going to be hard emotionally, but now that she had this time to reconnect with Sasha and knew they would continue to have a relationship after the baby was born, her anxiety on that front was manageable. From the beginning, Sasha had assured Molly she would have an auntlike relationship to the baby. That would go a long way to softening her sense of loss. Now she was even talking about opening herself to Libby, which made Molly even happier that she was doing this.

No, she wasn't particularly worried about the aftermath of the delivery. It was the emptiness in the other corners of her life that loomed like ghouls. She wouldn't have her job. She had planned to live with her mom and

Libby while she looked for a new position, but already knew her life would feel desolate because it already did. Gio wouldn't be in it.

"I think I expected that if Gio knew you were Libby's mom, and that I'm just trying to give you what you gave us, it would make a difference. That he would understand." She started to choke up again.

"Oh, Moll. Let's both have a good cry and get it over with for a few days. Shall we?"

"I'd love to, but now I have use the bathroom again," she said with a beleaguered sigh as she rose. "Maybe we should go back to bed and start over tomorrow."

"Sounds like a pl— Oh, my God. Moll."

Molly looked over her shoulder. Sasha was staring with horror at a bright red stain on the sofa.

Gio was in New York, heading to one of a dozen quarterly meetings, when Avigail walked in, wide-eyed with alarm. She held out her phone.

"My grandfather?" Gio asked with a lurch of his stomach.

"No, but she says it's urgent. Alexandra Zamos."

Gio jolted as though struck by lightning. His heart nearly came out his mouth.

In every way, he had tried to cut Molly from his consciousness, but she was still there, every single hour of every single day. The most coldly pragmatic side of himself told him that accepting the call was prolonging a weakness he needed to conquer, but another part grasped at this delicate thread of connection to her.

He walked from the room, then said gruffly into the phone, "Alexandra?"

"I'm evacuating Molly to the hospital in Athens." She sounded as though she was crying. "She's bleeding. Will you—"

"What happened? Does her mother know?"

"No. That's why I'm calling. Can you tell Patty? I can't ask Rafael. He's never even spoken to her and he doesn't know—" Her choked voice was almost drowned out by the growing sound of helicopter blades thumping the air. "Can you arrange to get them here?" she shouted. "Tell Patty— Tell her that she should tell Libby anything she needs to know. Tell her about me. *Everything.*"

She didn't sound like the spoiled heiress he had met in the past. She could barely speak through palpable anguish that was causing the blood to drain from his head into his shoes. He had to lean on the wall for support.

"I know this is a lot to ask when you and Molly are on the outs, but Rafael—"

"It's done. I'll handle it." Gio didn't know how he would have that conversation with Molly's mother. He didn't know how he would speak or breathe or function if Molly didn't survive this. "Keep me posted," he said, but he wasn't sure she heard him.

Molly blinked awake to the dimly lit private hospital room. She sensed it was the middle of the night and wasn't certain what had pulled her from sleep except lingering anxiety over all that had happened today.

First there'd been the shock of realizing she was

bleeding, then the drama of a helicopter evacuation to the mainland. A scan had revealed a placental abruption. For the moment, the baby was getting enough oxygen, but they had given Molly steroids and put her on strict bed rest, hoping to buy the baby at least one more week of development. She would definitely deliver early, probably within the next two weeks.

She touched her belly with concern. Her hand still held the IV tube and the firm swell of her bump wore the monitor, reassuring her that the baby was safe inside her, but she was not quite twenty-five weeks along. Far too early.

"The baby's okay. You're stable," Gio said in a quiet rumble, coming to her side from the darkened corner by the window.

Her heart soared, then plummeted as she tried to read his expression and found it deeply guarded.

"When did you get here?" she asked with shock. *Why are you here?*

He touched a finger to his lips and nodded at the sofa. She lifted her head to see Libby sleeping under a draped blanket.

"Your mother is here," he said in an undertone. "She's down the hall with Alexandra. Libby wanted to stay here with you. It was a long flight and…" He hitched a shoulder. "A lot for her to process. She's worried about you."

Oh, kiddo. Molly dropped her head back onto the pillow.

"Thank you for bringing them," she whispered.

Rafael had been Sasha's first call after ordering the

helicopter, when they realized Molly was hemorrhaging. In her panic, Sasha had said all the wrong things, including "Of course, I remember everything!"

She had blown up her marriage in a way that was inevitable and possibly irrevocable. Rafael had promised to meet them here at the hospital, then hung up on her. At that point, Sasha had had no choice but to involve Gio.

Sasha had said that Gio had promised to handle everything, but Molly hadn't expected him to escort her mother and sister to her side himself.

"I really appreciate this. I need Mom and Lib here, but…" She couldn't keep her mouth from quivering. "You don't have to stay if you don't want to."

His cheek ticked. "If you don't want me here then say so."

"I want you here." Her voice was a mere scuff in the back of her throat.

He started to reach for her hand, but there was a rustle of noise behind him.

"Moll?" Libby asked sleepily.

"Hi, pumpkin. I'm awake. I'm okay."

Gio stepped back so she could see her sister sit up and throw off her blanket.

"That's good, because I need to tell you that I'm really mad at you," Libby informed her.

Ten days passed. Ten precious days of consistently lying on her left side, playing cards with Libby as they talked out secrets and lies. Ten days of letting her mother check her pulse and smooth her hair while they exchanged suggestions on what to read next on their e-readers.

Ten days of seeing Sasha and Rafael separately, both concerned about her and the baby, but not bringing any of their marital issues into her room.

That was her mother's doing. Patricia had read a riot act that Molly needed to remain calm and keep her blood pressure down. Conflicts should be taken down the hall and preferably kept from the hospital altogether.

Thus, Libby wasn't saying much to her birth mother, either.

"I just wonder why she didn't come and see me if she wanted a baby?" Libby had said to Molly one day, voice ringing with confusion and hurt.

Molly had a feeling that Patricia was spending a lot of time stroking Libby's hair, too. Maybe even Sasha's.

Then there was Gio. He was the first person Molly saw every morning and the last person at night. He usually stepped out when someone else arrived, but he never went far, because once they left, he flowed back into the room like a loyal sentry.

He brought flowers, which he insisted were from Otto.

"Does he know why I'm here?" she asked with alarm. It was her fourth day in hospital. They were all doing their best to continue keeping her surrogacy confidential. The last thing Sasha wanted was for her parents to catch wind of this and turn up. "How is he?"

"He's back to his old self. He only knows that you're receiving necessary treatment and that's why I'm here."

"What about work? I feel like I'm keeping you."

"I'm working." He held up his phone. "Valentina is overseeing our three musketeers. We're managing."

He could have at least pretended the place was falling apart without her.

"Gio—" She hesitated, not sure she wanted the answer, but she had to ask. "Why are you here?"

"If I were in hospital, where would you be?"

By his side, if he would let her, but that was because she loved him. Did that mean...?

"You heard your mother. I'm only allowed to stay if I let you nap. Go to sleep." He'd patted her calf and moved to the chair in the corner.

A few days later, he came in after Alexandra had left and said, "I keep thinking about that day on the yacht, when she was so shocked to see you. You never kept in touch after she placed Libby with you?"

"No. I was sad about that, but it was a painful time for her. Please don't judge her for pretending she lost her memory. If I had some of her memories, I'd want to forget them, too."

"I don't." He pushed his hands into his pockets, cheeks hollowed with reflection. "When we were on the plane, I overheard your mother tell Libby that Alexandra's parents are very wealthy and influential. That if they learned about her, they might destroy Patricia's career and make an attempt to take custody of Libby."

"They wouldn't win. Libby's birth father agreed to the adoption and even set up a trust for her, but they would put everyone through hell. Mom's practice would be impacted, which would be the point, given what I know of them," Molly said dourly.

"They sound delightful. We should introduce them to my parents." Gio curled his lip in contempt.

"When Sasha came to stay with us, I was really jealous of her. She was like you. She never had to think about money. That's not an insult," she said as his expression stiffened. "It's a fact. But as I got to know her, I realized she was deeply unhappy. She made me realize that having enough is enough and that I was lucky to have a mother who loved me. That's why she wanted to place Libby with us. She knew we would love her in a way she had never been loved herself. And we love Libby *so* much." Hot tears pressed into her eyes, her love for her sister was so big inside her.

"I know." He caressed her arm. "You don't owe me explanations. We can talk about this another time if it's upsetting you."

"No, I really need it off my chest because I couldn't tell you before." She covered where his hand sat on her upper arm. "I always believed that Sasha had had this one dark spell in her life and that she had made the best of it by giving both her baby and herself the best chance at a fulfilling life. Then I saw her on the yacht and she was miserable. She wanted a baby so badly and her body was betraying her. She had given us such a precious gift. I had to do the same for her. *I had to.*"

"I won't pretend I didn't struggle to understand it," he acknowledged somberly. "Especially when I thought you were doing it for money. My baggage put a dark spin on that."

"I know." She swallowed a lump in her throat. "I hated lying to you about that."

"It didn't fit with who I believed you were. You're ambitious, but if money motivated you, you'd be married to me right now. You have a soft heart, but you're not so soft you don't know how to say no. I spent a lot of time questioning whether I could even trust my own judgment. That's why I went to see your mother. I was certain I was missing something and I was."

He hadn't come to see her afterward, though, once he knew the truth. Why not?

Rafael had arrived at that point and Gio stepped out.

Rafael never stayed long. He only asked how she was feeling and glanced at the reports on the baby's vitals, then offered to bring anything she needed.

"Rafael, I'm worried about you and Sasha," Molly blurted, because it was genuinely eating at her.

"You're forbidden to worry," he reminded her dryly. "Alexandra and I want this baby very much. We'll do whatever we have to, to give our child a good life, including reconcile our differences. I know I speak for her when I say we're equally sorry this pregnancy is costing you so much. I don't know how I'll ever make that up to you. It eats at me every day, so, please, don't worry about me on top of it. I'll expire from guilt."

Until these daily visits, she hadn't really gotten to know Rafael. He was still aloof, but he sometimes offered these small glimpses that reassured her a human lurked behind the iron wall he presented to the world. That helped her see why Sasha had fallen for him. Molly only wished the pair would find their way back to each other before this baby arrived.

Who was she to talk, though? She was terrified to ask Gio point-blank what his feelings for her really were.

When Rafael left a few minutes later, she heard him speak to Gio in the hall. It sounded like Rafael had said, "So you do care."

Gio's response had been too low for her to hear. By the time he came back into her room, he was on the phone with Nelo and asked her if she recalled some detail about a contract. From there, the day wore on in its glacial fashion.

Every day was one minute at a time. For those ten days, Molly felt as though her life had stopped altogether. Or rather, that her life became focused on "life" in its most elemental sense—on the life inside her.

Then the decision was made for both of their sakes that the baby should be delivered by cesarean section. Molly was prepped for surgery and everyone gathered in her room. Since she was having a full anesthetic, no one would go into the theater with her.

"It's going to be fine," Sasha insisted with a strain in her voice. Her lips were white.

"I have every confidence in these doctors," Patricia assured her, which bolstered Molly a little.

Libby put on a brave face, smiling through her tears while Rafael was at his most stoic.

So was Gio, until they started to wheel her out.

"Molly!" He lurched into the hall and stopped the gurney to lean over her. His expression was tortured as he cupped her cheek. "Make sure you come back to me."

It was hardly in her power, but she promised, "I will."

He pressed one hard kiss on her dry lips, then she was on her way again, heart pounding.

CHAPTER ELEVEN

ATTICUS BROOKS ZAMOS was tiny, but utterly perfect. He was in neonatal intensive care, requiring extra oxygen and accepting his nutrition from an IV, but his lungs were working and his heart duct had closed. He needed time and a lot of close watching, but he was as healthy as could be expected for a baby born so early.

When Molly was wheeled down to visit him, and she saw his naked brow bunched with stern determination to stay alive, she knew she would love him for her whole life. She would have kept him as her own in a heartbeat, but as she watched Sasha shakily cradle his achingly small form against her bare chest, crying with love for him while Rafael stood over them like a wolf guarding his mate and cub, she knew she had done the right thing.

Which wasn't to say the baby blues didn't hit her like a ton of bricks. She was kept in hospital a few days to ensure she was recovering from the surgery, and she expressed a little colostrum to give Atticus his best start, but she was planning to go home to New Jersey with her mom and Libby, so she only pumped to keep herself comfortable, not to encourage more milk.

That caused a hormone roller coaster that had her unable to stop crying the day she was discharged. It felt wrong to leave Atticus here, but even Sasha couldn't bring him home yet. He would be in hospital for several weeks, likely until what would have been his due date if he'd gone to term.

"We'll stay at the apartment. It's just a few streets over," her mother said to console her, pacing alongside the wheelchair as Molly was brought to the exit. "We can visit him every day."

"I thought you were at a hotel?" Molly said with confusion.

"Gio moved us into his penthouse the second day we were here. It's closer and has a pool. Libby loves it. I thought it was too much of an imposition, but he's very persuasive," Patricia said ruefully.

"Oh, you've met him," Molly said, brightening with humor for a moment, then wondered why Gio hadn't come to fetch her if he was still here. Was he? Or had he left, now that he knew she had safely delivered and was on the mend?

"It's been nice getting to know him," her mother said. "And I won't pry, but…" She swept her hand over Molly's hair. "I like him. I hope things work out between you."

A nurse had helped Molly shower this morning. At least her hair was clean, if damp, but between that and the surgery, and the activity after so many days of bed rest, then the shuffle from the car into the apartment building, then into the penthouse, Molly was exhausted by the time she found Libby playing a lively hand of cards with Gio.

"Oh, no," Libby said with guilty horror when she saw her. "I was supposed to move my stuff into Mom's room so you could have mine. I'll do it now."

"Rest in my room while she does that," Gio said, rising to help Molly down the long, marble hallway into the sprawling bedroom where wide windows offered a stunning view of the Parthenon. "Can I get you anything?"

"No. I'm f-fine." She wasn't, though. Tears started to leak down her cheeks.

"Molly. Do you want me to get your mom?" he asked with concern.

"No," she sniffed. "I want to lay down."

He closed the door and came to help her sink onto the bed, then picked up her feet for her. She habitually rolled onto her left side.

"The counselor told me I should expect to be sad, but I don't want to cry. It hurts my stomach."

"Ah, *cuore mio*." He moved around the bed and lay facing her. "Of course, you're sad." Very gently, he drew her closer, arranging her against his warmth in a way that brought fresh tears to her eyes, but of a completely different sort. "I imagine you'll feel sad for a long time, but I hope you're proud, too? That was quite a gift you have given them."

She hitched back her sob, fighting to control herself, and adjusted how her head was pillowed on his shoulder, then relaxed with her arm across his waist.

"Thank you for saying that. I don't have any regrets about doing it. I really don't. Except…" She swallowed.

"Hmm?" he prompted, dipping his chin.

"I'm sorry I hurt you."

"You did hurt me." The admission sent a slicing pain through Gio's chest. He looked to the ceiling and blinked to hold the dampness in his eyes. "And I hurt you. I shouldn't have stayed away all those weeks." He tried to swallow away his regret for that lost time, but it would be with him forever. "Having that much power over each other felt dangerous. It was something I wanted to put back in the box, but I couldn't, no matter how hard I tried."

She brought her hand off his chest and into the nook of her throat, but he caught it, prickled by that small withdrawal. Her desire to self-protect was his fault, he knew that, but he didn't know how to open himself to her. How to keep her feeling safe while he told her the truth.

They needed the truth, though. There had been too many secrets and prevarications. Only complete honesty would move them forward and that's what he wanted above all—a future with her.

He drew a deep breath that felt as though it was nothing but powdered glass, trying to find the words to make things right between them.

"I need you to remember two things, Molly. That I was taught not to expect love and that I wanted you from the first time I saw you."

She went very still. A discernible tension remained in her, but it told him she was listening very attentively.

He played with her fingers and caressed her upper arm.

"Given my history, you and I would have struggled whether you were carrying your friend's baby or not, but that certainly didn't help," he said with a humorless choke.

She coughed a similar dry chuckle.

"I knew you were different the first time I saw you. I knew you affected me in a way that was deeper than anyone else ever had. That's why I liked having you on the other side of Valentina. I could see you, but there was no emotional risk. Did I want to have sex with you? All the damned time."

She released another small sniff of laughter and snuggled her head deeper into his chest, which encouraged him to continue.

"The fact you were my employee was a convenient firewall. When I promoted you into Valentina's position, I was looking forward to getting to know you better, but I was confident I could keep it professional. That didn't turn out as well as I'd hoped."

"You were going through a lot," she said, vouching for him, because she was far too generous. Her lashes lifted and the way she tilted her face up invited him to kiss her, but he made himself resist the urge and finish saying what he needed to say.

"I was devasted by the thought of losing Nonno, that's true. But I was just as troubled that you were talking of leaving. I could barely admit that to myself at the time. Saying all of this aloud here and now is still very hard."

She splayed her hand on his chest with such empathy, such care, he would swear she was leaving fingerprints against his heart, ones he would happily wear forever.

"Nonno's illness gave me the excuse to do what I wanted to do, which was shift our relationship into a personal one, but in a way that demanded very little emotional exposure."

A skeptical shadow entered her gaze.

"You don't believe that? Molly," he chided. "I hold Valentina in the highest esteem and she is loyal enough she would have gone along with a similar pretense. Frankly, it would have been an easier sell that she and I were spontaneously deciding to marry given our long association, but that subterfuge wouldn't have occurred to me if she'd still been with me. Engaging myself to you was about me hanging on to you in the most expedient way I could without admitting to anyone, especially myself, that I was afraid of losing you. I'm not proud of that. It was dishonest and I shouldn't have pressured you that way."

"I wouldn't have let it happen if I didn't already care for you," she chided, moving her hand so it became a pillow for the sharp weight of her chin on his chest. "I knew where the door was. I had credit cards and people I could call. I could have told Otto at any time that it was a lie. I let the engagement happen because it was *my* only chance to have a personal relationship with *you*."

"I wanted to believe you were with me by choice,

but thank you. I needed to hear that." He combed his fingers into her soft, sweet-smelling hair.

"I shouldn't have let it go so far, though," she said with remorse.

"In what way? Sleeping with me? Telling me you love me?"

She bit her bottom lip and nodded.

"I've seen the lengths you'll go to when you love someone, Molly." He tried to swallow the lump in his throat, but it stubbornly stayed there. "Would you have *my* baby if I asked you to?"

"As a *surrogate*?" She picked up her head.

"As my *wife*."

She withdrew, rolling onto her back with a sharp wince.

"I'm handling this badly." He came up on an elbow, still loathe to fully expose his heart because it was so damn frightening.

On the other hand, he'd walked through the cold shadows of all the ways he could lose her. He knew now that even if she cheated on him or revealed some venality of character, if she abandoned him or lied or if death stalked her, he would still feel the same about her. He would carry this want, this need, to have her near.

It was terrifying and humbling to be this susceptible to someone, but he was beginning to understand that that was what love was. It was this horribly exposed sensation of having a hole in your soul, one that also let in an abundance of joy and light, passion and harmony. Belonging. It sounded too sentimental to call it "completion," but it was an end to feeling as though something was missing.

"You know that I'm at a higher risk to have the same complication with a future pregnancy?" Her brow angled into worry.

"Is that what you took from what I just said? *Bella*, we can find our own surrogate. We can adopt. That is a discussion for a year from now, when you're fully recovered and want to think about children. I was asking if you still love me. I want to say it to you, but—" He closed his eyes, hardly able to breathe, he stood on such a high precipice.

He knew he had to step off and trust that she would catch him. He knew that's how it was done. He knew she *would* catch him, but, *mio Dio*, it was hard.

"Gio," she whispered. Her hand came to his cheek.

"No. Shh. Let me do this," he urged her softly. "I can."

He opened his eyes and saw such a glow in her expression, it brought tears to his eyes and a swelling elation into his chest.

"I love you, Molly. I don't want you to go home with your mother. I want you to come home with me. I want you to be my wife and make a family with me however we can. I want you to be beside me for as long as we both shall live."

Her mouth trembled and tears flooded into her eyes. "I want that, too," she choked. "I love you so much."

How could something so hard be so easy in the end? He brought her hand back to his chest and gently,

gently brought them into full contact so he could feel every curve and muscle and twitch and sigh. He covered her mouth with a hungry kiss and dragged her an inch closer, being careful, so very careful, because she was infinitely precious to him.

She was his heart. He understood that, now. But that was okay, because he was hers.

Two hours later, Molly woke cotton-headed from her nap. Gio was still holding her.

"Did you sleep?" she asked as she stretched and winced.

"No. But I didn't want to disturb you. It was nice to hold you again. I missed you." He rolled onto his back, moving with enviable lack of discomfort.

"I missed you, too." She was touched that he was so unabashed in saying it. Even so, she experienced a stab of shyness and asked, "Did I dream that we're in love and getting married or...?"

His mouth kicked sideways. "If it was a dream, I would like to make it real." He fished into his trouser pocket and brought out Nonna's ring. "Let's hope three times is the charm. Will you marry me, Molly?"

"Yes!" Here came the tears again, but they were happy ones.

After a dab of hand cream, the ring went on and they went out to tell her mother and Libby.

Patricia gave her a heartfelt hug, but Libby, being on the verge of twelve and still stung by all the secrets that had been kept from her, asked skeptically, "Do you mean it this time?"

"We do," Molly insisted, and tucked her hand into Gio's.

"All right, then." Libby hugged her, then hugged Gio. "You don't mind if I come live with you guys, right?"

"I'm sure your mother would mind, but I would not," Gio said with good humor, then he winked at Patricia. "Why don't we visit my grandfather before you fly home, so you'll know where to find her if she runs away?"

They married at Nonno's villa that December, when Libby was off school for Christmas holidays.

It was a beautiful, intimate ceremony with only Otto, her mother and sister, Sasha and Rafael, and the sweet and mighty Atticus. He had been out of hospital more than a month and Molly saw him as frequently as she could. He was still small, but he ate nonstop and had a terrifically demanding cry, one that cut off with comical abruptness when Libby gathered him into her arms.

"Do you remember me?" Libby asked him with quiet joy. "I'm your sister." She leaned close and whispered, "I'm also kind of your aunt."

They had confided the surrogacy arrangement to Otto, so he knew Molly was only a few months postpartum, but he still gently chided Molly. "When will you give me one of those?"

Her doctor had pronounced her fully healed from the surgery, but suggested she wait a little longer before attempting pregnancy, to give any potential baby its best chance for success.

She didn't mind waiting. She had a passionate husband who tumbled her to the bed in his jet when they left the villa for their honeymoon in Australia.

"We have twenty-something hours in the air," he informed her. "I intend to take advantage of you for every one of those hours."

"Show me."

He did, stripping her without ceremony. They knew each other very well now and flagrantly ran their hands over each other, enticing and caressing, trying to see who would break first.

It was her. It was always her. He loved making her shudder and cry out and weakly succumb to whatever he wanted. Today, after two shattering orgasms, he left a final damp kiss between her thighs, then rolled her stomach onto a pillow and guided himself to the still sensitized flesh he had pleasured so mercilessly.

"Ready, *cuore mio*?" he asked against her nape, sending shivers of fresh anticipation down her spine.

"Yes," she moaned, arching with invitation, longing for his thick length to fill her.

He did, then he roamed his hands over her cheeks and grasped her hips and unleashed his full power, claiming her with proprietary thoroughness.

She loved it. Loved him. It was the randy, earthy lovemaking they hadn't been able to enjoy when she'd been pregnant and still healing. It was rough, yes, but it was a joyous, carnal experience, one that reinforced the trust between them. The fierce bond that had already withstood so much.

When they peaked together, they were together in the most elemental, indelible way. It was pure and perfect. Eternal.

But as their skin cooled and their hearts returned to a resting rate, she noticed he wore a slight frown.

"What's wrong?"

"Nothing." He closed one eye, rueful at not being immediately honest. "I'm envious of Sasha and Rafael," he admitted. "Every time I see them with Atticus, I'm impatient for us to have a baby of our own, but I don't want to give this up yet, either." He brought her hand to his lips. "I don't know if you noticed, but I *love* having wild sex with you."

"You don't want to give that up and go back to visiting me in the hospital while I'm on strict bed rest? That's weird."

"I do not," he said somberly. "Perhaps we should consider other options."

"I'd like to try getting pregnant first. Not yet," she added quickly. "But soon. If we run into complications, I won't put myself through a lot of procedures. We'll look at other options right away, but for now…" She rolled atop him, reveling in the fact she could push her own body to its limits while testing his. "You made a certain promise about this flight. Have we crossed the equator? Because I'm about to." She began kissing her way south.

He made a noise of agony when she took him in her

mouth, then said on a sigh of bliss, "I love you so very much, *mia amata*."

She smiled, not surprised that he would say that to her when she was anointing him in this very intimate way, but later, when they were both sated and falling asleep in each other's arms, he said it again with deep sincerity.

"I do love you, you know."

"I know," she assured him. It was as real inside her as breath and blood. "I love you, too."

EPILOGUE

TWO DAYS BEFORE their second anniversary, Molly gave birth at the villa in Genoa to a boy with brown hair like his mother and blue eyes like his father. Patricia had monitored her very healthy pregnancy, then attended her through the labor and caught the baby. Libby brought ice chips and texted reports to Sasha. Gio cut the cord.

Otto came in the moment he was invited, then wept when they told him he was holding his namesake.

Everything about the experience was as perfect as Molly could have imagined it, but when she woke in the night, Gio was awake, holding baby Otto and wearing a pensive frown.

"What's wrong?" she asked with a skip of alarm, starting to sit up.

He lifted his face to reveal damp eyes. "I was so afraid I wouldn't have this feeling," he choked. "Now it's here and it's so fierce, I don't know what to do with it."

"Love?" She tucked her chin, absolutely undone when he showed her his heart like this.

Gio was a man of great affection and generosity. He

spoiled Libby, which she did not need, given everything Sasha and Rafael did for her. He was constantly trying to soften Patricia's life any way she would allow, too, coaxing her to let him buy her a new car and book her vacations. He wanted to buy her a home in Genoa so they could all see each other more. Now that her first grandchild was here, Patricia was coming around to the idea.

Gio had proven himself a doting husband and family man even before he had refused to travel farther than the office here in Genoa for the duration of Molly's pregnancy. She and their son were his top priority and always would be. She knew that.

"It's okay to love him that hard. He won't break," she reassured him, then teased, "Look at me. I'm alive and well and you love me a *lot*."

"*I* might break, I carry so much love for you." He came to sit on the edge of the bed with Otto still in the crook of his arm. He cupped the side of her neck and leaned down to drop a kiss on her lips. "*Ti amo, cuore mio*. Thank you for all that you've given me. Not just our beautiful son, but the ability to love you both with all my strength."

Her mouth started to quiver. "I don't know where I would have put my love for you if you hadn't opened your heart to take it." They shared a longer kiss, one so ripe with emotion, it brought tears to her eyes.

She peeked at their son, who was fast asleep. Her heart swelled a dozen sizes. What an astonishing little miracle.

"Have you slept at all?" she asked, recalling that Gio

had been awake since her first labor pain in the early hours of yesterday.

"I will soon, but I want to hold him." He rose and came around the bed so he could sit against the pillows beside her. "I want him to know I'm here. I'll always be here," he vowed to their boy, kissing the infant's cheek. "For both of you."

She believed him. With a smile on her lips, and the weight of her husband's hand over hers where she rested it on his thigh, she drifted to sleep.

* * * * *

Did you fall in love with
The Baby His Secretary Carries?
Then you're sure to adore the next book in the
Bound by a Surrogate Baby duet,
coming soon!

In the meantime, check out these other stories
by Dani Collins!

Cinderella's Secret Baby
Wedding Night with the Wrong Billionaire
A Convenient Ring to Claim Her
A Baby to Make Her His Bride
Awakened on Her Royal Wedding Night

Available now!

#4177 CINDERELLA'S ONE-NIGHT BABY
by Michelle Smart

A glamorous evening at the palace with Spanish tycoon Andrés? Irresistible! Even if Gabrielle knows this one encounter is all the guarded Spaniard will allow himself. Yet, when the chemistry simmering between them erupts into mind-blowing passion, the nine-month consequence will tie her and Andrés together forever...

#4178 HIDDEN HEIR WITH HIS HOUSEKEEPER
A Diamond in the Rough
by Heidi Rice

Self-made billionaire Mason Foxx would never forget the sizzling encounter he had with society princess Bea Medford. But his empire comes first, always. Until months later, he gets the ultimate shock: Bea isn't just the housekeeper at the hotel he's staying at—she's also carrying his child!

#4179 THE SICILIAN'S DEAL FOR "I DO"
Brooding Billionaire Brothers
by Clare Connelly

Marriage offered Mia Marini distance from her oppressive family, so Luca Cavallaro's desertion of their convenient wedding devastated her, especially after their mind-blowing kiss! Then Luca returns with a scandalous proposition: risk it all for a no-strings week together...and claim the wedding night they never had!

#4180 PREGNANCY CLAUSE IN THEIR PAPER MARRIAGE
by Kate Hewitt

Honoring the strict rules of his on-paper marriage, Christos Diakis has fought hard to ignore the electricity simmering between him and his wife, Lana. Her request that they have a baby rocks the very foundations of their union. And Christos has neither the power—nor wish—to decline...

HPCNMRA0124

#4181 THE FORBIDDEN BRIDE HE STOLE
by Millie Adams

Hannah will do *anything* to avoid the magnetic pull of her guardian, Apollo, including marry another. Then Apollo shockingly steals her from the altar, and a dangerous flame is ignited. Hannah must decide—is their passion a firestorm she can survive unscathed, or will it burn everything down?

#4182 AWAKENED IN HER ENEMY'S PALAZZO
by Kim Lawrence

Grace Stewart never expected to inherit a palazzo from her beloved late employer. Or that his ruthless tech mogul son, Theo Ranieri, would move in until she agrees to sell! Sleeping under the same roof fuels their agonizing attraction. There's just one place their standoff can end—in Theo's bed!

#4183 THE KING SHE SHOULDN'T CRAVE
by Lela May Wight

Promoted from spare to heir after tragedy struck, Angelo can't be distracted from his duty. Being married to the woman he has always craved—his brother's intended queen—has him on the precipice of self-destruction. The last thing he needs is for Natalia to recognize their dangerous attraction. If she does, there's nothing to stop it from becoming all-consuming...

#4184 UNTOUCHED UNTIL THE GREEK'S RETURN
by Susan Stephens

Innocent Rosy Bloom came to Greece looking for peace. But there's nothing peaceful about the storm of desire tycoon Xander Tsakis unleashes in her upon his return to his island home! Anything they share would be temporary, but Xander's dangerously thrilling proximity has cautious Rosy abandoning all reason!

YOU CAN FIND MORE INFORMATION ON UPCOMING HARLEQUIN TITLES, FREE EXCERPTS AND MORE AT HARLEQUIN.COM.

HPCNMRB0124

THE
DEATH
HOUSE

THE

DEATH
HOUSE

A NOVEL

SARAH PINBOROUGH

TITAN BOOKS

The Death House
Print edition ISBN: 9781789091830
Electronic edition ISBN: 9781783298044

Published by Titan Books
A division of Titan Publishing Group Ltd
144 Southwark St, London SE1 0UP

First Titan Books edition: September 2015
This paperback edition: October 2019

2 4 6 8 10 9 7 5 3 1

A CIP catalogue record for this title is available from the
British Library.

Printed and bound in the United States.

For Johannes,
My partner in crime and wine.
Much love.

'Be happy for this moment. This moment is your life'

OMAR KHAYYÁM

ONE

'They say it makes your eyes bleed. Almost pop out of your head and then bleed.'

'Who says?'

'People. I just heard it.'

'You made it up.'

'No, I didn't,' Will says. 'Why would I make that up? I heard it somewhere. You go mad first and then your eyes bleed. I think maybe your whole skin bleeds.'

'That is such a heap of shit.'

'Shut up and go to sleep.' I roll over. The rough blanket scratches me on the outside and my irritation at Will's overactive imagination scratches me from the inside. I let out a hot breath against the wool. My irritation is irritating me. It comes fast these days, flares from the ball of a black sun that's been growing quietly in the pit of my stomach. The two boys fall satisfyingly silent. I'm the eldest. I'm the top dog, the boss, the daddy. Of Dorm 4, at least. My word goes.

I yank the starched sheet up until it covers the edge of the old blanket. The dorm isn't cold so much as cool – the kind of chill ingrained in the bricks and mortar of centuries-old buildings, a ghostly, melancholy chill of things that once-were, now part-lost. We suit the house, I think, and that makes the ball contract in my gut. I shiver and pull my legs up under my chin. My bladder twinges. Great.

'I can't sleep,' Will says plaintively. 'Not with that going on.' He yawns then and I can see him in the gloom, sitting up cross-legged on his bed, fiddling with the metal bars at the foot of it. He's the youngest in our room, and is small for his age. He acts younger, too.

The constant whispering comes from the bed opposite Will's on the other side of the room. The cuckoo in our nest, Ashley, is on his knees beside it, praying. He does this every night at lights-out. Religiously.

'I don't think God is listening,' I mutter. 'You know, given the situation.'

'God's always listening.' The prim voice floats in the frigid air – a stretched reed with a breeze cutting across it. 'He's everywhere.'

My bladder twitches again and I give in and push back the covers. The floorboards are cold – fuck knows how Ashley's knees must feel – but I ignore my slippers. I'm not a granddad.

'Then your praying makes no sense,' Louis says,

matter-of-fact. His bed is closest to the door and he's staring up at the ceiling, his hair here and there and everywhere. He still gesticulates as he speaks, even though he's lying down. 'Because if your God *is* everywhere then he's also inside you and therefore you could speak to him from the quiet privacy of your own mind and talk all night if you wanted without making a sound and he would still hear you. Of course, there is absolutely no scientific proof that any form of deity exists, or that we are more than a collection of cells and water, so your God is just a figment of someone's imagination that you've bought into. Basically, you're wasting your time.'

The whispering gets louder.

'Maybe he's having a wank under the bed and trying to cover the noise,' I say as I reach the door. '*Fwap fwap fwap.*' I grin as I make the hand gesture.

Louis snorts a laugh.

Will giggles.

My irritation lifts. I like Will and Louis. I wish I didn't, but I can't help it. I glance back as I close the door. They look small in the large room. There are too many beds for just the four of us – six against each wall. It's like everyone else has gone home and somehow we were forgotten. The door clicks shut and I creep along the corridor. It's a long way to the bathroom and even though I have bigger things to frighten me than the shadows and emptiness of the tired manor house, I still move

11

quickly. The last rounds haven't been done yet.

I hurry down the wide wooden stairs, clinging to the bannister in the dark as if it were the railing on a ship wearily cutting through the night ocean. The whole house is silent apart from the gentle creaks and moans of the old building itself. I think of the others sleeping in the dorms spread throughout the draughty wings, and the nurses and teachers in their quarters, and then my mind can't help but imagine the top floor. The one where only the lift goes. Where the kids who get sick disappear to in the night, efficiently removed while the house sleeps. Swallowed by the lift and taken to the sanatorium. We don't talk about the sanatorium. Not any more. No one ever leaves the house, and no one ever comes back from the sanatorium. We all know that. Just like we know we'll each make a trip there. One day I'll be the kid who vanishes in the night.

I pee without closing the door or turning on the light, enjoying the relief even though the liquid stream on ceramic is loud. I don't flush – Mum's rule of no flushing at night still sticks – and then I yawn into the mirror without washing my hands. That rule has changed. Germs are not our biggest problem here. Not that, to be honest, I ever remembered much *before* anyway.

They say it makes your eyes bleed.

I lean in closer and stare at my eyes. They're

normally bright blue but look drowned grey in the grimy night. I pull down one lower lid and can make out the streaks of tiny veins running away to my insides. No blood there, though. It probably isn't even true. Just Will's stupid imagination making shit up. I'm fine. We're all fine. For now.

'You should be in bed.'

The voice is soft but it makes me jump. Matron stands in the corridor by the window, the moonlight through the glass making her white uniform shine bright. Her bland face is barely visible.

'Aren't you tired?'

'I needed to pee.'

'Wash your hands and go back to bed.'

I blast cold water onto my palms and then scurry past her, taking the stairs two at a time. It's the most she's said to me since I arrived here. I don't want her to speak to me. I don't want her to notice me at all, as if somehow that will make a difference.

'Matron's coming,' I whisper, back in my own room.

'They're asleep,' Louis says. The words blur together. I'm not surprised. It's about the right time.

'I don't understand why they give us vitamins before bed,' Louis slurs. 'I don't understand why they give us vitamins at all.'

I half-smile at this from under my rough blankets and too-crisp sheets. Louis – with his six A levels by the age of thirteen, and who'd been racing through university stupidly early before this stopped him

13

– might be some sort of genius, but just like the others, he's missed the obvious. I don't point it out. They're not vitamins; they're sleeping pills. Matron and the nurses like the house silent at night.

I wait, tense, for another ten minutes or so before I hear the door handle turn and the soft shuffle of soles as she checks each bed. The last round before morning. Only after she's gone do I open my eyes and breathe easily.

It was a Friday when they came. It was hot, hotter than normal, and he'd taken his time on the way back from school. He'd bought a Coke from the shop on the corner but the fridge wasn't working so it was warm and sticky. He drank it anyway, belching loudly after draining it and kicking the can across the street. His mind was drifting through the landscape of the day. Mr Settle droning on about the continuing global climate instability as they all baked and dozed, bored in the classroom. The History essay he owed. The fight with Billy. That was going to come back on him at some point. He didn't even know why he'd started it other than Julie McKendrick had been watching, and it felt like Julie had been watching him for a few days now, even though he couldn't quite believe it. Tomorrow night was the party. Tomorrow night, everything could change.

Julie McKendrick was always there in some part

of his brain. It was too hot to work. Too hot for school. But it wasn't too hot to think about Julie McKendrick and the fact that she might actually like him. He was so lost in his own world he didn't notice how quiet the street was, how all the little kids were inside, not sitting out on the pavements or racing around on their bikes as usual. Billy and the essay had faded and he was mainly wondering if what he felt for Julie really was love or just that she was the fittest girl in the school and he might actually get to kiss her. Maybe even put his hands inside her bra. Just thinking about it made his mouth dry and his heart race. He wondered how it would feel. He wondered if he'd actually find out the next day at the party. Even when he saw the van outside his house, where his dad's car would be parked later when he got home from work, he still didn't put two and two together. Not until he heard his mum crying. By then it was too late. And it was too hot to run.

TWO

'My money's on one of the twins,' Louis says, and glances at me. 'You still taking bets, Toby?'

We're at breakfast, the gong having summoned us down to the wood-panelled space that might once have been an oversized drawing room but is now our dining room. The ornate stone fireplace remains unlit and the only evidence of a previous existence is a tired purple velvet chaise longue pushed up against a wall, and brighter patches on the faded yellow paint where pictures must once have hung. The sun breaks momentarily through the gathering clouds outside and light streams through the vast windows, sending dust-motes dancing curious in the air. The warmth feels good on my face and as I finish my tea, I wonder if maybe Matron and the nurses put something in our breakfast drinks, too, like I heard they used to give men in prison to stop them wanting to fuck or fight.

Louis is trying to eat a fried-egg sandwich made with toast that's not quite done enough and an egg that's too runny. Most of it's going down his T-shirt but he doesn't seem to care. We're on a table of our own – our table ever since we arrived. New habits form quickly. There are sixteen tables but only eight are used, one for each of the occupied dorms. We don't talk to the boys from the other dorms much any more, even though there's only twenty-five of us left. The girls, Harriet and Eleanor, sit at a table at the back. I'm not sure how old they are, but Eleanor's still young and Harriet might be older but there's nothing hot about her. She's bookish and dumpy and her mouth is nearly always turned down in an unpleasant pout. They have always excluded themselves, and mainly I forget they're even here.

'Yep,' I say. 'Which one?'

'Either. I can't tell them apart. The one who's trying not to look like he's sniffing. Is that Ellory or Joe? Whichever, he's been getting sick and trying to hide it for days.'

The twins are in Dorm 7. Dorm 7, like our own, is still complete. It's become a matter of unspoken rivalry between us – which dorm will keep a clean survival sheet the longest. Of all the dorms, only Dorm 7 really counts to me. I stare at the table opposite and realise Louis is right. One of the two identical lanky, spotty boys sneakily wipes his nose with the back of his hand. He doesn't reach for a tissue even though there are paper napkins on the tables. I watch him. It's really hard to tell.

The symptoms can be so different.

'I'll take your bet. Two washing-up duties?'

'Done.' Louis smiles. 'I call double or quits. If he goes, the other one goes next.'

'Why?' Will sits down with a second bowl of cereal. Will may be tiny but he eats more than anyone I've ever known. ''Cos they know each other?'

'No, because of science. They're identical. When it goes in one of them, it's logical it'll go in the other soon after. It's genetic, after all.'

'Oh,' Will says. 'Right.'

'But that reminds me.' Louis gets up, egg still dripping from his chin, and before I realise what he's doing, he's over at the Dorm 7 table, smiling at Jake.

'Oh, shit,' I mutter.

'Jake,' Louis starts, 'I was just wondering if you could help me with something. I'm doing a kind of study of where we've all come from and roughly how long it took us to travel here. Firstly it was to find out where exactly we are, but we've sort of figured that out now, so I . . .'

'Oh, this isn't going to end well,' Will says, peering over his glasses.

I groan inside. Louis and his stupid information-gathering. No one in the house comes from the same part of the country. We know that. So why does Louis need to know the details? What is it with him and his precision in everything? Over the past week, Louis has become obsessed with trying to collate as much data on the inmates, as he calls us, as he can. This in the main has not gone well. For a start, he's failed to factor in that people lie. I've lied. I'm sure the rest have, too. No one wants to talk about their private history from *before* anymore and definitely not to someone from another dorm. The nervous friendliness we'd shared at the start is gone. The dorms have become packs and we stay within our own.

'What the fuck has it got to do with you?' Jake slowly gets to his feet. He's speaking quietly – there are nurses by the food station – but the threat is palpable in the air. Cutlery goes down. Heads turn.

'I thought it would be interesting to—' Louis, the genius, the prodigy, is oblivious to the tension.

'Why don't you just fuck off?'

Jake's the same age as me, but the stories about him spread on day one, in nods and whispers. He's been in reform school. He's stolen cars. I don't believe a lot of the wild tales of *before* that I've heard in the house, but Jake is different. Jake's knuckles are scarred and when we first arrived, the back of his head had a gang symbol shaved into it. If you look closely you can still see the shape of it in the new hair. I have no intention of messing with Jake. Jake is no Billy in Year 13.

'Is Jake going to punch him?' Will looks at me and, worse, so does Ashley. I've got no choice, not if I want to keep whatever respect they have for me.

'I'll talk to him.' If there is some kind of drug in the tea, I'm not feeling it now. My nerves jangle as I walk over to them. Not for what might happen now – the nurses don't tend to interfere, although I doubt they'll stand idly by in a fight – but for what might happen later. I never got my beating from Billy. Maybe I'll get it from Jake instead.

'Sorry, Jake,' I say, trying to sound casual. 'Louis wasn't thinking.' I look at the wild-haired boy between us. 'Go and wipe that egg of your face. You look like a dick.'

'He looks like he's been sucking a dick,' Jake says. His table-mates snigger. They're gazing up at Jake like he's a god.

I force a smile.

'Yeah, I guess he does.' The worst thing is, now I look at Louis, Jake's right. A strand of not-quite-cooked-enough egg white is glued to Louis' chin.

Louis crumples a little, looking hurt, and wipes his mouth. 'It's egg,' he says.

'Just shut up and sit down, Louis,' I snarl at him, and Louis, shaken by my tone, drops his head and shuffles back to where Will and Ashley are waiting, finally aware that all the eyes in the room are on him. I look at Jake, not sure where to take this next. 'Like I said, sorry.' I turn and walk away.

'Fucking retards,' Jake says to my back.

Not retards, Jake, fucking Defectives. We're all Defectives here.

I don't say it, though. I just sit down and sip my tea and hope that's it done. Nobody speaks as we watch Dorm 7 gather up their plates – the youngest, Daniel, a chubby boy of about eleven, clears Jake's away – and then head out in a line behind their leader, each of them sneering as they go by, as if they think they could all take me on, not just Jake. I ignore them. Only when they've gone does Louis look up.

'You didn't have to agree with him.' He's smarting.

'Yes he did,' Ashley says. He's nibbling a piece of carefully buttered toast. 'Just because you're clever, you think you know everything. You don't. Sometimes you're plain stupid.' He sounds smug, no doubt still annoyed with Louis for taking the piss out of his praying last night.

'Let's just forget about it.' I want breakfast over. I wish I could be friends with Jake – not that I like him, but at least we're the same age. If we were friends I wouldn't feel as if I'm such a fucking *nanny* so much of the time.

'Maybe we'll get letters today,' Will says. 'They said our parents could write to us. They must have written by now. We've been here weeks. Maybe they'll even be able to visit.'

'Do you still want to learn to play chess?' Louis says. 'I'll teach you, if you like.'

Will smiles, the letters momentarily forgotten. I might be the boss of the dorm, but Will is most fascinated by Louis, and although their minds are miles apart, it's clear Louis likes Will, too. I wonder what Louis' life was like before this – all that brilliance but always several years younger than his classmates. No real friends. Always treated like a bit of a freak. I suspect Louis mentioned the chess on purpose to distract Will. There weren't going to be any letters, and definitely no visits. That had all been clear on my mother's face as she screamed my name when they put me in the van. This way no one has to know when it happens. It's *cleaner*.

For our families, at least.

THREE

After breakfast there are lessons. We have these in dorm groups and the teachers rotate around the various rooms that might once have been bedrooms or dining rooms or whatever else someone filled this old house with, but now serve as small classrooms. Even though some of the dorms are down to just a couple of people, they don't change that rigid routine by mixing us up.

Mainly, given the age differences between us, we work from textbooks, answering comprehension questions or learning French we'll never use or just staring out of the window and waiting for the next change of teacher. There's a ten-minute break but no playground to dick around in. It's basically just a toilet break. There's no detention. If you don't work and just sit there quietly the teachers don't care. It turns out that you end up working anyway, just to make the morning pass quicker. Four hours is a long time to just sit and think, especially when you don't have any good stuff to think about.

The teachers are all middle-aged and I wonder about that. Maybe it makes it easier for them to distance themselves from us. We don't know their names – *just call me Sir or Miss should you need help* – and I think they must be as bored as we are. They sit at the front and watch us until we have a question, but mainly if we don't understand something we just move on to the next bit. Or, in our dorm, ask Louis. The textbooks we use are old, maybe twenty or thirty years older than the ones at school, and I think that's intentional, too. It's school but not school. Like this whole place is life but not life. At least the teachers, who disappear off to their own wing once lessons are done, will get out of here. Sometimes I'll catch one watching us as we work as if we're animals in a zoo. I can never decide quite what the look is. Fascination or fear, or maybe a bit of both. They watch for symptoms, too, I bet. Just like the nurses. I wonder if the teachers talk about us at night. I wonder if they take bets on which of us will go next – or say which one of us they *want* to go next. I think about rolling up balls of paper and launching them across the room to see if I can hit Ashley's head, but I never do it. Aside from my lack of interest in mucking around here, I suspect that messing about in class is a sure-fire way to get Matron's attention. I don't want to be a troublemaker. I don't want her noticing me. Instead, I scratch answers onto paper and sit the morning out.

The sunshine is gone by the time we finish lunch and scurry away like rats in drains through the vast corridors of the house, and by two, rain is falling in sheets from the heavy grey sky outside. It's not cold but it's rained for days. Not that I feel much like going outside. I'm tired.

Will and Louis are set up at a small table in the corner of the common room that no one really uses, the plastic chess pieces laid out between them. Louis is carefully explaining how each one moves and Will already looks confused. The common room is a strange affair, out of time, just like the rest of the house. There are shelves of board games in battered boxes and an old record player on the side, but the music is unfamiliar and who knows how to use a record player, anyway? Although there are only four or five kids in the room with them, neither Louis or Will glance towards me as I pause at the door. This isn't a surprise. When Louis engages in something, it absorbs his whole attention. We might not have known each other very long, but we're getting to know each other well.

In the library, Eleanor is curled up next to a radiator with a book, ignored by the two boys playing cards cross-legged on the floor. It's a thin paperback with a colourful cover and yellowed pages and she pulls at a strand of her hair as she reads, lost in whatever world is coming alive on the paper. I think about taking a book, but nothing grabs my attention. I didn't read much *before* – not even for school – and now it just looks like hard work. Plus I don't want to read about things I'll never do. It'll just make the dark ball in my stomach grow.

Ashley is in the art room, labouring over a sheet of buff A1 paper like they use in primary schools, a selection of coloured markers beside him. Harriet is working on a painting of an empty vase that she's set up on a table with some books around it. Her tongue sticks out as she concentrates on bringing it to life, adding imagined brightly coloured flowers springing from the gaping china. Ashley glances over and nods seriously at me, and I wonder what he's up to. Whatever it is, I think he should let Harriet finish it for him. Her painting is quite good. I leave them to it.

I stand in a corridor for a while, leaning on the chipped paint of the windowsill and looking out at the rain. The house gardens are empty. The old oak tree at its heart is still. There's no wind, no movement in its leaves and branches, as if it's simply staring back at me and waiting for something. In the quiet I can hear my heart beating, punching out angry not-quite seconds of natural time. My eyes itch. I need to sleep. I don't mind being tired or bored. I'm always bored. I sometimes wonder if I like the boredom because it makes time go more slowly.

The swell of Julie McKendrick's breasts rises in

my mind and I go and lock myself in one of the bathrooms. I sink into the memories of her low-cut T-shirts and her shorts so short you can just see the curve of her arse. Sometimes I worry because I can't remember her face so clearly even though it's only been a month or so, but I concentrate on her breasts and her arse and her warm skin and drift into a fantasy of her mostly naked and wrapped around me, my fingers inside her and her breath hot in my ear telling me how much she likes it and what she wants to do to me, and then I'm in her mouth. I don't know if Julie McKendrick has ever given a blow job, but by now she's only part-Julie and part-porn from *before* that I've seen and laughed at with the boys from school and watched in throbbing wonder on my own. I figure it doesn't matter much what I do with her in my imagination. She's never going to know.

Afterwards the tiredness is overwhelming and I head back to the dorm and close the door, then climb wearily onto my bed. I don't get under the covers. The house is drowsy warm during the day, whatever the weather is like outside. I yawn and my eyes close. I listen to the patter of rain against the old glass and let it drown out my thoughts as I drift off. I always sleep after lunch. This is my routine and the others never disturb me. I don't want to socialise anyway. What's the point?

There is no point, I think as I sink into the

darkness. And then, just before I drown into nothing, *They say it makes your eyes bleed.*

I'm so fast asleep when the gong wakes me that for a moment I think I'm back in school and a fire alarm is going. I tumble off the bed and stare, confused for a few moments until the house settles into place around me. I blink, not yet ready to move, and the gong falls silent. My mouth is dry and I'm still too sleepy to be hungry but I know I have to go to tea. Matron and the nurses might seem to vanish for most of the day, hidden in the walls of the house somewhere, but I know they still account for each child and, like ghosts, they watch us quietly without us really seeing them. I stretch and then head to the door. Halfway down the stairs, I'm greeted by the rest coming the other way, filled with excited chattering that I'm not awake enough to really absorb.

'We've got to stay in our room!' Will says. 'We've got to stay there until tea!' He flies past with Louis at his heels and my tiredness vanishes into their energy and my own confusion. The stairs thump with feet heading to dorms, and for a moment the house is alive. The nurses have appeared, standing at each landing and watching silently as we hurry past them. Their eyes follow each of us, mentally ticking us off. They don't smile, though, or offer any words of encouragement. That's not what the nurses are here for.

Ashley is the last up the stairs and by the time he closes the dorm door behind him, the rest of us are at the window.

'Look,' Louis says, so close his breath fogs the glass. 'New people. That's what it is.'

There are two black vans outside, pulled up right by the doors to the house. Someone's standing on the steps under a big umbrella and we all know it's Matron. It was Matron who greeted us when we arrived. There had been more than two vans then, though. There had been a seemingly endless line of them, eight or nine stretching out back through the high electric solid gates at the end of the drive.

'New kids,' Will breathes. His eyes are wide. We've got used to our numbers going down, not up.

'Can you see how many there are?' Ashley asks, touching the glass with fingers green-streaked from the coloured pens. Even he is intrigued. Although the others find activities to fill their afternoons, they're all as bored as I am.

'Not many, by the looks of it,' I say. Below, the door of one van slides back, but Matron has stepped forward with her umbrella and it's blocking our limited view.

'I wonder where they've come from?' Louis asks, already thinking of his useless data survey.

'They'll be getting the talk in a minute, I guess,' Will says. 'Like we did.'

*

His legs had been stiff when he climbed down from the van. The uniformed men who'd dragged him away from his screaming mother and strapped him into his seat had injected him with something as they sped away, and much of the trip passed in a haze. He hadn't slept but neither had he felt like talking. For a while he thought he might be having a bad dream, but then the drug slowly wore off and although there were no windows to see out through, at one point he could feel the thrum of a bigger engine and the tilt of waves beneath them before the van started up again and cooler, fresher air crept in through the gaps around the door. He asked questions then but the men didn't answer him, staring ahead as if he wasn't there. In the end he gave up.

The men didn't climb down with him from the van, and as soon as he stood blinking on the ground, the door slid shut and they drove away, leaving him in the shadow of the overbearing manor house. More vans pulled up behind; three kids stepped down from the next one and he wondered if his own face matched the masks of nervousness they wore. In front of them a woman in a starched white uniform watched from the steps, and when the last van was unloaded, she led them inside.

They gathered in the dining room, fifteen or so refugees with no suitcases and only the clothes they'd been taken in, a mishmash of youth and styles. The woman at the front of the room waited patiently as the nurses handed out cups of orange squash which they all drank and then she called them to silence.

'I think there's been a mistake,' a boy beside him said. 'My results must have got mixed up.' He was maybe thirteen, geeky and wearing an oversized black T-shirt with some sci-fi shit on the front. His name turned out to be Henry and he would be the first of them to be taken in the night. No mistakes made there. His voice trembled as he tried to sound confident but he just sounded scared. Someone at the back snickered and the rest joined in, Toby included. Eyes flashed looks at each other and sudden bonds were formed, even though on the inside they were all thinking exactly what Henry had said aloud.

'You will call me Matron,' the woman said, ignoring Henry's plaintive statement. 'You are here because your blood tests have shown the Defective gene to be active. You are Defectives. Do I have to explain what that means?'

Her voice was neither kind nor unkind, exactly matching her neutral face and expression. Another titter of nervous laughter rippled through her audience. They all knew what it meant even if they couldn't believe it had happened to them. Toby had never known anyone test positive. Positives *were so rare these days, that's what his mum had always said. They never happened to anyone you actually knew. Like plane crashes.*

Matron was still talking. 'This is your home now. You will be provided with clothes and food and activities to enjoy. You may play in the grounds of the house should you wish to do so. You will have some chores as you would at home and a rota in the hall outside this room will give you your allocations. You will change your bedsheets once a week. Your top sheet will go to the bottom and the bottom sheet should be put in the laundry sack provided. You will also continue with your studies every morning.'

'Fuck no,' someone said loudly. More laughter. Toby looked at the speaker, whose eyes shone. He had none of Henry's nervousness, an arrogant swagger visible even in the way he simply stood. There were cigarettes in the back pocket of his jeans. Toby hadn't seen the symbol shaved into his hair then, but Jake was already staking his claim as top dog in this ragamuffin collection of doomed youth.

'The nurses and I will not – unless necessary – interfere with your time. It is our role to make sure you are cared for and comfortable. We will keep you in the best health possible while we can.'

While we can.

The tittering died as a surreal reality began to

34

creep into the gaps around them. It wasn't panic – and that was the first time Toby wondered if maybe there had been something in the orange juice to keep them calm – just a touch of surf washing in from the ocean of dread that suddenly lay before them.

FOUR

'What's your name?' Louis asks.

'How old are you?' Will, once again cross-legged on his bed. 'You look older than Toby.'

The new boy is an infiltrator in the calm of Dorm 4. He's pale, but his eyes and hair are dark and his mouth is set in such a tight frown that his jaw, already square, looks more angular than it actually is. Clothes are laid out on the bed – jeans, T-shirts, hoodies. All the right size. Everyone is measured and weighed on arrival at the house. The nurses have been busy today.

'Tom.' The new boy speaks from between thin lips. 'I'm seventeen.' His eyes darken in the pause. 'And a half.'

'Oh, shit,' Louis says.

There is a moment of silence, broken only by the patter of heavy rain outside as we take this in. I can understand the boy's bitterness now and my stomach tightens slightly. If it hasn't happened by eighteen then it's not going to happen. We're all unlucky, but Tom is unlucky with a kick in the balls thrown in.

'Tell us about the others,' Ashley says. He's leaning on the radiator, not messing up his neatly made bed by sitting on it.

'Six more months.' Tom doesn't look at them but stares at the unfamiliar clothes that are now his. 'That's all I had to get through. Six fucking months.'

'Shit happens.' It's the first thing I've said. I don't like Tom. I don't know him, but I don't like him. What if his arrival breaks our streak? It's illogical, but the fear is there regardless. Dorm 4 is no longer the same as it was this morning. Tom has arrived like a fracture through stone.

'Yeah, tell us about the others,' Louis says.

'You know what they call this place, don't you?' At last Tom looks up. 'The Death House.'

'Who gives a shit what they call it?' I say. 'It's home now.' I'm bristling slightly. We've all learned to manage our fear – to live with it. Now we have to manage Tom's.

'That's what they call it in London. Not just this house. All the houses.'

'So you're from London, then?' Louis' eyes have lit up as he pulls a small notebook from his pocket and scribbles in it. 'Whereabouts?'

'Like it matters.' Sour, downturned mouth.

'What about the others?' Will is the third to ask the question. We're not intentionally unkind people, but there is no point in sympathy. Sympathy is something you give someone worse off than yourself. Here, we're all in the shit. It's a level playing field. And at least Tom got to seventeen and a half.

'Just a girl,' Tom says. 'She seems okay.' His eyes slide to one side.

'A girl?' Will says. 'It doesn't get a lot of girls.' His face scrunches slightly. 'I wonder if it makes their eyes bleed, too.'

Louis giggles at this, or perhaps at Tom's shocked expression, and I can't decide if Will said it on purpose to freak the new boy out. Cruel humour, but funny.

'Let's get back to our game,' Louis says and Will smiles. The novelty of the stranger is wearing off and Tom's not going anywhere. There'll be plenty of time to get to know him, and if there isn't, then what's the point in trying?

'Which way do the horses go again?'

'They're knights, not horses, and they move in an L shape. Two and one.' Louis' still explaining it as the dorm door closes behind them.

'I'm going back to the art room.' Ashley pushes away from the radiator and picks up his Bible from the top of a wooden chest of drawers. Even he, with all his prim Christian charity, doesn't offer to show Tom around the house.

And then there were two.

'You're Toby, I take it,' Tom says. I close my eyes. I don't want to talk. I don't really want to go back to sleep either, but it's preferable. I'm going to have to get used to Tom, but I'll do it in my own time.

'You're older than the others,' Tom tries again. I say nothing. I think about how I'd hoped to be friends with Jake so I'd have someone my own age to dick around with, and now Tom's here and I'm shutting him out. But Tom isn't one of us. Not yet, at any rate. Jake, for all his assholery, is. Tom is older than me too. I'm going to have to make sure I keep my place as the boss of Dorm 4. Despite my calm stillness on the bed, the new arrivals have disturbed me.

Tom doesn't speak again but lets out a frustrated too-loud sigh, and then the drawers scrape and slide as he puts the clothes away. He's settling in. He has no choice.

The evening passes slowly and my unease grows. At tea all the attention is on Tom and the new girl, whose name is Clara, apparently. I ignore her. Her table is too far away to see her properly and she's got her back to me anyway, only her scruffy ponytail on show. There is more laughter from the girls' table than normal, though, and I can see Eleanor's face shining and even Harriet looks less dour. Jake preens, swearing loudly, and although Tom is sitting with us, when he gets up to fetch a cup of tea, he stops at the girls' table and talks to Clara, his face suddenly a patchy red. It doesn't take long before Jake follows suit. If Tom thinks he has some kind of claim to the girl because they arrived together, he's got a lot more to learn about the house than he thinks. Will and Louis giggle at the two older boys so obviously vying for her attention, but I just let it wash over me. She must be an idiot, smiling and laughing as if she's at some holiday camp or on a school trip. I won't join in with the fawning.

I keep my attention on the twins instead – they're the reality of the house, not some stupid girl who has everyone twisting in their seats. Ellory and Joe are identical. Or they *were* identical. One of them – I think it's Ellory because he has more acne than his brother – is sweating hard. Even from ten feet or so away I can see it. There's a thick sheen on his skin, almost greasy as it oozes from his pores. He's sniffing hard, too, and occasionally his chest contracts and his face tightens as if he's desperately holding back a coughing fit. His brother is eating both dinners, his body turned slightly to block the nurses' view as he takes mouthfuls from his twin's plate. I watch with a kind of fascinated dread. The nurses are watching too, their eyes cold and dark like eagles observing prey. The others on the Dorm 7 table have shifted themselves a few inches away from their room-mates even though the same illness is percolating inside them. They talk around the twins, as if they're no longer there.

I'm going to owe Louis some washing-up duties.

'Do you think they'll take him tonight?'

It's only when Ashley speaks that I realise I'm not alone in watching Ellory. Ashley is as well, his thin lips pursed.

'Probably.'

'I'll pray for him.'

'Yeah, that's going to help.' I concentrate on my food, scooping up a forkful of mashed potato and chewing the lumps out of it. I don't want a conversation with Ashley. He can keep his smug piousness to himself.

After tea, the nurses put on some ancient film and although Will and Louis try to drag me with them, I don't go. Instead, I have a long, hot bath and then lie on my bed staring at the ceiling. It's still raining outside. I wonder what Ellory is thinking. I wonder if he went to watch the film. My stomach contracts at the thought that one day soon I'll be in Ellory's position. I wish I could stop thinking so much. Not even the memory of Julie McKendrick can distract me. I just end up wondering if she remembers me at all or if she's started smiling at Billy in Year 13 now and he's going to get to slide his hand into her bra rather than just dream about it.

Eventually, the others come back up and start the ritual of teeth-cleaning and washing and getting ready for bed. A nurse brings around her tray of pills and small cups of water and we all dutifully take them before she closes the curtains and turns the light off with a cursory, bland, 'Goodnight.'

'Clara's dad was a Black Suit,' Will says. 'Isn't that right, Tom? A proper government minister.'

'Yeah, that's right.' A pause. Whispering fills it. 'What the hell is he doing?'

'Just praying. Ignore him, he'll stop soon. A Black Suit. That's kind of cool, though. What did your dad do?'

I wonder if Will realises he's using the past tense – as if our families are gone, not living out their lives without us, back in the real world.

'The usual. Some tech firm. He worked away a lot.' Tom's only been in the house a few hours but already he's closing down. Locking *before* away. Taking his cue from the rest of us and keeping it inside.

'I liked that film,' Louis says. 'But I can't help wondering why they showed it to us.'

'Vampires are cool,' Will says. 'And the dog was cool, too. But I didn't like the part where that one bit the man's head right through his skull.'

'But a film about a bunch of teenagers who live for ever. *Lost Boys*,' Louis muses. 'Where something inside makes them turn into monsters. I wonder about Matron sometimes. She's either got a very sick sense of humour or absolutely no sense of irony.'

'Ha, yeah.' Will laughs but it's clear he doesn't understand what irony means.

'We can all live together in God,' Ashley says. 'That's the true life everlasting.'

'Is he always like this?' Tom's disdain is clear. He may be the new boy but Ashley is forever the outsider.

'Sadly, yes.' Louis settles down under his covers, rustles of starch competing with the renewed whispering.

'You okay, Toby?' Will watches me in the gloom. 'You're very quiet. I thought you'd want to watch the film and meet the new girl.'

'I'm just tired.'

'You're always tired. You sleep most of the day.' His breath hitches. 'You're not—'

'No.' I don't let him finish his question. 'I'm not sick.'

'Good,' Will says. He picks at his blanket. 'I wouldn't like that.'

Something in his tone makes my heart squeeze in on itself, tight and hard.

'Goodnight, Will,' is all I say in return. Eventually we fall into a sleepy silence, even Ashley, and the breathing in the room slows. Another day is gone. Evaporated away from us. I close my eyes.

FIVE

It's nearly two hours after Matron has done the final rounds when I hear the smothered belch of the lift starting its rumbling journey down through the core of the house. I knew it would come tonight, and part of me wants to hide my head under my pillow until it's done, but my feet are itching to get up and my insides are tangled in knots around the dark ball in the pit of my stomach. I have to see it. Watching is better than lying here, just listening. The chill air prickles my skin as I creep over to the door and open it. The other boys don't stir. Tom snores, but the rest are silent.

On the landing my heart beats so hard I can feel it throbbing in my neck. The lift has come to a stop upstairs and the soft *whoosh* of the large metal doors, their modernity so out of place here, is a sigh in the night. I creep up to the next half-landing and press myself into the dark shadows that cling to the wall. I stay very still. I can't see the lift from where I am, but the nurses will have to pass by on the next floor when they go back to it. I wait, and then the quiet squeak of old wheels turning puncture the night. Ellory is leaving Dorm 7 for the last time and he's not awake to know it. Perhaps he knew it when he went to bed. Maybe he thought he had one more day. It's hard to imagine not having one more day.

Soft white shoes come into view, plimsolls under white scrubs, as the nurses from the sanatorium wheel the bed towards the lift. I can't see Ellory but I know it's him. No one else is sick. Not like he's been. The nurses don't rush, maintaining a steady, calm pace. Ellory isn't going anywhere and neither is the sanatorium. These are different nurses from those who look after us during the day. I've seen them enough times now to know. Angels of death who only appear in the night to collect sleeping, sick children. Sometimes I think of the sanatorium as some awful creature that feeds on us. In some ways, that's preferable to the empty unknown. In my small window on the action above, the bed is wheeled by, but I don't move. I know the routine and they're not finished yet. A minute or so later, two more sets of feet whisper past accompanied by the rustle of plastic bags as Ellory's clothes and toiletries are removed. Nothing will be left for Joe to remember him by. He's being efficiently exorcised from our community. I wonder what they do with the clothes. Are we all wearing dead boys' clothes, recycled from a previous wave of Defectives? Is there a stockpile in the house somewhere ready for children of all shapes and sizes? The lift doors slide shut again and I let out a shaky breath as adrenalin rushes through me.

Goodbye, Ellory. It was nice not knowing you.

I feel almost sick, a tang of nausea in my mouth. I need the bathroom and a glass of water. I turn away, and only then does my eye catch on the landing two floors above. A thick strand of something has escaped from between the banisters and floats in the air like seaweed drifting in the shallows. I almost gasp with the unexpectedness of it, and maybe I do let out a short, sharp breath as my mouth falls open. It's hair. Someone else is awake. I freeze, then frown, my thoughts jolted away from Ellory, the sickness, the dreadful nothingness that waits upstairs. Thoughts I can't define but which are wrapped up in the ball in my stomach and sit like a sour taste on my tongue. They are gone in an instant. No one else is ever awake.

The shadow moves, the hair pulled away as its owner retreats, and the stairs creak. I dart back into my dorm and peer out through a crack in the door as the figure goes by. Who is it? What are they doing? More change – first Tom, now this. I seriously think about going back to bed and staying there, but I'm not tired, and why the fuck should I, anyway? The nights are mine.

*

I find her in the kitchen. She's got slices of ham and cheese out and is making a sandwich.

'Want one?' she says, as if it's the most natural thing in the world that we're meeting here in the dark at gone two in the morning. I don't answer, just stare at her from the doorway as the wind outside whips around the building and whistles through the gap under the back door.

She spreads about an inch of butter on one slice of white bread. 'My mum never let me have butter. Not good for the hips, apparently, and definitely not good for a dancer. Well, I'm having it now. Don't think fat thighs are my biggest priority any more, do you?' She smiles as she slaps the sandwich together and then jumps gracefully onto the stainless steel kitchen prep table to eat it. It's hard to see but I think she has a rash of freckles across her face. Her teeth are white and even, and her thick red hair tumbles scruffily around her shoulders.

I look at her sandwich and my stomach tightens. The nights are no longer under my control. I have someone else's mistakes to worry about. She follows my eyes.

'Don't worry. I was careful and I'll clean up. They won't notice I've been here.'

'You came with Tom,' I say.

She nods. 'Poor Tom. He's so angry about everything.' Her legs swing back and forth and under her nightshirt I can see they're slim and toned. There's pink varnish on her toenails. An echo from her *before*. Energy fizzes from her. She chews another mouthful and watches me. I want a sandwich or something but I'm not going to have one. She's killed my appetite.

'You didn't take the vitamins,' I say. I've moved one step inside the kitchen but I won't come any closer. I'm sullen but she doesn't appear to notice. She laughs a little instead. It's warm. Friendly. What is wrong with her? Doesn't she know where she is?

'Vitamins, my arse. My mum's been taking "vitamins" for years. Normally with Scotch.' She puts the sandwich down, forgotten. 'Why don't you take yours?'

I've learned to slide the pills between my upper lip and gum line so quickly that the nurses don't notice, practising with peas from dinner. Now they're all collected in a wrap of toilet paper stuffed into the ball of my bedpost. Same routine every night. I should probably just shove them down the sink but they're a way of counting the days. Marking out my survival.

'I like the nights,' I say.

'So what shall we do?' She grins again, impish with delight. 'Now that the house is ours?'

'Do whatever you want. Just don't fuck it up for me.'

Her smile falls. 'But it'll be more fun—'

'I mean it.' Suddenly I hate her. She has no right

to be awake. This is *my* time. The ball inside me flares all the way up to my tongue and I spit out angry flames in words. 'This isn't your perfect fucking life now with your posh government dad and big house and whatever you want. You're as Defective as the rest of us. You can sit there and laugh and joke and think it's all so fucking funny, but you're going to get sick and die just like Ellory, and me, and all the rest of the stupid fuckers here. You're not special. So stay out of my way and get used to it.'

I glare at her, panting with the angry heat that's making my body shake, and her swinging legs fall still. She's not smiling any more. I turn away, not wanting to look at her. Not wanting to feel bad. The house is big. I don't have to see her. Maybe she'll start taking the pills now she knows she's not welcome at night.

'No,' she says, soft and hurt as I walk away. 'I think it's *you* who needs to get used to it.'

Bitch, I think. *Fucking bitch. What the fuck does she know?*

His test was after PE on a Tuesday, and he was happy for two reasons. First, it got him out of ten minutes of Triple Science – maybe twenty if he stretched out the walk back, and second, they always did the test in alphabetical order so Julie McKendrick was always tested at the same time.

The downside was that Billy Matthews would be there too, so it was unlikely he'd get to speak to Julie even if he could think of something interesting to say. Still, he'd be able to look at her and that was better than nothing.

The corridor outside the nurse's room was hot, the windows lining the wall magnifying the sunshine outside, and even though he'd just showered in the gym, Toby was sweating as he joined the queue, kids of all ages chattering together. No one looked worried. The tests were routine, after all. He looked ahead in the line but couldn't see Julie. His heart sank. She'd spoken to him yesterday in Maths – the only subject they had together – and he'd got through the whole conversation about the dullness of algebra without stumbling over his words or looking at her chest once. She'd laughed at something he'd said about Mr Grey and told him he was funny. Maybe being the class joker was finally going to pay off.

'Hey, Toby.'

She was behind him with Amanda, whose surname didn't begin with an M but who must have bunked off to come with her. Julie and Amanda, both blonde and pretty, but Amanda just didn't have that extra something Julie had, plus her chest was flatter and her legs too thin.

'Hi.' The word felt like glue in his throat. He shoved a hand in his pocket to try and look casual

but felt as if every joint in his body had stopped working properly. 'What have you got out of?'

'English. And it's a test.'

'Result.' Over Julie's perfect shoulder he saw Billy sauntering up to join the line. Great.

'Amanda's having a party on Saturday. You live close, right? Why don't you come?'

Amanda rolled her eyes but Julie didn't appear to notice. Toby's face was burning so much he thought it might actually melt off his bones. An invite to a party from Julie herself. A cool party. Everything Julie and Amanda did was cool.

'Sure. I don't think I'm doing anything much,' he said. He'd planned to hang out with Jonesy down at the rec but Jonesy could wait. He thought for a second about bringing him along but nixed it almost immediately. Jonesy was in no way cool enough for a party at Amanda's. Neither was Toby, but he was fucked if he was going to miss an opportunity like this.

'Of course he doesn't have plans,' Amanda drawled. 'Like he ever has plans.'

'Shut up, Mandy.' Julie ignored her friend's clear displeasure and smiled at him. Right at him. Her skin was flawless and her eyes bright under the mascara and liner that the cool girls wore no matter how often they were told to wash it off. Toby wondered if it was at all possible to love anyone more than he loved Julie McKendrick.

'Great,' she said. 'See you there. From about eight.'

He nodded, not trusting himself to say any more, and then turned back to face the front. He could hear Billy talking loudly and both girls laughing but it sounded like they were just humouring him. His whole body buzzed with excitement. A party with Julie. That she'd actually asked him to go to. He couldn't wait to tell Jonesy.

He was still grinning like an idiot as he walked in to give his blood. Life was looking up.

'Double or quits, remember,' I say as we come out of breakfast. Louis is heading to the rota, ready to scratch his own name out and replace it with mine, but I stop him. 'It's not a done deal yet.'

That's all anyone says about Ellory that morning. Me and Clara might have been the only ones to see him wheeled away, but no one else is surprised by his disappearance. Dorm 7 had looked shaken as they came into the dining room, but apart from Joe they'd kept their chins up and expressions arrogant, Jake particularly defiant. There's one chair fewer at their table and the rest have been pushed closer together. Even the signs of Ellory's absence have been removed.

By the noticeboard, we watch as Dorm 7 trail past and head upstairs. 'Consider it pencilled in,' Louis says, eyes on Joe. The abandoned twin looks defeated, shoulders slumped and eyes rimmed red. There might be blotches on his cheeks but it's hard to tell amidst the acne.

'What are you staring at?' Jake snarls at us. I shrug, and say nothing. I don't have to. The Dorm 7 spell is broken.

Now only Dorm 4 remains intact.

SIX

Outside, it's stopped raining but the air is misty wet, as if the clouds have been pricked and are slowly deflating, slumped on the ground. Tom stares out of the kitchen window as I rinse the last of the lunch dishes and add it to the rest on the side.

'Any time you're ready, mate,' I grumble as the steam collects in hot drops on my face. Tom picks up a plate and starts to dry it but his concentration is focused on the garden. I've been determinedly not looking but it's hard when the window is right in front of the sink and the girls are laughing outside directly in our line of sight. Eleanor's sitting on an old tree stump clutching her book but not reading it. Instead she's watching Clara trying to teach Harriet to do a handstand against the rough brick wall. Harriet is failing miserably, but they're all smiling as her legs wave in the air while Clara tries to grab them and hold them straight.

They move on to cartwheels, Clara turning perfectly across the grass, her limbs straight and strong. She does have freckles across her nose and her hair shines a deep copper red even though the grey damp deadens the colours around them. As she turns upside down, for a moment her top rides up and shows her taut, pale stomach. Tom's swallow is audible.

'Maybe she's a gymnast,' Tom says. I don't have to ask who. He's sure as shit not talking about Harriet, who's doing her best with her unwieldy body to mimic the older girl.

'She's a dancer.'

'How do you know that?' Tom looks at me, curious.

I shrug, awkward. 'Must have heard someone mention it.'

My rudeness when we met two nights ago hasn't made her take the sleeping pills, and although I've tried to stick to my resolution to avoid her, it's hard knowing someone else is awake in the night. Instead, I've almost shadowed her, waiting for her to leave one part of the house before I go there, checking that she hasn't left anything out of place that could raise suspicion. Last night, I was about to go into the playroom – when the nights were purely mine, I liked to sit on a beanbag by the window and look up at the sky – when I saw her through the gap in the door. The record player was on, turning silently, the needle scratching in the quiet. Clara stood in front of it, large headphones covering her ears, swaying and dancing to the music, her body relaxed and her eyes closed. She was lost in her own space, oblivious to the house. The moonlight pooled on the floor through the open curtains – a spotlight she moved through. There was no form as such to her dance, but she'd found the rhythm and smiled as her arms rose above her head, her hips swaying in time to the song I couldn't hear.

My mouth had dried up and I felt unsettled. I wasn't sure why at first. It wasn't her bare legs and arms or the outline of her body through her night-shirt. Those details made me feel uncomfortable in a different way that I refused to acknowledge, but didn't stir up the tight ball in my stomach. Then I got it. Envy. That's what I'd felt. A sour apple of jealously. She was smiling. Perfectly happy. Enjoying a moment of freedom in the music. How could she be happy?

Finally, she turned the record off and left the playroom. I waited in the shadows until she'd disappeared up the stairs and then gone to see what it was. I'd never heard of it, some album from generations ago. My fingers hesitated over the headphones for a second and then I stepped away. I wasn't going to play it. I wasn't going to be drawn in. I refused to be curious.

I went to bed but couldn't settle. I tried to think of my family and then Julie McKendrick but the dread had crept in and constricted around my spine, and all I could hear in my head were the wheels turning as Ellory's bed was pushed away, and all I could see was Henry's plaintive face, *I think there's been a mistake*, and all I could think was that I didn't want to die and be just a terrifying nothing – not now, not ever.

'How do you know that?' Tom repeats, snapping me back to the present. I glance out of the window.

'I must have overheard the girls, I guess,' I say. She has no right to look so carefree. None of them do. I wipe the stainless steel surfaces down as Tom finishes the last of the drying up and then a nurse appears from nowhere and checks our work before nodding her approval and releasing us from the kitchen, our chores done.

I don't wait for Tom, who's still looking into the garden, but head back to Dorm 4 to try and sleep. I'm halfway up the first flight of stairs when Ashley comes striding along the corridor and stops outside Matron's office. I pause. No one ever goes to see Matron about anything. Not since the first few days. Matron doesn't have any answers, or if she does she's not sharing them, and she made it clear she has no wish to be involved with us any further than her job requires. Why would anyone draw Matron's attention to them? Matron makes all the decisions in the house . . . and sometimes I wonder if maybe she even decides who gets carted off to the sanatorium next. I don't know what's in the food we're given. We're all happy to stay under her radar.

Ashley takes a deep breath before knocking three times on the door and then rearranging the rough paper rolled up under his arm. He has several sheets in different colours, all poster-sized and thick. I catch a glimpse of careful writing on the inside of one but can't make out the words. I lean over the banister to try to get a better look but then Matron's door opens and Ashley is swallowed up inside.

I stay for a moment. Up the wide old staircase, the dorm and my bed are waiting. I shouldn't care what Ashley wants from Matron – I *don't* care, and yet I still want to know. I take two more steps and then stop again. I look back at the spot where Ashley had stood so nervously. My feet tingle inside my trainers, not knowing whether to go forward or back. Ashley's in Matron's office. My brain whirs through the possibilities despite myself. I don't want to get involved with the other kids – what's the point of that, after all? – and aside from Will and Louis who are too close to avoid, I've done a pretty good job so far of keeping myself to myself and out of everyone else's business. We're all going to die alone, so I might as well live alone. There's nothing to do here anyway.

But still, Ashley is in Matron's office and I want to know why. He didn't look sick, and even if he is, he'd hardly march up to Matron to announce it. And what's all the paper about? He can't have drawn up a list of complaints about the house. Even a smug dick like Ashley wouldn't be that stupid. I frown. Would he? Was this something to do with the dorm? Maybe this *is* my business, after all.

I turn away from the gloomy, yawning stairwell that twists and turns like a crooked spine through the vast house and go back down the way I came. The hallway is empty and I peer along the various corridors to check no one is coming before pressing my ear close to the door. I can't make out any words, just the deadened murmur of voices. Neither of them sounds angry, but then Matron never sounds angry – or happy or upset, for that matter. She's always just Matron, calm and impersonal. I wouldn't be surprised if underneath her skin she's simply a network of metal and wires and processors.

I don't linger, already feeling like I'm spying – which I am – and I definitely don't want to be caught here. I find Louis and Will in the playroom, in their corner away from the boys at the record player trying to find something they recognise or like in the antique collection and squabbling over what to play next.

'I just saw Ashley going into Matron's office. What's that about?'

'Look! She's just swung herself up onto that branch! How did she do that?'

The chessboard is out – and judging by the lack of white pieces my bet is on Louis as black – but neither boy is at the table.

'We should go and play with the others.' Will's feet are twitching with excitement. 'It's not raining.'

'Jake's out there.'

'Yeah, but so's Tom.'

Only a few days in and Tom was one of them. Their pack. For Will and Louis, at least.

'He totally fancies her. He's trying to look all cool.'

'Epic fail.' Snorts of laughter.

'I said' – I try to get their attention again – 'that Ashley's in with Matron. Got any clue why?'

Finally their heads turn. 'Uh-uh,' Will says. 'Haven't seen him.'

'He hasn't said anything weird?'

'No more than usual.' Louis suddenly smiles as the change in my routine dawns on him. 'You're not asleep. Let's go into the garden.'

I almost groan. 'Why? There's fuck all to do out there.'

'Clara's climbing the tree. Look.' Will points out of the window as if I can see from where I'm standing in the doorway.

'I'm not stopping you if you want to go and play like kids.' Maybe I should have just gone to bed and not worried about whatever 'Reverend' Ashley was up to.

'But we *are* kids.'

'Then fuck off and play. What do you need me for?'

'Come on, it'll be fun!' Will says. 'All of us together. And it's not raining.'

'It's not exactly sunny, either.'

Louis looks down at his feet. One of his shoelaces is undone, but he doesn't appear to notice. They were new when he arrived – his mum had only just bought them, he declared plaintively on the first night – but now the brown leather is scraped and worn. How he's scuffed them so badly when all we do is drift around the house like ghosts most days, I don't know. But then Louis is clumsy and all over the place, his mind moving too fast most of the time for his body to keep up with it. Blotches of embarrassed red colour his cheeks and he pushes his hands into his jeans pockets before looking at me and shrugging slightly. 'Jake's out there,' he repeats. Quieter this time, and ashamed.

'And Tom,' I say. It's a test. Tom's older than me.

'Yeah, but . . .' One of Louis' shoulders has risen so high in his awkwardness that it's almost touching his pink ear. 'Tom wouldn't . . . you know. Look out for us.'

'Please, Toby,' Will says. They both watch me hopefully.

I glance from one to the other and wonder how I got landed with them. I sigh. I still want to know what's going on with Ashley and Matron before I go to sleep. I need to kill some time anyway.

'Ten minutes,' I say, and think I sound like my dad. 'That's all.'

'Fucking A!' Louis says, the swear word sounding all wrong coming from his mouth.

'Thanks, Toby.' Will is already tugging his sweater on and the words are muffled. When his face pops out through the neck, though, he's beaming. 'Come on!'

As I follow them along the corridor and down to the back door, I wonder when going out into the garden became such a big deal. If it was so much fun, then why the fuck hadn't we done it before? Maybe I'm not the only one who's been hiding from their situation. I hide by sleeping all day; maybe the others hide by staying inside. Maybe outside is too much bright real world and we don't belong in it any more. Or maybe it's just that it's been raining.

As I step outside, I wish that, for once, my brain would do less wondering. I need to drink more tea at breakfast.

'Look how high up she is,' Will says as we stroll over towards the tree. From inside, the old oak hadn't looked so large, but now we're in the damp garden air it's huge, the gnarled trunk wide and thick enough that it would take at least three of us to be able to wrap our arms around it and touch fingers. The overgrown grass sparkles bright green and moist under our feet and I can feel the wetness creeping in through the fabric of my trainers. It's not cold, though. Even if there is a breeze, the high walls around the grounds are blocking it. I don't walk fast, and Will and Louis match my pace. If it had just been Jake and some of the Dorm 7 boys out and about, I wouldn't have come; but the girls are here, too, and a few of the other kids, and suddenly people are mixing again, apparently.

High in the branches of the tree, Clara sits, her head tilted upwards slightly, her body half-hidden among the leaves. They're all out here because of her. Girls are always the problem. It's like they have a secret power that kicks in at some point around fourteen. Will and Louis might think they're immune to it, but it's starting. They're out here, after all. I think of Julie McKendrick and my mixture of terror, awkwardness and abject nervous excitement whenever she was near me.

The garden is much bigger than I'd thought, almost the size of the house, and stretches out to either side of the building. There's a pair of rickety swings over to the left and Joe rocks half-heartedly backwards and forwards on one, kicking tufts of grass as his too-long legs hit the ground. His head is down and his jaw tight. I don't want to look at Joe. It makes me hear the awful squeak of bed wheels in the night.

Someone has found a football and Jake and Tom kick it between them with the little lardy kid, Daniel, running around trying to get involved.

'Over here, Jake! To me!' he wheezes, his face red with exertion. Maybe he feels more involved now that Joe is keeping to himself and Ellory is gone, but if he does then he's an idiot. Jake kicks the ball at him, intentionally too high, and it soars over his head and bounces off the wall twenty feet away. He runs to fetch it as Jake laughs. It's not the kindest laugh, but then half the kid's fat arse is hanging out of his jeans, and as he bends over to pick the ball up the crack is visible and his fat rolls over the waistband. It makes me want to laugh, too.

I stay back from the tree and the other boys. There's plenty of space and I don't want to get involved. Will, however, is staring up through the branches of the oak tree.

'How did you climb so high?' he asks Clara's swinging legs.

'She just jumped and then swung herself up,' Eleanor says. She and Harriet look like some kind of tree creatures or wood nymphs, their faces peering around either side of the trunk. 'Then she kept on climbing.'

Will jumps but doesn't even get near the lowest branch. 'Maybe if you gave me a leg up?' He looks at Louis.

'It's too high.'

It is high. Maybe not for Tom or Joe or me, but definitely for the rest of them. I look at the branches. That's why neither Tom nor Jake have tried it. Even if they got to the first branch without making dicks of themselves, the higher ones are slimmer. You'd have to be light to be confident about not breaking them, and Clara must be strong to have jumped that high herself.

'We won't know unless we try,' Will says. 'Come on, give me a leg-up then I'll pull you. I've never climbed a tree.'

Louis still isn't convinced. 'I'm not very good at lifting.'

'What are you looking at up there, anyway?' Will asks.

Jake catches the football and tucks it under his arm. He strolls towards the tree, thrusting the ball at Tom, who takes it, stumbling backwards slightly, as he passes. All the posturing is pointless. Clara isn't looking down. She's staring out into the distance.

'I can see the sea from up here,' she says. She's sitting astride a branch as casually as if it was a foot from the ground. She's not even holding on, but pushing leaves aside so she can see out. 'It's beautiful.'

'How far away is it?' Louis calls up.

'Not far. I think there's cliffs. Can't see any houses, though. We're all alone.'

'We are,' Louis says. 'There's no one on the island.'

'How do you know?'

'Two kids tried to run away once,' Jake cuts in, wanting her attention back. 'But they got caught. There was nowhere for them to go.'

'What happened to them?' Clara asks, still looking out over the view.

'Matron,' Jake says. 'Matron happened. She got a coin and made them pick heads or tails. Heads won. The boy who called tails went straight to the lift. She hauled him into it, kicking and screaming and begging her to take the other one instead, right in front of all the other kids. He never came down again. He wasn't even sick or anything. She said it was a lesson.'

We've all heard the story, although none of us were at the house when it happened. The boys who were already here when we arrived told us, just like boys before told them. I don't even know if it's true, but no one, not even Jake is going to take that risk if there's not even anywhere to run to. And it *sounds* like something Matron would do.

'Maybe I should come up there and have a look,' Jake says. I think he wants to change the subject too. We all do enough thinking about the sanatorium – we don't want to talk about it as well. He's grabbed the lower branch and dangles from it like a chimpanzee. He's making it look casual but I can see he's figuring out if he can swing himself up without looking like a twat.

'I wouldn't try it,' Clara says. 'This branch is pretty thin.'

'Joe's sneezing!' Daniel shouted. I'd forgotten the fat kid was there, but now he's standing by the swing, his trousers pulled up but his belly still poking out, and pointing at the lost twin. 'Jake, Joe's sick!'

'Shut up, you little prick,' Joe growls, sending the squealing pig of kid running back to the group.

'He's sick!'

'Leave him alone,' Harriet says, stepping out from behind the protection of the tree. 'And don't shout things like that.' Her face isn't so dour close up, not pretty but not as sour, either. 'The nurses might hear.'

'I was just telling Jake—'

'Oh, fuck off, Daniel,' Jake says, dropping from the tree. 'I don't need you telling me stuff.'

Piggy, I think. This Daniel kid is like Piggy out of that book I keep having to do comprehension on in morning lessons. Desperate to be in with the cool kids. Never going to be.

'Sorry, Jake, I just thought—'

'I said fuck off.'

Louis has been watching the exchange with rapt wonder and his eyes light up as Daniel, muttering miserably to himself, skulks back indoors. Louis' eyes drop when Jake looks at him, though. The egg on his face, both literally and metaphorically, is still a smarting memory.

'Is that a conker tree?' Will says, frowning and looking over to a second tree, this one squat to the ground near the right-hand wall. 'My granddad played conkers with me when I was little.' A cloud forms on his face for a moment. 'You ever played conkers, Louis?'

'Nope.'

'It's easier than chess.' He tugs at Louis' sleeve. 'Come on. There might be some big ones.'

'I'll come, too!' Eleanor bursts out from behind the tree, still clutching her book, and darts to catch them up.

Harriet stands awkwardly for a moment and then wanders towards the swings. She takes the free one and says nothing, but gives Joe a half-smile that he doesn't return.

There's a tension between Jake and Tom, like a stand-off in an old cowboy film with neither of them wanting to move away, and I'm about to turn and head back inside now that Will and Louis are settled when Clara speaks.

'The sea is so beautiful. I wonder what it looks like at night.' She leans through the branches and tilts her head so she can see me. Her red hair hangs long down one side of her face, a waterfall of fire. 'Don't you, Toby?' She smiles. Both Jake and Tom glare at me. I say nothing, and we all watch as she swings herself down from the tree with the quiet precision of a cat. She's still looking at me and I wish she wouldn't. The air crackles electric between me and Jake and Tom with her in the middle, the cause of it all.

'I think I know where I can get some booze and fags,' Jake blurts out.

'What?' Tom says. 'In here?'

Clara doesn't shift her gaze, her hands in her jeans pockets and her hips tilted forward. She's challenging me. Laughing at me. Suddenly I feel uncomfortable and slightly stupid without knowing why. I'm not going to get in a cock fight with Tom and Jake over a girl I don't even like much.

'Yeah,' Jake continues, louder. 'From the teachers' rooms. I've smelt cigarette smoke on some of them. They stink of it. Bet they've got drink, too. They must be bored out of their fucking minds here. I know I am.' He looks at Clara. 'What do you think?'

Finally, she graces him with a look and shrugs. 'Sure. If you can get some, I'm in.' He grins, wolfish.

'I'll help.' Tom doesn't want to be left out. 'You in, Toby?' Jake looks at me and so does Clara. I wish I'd stayed inside or headed upstairs two minutes later and not seen Ashley going into Matron's office. I think about the jazz and blues I sometimes hear coming from the teachers' quarters when I wander the house at night. Jake's probably right. I'd drink too if I was stuck here when I didn't have to be.

'Maybe.'

'Hey!' The voice comes from near the back door, and moments later Daniel is waddling across the grass towards us.

'Oh, fuck, what now?' Jake mutters, and I suddenly feel some sympathy for him. He's a *nanny* too.

'You have to come and see this!' He's smiling, eager to be back in Jake's good books. 'All of you!'

SEVEN

We stand in front of the poster that's been Blu-tacked to the wall above the gong in the hallway.

'There's more,' Daniel says, still breathless. 'There's one in the playroom and another up on the landing.'

'What the actual fuck,' Jake says, taking the words from my mouth. So this is what Ashley was up to. The words are printed carefully in black marker:

Church open!
Last room on the second floor
next to the nurses' quarters.
Service every night at 7.30.
All welcome!

Surrounding the precise writing are childish drawings of angels and crosses, and a small piece of paper has been tacked to the bottom:

Tonight we'll pray for Ellory.

'Jesus Christ,' I say, and Louis immediately snorts with laughter at my unintentional irony.

'Maybe this will stop him praying in our room, at least,' Tom says.

He has a point. But still, I can see Jake's sneer and I hate Ashley and his smug piety all over again. Joe says nothing. His eyes are fixed on the small bit of paper at the bottom.

'Let's go and look,' Will says, always curious. For a moment all our divisions are forgotten and we climb the stairs. The girls have said nothing but they follow along anyway as we leave a trail of damp footprints on the wood. What else is there to do?

'Down here!' Daniel says, as if we can't figure it out ourselves. The long corridor is gloomy but light shines out through one doorway. I've never come this far in my night-time wanderings – it's too close to the nurses' rooms. Ashley's chosen well. Not even Jake would come here and give him shit. Not when all Ashley would have to do is shout to get some attention.

'Come in, come in,' Ashley says as we gather in the doorway. I have no intention of crossing the line, but Harriet and Eleanor squeeze past me and Will and Louis follow them. Instead of beds, twelve chairs are set out in rows of three and there's a desk at the front that he's slung a bed sheet over. He's sweating from carrying the chairs, but he smiles. 'Everyone's welcome.'

Some sniggers then, and his smile falls a little and he busies himself with a pile of papers on one of the chairs.

'You're a fucking freak,' Jake says. Daniel laughs. I look behind me and see Clara wandering back down the corridor. I don't think she likes the church but I don't think she likes our aggression, either. Maybe after she's been here a week or so she'll understand it.

'What a beautiful window,' Harriet says, looking up. She's right, it is. A perfect arch in the centre of the wall.

'It's why I wanted this room,' Ashley says. 'It's like a church window.' He pauses. 'You could paint it, if you like. Matron won't mind.'

'You and Matron all cosy now, are you?' Jake says. 'That won't change anything.'

Ashley says nothing.

'You're still Defective,' Daniel chimes in. 'You're just the same as the rest of us.'

'I know,' Ashley says.

'Fuck him,' I say, suddenly torn. I hate Ashley for this, but he's one of our dorm. 'He's going to be here on his own. Better here than trying to hang out with us.' I turn to walk away and Tom follows.

'Yeah, fuck him,' he repeats, and I know I'm still the boss of Dorm 4. The group melts away from the doorway, each going in their own direction. Will and Louis race off together in search of string for their conkers and I head back to our dorm. Sleep. That's what I need.

The air is colder tonight, creeping in through the old stone like an invisible mist, and I have my socks on as I wander the house in the dark even though the polished wooden floors can be slippery and the thump of a fall might alert one of the nurses. I've stayed in bed longer than usual, wondering if they might come for Joe, but the lift doesn't rumble like the hungry stomach of the sanatorium and the house is quiet.

I get some bread and butter from the empty kitchen and look through the window at the oak tree – now a hulking spread of black in the moonlight – as I eat it. The ground floor is quiet, the playroom empty, and I wonder if Clara has finally decided to take her sleeping pill like everyone else does and leave the night alone. I should be relieved by that thought, but instead my stomach expands and feels hollow. I think about playing some music through the headphones as I look out at the night, but don't. I'm not Clara. Not only does the idea of dancing alone in the dark make me feel a bit of a dick, I like to be able to hear if someone is coming.

I wander back upstairs and find myself heading towards Ashley's church. He'd been smug and smiling when he returned to the dorm and although none of us had asked him about his stupid service, he was pleased with himself. A little bit of me wants to smash up the chairs but I don't know why. Maybe I'll just rearrange them to freak him out.

I see the tiny flickering light as I get closer to the door and I know that Clara's there ahead of me. This time I don't turn back. The night is still my place – she's still the interloper. If anyone should leave, it should be her.

'Where did you get the candle from?'

She's standing with her back to me, looking down at a piece of paper, trying to read it in the yellow flame. The candle's stuck to a saucer sitting on the covered desk that's trying pathetically hard to be an altar.

'It was already here. I brought the matches from the kitchen.' She doesn't even jump. Did she hear me coming or does she just not care? She turns a little towards me, still focused on the paper.

'"For Ellory,"' she reads, '"beloved brother of Joe, son of Mary and Stephen and member of Dorm Seven. 'He will wipe away every tear from their eyes, and death shall be no more, neither shall there be mourning, nor crying, nor pain any more, for the former things have passed away.' Revelation twenty-one, verse four." That's quite beautiful when you think about it. If sad.'

'Don't tell me you buy into this God shit,' I say, sneering. She shakes her head, her red hair shining in the candlelight.

'No, I believe in nature. We die, we rot, we feed the earth and the plants and the insects and that's that.'

'Cheerful,' I say, trying to sound casually dismissive, but her words have sunk to ice in my stomach and I wish I'd stayed in the kitchen.

'We're still here now.' She shrugs. 'No different from anyone else.'

'Pretty different. I think that's why they call us *Defective*.' My sarcasm is obvious, but she doesn't appear to notice it.

'Not really. Every day is a new day for everyone. No one knows what tomorrow brings.' She flashes a smile, her eyes sparkling. 'Maybe tomorrow they'll find a cure. Or maybe tomorrow this house will be struck by lighting and we'll all burn to death. Maybe tomorrow an earthquake will hit London and all my old school friends will be gone before me. See?'

I smile, I can't help myself. There is a logic to it, a piece of driftwood to cling to in the ocean of dread.

She looks back down at the small sheet of paper. 'Not for Ellory, though.' Her voice is soft. 'Harriet went to the service. She said only Joe came from Dorm Seven. That's sad, isn't it? They should have gone for Joe's sake.'

'That's not how it works.' My smile fades. She doesn't understand the house. Not yet. She still thinks it's like *before*. It isn't. I'm not sure I could explain the differences even if I wanted to. You have to *learn* them. I'm about to say something mean, a barb forming on my tongue, when I hear a bell sounding from beyond the door that leads to the nurses' quarters. I freeze, my heart pounding.

'What?' Clara says. 'What is it?'

'It's an alarm clock.' I rush past her and extinguish the candle, ignoring the pain of squeezing my fingers around the hot wick to stop the smell of burning. And then, without thinking, I grab her hand. 'Come on.'

We rush back out into the corridor. Even as we run for the stairs we can hear more sounds of movement. Even the sanatorium nurses and Matron are waking up.

'What's going on?' Clara whispers as we press ourselves against the dark wall.

'I don't know.'

'This way. Quickly.' She yanks my arm and we race up the next flight of stairs. Her dorm is closest and she pulls me inside and shuts the door. Neither Eleanor nor Harriet stir as we hurry, breathless, to the far corner. We're just in time, heavy heels betraying someone's passing outside.

Bright lights shine through the window and wheels churn through the gravel. Clara's dorm is further along from the main entrance than mine, but we peer carefully out through the curtains and just at the limits of our vision we can see a large truck pulling up, its huge headlights two moons in the night. The engine chugs steadily as the driver jumps down and heads to the back. The rough sound of steel doors opening. Voices.

'What is it?' I whisper. Can't be more kids arriving, surely. Not in a truck like that. We all came in black vans.

'Must be supplies,' Clara says. We're standing so close I can see every one of her pale eyelashes. Her mouth is slightly open and her breath mists the glass as she speaks. 'We're in the middle of nowhere. I guess they have to get all the food and stuff delivered. You haven't seen this before?'

I shake my head. 'First time.'

'How long do you think it will take?'

'It's a big truck. A while.'

'Then we're stuck in here until it leaves and they've gone back to bed.'

'Unless they don't go back to bed, in which case we're fucked.'

'Let's worry about that if it happens.' She shivers. 'It's cold.'

She lets the curtain drop and goes to her bed, pulling back the blankets and climbing in. She's right. Now that we're still, it is cold, but the spare beds have no covers. I stand there, awkward, not quite sure what to do.

'Well, come on, then,' she whispers. 'Get in.' She looks at me, expectant.

I'm glad it's dark and she can't see my face as I wedge in beside her on the small mattress. I know I'm blushing furiously. My arms and legs feel too long, my mouth is dry, and although I was freezing seconds before, my skin is now too hot. She wriggles across to give me space and we lie side by side, staring up at the ceiling. Her hair, too much to be contained on half a small pillow, tickles my face, but it's soft and almost warm.

'That's better,' she says. 'Better?' Her head twists sideways slightly to check.

'Yep,' I say and then swallow loudly. I have never lain in a bed with a girl before. My body is a screaming mess of anxiety and excitement that I have no control over. I take deep breaths as quietly as I can. This reaction is stupid. My right side is pressed against her left and I can feel her toes against my ankle. Her skin is impossibly warm through my pyjamas, and I realise that this is the closest I've been to anyone in weeks. I can feel her body move slightly as she breathes, slow and steady and completely relaxed, while I struggle to shift air from my lungs.

'When I was little,' she whispers, her head leaning towards mine until our skulls touch, 'until I was about ten or eleven, I always wanted to go to boarding school, the kind just for girls. I read all those stupid kids' books where they had midnight feasts, broke the rules, made lifelong friends and had adventures. And now here I am. Not quite what I was hoping for. Funny, huh?'

She's staring at the ceiling again, and that calms my awful self-awareness slightly. 'Well,' I say, 'I don't think you can get better lifelong friends than those you'll make here – that's pretty much guaranteed.' My tone is light as I say it and she giggles beside me. For a moment I'm almost the old Toby again, the classroom joker, even if this is the darkest kind of humour.

'You may have a point,' she says. 'Weird thought, though.'

'I'm surprised you didn't go to a posh boarding school,' I say, wanting to change the subject. 'I heard your dad is a Black Suit.'

'Oh, my school was definitely posh,' she says. She plays with a strand of her hair, pulling it straight upwards. It's so long her pale arm is nearly straight. 'One of the very best, of course. But I didn't board there. You can't control someone if you send them away and I had to be the perfect daughter. If they'd sent me away I'd have been free to be myself.' She smiles. 'That's bitten them on the arse now, hasn't it? I'm locked away *and* Defective. My poor father. You should have seen his face when they came. It was almost worth it. I think he was already wondering how he could contain the information. He's probably told the world I've died in some tragic accident. *And* convinced himself it's true.'

There's a pause after that. I had imagined her life to be fairy-tale-princess spoiled.

'He sounds like a bit of a wanker,' I say, eventually.

'He's a politician. They all are, aren't they?' She sighs. 'He wasn't always that bad. He was fine until I was about five; they both were. They just wanted too much for me.' I glance at her and her face is taut and serious in the memory for a moment and then the furrows in her brow disappear. 'What was your school like?' she asks.

'Pretty average,' I say. Jonesy and Billy and Julie McKendrick rise up in my mind like ghosts. 'Normal. Boring, mainly.' I don't want to think about it. Long, hot days playing football and dicking around. In the cold night, even with Clara beside me and my stomach flipping and tingling in ways I wish I could control, I'd give everything to go back to that. I'd walk away and leave them all to die here without a second thought if I could just go home, whole and healthy. Their names would be forgotten in days.

They say it makes your eyes bleed.

I think there's been a mistake.

From outside we can still hear the engine running and people crossing the gravel. 'That truck must have come here by boat, like we did,' I say. 'If there was a road, we'd have taken it. Louis reckons we're on an island. He's probably right.'

'We should explore it one night. Go over the wall.'

This time it's me who turns my head to stare. 'Yeah, right.'

'I'm serious.' She looks back at me, her eyes sparkling. 'Why not? Who's going to know?'

'Didn't you listen to what Jake said happened to the two boys who tried to run away?'

'Yes, but we won't be running away. We'll just be going out for a while and then we'll come back. And *we* won't get caught.'

Our faces are so close that our noses are almost touching and my stomach flips again, dipping down into my groin. I know what's happening there and will it to stop. She's just an ordinary girl. Not even hot like Julie McKendrick. Until two hours ago I didn't even like her much. I'm still not sure I do. She's like a creature at the bottom of a motionless ocean, dredging up the mud as she moves through it, making everything hard to see. Life at the house was clear-cut until she arrived. She's changing things.

'We should go tomorrow night.' She looks back up at the ceiling, decided. 'There's no time like the present, is there? Live for the moment and all that.'

'You're crazy,' I say.

We lie there in silence for a while, and soon we both drift into a doze. When I next open my eyes, grey light is washing the sky and the truck is gone. The house is quiet. I creep out of the bed, not wanting to wake Clara, and as an afterthought I turn around and rearrange the covers so she'll stay warm. She half-smiles then, sleepily, as she snuggles down, her eyes closed.

'I told you,' she slurs quietly.

'Told me what?' I whisper.

'That it would be more fun together.'

I leave her there and creep back to my dorm. If the nurses and Matron are still awake there's no sign of it, nor of their nocturnal activities. The house has returned to its undisturbed state, locked out of the world. My bed feels cold and unfamiliar as I peel my socks off and slide between the sheets. She's crazy, I think, imagining the madness of going over the wall. But my heart races and I can't sleep.

Even though Clara has been up every night since she got here, this breakfast is the first time I feel we're sharing a secret instead of me resenting her for stealing mine. We don't look at each other at all as the dorms file in, although she laughs and jokes with Tom when he goes to the food station while she's there. He comes back looking slightly flushed and pleased with himself, and somehow that makes me feel pleased with myself.

'Anyone want milk?' Tom says.

'Why did you get it if you don't want it?' Louis asks.

'He fancies Clara.' Will snickers.

'No, I don't,' Tom says. 'I just changed my mind after I got it.'

'Yeah, right.'

Tom's face is so red-blotched he looks like he's got a fever. I don't pay any attention. It's not like Will said anything I wasn't already thinking.

'Hey, check Joe out,' Louis says, nodding at the Dorm 7 table. I look across and Tom turns around in his seat to stare. The final three of Dorm 7 have moved themselves to one end of the table, leaving Joe isolated at the other. They're chatting away like he doesn't even exist, Jake at the centre, with Daniel – who's beaming to be suddenly closer to Jake – on one side, and a black kid called Albi who spends most of his spare time playing jazz on a sax in the music room on the other. If the nurses had somehow missed the fact that Joe's sick, it's obvious now.

As well as being isolated from his room-mates, his shoulders are hunched and he's listlessly spooning Weetabix into his mouth. He flinches as he swallows and his nose is so blocked he has to suck in a breath as he chews. It's like a flashback to Ellory, except no one's trying to protect Joe.

'Get your washing-up gloves ready, Toby.' Louis bites into his toast. 'You have some chores coming.'

A chair grates beside me as it's pushed away and Ashley gets up. At first I think he's going to get more toast or something, but then he picks up his plate and his cup of tea. His mouth is tight.

'You done?' I ask. He doesn't answer. With his back ramrod straight, he walks over to the Dorm 7 table. Their chatter stops for a moment as they stare at him, but he ignores them and sits down opposite Joe.

'Why can't he just be normal?' Will whines. 'He's going to get us all in the shit with Jake. Why would he do that?'

'And why at breakfast?' I grumble, my good mood evaporating. 'I don't need this crap first thing in the morning.'

At the other table, Joe smiles gratefully at Ashley and his shoulders lift slightly. I look from Joe to Jake and can see that Daniel and Albi are watching him intently, their eyes shining, sure he's going to kick-off. It's literally survival of the fittest here. There's no room for sympathy for the weak, and the twins broke Dorm 7's run of luck. Jake's jaw tightens and he's about to get to his feet when suddenly Harriet appears and takes the final free chair at the end of the table, Joe on one side of her and Ashley on the other. She's brought a stack of toast with her and puts it in the middle, smiling at both of the boys.

Jake glances back to where Clara and Eleanor are still eating their breakfast, continuing as if nothing out of the ordinary is happening. My heart's beating faster and we're all watching. This is not how it goes. Not since Henry and his terrible tears and pleading when he got sick. It's easier to simply cut them off. If it had just been Ashley, Jake would have said something, and I'd have let him, but one of the girls is different – especially now that Clara is here. After a moment, Jake goes back to his breakfast and ignores the two extras at the table. It's as if the whole room lets out a sigh.

'Why didn't he do anything?' Louis frowns.

'Tom's not the only one with a crush on the new girl,' I say, and Tom flashes me a glare as Will giggles. My appetite's gone and I feel unsettled again. The packs are changing. Ashley has his little God Squad now. Even if it's doomed to failure and will only alienate him further, it's still creating waves. It's not just Clara who's shifting the silt. I want things to stay the same. When things stay the same, you can't feel time moving forward.

'Fuck 'em,' I say. 'Better to have him over there than here with us being all holier-than-thou. Maybe he can move into Jake's dorm, too.'

'Oh, man, just imagine it.' Will grins, his face alight with mischief. 'All that praying.' Sometimes I wish I was Will's age. Too young to really get any of this.

It's colder today and the teacher waiting for us at the front of the class is wearing a thick wool jumper. He looks tired, and I wonder if they had to get up in the night to help with the truck, too. As we file in and take our seats, Will pauses at the back and puts something carefully on top of the radiator.

'Drying my conkers out,' he says when he sees us all staring at him. 'Makes them harder.'

'You didn't tell me about that.' Louis looks hurt.

'I forgot. But now you know – drying them out makes them harder.'

Louis immediately pulls two out of his pocket and puts them at the other end of the radiator.

Will grins at him. 'You still won't beat me.'

'Take your seats, boys,' the teacher says. 'Comprehension this morning, please.' He sits down and watches as we pull exercise books and textbooks out of our desks, and then his gaze drifts towards the window. He'll sit like that for a while and then make a half-hearted effort to come round and check on what we're doing. I'm not even sure he's a real teacher. Surely a real teacher would give it a proper go. We settle down quickly into quiet and all I can hear are shuffles and scratches of pens writing on paper. I doodle on the back cover of my book for a while and realise I'm drawing waves and the sea, and start thinking about later. Will we really do it? What if we get caught? Maybe she'll have changed her mind by the end of the day. I can't decide whether I want that or not.

'Get on with the work, please.'

He's staring at me.

'Sorry.' I drop my head and stare at the extract and questions in front of me. Piggy is not having a good day in *Lord of the Flies*.

After the first hour, the teacher drags himself out of his chair and starts his rounds. As he leans over me, his jumper smells of cigarette smoke doused with aftershave. He's old. Well older than I'll ever be, his short beard almost grey with rough patches of skin showing through the gaps. Over forty, that's for sure. He nods and then moves on, doing the minimum to disguise how pointless all this is.

'Are you going to sit with Joe every mealtime?' Louis asks Ashley at the end of the first two hours, when the teachers swap rooms and we have our pointless ten-minute break. 'Why would you do that? He's sick.'

Ashley doesn't even look over. 'I will no longer pass by on the other side of the road.' Even the way he speaks irritates me. His voice always sounds like a whine coming from somewhere behind his nose.

Will looks at me, baffled. 'What does that even mean?'

'Bible shit,' Louis says. 'He's just being mental.'

'No one should be afraid alone,' Ashley says as he opens his maths book.

I want to punch him for his stupidity. Everyone is afraid alone. If it wouldn't break our run with no losses, I'd wish that he would go next. I really, really would.

*

I sleep in the afternoon as usual, happy to keep my routine and stay out of the way of the others. I don't think about Clara or the night before or the night to come, but instead try to empty my head of everything except my tiredness. It works and I don't wake up until just before tea, after which I go for a bath. I had a shower that morning, but locked in the bathroom I can at least avoid the playroom and the church and the dread fascination of Joe's steady decline. I lie in the water until it's too lukewarm to stay in and then examine my body for any changes. I know every freckle and mark on my skin. I run my hands under my armpits looking for any bumps. I check the soles of my feet. The glands in my neck. Everything feels normal. For now, at least.

When I get back to the dorm, Louis, Will and Eleanor are there, stringing conkers, and Tom is lying on his bed pretending to fill in a tattered puzzle book from the library.

'What are you all doing in here?' I only have a towel around me, not expecting anyone to be in the room – least of all one of the girls.

'Can't get in the playroom,' Louis says, focusing on forcing a hole through the brown nut. I stare at Eleanor and her head drops as she quickly gathers up her stuff. She leaves her battered paperback behind.

'You can read that if you want, Will. I've finished it. It's really good.'

'Cool, thanks.' Will beams. 'Goodnight.'

She hurries out and as the door closes I relax.

'Maybe now Ashley and Harriet are sitting on the Dorm 7 table, Eleanor could come and sit with us. Clara, too.' Will looks at me, hopefully. I glare at him.

'Joe will be gone in a day or so and then Ashley will be back.'

'Lucky us,' Louis says, pushing a strand of wool through the hole on a thick needle. I haven't seen any wool or needles in the playroom. Who did they ask for them? Matron? Have they all forgotten why we're here?

'It was just a thought,' Will mumbles.

'A dumb one.' I pull my pyjama bottoms on. No point getting dressed. Not until much later, anyway. I feel a fizz of excitement in my belly and for a second or two the dread vanishes. That scares me slightly. The dark ball in my stomach is the anchor weighing me down. I need to make friends with it. I need to accept it. There is no point wishing for anything else.

'Why can't you get in the playroom?' I ask.

'Jake,' Louis says as if this is answer enough. 'He even kicked Tom out.'

'*Especially* Tom,' Will adds. He raises his conker. 'Ready when you are.'

'But why? Because of Ashley sitting at their table?' Jake is going to have his revenge for that, I'm sure.

'No, he kicked all the dorms out. Some of the

others took games into the music room but we figured we'd just come up here.'

'He's in there with Clara,' Tom says. 'Watching some old comedy film.' He keeps his eyes firmly on the puzzle but it's clear he's pissed off. 'Didn't want anyone else in there.'

'I didn't know she liked him,' I say lightly, focusing on drying my feet. I don't want the others spotting the pricks of red on my face. Jake and Clara watching a movie alone. Is that like a date? I'd see it as a date. I feel weird about it.

'They're on washing-up together. Came in covered in soapsuds and laughing.' Louis' conker hits Will's but does no damage and Will smiles. 'I like Clara. It's less boring now she's here.'

I don't say anything to that.

'I thought washing-up was done in dorms?' Tom says. 'How did she end up with him?'

I want to go and look at the rota. See who Jake bullied into swapping places with him so he could be with Clara. I lie on my bed and listen to Will and Louis chatter and laugh as they twat the conkers and each other's fingers and wonder what's happening in the playroom downstairs. Has Jake now got his own secret with Clara? Does she like him? Having spent days wishing she'd just fuck off, I now suddenly feel some weird sense of betrayal, which is wrong. I think of Julie McKendrick and Billy and wonder if this is like that all over again.

Then another thought occurs which shakes away the jealousy – will she tell him about the night-times? Will she tell him to stop taking the pills? Whatever excitement I had fades at the thought of Jake showing up in the kitchen tonight, then swaggering off with Clara. Jake wouldn't be able to keep it a secret, that's the worst part. If she tells him then everyone will know.

I close my eyes. Maybe I won't show up tonight. I can just withdraw back into my safe bubble of solitude. She's not even all that pretty. Fuck Clara. Fuck Jake. They can fuck each other for all I care.

EIGHT

'Don't squash the sandwiches!' she whispers down to me, astride the wall above. 'Come on!' She swings her leg over and disappears on the other side. We've moved the old garden bench against the wall, muddy indentations from the legs showing us exactly where to return it, and I climb onto the back before reaching up to grab the edge of the rough bricks. My arms, out of practice at any kind of exercise, strain in their sockets, but eventually I pull myself high enough to get a leg up. Despite the cold, I'm sweating by the time I drop heavily to the ground on the other side and my shaking shoulders take a minute to stop screaming at me. I half-expect floodlights to suddenly flash on and Matron to run towards us holding out a coin and shrieking, '*Heads or tails? Heads or tails?*', but there's nothing – just the darkness and the crisp, fresh air.

'So, where to now?' I say, staring into the darkness.

'Let's follow the road. Maybe that will take us to

a path leading down to the sea. It's over there. I saw it. Can't be too far away.'

I glance back at the house. It remains still and silent. They haven't made it easy for us to get out, but neither have they made it impossible. Louis was right – we must be on an island. It's not a surprise. They wouldn't want to risk us getting back into the general population if something went wrong and the sickness was allowed to run its course. There's no chance of that here.

'We shouldn't stay out too long.' I hurry to catch up with her as she strides, fearless, across the sloping thick grass towards the midnight strip of the road.

'We've got a couple of hours, panic-pants. Relax!' Her teeth flash white as she laughs. 'Doesn't it feel great, though? To be free?'

As our feet hit the smooth tarmac the clouds break overhead and the moon, hanging low in the sky, shines bright and beautiful above us, illuminating the wild and natural surroundings. I suck in a huge breath of cold air. My whole body tingles and I want to run and jump and shriek like a crazy person. She's right, it does feel good. For a little while I can leave it all back there – the house, the Defectiveness, the dread. Right now, we're just two people on a night adventure.

We walk for several minutes, staying quiet until the house is barely visible behind us, and then I hear it. Water rustling on shingle. The steady breath of waves as the sea sleeps. Salt tickles my nose, overwhelming the cold air and the tang of heather.

'Look!' Clara stops and points. 'There. Is that a path?' She grabs my cold hand and we run from the road to a chalky line cutting through the overgrown shrubs. The wind picks up and the call of the sea grows louder. We're near the edge of a small cliff and the wet pebbles on the beach below wink at us in the moonlight.

'For fuck's sake, be careful,' I mutter, but she's steady on her feet as she breaks away and picks her way down the steep chalky slash that cuts its uneven way into the darkness. 'And wait for me.'

'Slowcoach.' Her laughter tinkles back at me and I grin – a proper smile. An old Toby smile. As I move carefully forward, my ears freezing in the cold sea breeze, I feel good. Properly good. We're outside, we're alone and we still have our secret. Whatever happened in the playroom, she didn't tell Jake. When I finally got to the kitchen, hating myself for even showing up, I expected to find them both there. My hands were balled into tight, angry fists and I was ready to kill them for taking what had been just mine and making it something for everyone. But there was only Clara, layered in jumpers, wrapping sandwiches in greaseproof paper, waiting for me. No Jake. No betrayal.

I clamber down lower, trying to keep up with

Clara as the ridge of the cliff disappears above me. I don't even want to think about Jake, or Will, or Louis, or any of them. All that belongs back at the house with Matron and the nurses and the hungry sanatorium and the dread. It's strange not to feel that black fire raging in the pit of my stomach. I feel lighter. I know it'll return, but right now I feel alive and I don't want to curtail it.

My feet hit the shingle and, with her hair whipping around her head, Clara reaches back for me and I take her hand again. It's small but strong in mine and my heart races as we laugh and run awkwardly away from the stony ground and across the sand to the white surf which creeps in and away from the endless black water beyond. We stand there, breathless, faces burning, and stare out. The sea is calm, its endlessness mesmeric. Nature is beautiful. Life is beautiful. I ache slightly at the monumental mystery of it all and squeeze Clara's hand tightly, reminding myself that right now, right here, I am alive.

We wander along the beach a little, not wanting to stray too far from the path, and as Clara scours the sand for treasure, I spot a break in the rocky wall, a small, yawning opening. 'Over there.'

Clara puts down the shell she's been examining – we both know, without saying a word, that we can't take anything back with us – and follows me as I peer through the opening. It's a cave, perfectly arched, carpeted with silt, sand and washed-up flotsam. The wind drops as soon as we're inside and my stinging face warms immediately.

'It's beautiful,' Clara says, her words echoey in the sudden stillness. 'We should bring that candle from Ashley's church down here or search the kitchen stockroom for more. And some cushions and stuff from the playroom. Make it our own secret night-time den!'

I look down at the dregs of seaweed clinging to my shoes. 'Wouldn't work. The tide must come right in here. It would wash everything away.' The walls are damp and slick with sea slime, but we find a couple of rocks near the mouth and sit down and eat our sandwiches gazing out at the sea.

'This is beautiful, isn't it?' she says, chewing.

'Yes. Yes, it is.'

She looks at me and smiles happily, and my sandwich almost sticks in my throat as I swallow. I'm not talking about the beach or the water. Her long hair falls around her face in thick, red, wind-battered coils, almost matted like dreadlocks by the salty wind. Her cheeks are flushed, her eyes bright and alive. How can I not have seen how beautiful she is?

'You look like a mermaid,' I blurt out, from nowhere. 'A mermaid who comes ashore at night and sits in this cave wondering what it would be like to be human, before the tide comes and carries her back out to her people in the deep.' I don't know where the words are coming from. I wish I could just shut up. She's going to laugh at me. She doesn't. She just studies me for a moment as she finishes her food.

'I love that,' she says when she's done. She looks out again to where the star-littered sky meets the whispering sea. 'It's magical. I wish I was a mermaid.'

'We should get back.'

'We have to come here again,' she says.

'We will.' I don't look behind me at the cave as we amble along the beach to the path. I don't need to.

When we reach the road we stop to shake sand out of our shoes and clothes, not wanting any evidence of our escape to be spotted by the eagle-eyed nurses, and after brushing each other's backs down, we walk a little further on from the house in the night that's slowly creeping towards dawn to take in the surroundings we haven't yet seen. The island is not very big, probably not much more than a mile or so in any direction. We can't see any houses. There might be one or two dotted out of sight, but it's unlikely. Who would live here? What would they do?

'Over there,' Clara says softly. At first I don't see what she's looking at, but then I notice the shine of paint between a grassy knoll and a clifftop.

'We should go back.'

'It'll only take a minute.' She jogs forwards for a better view and I follow. 'That must be where boats from the mainland dock,' she says as the small building and the wide, sturdy jetty cutting a little way out into the bay come into view. 'Look – the road leads up from it.' The slope down to the sea is gentler there and a flat stretch winds up the hill to where we stand now. 'Do you think anyone lives in that house?' she asks. 'Like a gatekeeper?'

She makes it sound like we live in a fantasy castle rather than a Death House. 'Maybe. I guess they need someone to guide the boat in.' I'm making it up. I know nothing about boats.

'We should find out when that supply boat's due again.' She's not smiling now, her eyes narrow and thoughtful. 'We could escape on it. Go somewhere no one knows us and have the rest of our time to ourselves.'

I don't know what to say to that. Too many thoughts whirl in my head to focus on, but one floats to the surface now that we're in the shadow of the house. We can make whatever plans we like, but first we have to survive until the boat comes back.

'Come on,' I say quietly and tug her arm like a child. I don't want to get caught. I don't want to play heads or tails with Clara.

The sun was warm on his back and his skin itchy with dried salt from where they'd run in and out of the sea, whooping and shrieking in water so cold they couldn't help but laugh. His mum had even sworn a couple of times as she'd sprinted in behind him, throwing herself into the waves to get the shock of it over faster, and that had made him howl with laughter.

He was thirteen, probably too old to be enjoying a family holiday so much, but school was an age away and it had been a brilliant two weeks. Long days on the beach, the trip to the waterpark, the funfair, the circus, candyfloss, ice creams, fish and chips, and wandering through the cobbled alleyways where all the shops were filled with souvenirs and hand-crafted jewellery, and cafes served clotted cream teas and Cornish pasties. The cottage they'd rented had a hot tub and a huge shelf of DVDs, and every night, if they didn't play cards, they sat together on the sofa and watched movies until they fell asleep.

Sometimes when he'd been growing up, Toby had wished for a brother – or even a sister – to play with, but those days had gone. He couldn't imagine someone else being part of their family – his dad ruffling another kid's hair the way he did Toby's, or his mum smiling at someone else with so much love it made her nose crinkle. They were his parents and his alone and he was lucky to have them. They loved him and he loved them, and although the way he showed it would change in the years to come – he could already feel the pull of 'coolness' and wanting to hang out with friends *rather than family – on that holiday, growing up was part of an unknown future, and his mum and dad were the best people to be with.*

It was the last day, and while his dad lay on a sunlounger reading an old spy thriller, Toby and his mum wandered the beach looking for shells to take home.

'Hey, Toby,' she called to him. He was paddling in the shallows and enjoying the feel of the sand being sucked away from his feet as each roll of the water pulled back, and watching the sunlight glitter on the surface, and thinking about everything and nothing in that way you can when the weather's warm and there are no clouds in the sky or your mind.

'Come over here! I've found something.'

It was black and leathery in his hand, a flat oblong with four thin prongs like strips of leather curving away from each corner. 'What is it?' he asked, rubbing the smooth surface clean of sand.

'It's called a mermaid's purse. They say that mermaids leave them behind when they come up to the water's edge. Like lost handbags. Sailors used to search the beaches for them. They thought they were lucky.'

'There's no such thing as mermaids,' Toby said.

'How do you know?'

'Everyone knows!' He was thirteen. Too old to believe in all the magic of childhood any more. He knew there was no Father Christmas. The tooth

fairy didn't exist. The only one he still partly believed in was the bogeyman, and then only at night in the dark when he couldn't sleep. 'What is it really?'

His mum's shoulders slumped slightly, the wind taken from her sails by her growing-up boy. 'It's an egg sac. Fish lay their eggs in them and they grow there until they're ready to come out and swim by themselves. I prefer the mermaid story, though.'

Toby stared at the sac a moment longer and his mum started to wander away.

'Hey, Mum,' he called after her.

'What?'

'Maybe we should put it back where you found it. You know, in case the mermaid comes looking for it.' She smiled at him then, a beaming grin that made her look like a teenager rather than an old woman in her thirties, and Toby was happy. He had the best mum in the world and he'd believe in the magic if she wanted him to.

'Let's get Dad and grab another ice cream. I'm sure there's still a couple of flavours at that stand I haven't tried yet,' she said as they bedded the mermaid's purse into the damp sand. 'It's our last day. We may as well eat until we feel sick. Deal?'

'Deal.'

The perfect end to the perfect holiday.

NINE

We find the bird the following night after we've scaled the wall and put the bench on the lawn and are just about to climb into the house through the kitchen sash window. It's fallen close to the large black bins next to the locked side gate and one wing hangs awkwardly from its body, a gash down the centre. It's still breathing, though, the small body warmish under the feathers, and for a moment, after Clara has picked it up, we don't know quite what to do. In the end I pull off my hoodie and we wrap it carefully inside.

'Let's hide it somewhere. But we'll have to be quick.'

We're a whirlwind in the kitchen, Clara finding an old food box we can turn into a bed, me soaking some bread in milk in a saucer and getting another to put water in, to take with us.

The house is still and silent and we creep through it until we find an empty room far from the others where an old wardrobe, abandoned and lonely, is pressed up against a wall. We make a home for the bird on its floor and Clara carefully wipes his cut clean before settling him down into it.

'It's a baby,' Clara says as she picks up a small piece of the milk-soaked bread and holds it close to his beak, tempting him. 'Poor little thing.'

'He's probably in shock,' I say. 'If we leave him in the quiet, he'll calm down. At least he's warm here.'

'Don't worry, little bird,' Clara coos softly. 'We'll make you all better again, and then you can find your mother.' She pauses. 'Let's just hope she's a better mother than either of ours.' She glances at me and spots my immediate confusion. 'Harriet says that your mum was a bitch.'

I shrug, awkward. I don't want to talk about it. I've forgotten how people still hold on to those early-days conversations. But still, she's talked to Harriet about me. That gives me a good fizz inside.

'What shall we call him?' Clara asks as we close the wardrobe door reluctantly and get to our feet.

'You pick something. Maybe he's a she?'

'Georgie, then,' Clara says. 'That works for both. We'll have to take it in turns to check on him during the day. I'm on washing-up again so you do the morning, okay?'

I'd almost forgotten about Jake and the washing-up and a small flare of jealousy burns through me, but then I remind myself that Jake doesn't have the boat and the bird and the cave.

'Sure.'

'Okay, then. Until tomorrow night!' She grins and wraps her arms around my neck and kisses me right on the lips before turning and heading back to her dorm. I stand there, suddenly breathless and as stunned as the bird wrapped in my sweatshirt. My lips tingle from the contact. My head is throbbing. She kissed me.

By the time I crawl into my own bed, I've convinced myself I'm being stupid and it doesn't mean anything. It wasn't a proper snog or anything. It was just friendly. But still, she did kiss me. It's enough to keep the dread at bay when Joe's hacking cough cuts through the silent dawn.

TEN

'What the hell are they doing?' I ask.

The temperature's dropped over the past few days and I've wrapped up warm to come outside, but still my nose runs each time I bend over to dig around in the soil. I can't remember it ever being this cold and I just want to get back inside and go to sleep for the afternoon. I've found three worms and they're wrapped in toilet paper in the pocket of my jacket. I hope I don't crush them before I can escape up to Georgie and see if he'll eat them.

'Baptising him,' Louis says.

'They're always in the church now. Talking about Bible stories and stuff.' Will scuffs his feet to keep warm. 'You never notice anything any more.'

I don't answer that. It's true. Not that I paid much attention before, but that was different. Now even when I'm awake I'm thinking about Clara and the bird and what the night may bring, and everything else feels unreal. I like it. I feel as if I'm not part of the house any more. Mainly, at the moment, I'm thinking about the bird.

'I'm not sure that standing out here in the freezing fucking cold and pouring water over his head is going to make Joe better.'

'The point of baptism isn't to make him better,' Louis says. 'It's to introduce him to God or something.'

'There's more of them.' They're gathering by the swings – Ashley, Joe, Harriet and a couple of boys from another dorm whose faces I know but can't remember ever speaking to.

'Wake up, Toby,' Will says. 'Ashley's got his own gang now.'

'Hardly a gang. More like a bunch of sad twats.'

Joe sits down on one of the swings and the others bow their heads as Ashley speaks softly. I can't hear his words but his face is serious and his eyes closed. Joe's skin is blotchy with fever and even with no sun out his hair is shining with sweaty grease.

Ashley's voice rises as he pours water from a bottle over Joe's tipped-back head. 'I baptise you in the name of the Father, the Son and the Holy Spirit.' Three splashes of water. The small congregation smile at each other as if this is some magic fucking cure for Defectiveness, and then Joe stands up and Harriet takes her turn. I didn't think it was possible for Joe to get any thinner but his clothes are hanging from his bones.

'Why haven't they just taken him to the sanatorium already?' I grumble. It feels like Joe's been ill for ever. I don't want to see the reality of the house. What's waiting for us all. Not now. Not after the kiss.

'That's obvious, isn't it?' I hadn't noticed Tom join us. He looks as displeased with the baptisms as I feel. 'Whatever he's sick with, that's not *it*.'

All three of us turn to look at him. Even Louis with his super-sized brain hasn't thought of that.

Tom shrugs. 'Makes sense to me. He's grieving for his twin – of course he's fallen sick. When my brother died, I caught the worst flu I've ever had. Couldn't get out of bed for two weeks.' He shivers and turns away. 'I'm heading back inside. Albi's teaching Jake to play some stuff on the guitar. He's going to teach me the drums.'

'The drummer never gets the girl, you do know that, right?' I say, unable to stop myself. I'm not sure whether he hears me or not, but he doesn't react.

'Did you know Tom had a dead brother?' Louis asks.

'His poor mum.' Will's small face is awash with sadness.

'Who gives a fuck?' My words come out harsher than I mean them to. Why would Tom tell us something like that? I don't need to know things like that. I don't want to feel sorry for him. Or Joe. I don't want to think about them at all.

*

I don't get to take the worms upstairs. As we go back inside, fingers and toes numb after watching Ashley's crazy display in the garden, the gong rings out and we all have to return to our dorms where the nurses are waiting for us. Even for Ashley and his God that he carries with him everywhere like some shield that can save him.

'Blood tests,' the nurse says as she snaps on her plastic gloves and prepares the first syringe, as we sit in dread. What do they need to test our blood for? We're all Defective – they know that already. Are we like some kind of lab animals here? Are they studying us to try and understand it better? I stare at the nurse while my heart thumps. She's not that old, under thirty, I'd guess, and wisps of her fine ginger hair escape from under her hat. 'We need to see how you're all progressing,' she says as if reading my thoughts.

As she jabs the needle into Ashley, Will goes pale and squeezes his eyes tight shut. Louis sits close to him and holds his hand. I can't remember if either of them had brothers or sisters on the outside, but they're brothers now.

'I'm not sure "progressing" is the right word.' I try to dispel some of the tension in the room. I don't want Will to be scared. *I* don't want to be scared, either. 'Do we get a badge if our genes are more fucked than anyone else's?' I smile at the nurse as she comes over to me. It's my best cheeky-Toby grin but she doesn't even look up. 'An A-Star? A full pass grade in Defectiveness?' I wink at Louis and Will and they both manage small smiles, maybe one proper one between them.

'Keep still,' is all she says as she tightens the pressure on my arm and the needle goes in. I watch my blood come out, thick and red as it fills the small tube. It looks perfectly normal. No different than it ever has done through all the tests and scrapes and cuts over the years. I can't even remember looking at it before. The last time I was tested I was too busy feeling high over the prospect of Julie McKendrick's party. Maybe if my surname had started with a different letter, I'd have even got to go to it before they dragged me here. A few more days of normality.

'I hate needles,' Will whispers. 'I thought I was done with needles.'

'I'll go next,' Tom says. 'You go after me, then Louis, okay?' Will nods. My heart and stomach ache a little. By the time the nurse has finished with Tom, Will's breath is coming fast. Tom picks up the book Eleanor gave him and opens it to where the corner of one page is turned down. 'How about I read this to you?'

'You'll think it's silly,' Will says, defensive. 'It's a kids' book.'

'I want to hear some,' Louis cuts in.

'Me, too,' Ashley says, and for a moment I almost feel warm towards him.

'Read some, Tom,' I hear myself saying. We are family now, however much I pretend we're not. We're Dorm 4. We stand together.

'Okay, here goes.' Tom takes a deep breath and starts to read. '"This must be a simply enormous wardrobe!' thought Lucy, going still further in and pushing the soft folds of the coats aside to make room for her. Then she noticed that there was something crunching under her feet. 'I wonder is that more mothballs?' she thought, stooping down to feel it with her hand. But instead of feeling the hard, smooth wood of the floor of the wardrobe, she felt something soft and powdery and extremely cold. 'This is very queer,' she said, and went on a step or two further." Who's Lucy?' Tom looks down at Will. The nurse is ready with her needle. She waits until Will looks up at him.

'She's a girl. She's been sent away with her brothers and her sister to a big house in the country because of the war.' He flinches slightly and I see Louis squeeze his hand.

'Bit like us, then,' I say. Will nods. His bottom lip trembles slightly, but the nurse is working fast and soon the needle is out, and within seconds she's labelling up his sample and putting it with the others.

'Lucy's the youngest,' Will says and sniffs. Tom gives him the book back and he stares at it while Louis' test is done. He's still shaking, though. I think about how casually I've walked into every six-monthly blood test I ever had at school. It wouldn't have been like that for Will. Five months of freedom, then one month of building dread.

The nurse packs her kit away and goes to leave. She pauses at the door and turns back.

'It's a good book,' she says softly. 'My great-grandma read it to me when I was little.' And then she's gone, leaving us all staring after her, mouths slightly open. The nurses never speak to us like that. Never.

'I think he's getting better, you know,' Clara says as Georgie eats the last of the slightly squashed and paper-fluffy worms I dug up this afternoon. We haven't gone over the wall tonight. The island is coated with a blanket of thick, freezing mist and although it would have been fun to explore in it, we want to spend time with the bird. His box sits on top of the blankets we've pulled from our beds to keep us warm, half on one of my legs and half on one of hers.

'That's it, I'm afraid,' she says as the small beak opens and chirps for more. She looks up at me. 'He definitely prefers the worms to the bread.'

I touch his small, warm head. His feathers are soft under my fingers and he doesn't shiver or shake like he did when we first tucked him into the box. My hooded sweatshirt is still wrapped around him but he's not afraid of us any more. His dark eyes dart from Clara to me and back again, and when he realises that the food really is all gone he settles down in the warmth of his bed. We've cleaned his wing again with some warm water and soap to get rid of the weird pus coming from the gash and he didn't even try to wriggle free. I think he's becoming tame – to us, at least. He looks happy enough and he's eating, so maybe Clara's right. Maybe he is getting better. That gives me a warm glow. Another crack in the defences I've worked so hard to build since I arrived at the house. I'm becoming 'me' again. I want to fight it. I *should* fight it, but here in the night with Clara I can't stop myself.

'I wish we could ask the nurses for some cream or something to put on his cut,' Clara says. We've searched the house for a medical kit but couldn't find one. The only thing we came up with were some blue plasters in the kitchen.

'You know we can't.' I touch the soft head again.

'Did you have a pet at home?' she asks.

'No.'

We've stacked our pillows behind us to make a kind of sofa on the floor but I can still feel the cold seeping through. I pull the blankets up a bit and Clara leans against me. 'My mum was allergic to animal fur,' I finish. 'You?'

'God, no. A pet? Making a mess? In the house?' Her voice has changed into something sharp and affected – an impersonation of her mother. 'That would be impossible. Muddy paw prints and fur everywhere.' She laughs. 'Which I could understand a bit more if it had been my mother doing the cleaning.' Listening to her, I wish I could hate my mum. It would make all of this easier. All I can think of is the stuff I never said to her. The *good* stuff.

'Well, we've got a pet now,' I say. As if agreeing, Georgie ruffles the feathers on his good side.

'I don't want him to be a pet. I want him to get better and fly away. We'll nurse him better.'

'I wonder why she spoke to us. They never speak to us.' Her words have made me think of the nurse again. Until today the nurses have just been 'the nurses'. Now there's one who's a real person. After the blood tests, Will read his book right up until lights-out, Louis, curious, sometimes looking over his shoulder. I think Louis was reading the pages in seconds whereas it felt like an age before we heard the rustle of paper from Will. It isn't a big book but I suspect this is more reading than Will probably ever did *before*. Now he's not just reading it because Eleanor liked it, he's reading it because of the nurse, too. The book is the link to that moment. Who'd ever have thought a few words from an adult could make such a difference?

'I suppose she feels sorry for us.' Clara's voice is soft and for the first time she sounds reflective about our situation. 'It must be strange for them, too. I wonder how they're chosen?'

'I always presumed they were just skilled psychopaths. You know, no feelings.'

She giggles. 'Maybe Matron is. And the ones upstairs in the sanatorium. I wonder if they ever party? The nurses and the teachers getting it on. It would be like role-play heaven, I guess.' She laughs again. 'Maybe they play "you wear my outfit and I'll wear yours" and then get dirty.'

I feel suddenly hot and uncomfortable. Clara's a girl. They're not supposed to talk about stuff like that, the stuff you see on the Internet. The idea that Clara might ever have watched porn makes me squirm.

'You'll have to point her out to me.'

'Who?'

'The nurse, dummy.'

'Oh, yeah.' I wonder how I'm supposed to do this. We never speak during the daytime. 'If I see her. Anyway, you're always with Jake.' The words have blurted out of nowhere, my brain still fried with images of Clara and porn. Girls don't think about sex. Not like boys do.

'You're always asleep. You should sleep less. I'm sure they put something in our drinks or food to keep us calm, but that doesn't mean you should sleep the whole time. You're worse than a stoner.'

I don't know how she doesn't sleep *more* after being awake for most of the night. She must only get three hours tops by the time we go to bed.

'Anyway,' she continues, 'it's safer that way.'

'Safer?'

'I don't want people to notice. And if we talk to each other too much we'll end up letting something slip. I don't want them to start force-feeding me their "vitamins".'

She's got a point. It would be bad if the others picked up on something – worse if it was the nurses. Perhaps only one has ever spoken, but they all listen. And the one who talked to us is the one I'm the most suspicious of. Why would she want to be nice? What was she trying to achieve? I put her out of my head.

'True. But Jake's such a cock.'

'No, he's not.'

'Maybe not with you, but that's only 'cause he fancies you.' The last bit comes out in some awful sing-song voice that makes me cringe. I wish I could shut up. 'Before you got here he was just a cock. Trying to rule the place.'

'He's all right,' she says. 'I think he's had a shit life. Even before this.'

I think of her loveless parents. 'So did you.'

'Different shit. Scarier shit.'

'Maybe.' I wonder how different this house is from reform school. Jake must have been young when he went, maybe Louis' age. He wouldn't have been top dog there.

But at least he got out. The dark ball knots in my stomach. 'He's still a cock,' I mutter.

'You sound jealous.' She twists around to look at me, surprised. 'Are you jealous of Jake?'

This is going nowhere I want it to go, and while my insides shrivel, I only shrug. 'Why would I be jealous? I just think he's a bit of a dickhead, that's all.'

'Maybe you're right,' she says. 'But why waste time not liking people? We may as well all try and get along.'

I don't know what to say to this. To be honest, I don't see the point in trying to like people, not here. Mainly I'm thinking that she hasn't really said anything about Jake fancying her. Maybe she already knows. Maybe she fancies him back. Maybe I should just stop thinking about that stupid kiss. It wasn't a proper one, anyway. Could easily have been friend-zone. And why do I even care?

In the box, Georgie chirps and then hops out onto my lap and stares up at us. After a second, he cocks his head. I laugh, I can't help it.

'See?' Clara says, smiling. 'She agrees with me.'

'Or *he's* agreeing that Jake is a bit of a dick.'

The bird cocks its head the other way and chirps twice. We both laugh this time. Bored, Georgie starts to peck at our blankets.

'I knew if I met anyone awake that first night it would be you.' She's gazing down at the bird and smiling. 'I saw you at tea. You were the only one who looked at me like I was an idiot rather than just staring at the new girl. Then you didn't come to the playroom after to watch the film. Everyone else did. Even poor Ellory. All curious about me and Tom. The fresh blood.' She's speaking quietly, remembering.

This all goes through me like a jolt of electricity. The idea that she'd noticed me before we met in the kitchen hadn't even occurred to me.

'I was glad it was you,' she continues as I sit listening, my heart racing as fast as the bird's and my skin starting to burn all over again. 'Even though you were so pissed off I was there. Wouldn't have been the same with anyone else.'

'I wasn't pissed off,' I stutter, 'I was just—'

'Yeah, you were. You were determined to hate me.' She smiles up at me and my stomach flips. 'I knew I'd win you round, though.'

'Don't count your chickens,' I say, trying to be funny as my throat dries and constricts, threatening to choke me.

'Georgie's not a chicken. I don't have any chickens.'

We sit in silence for a moment, both looking at the lopsided bird hopping about in the gloom. He's so light I can't even feel him through the covers.

'Have you ever had a proper girlfriend?' she asks.

I almost answer, *Yeah, loads, of course I have*, but then I remember where we are and how I hate the lies I've already told and I don't see the point.

'Not really. A couple I've sort of seen for a while, but nothing serious.'

'No girl broke your heart, then?' It's weird talking about this stuff. Me and Jonesy never talked about girls – not properly. Only in that 'what you did or didn't do' or 'what you would or wouldn't do' kind of way.

'No one special left behind?'

I think of Julie McKendrick. A dream-girl. A ghost. 'No,' I say. 'What about you? Proper boyfriends?' I don't even know what she means by that. What is a 'proper' boyfriend or girlfriend anyway? Does that mean you've done it?

'With my dad around? And at a girls' school?' She shakes her head. 'I guess a bit like you. One or two who tried. Most of the boys my parents approved of I didn't like.'

'At least you have Jake,' I say. I hate the idea of her and Jake. I hate it with more feeling than I've had for anything during my entire time at the house. I definitely hate it more than the thought of Julie McKendrick off with Billy. Julie doesn't even feel real any more.

'Yes, I suppose I do,' she says, and my insides tighten so hard I can feel my stomach shrink. I wish we'd gone out in the mist to the cave. I wish we'd never had this conversation. I wish she'd never come to the house. I just want to go back to the dorm on my own. Suddenly she bursts into laughter.

'God, you're so *thick* sometimes.' She twists

around so she's facing me. 'I *like* Jake. I don't *fancy* Jake. It's not Jake I'm asking about girls.'

I stare at her. Nothing is working in my head. There's just a mad humming as my blood rushes in all directions around my body with the switch of emotions. Before I can say anything – not that I have anything to say – she leans in and pulls me towards her by my pyjama top. My face doesn't know where to go and my nose bangs into hers and then she tilts her head and she's kissing me.

This isn't like that other kiss. This time, despite my terror of being shit at it, I feel like I'm going to explode. My whole body is shaking. Her face is warm in my hand and I slide the other nervously around her waist, feeling her nightshirt crumple and crease. She smells like freshly washed cotton with something alive and earthy wrapped in it. Her tongue is hot and still carries the lingering mint of toothpaste as it presses and turns around mine. We kiss for what feels like a minute and for ever, and when we finally break free I'm breathless and my body is on fire, throbbing.

'Wow,' I croak. She giggles.

'Good kisser.'

'You were okay, too,' I say, trying to get myself under control. The moment's broken by a small squawk between us.

'Oh, poor Georgie!' As we turned towards each other to kiss, the blankets folded over him, and now his beak pokes out from somewhere between our legs. As Clara carefully picks him up and puts him back in his box, his head turns this way and that and he ruffles what feathers he can and cheeps as if reprimanding us for forgetting him. We both giggle. I feel good. I feel amazing. I feel alive.

'We should head to the dorms soon,' she says.

I nod.

'You take your stuff and go. I'll put him back.' I'm panicking slightly. There is no way I'm standing up in front of her yet. Not in my thin pyjamas. If we'd done this in the cave, at least I'd have my jeans on.

'Are you sure?' She kisses me again, short and sweet this time, and my whole body aches. 'And for the record, you're way better looking than Jake. And funnier.'

'So are you.'

She laughs again. I like the sound of it. I like the way her hair falls so wild around her face. I like the way she's so full of energy. What I like the most is the way she likes me.

She bundles up her blankets and pillow and heads to the door. I watch her go, her bare legs doing nothing to help my throbbing subside. She pauses in the doorway.

'Isn't it strange?' she says. 'You'll be my first proper boyfriend. And my last.' She's wistful. 'Strange but wonderful. Like it's meant to be.'

And then she's gone, disappeared into the corridor, leaving me a trembling mess, alone in the night. Boyfriend. She called me her boyfriend.

ELEVEN

'I heard that pair from Dorm Two talking about it in the playroom,' Louis says. 'They were calling it a miracle. Said they might get baptised, too.'

'What a pile of shit,' Tom says, sneering.

We're all staring at the new poster in the hallway. It's brightly coloured, with glued-on glitter twinkling at the corners. Where does Ashley find all that crap? Why would the house even have glitter and glue? Who thinks of this stuff? The writing is large and almost artistic, the letters curling at the edges of each word declaring a 'Celebration Service for Joe's Recovery!' and I wonder if Harriet is now in charge of the posters. I'm with Tom. It's all bollocks. It's not a fucking miracle. Joe just got over his flu.

'Should we take it down?' Will asks. 'Before Jake sees it?'

'Why?' Jake won't do anything about Ashley's church. He's not stupid. He knows Matron knows about it. Who cares what Jake thinks, anyway? And if he wants to take Ashley on, then that's Ashley's problem, not ours.

'Why are people so stupid?' Tom mutters. I shrug. I'm only half-here anyway, the rest of me still reliving Clara calling me her boyfriend, and mostly I'm trying to keep a big, fat, smug grin off my face.

'Just forget about it and do something else. Watch a film or something.'

'I might hang in the music room.' He says this casually, but I know he's going because Clara is in there. I have to bite my tongue to stop myself blurting out that he's wasting his time because she's *my* girlfriend.

'You're going to sleep, I s'pose,' Will says.

'Dunno,' I say. For once, I don't feel tired. I should be, but I'm not. It's all I can do to stop my foot tapping with all the energy bubbling through me. 'Why?'

'We found an old board game yesterday. Called *Escape from Colditz*. It's really good.'

'Never heard of it.' I only ever played board games at Christmas *before* and even then only when Gran came to visit.

'It's fun, but would be better with more than just two of us playing.' They both stare at me but I can see they're not holding out much hope.

'Okay,' I say. 'Go on, then.' Why not? Otherwise I'll just lie on my bed and count the interminable hours before everyone else is asleep and me and

Clara can be together again. Just thinking that makes me feel like a twat but I can't help it. At least this will make the time pass more quickly.

As it goes, it's not such a bad game and Louis and Will make me laugh, and before we know it, it's teatime. Will scours the room for *the* nurse, but she's not at the food station tonight. She was there this morning and he'd smiled at her as he got toast and was convinced she'd given him a wink back. I don't know if she did or not, but as long as Will believed it, who cares? He's young. He misses his mum. He's the only one of us who's come right out and admitted that ever since Henry got sick back at the beginning. Henry has put us all off talking about our mums. Not after all that terrible calling-out.

Apart from the flash of dread it causes, I can't really remember much in detail about what happened with Henry. It feels like a long time ago even though it's only been weeks. I think maybe they upped whatever they put in our drinks in the aftermath. I bet the next morning, after breakfast, we were all pretty much tranquillised off our tits. I sometimes wonder why they don't just get us high and keep us that way. Maybe they are studying us like lab rats. The chosen few. The rare Defectives. Throwbacks from a terrible time that nearly broke the world.

These thoughts normally send me spinning into a quiet, terrible panic – fear of the waiting dark nothingness, of the sanatorium, the *changing*, of the certainty of non-existence that's waiting for me – but this time it doesn't. Weirdly, I just want to laugh. They're not watching very hard. They don't know about me and Clara and Georgie. It's like we've escaped them. I'm alive and happy and that's all that counts.

Ashley looks smug at bedtime and he has good reason to be. Although I'd kept to my normal routine and had a long bath after tea, Louis and Will were quick to tell me how much quieter the playroom had been for the film.

'I hear there's a kid in Dorm Three getting sick,' Tom growls as Ashley carefully folds his towel over the back of his allocated chair. 'You going to cure him, too, Jesus?'

'Don't call me that. It's disrespectful.' He doesn't even look at Tom. 'Anyway, I didn't say I'd cured him. I just said he'd got better.'

'It's only disrespectful if you believe in it,' Louis mutters. He's half-listening and half-reading over Will's shoulder.

'But I bet you're not telling your followers it wasn't a miracle.' Tom's eyes are dark. It's normally me who gets angry at this shit, but Tom is way ahead of me this time.

'I'm not telling them it *is*, either.'

'He only had the flu, that's all. It's sick how

you're claiming it. Giving all those kids hope just so they'll buy into your bullshit.'

Will's head dips closer to the pages. He's not good with arguments. Jokes he can do, giggling at Ashley from a corner, but not full-on confrontation.

'*You're* saying I'm claiming it. Not me. I just wanted to celebrate that he was better. What's wrong with that? And what's wrong with hope, anyway, if it makes people less afraid?'

Ashley is smarter than I've given him credit for, even though his endless calm makes me want to punch him as much as Tom clearly does.

'Because it's bollocks. And you know it. You're just on some fucking power trip. Billy No-Mates Sad-Fucker suddenly has people listening to him.'

'What does it matter to you what I'm doing? Why does it make you so angry?'

'Why don't we all just stop talking about it?' I sit up and stare at them both. 'Stop thinking about *all* of it. It's a waste of time. We should just be having as much fun as possible.'

For a moment no one speaks. All eyes turn to me. Even Will looks up from his book to stare.

'Mr Grumpy-Sleep-All-Day has gone mental,' Louis says eventually, and Will giggles. 'What do you think me and Will have been trying to get you to do since we arrived here?'

I smile, I can't help it. 'Maybe I'm a slow learner.'

Tom grunts and gets into bed. He doesn't look

happy but neither does he badger Ashley any more. I feel sorry for Tom. I know how angry he is. Until Clara came, I was the same. Probably *more* angry. Sometimes anger is the only release for the fear. If I didn't have Clara and the nights, I'd probably have punched Ashley by now. I know why Tom hates the Church – for the same reasons I do. Not because of believing in some god or something, but because always, always, it highlights that the end is coming. You've got to think about *after*. It's hard enough trying to not think too much about *before*, and thinking about after is scary. If you don't buy into their heaven, then seeing Ashley with his Bible and superior lack of fear is a constant reminder of what's ahead. No one in here needs that. It's really hard to just enjoy *now*. If the house has taught me anything, it's that. I think about that for a moment. Not the house. The house hasn't taught me that. Clara has.

'Do you think he's sick?' Clara's worried and I can see why. Georgie's wing smells bad and more pus oozes from it as I try to wipe it clean. He's not as alert as normal and his head feels hot as I gently stroke it.

'Maybe,' I say. 'But he's a tough little fella. He'll get better.' As if in agreement, he lets out a small chirp, which reassures Clara a little. I don't want her to spend all night just staring at the sick bird.

If he's sick, he's sick. Watching him isn't going to do any of us any good. Not for the whole night, anyway. She hasn't kissed me yet. Not tonight. It's wrong but I'm more worried about that than the bird. Am I still her boyfriend? Has she changed her mind but doesn't want to tell me? A million doubts whir in my brain. Why hasn't she kissed me? My heart is suddenly shredding, pieces drifting down to my stomach.

'It's not raining. We should go out,' I say. 'We can come and check on him again when we get back.' She doesn't take any persuading. She's a ball of energy that needs to be free, not locked up in this place which, despite its size, is so claustrophobic.

'Good idea,' she says, and then she's up on her tiptoes and her lips kiss mine. It's fleeting, but enough to send my heart racing and electric shivers running across my skin. 'Let's go, handsome.'

I'm suddenly exhilarated. Part of me now wants to stay, to just kiss her and touch her and feel her touch me, but I'm too clumsy to say it and I don't want to scare her off. I don't want her knowing I think about her all the time. I've thought about her naked, too. About being naked with her, and I feel like it's written all over my face when she sees me trembling and panting as we say our goodnights. I can't help thinking about her that way, even though it feels sort of wrong. Maybe going outside will be good. It'll cool me down.

*

It's a dry night but cold and cloudy, the moon only peeking out every now and then to cast some light on the road. The darkness doesn't matter so much any more. We're confident of the island's landscape now, as if we own it somehow. I'm no longer even nervous when we go over the wall, just excited and ready to shake off the house again. We stride hand in hand as the tarmac curves and descends towards the water. Neither of us has gloves and my fingers are freezing but I don't let go of her as we sniff back our running noses and giggle and talk rubbish. I feel free around her. Everything else fades. We're not going to the cave. Not yet.

We hush as we draw closer to the blue building down by the little harbour and stick to the edges of the road nearest the rock face, staying as invisible as possible just in case. It's Clara's idea to come down and check it out, and although – as always – I'm worrying we'll get caught, I can't deny there is something exhilarating about creeping towards the small building knowing that someone could be inside to see us and catch us.

'Come on,' Clara whispers. She squeezes my hand tighter and we duck down as we creep across the shingle surrounding the small house. Even in the dark I can see that the paintwork is chipped on the old stone, small flashes of cream here and there on walls that have been battered by wind and rain for longer than I can probably imagine. A forgotten building on a forgotten island where forgotten children live. It almost sounds like the start of an adventure story. Maybe it is. Mine and Clara's.

We grip the flaky white windowsill and carefully peer in, but it's so dark inside that all the glass shows us is our own ghostly-grey reflections. I press my face against it and squint. Maybe an old stove in a corner. A sink.

Clara nods upwards. 'The bedroom must be up there.'

'If anyone lives here.'

She moves, light on her feet, around to the back of the house and I follow her, aware of every crunch my trainers make. It's not windy and the sea is quiet, barely murmuring as it teases the shore, so my footsteps cut through the quiet. I can't believe no one hears me but when the house stays dark I start to think that maybe the place is empty. It would be cool if it is. Me and Clara could make it a proper den. Somewhere over the wall but still warm.

'Look.' She's by the back door, pointing. A pair of boots sit neatly on the step. 'Someone lives here.' They're a man's boots, old and heavy, and the thick soles are crusted with mud. I try to imagine the man tugging them off and leaving them out here. Where had he been? Where was there to go? It's weird to think that someone other than us wanders over the island. Maybe the teachers and nurses do, too, for all we know. Go off in the afternoons for walks. I've never seen them do it, but then I've never really paid attention. It feels like a violation. The nights are ours, mine and Clara's, and I've started to think of the island that way, too.

'Just the one pair.' She's crouched beside them, tracing her finger over the edges of the leather, her hair falling across her pale face. 'Imagine living out here all by yourself. Not even a dog.'

'Maybe he has one.'

'If he did, it'd be barking by now.' She straightens up and smiles at me. 'But only one person is good. Easier for us to sneak by to get onto the boat.' I grin and we stand there in the chilly air and kiss for a minute, our cold noses touching and arms wrapped right around each other. It's sexy, yes, but it's more than that. It's like she warms me all the way through and my insides just can't hold it all in, making me ache with happiness, but a happiness that's tearing something within me. Like I'll never quite get everything I want from it. I've never done drugs – other than whatever we're drip-fed in the house – but I reckon this must be how drugs make you feel.

We walk away from the house and to the end of the road where the solid wooden jetty takes over from the tarmac and extends out over the sea. Something thuds gently underneath, making us both jump. Down to one side, a small rowing boat is tied to a wooden post that sticks out from the water like a broken bone. The boat bobs in the water, ducking under the jetty like a shy child and then peeking out again. We lie down on the rough cold grit and peer at it.

'We won't get very far in that,' I whisper. It's a rickety old thing and there's only one oar. Whoever lives here might like to muddy his boots on the wild land but he's clearly not a fisherman.

The wind picks up and the cold slice of air sends the boat beneath us again as we shiver. 'No, but we could hide in it. If we knew when the supply boat was coming, we could sneak out and hide there. While they're all busy loading and unloading, we'll creep on and stow away. It's not like they'll be expecting it. I bet there's only the captain and the truck driver aboard.'

'We might actually do it.' My heart races. I've blocked out the fact that I'm defective and suddenly the future feels endless. 'We just need to find out when that boat's due back. My guess is once a month.'

'Which means only about two more weeks.'

I scramble to my feet and pull her up. 'Let's go down to the cave and plan.' I like the cave. I even like the way it washes clean every day so each time we're there it's fresh and new.

We race there, sure of the path by now, and we laugh loudly knowing no one can hear us. We're warm, glowing and giggling when we arrive. We've brought the candle from the church and we light it. Ashley hasn't noticed it burns down overnight. He's too busy thinking about things that aren't real to see what's right in front of him. Me and Clara, we're all about the real. Right now, the real is good. We put the candle on a natural ledge in the rock wall at the back of the cave and sit down together and talk. The words come out in a rush of excitement. We're not even in the cave now, we're already across the water and free. We'll go somewhere far away. She'll cut her hair and dye it. We'll steal identities from old school friends who won't notice their passports are gone and flee somewhere warm where we can sit by an ocean and sell stuff on the beach to get by. At night we'll sleep out under the stars. We'll make a bonfire if we get cold and play guitar and sing songs. Our friends will all be people like us, carefree drifters. Maybe we'll get married in a hippy ceremony at some old ruins. It's perfect. It's going to be perfect. We'll run and run and we won't look back. Maybe in a few years' time we'll send postcards to our families and tell them we're fine. But maybe we won't.

'It doesn't matter how long we've got,' she says happily, leaning into my shoulder. 'It's going to be brilliant.'

Behind us, the tiny candle flame clings valiantly to life in the cold, and in front the black sea rustles against the sand, lazily stretching into the night.

'It's pretty brilliant now,' I say, tightening my arm around her.

'Yes. Yes, it is.'

We kiss some more, but this time for longer and as we lean back against the uneven wall, she slides her hand inside my coat and under my shirt. She's breathing as hard as I am, but when her cold fingers touch my skin I let out a sound that's somewhere between a gasp and a moan. This isn't new. I may not have done 'it' but I've come this far with girls before. Only this is Clara, and this is a different world and everything feels new. She presses closer into me, tilting forward as my own clumsy, shaking hand fumbles with her coat buttons. She smiles, barely breaking from the kiss and helps me, deftly finishing the last two and pulling her coat open. She untucks her shirt, her eyes fixed on mine. I swallow and then we're kissing again, her fingers trailing up and down my chest and stomach, making my muscles contract and my whole body ache. As eager as I am to touch her, I'm also terrified, and as my awkward hand slips under her jumper I try to mimic her movements. She's so soft and warm, and as I touch her she moans into my mouth. A deep sound, earthy and natural. She takes my wrist and guides me up to her bra. My heart is pounding so hard I think it might explode. I feel cotton and lace holding in the curve of unfamiliar weight and she pushes harder against me, and before I die of fear or anticipation I pull the material down and my hand is on her naked breast. I hold it for a second, not sure what to do next, and as she pushes her tongue against mine, I brush my fingers across it. Her nipple is taut and hard and her breathing is nearly faster than mine.

She breaks away, impatient, and wriggles out of her coat. For a moment, as I stare, dumbfounded, lost and helpless, I see her skin, pale like marble, and the perfect curve of her breast – not like Julie McKendrick's at all, smaller and high and brilliantly real. She's not even Clara any more, not in my head. She is and she isn't. She's the Clara who's my friend but also some strange, mysterious creature filled with a terrible power. A mermaid come to shore. Her mouth is slightly open as she puts her hands in my hair and pulls my face down to her chest. I feel dizzy with the smell of her, and as I lick and suck and hope I'm doing it right, my other hand loses its terror and shyness and pushes its way into the other half of her bra.

Her hand is on my thigh, her fingers stroking up and down the denim but not going *there*, and I just want to push her to the ground and rub against her before the strain of it all kills me. Blood is pounding in my head. Blood is pounding everywhere. When I close my eyes I see stars behind the lids.

I come up and kiss her again, more urgently this time, my fear and shyness overwhelmed by this terrible, beautiful want. After a moment, she breaks away. We stare, breathless, at each other. Familiar strangers. Something different from what we were before, but not quite what we will become. She's entirely magical. I'm not even sure she's real any more.

'We should get back,' she says. 'Check on Georgie before bed.'

I nod. I can't speak yet.

We blow out the candle and start our walk back. We're quiet this time, holding hands and just smiling at each other now and then. It's good. It's all good. Even the crazy lust that's humming under my skin like a swarm of ants.

'Are you happy?' she asks as the house appears, looming over us.

'Yes. Are you?'

'Yes.'

The house looks smaller when I next glance up. It can't beat us. We're going to leave it behind.

'I'm not sick. I'm really not. It's just because I'm nervous. It'll go away.' Henry said the same thing to anyone who'd listen. No one believed him. It was obvious that something was going wrong inside him. Something very not right. He hadn't been twitching when he arrived, despite what he claimed. By the time he was shuffling around the house trying to control the random movements of

his arms and legs, they were all fascinated, Toby included. They all knew what it was, too. It was like in those films with hostages where one person is selected to be shot and they look around, full of disbelief, at the rest, who are just guilty-glad it's not their turn yet. Henry was going to be the first.

He'd started to tic on the third day. Until then, in a weird way, they'd found the whole situation of being in the house funny. They hadn't really believed it. The playroom was always full and the dorms mingled – although Jake was definitely top of the heap. They watched the films he chose. Played the games he suggested. They lied to each other about the brilliance or awfulness of their lives before. The house was louder, then. More laughter.

At first they didn't notice the slight jolts and tics. They figured maybe Henry had been twitching before. It wasn't like he was a centre-of-attention kid. No one really paid him any heed. He'd marked his card from that first whiny moment when they'd arrived. Even when the twitches first became more pronounced – like when he'd gone to take a mouthful of cereal and a jerk in his shoulder made him miss – the others had just shrugged it off and laughed. Henry was a nervous, geeky kid. Maybe the twitches were just some freaky reaction to being put in the house.

I think there's been a mistake.

'That isn't normal.' It was Louis who'd come

right out and said it first. Henry was holding his left wrist down with his right hand and trying to make it look casual, but Toby could see it was taking a lot of effort. The fingers of his left hand were flexing and spasming, as if Henry was trying to hold down a slippery suffocating fish.

'You okay, Henry?' Will asked. 'Maybe you should go and see Matron.'

'I'm fine.' Henry's mouth strained into a smile. 'It's nothing. Happens sometimes.'

'Oh. Okay.' Will just shrugged and went back to staring at the old sci-fi film on the screen. Louis glanced at Toby. They could both see what Will hadn't – the dread in Henry's eyes. The fear. Whatever the twitches were, they weren't normal.

The nurses were watching, too. Their eyes rested on him dispassionately. Assessing.

Henry cracked on the third day. Out of nowhere. It was teatime and he was sitting with his dorm, trying to scoop soup into his mouth. The boy next to him helped. Everyone was watching – you couldn't not. Even though Toby had been determined not to look, there was something horrifically compelling about seeing someone slowly falling apart. Especially for the first time.

Jake's table was between theirs and Henry's and Jake was watching, too. 'Hey, Henry,' he called out. 'You turning into a dribbling spastic?' He stuck his tongue down behind his bottom lip and grunted while flapping his arms around. Everyone laughed. Toby smiled. It was the first time they'd turned on someone as a group. The boy helping Henry with his soup put the spoon down. No one was going up against Jake.

Henry stared at Jake for a moment. Where Jake's eyes were alive with malicious humour, Henry's were dark hollows staring out with a crippling fear none of them could understand. He was in a bubble of Henry. The rest of them were on the outside, and when he suddenly burst into tears, the line was set.

'I want my mum. I want to go home.' It was a snotty wail, not even that loud, but it cut through them all. There were a couple of awkward giggles and then silence. The shuffling of chairs. Toby felt his throat close with a sudden stab of nausea. 'I don't want to be here. I don't want to die here.' Henry twisted around in his chair and stared at the nurses, his voice dropping but his words clear in the quiet. 'I don't want to die. I want to go home. I want my mum.' The nurses stared back, their faces impassive, and in some ways that was scarier than Henry's panic.

No one ate much after that. Henry looked around for some support, but everyone's eyes dropped to plates of food that were no longer appetising. Toby glanced at him. It was there in the boy's sweaty face – he knew he'd fucked up. He knew something had changed with his outburst – he'd made them *face something they didn't want to see and no one would ever forgive him for it.*

Sometimes, when Toby thought about it afterwards, about how poor Henry had become an outcast in that moment, about how they'd all wanted to batter him into silence, it was clear that Henry made the house change. He'd spoken what they'd all been feeling; he'd wanted to share his terror with them when they were all trying to deal with their own. That was when the dorms closed inwards, protecting themselves. Henry was the first name that no one ever mentioned again.

They'd scurried straight back to their dorms after tea, whispering among themselves. Henry had tried to grab a couple of the younger kids as they passed, saying his tics were nothing, he was just upset, he wasn't sick, but no one would even meet his eyes as they pulled their arms free and shoved him away.

He was quiet for a while, but within an hour they could hear him crying again. He called, and then screamed, for his mum. Over and over until his throat was hoarse. Toby wondered if maybe a fever had got him by then.

'I wish he'd shut up.' Louis' face was strained, as if the muscles were pulling back into his skull. 'Why won't he shut up?'

Will was singing quietly to himself. Toby went and had the first of his long evening baths, letting the running water drown out the sounds that made his stomach knot. The knot never left him after that. His ball of dread was born that night. In the end, the nurses must have sedated Henry because by the time Toby unlocked the bathroom door and returned to Dorm 4, the house was silent.

In the morning, Henry was gone. So was all trace of him – his clothes, his toothbrush, his flannel, the geeky T-shirt he wore all the time. It was as if he'd never existed. All Matron said was that Henry had been taken to the sanatorium. A short, sharp sentence that forbade any questions. After the first hubbub of whispered discussion, no one mentioned Henry's name again. It was easier that way. They could pretend it had never happened.

It was easier for the others than for Toby.

The night they'd taken Henry was the first night he hadn't taken his 'vitamins'. He wasn't even sure why. His throat was dry and tight. He wanted to reject something about the house and that was his only option. A small moment of rebellion. He got more than he'd bargained for.

That was the first time he heard the chugging heart of the lift and the steady squeak of bed wheels. It wouldn't be the last. Henry taught them lots of things even if they'd pushed him out of their memories. He'd taught them that there was no point in crying. There was no point in calling for help. Mainly he taught them that when it came for you, you were on your own. When the second boy fell ill, another lesson was added. There was no one way to go. There were no definite symptoms.

If you thought about it hard enough, you could be scared of everything.

TWELVE

'I can't remember it ever being this cold.' Eleanor has her nose pressed against the playroom window. Outside the rain is thick and heavy, more like shards of ice hammering at the ground than water. It's laundry day and we've all dutifully changed our sheets – top to bottom and bottom in the laundry sack with pillowcases – and now the afternoon stretches out ahead of us. Will is in the battered armchair by the radiator concentrating on his book as Louis tries to teach Clara and me to play chess. I'm bored already. I can't sit opposite Clara and think about anything other than Clara. I'm pretty pathetic. I'm also pretty sure I'm in love.

'Can you?' Eleanor looks around and we all shake our heads. The weather is definitely weird, but then I've never been this far north before so fuck knows what's normal.

'Jesus, these are all so old.' Tom is browsing the records in the corner trying to find something he's heard of to play. I want to tell him some of them are quite good, but I don't. Dancing in here in the dark is a secret. It was Clara's secret first, and now it's mine and Clara's. We danced together last night. I didn't even feel too much of a dick once she'd made me close my eyes and just go for it. I probably looked like one, but I didn't feel like one. Who cares, anyway? How you feel matters way more than how you look. That's what Clara said. But then, she looked great.

'What do you expect?' I say. 'You ever even seen a record player before you got here?'

'It's your turn, Toby,' Louis says, and I realise I haven't even seen Clara make her move.

The door opens and Jake swaggers in with Albi and Daniel. He tries to make it look casual but his eyes go straight to Clara. There's no need to wonder where Joe is. His loyalties are with Ashley and the church now. Every day, more and more are spending their time in the room upstairs. We never ask Ashley about it – why give him the opportunity to smugly ramble on? – but whereas we used to be divided into dorm loyalties, it's shifting more and more to who does or doesn't believe. It bugs the shit out of Tom, but I let it slide over me. The days don't really count any more, even though I've stopped sleeping the afternoons away. I'm too excited about the nights to sleep much. It's easier to try and keep busy. It makes time go quicker. I remember when I used to try and make time slow down by getting as bored as possible. Everything is on its head these days.

'You guys want to do something?' Jake says. 'Dick around in the music room, maybe?'

He *means* does Clara want to do anything. He doesn't give a shit about the rest of us.

'Not enough space for all of us in there,' Clara murmurs, not looking up.

'We could play hide and seek?' Eleanor says, hopefully.

Daniel sniggers as if this is the stupidest suggestion he's ever heard. His fat face is a moon of mean. The only thing worse than a bully is a wannabe bully.

'I'm up for that,' I say. 'I'm shit at this anyway. Will?'

'Yep!' He's already putting his book down. Eleanor claps her hands together, excited. 'I'll be It! You all hide! I'll count to a hundred.'

'But count slowly.' Clara gets up. 'No cheating.'

'Yeah, no cheating,' Jake repeats. It makes me laugh seeing Jake going along with whatever Clara does. It must be hard for Daniel to know whether to sneer or smile.

'It's a kids' game, man,' Albi mutters.

'You got a better idea?' Jake snaps.

Albi withers into his hoodie and shakes his head. 'I was just saying.'

'Guess it's worth one go.' Daniel sniffs, his hands

thrust deep in his jeans pockets, making his belly stick out even more than usual. Daniel may not be destined to grow up, but he's already the shadow of the man he would have become.

'No one's forcing you to play.' Tom stares at the fat boy, his dark eyes full of disdain, as if Daniel is a cockroach that needs crushing. Tom's like me. He might be wary of taking Jake on, but no little shit gets to try and be the man around us.

'I said I'll play,' Daniel says, his voice more of a whine this time as he gets no support from either Jake or Albi. I wonder if he was bullied in school *before*. Maybe that's it. Shit-eater turned shit-head in one easy diagnosis.

'One one thousand, two one thousand . . .' We leave Eleanor facing the wall and counting steadily and hurry out into the corridor. When no one's looking, Clara gives my hand a small squeeze and it runs right up my arm to my heart. I wink at her and her face tinges red. She likes me as much as I like her. Of all the weirdness in the house, that's the thing I find the strangest. Epically brilliant, but fucking strange. I keep expecting her to wake up and change her mind. But she doesn't.

We split up at the stairs and Jake goes in the same direction as Clara, obviously wanting to hide in the same place and get some 'alone time' with her. Daniel heads towards the showers. None of us goes down the corridor to where the church is. I can hear them singing as I go up a floor. He's teaching them fucking hymns. I can't remember the last time I heard someone singing a hymn. Maybe at a wedding my parents dragged me to. I try and zone it out but the music floats after me.

The problem with the house is that it's so big there's almost too many places to hide, and yet not enough. There's no quirkily cluttered rooms. Everything is practical. I end up under a bed in one of the empty dorms. I bet nearly all of us are hiding under beds. The floorboards smell of polished wood, rich and tangy. I wait and my ears buzz in the silence. It's not comfortable under here and I hope Eleanor finds me soon. I stare up at the crisscross of metal bedsprings so I don't have to look at the locked wheels and hear their squealing in my head. I backed Eleanor's idea in order to piss Jake off, but I'm too old for this shit. At least if I'd been the seeker there would have been something to do. Or if we'd played Sardines and made Eleanor hide. Maybe I'll suggest that for the next round. I wriggle about, trying to find a spot that doesn't dig into my hipbones or shoulders and my nose itches with the shifted dust. I should have gone behind a curtain.

'Clara! Will! Come here! Quick!'

I've been hiding about ten minutes when Eleanor's shout reaches me. She's nearby somewhere.

'I've found something!'

At first I don't twig, but as I scramble out I realise with dread what's got her so excited. I race up the half-flight of stairs and run fast down the long corridor. I don't listen for her voice to guide me. I know where she's shouting from. Why the fuck did I agree we should play this stupid game? Why didn't I think?

She's got the wardrobe open and she's down on her knees with the box in her lap when I rush in, breathless. Clara's already there, and so's Jake, but no one else. Wherever the others are hiding, they couldn't have heard her calling. I look at Clara. We're both full of dread.

'It was in here. Just sitting in the box!' Eleanor's face is bright with excitement. She leans forward and stares at the wooden back of the cupboard. 'It's like the wardrobe from Narnia,' she says. 'It's magic!'

'Don't talk wank,' Jake says gruffly. 'Someone put it there.' He crouches beside her and takes the box. 'Get out and shut the door behind you.' Seeing him with Georgie, I feel sick. He looks up at Eleanor. 'Go and carry on looking for the others. And no more shouting.' Eleanor almost says something, but with me and Clara silent, she just does what she's told.

We stand there in silence after the door clicks shut. Jake looks down into the box for a few moments and strokes the bird's head. He's very gentle and that surprises me. The air between us crackles with tension, though.

'His wing stinks,' he says eventually, and goes to lift Georgie out of his box. He's right, it does smell. Georgie's got steadily worse and no matter how much we try and clean his wing, the pus keeps bubbling out of the gash that won't heal.

'He's mine,' Clara says quickly. 'Don't hurt him. I found him in the garden. I wanted to make him better.'

'When did you find him?' Jake doesn't look up. I can't read his expression as he lays the bird on his lap and carefully spreads out the damaged wing. I can see where the feathers are matted. Georgie lets out a chirp so quiet that if we weren't all trapped in this terrible acute silence, I wouldn't have heard it at all.

'A little while ago.' Clara drops to her knees beside Jake as I continue to stand like a useless twat, not knowing what to do or say. 'Don't hurt him.'

Jake looks at her then, a vague disgust in his eyes. 'Why would I hurt him?' Clara says nothing, just shrugs, uncertain. We're on a tightrope, I can feel it. Worse than that, we're about to slip off and I can't put my finger on why.

'He's dying,' Jake says. 'That stink is all the poison in him. His wing's rotting away. You should have left him where he was – it would have been quicker.'

'What makes you the expert?' The words are out before I can stop them. Georgie's ours, mine and

Clara's, and we're going to make him better and set him free. Clara's eyes well up and my face is hot.

'My uncle knew about animals. He used to go hunting.' He doesn't look at me when he speaks, as if I don't even matter. 'So he's yours, then, Clara? You hid him here?'

She tries to smile. 'Yes. I just wanted something of my own.'

He nods, slowly and precisely, as if processing something. He's so controlled. Quiet. I've never seen him like this.

'So, if it's *your* secret,' his voice is low, 'then how come *his* hoodie is in the box?'

Clara's mouth drops open as she fumbles for something to say. I see my hoodie, crumpled in the bottom of Georgie's nest, covered in bird shit and feathers. That's it. We're off the tightrope and plummeting to the ground. Jake's face is the worst. Embarrassed. Humiliated. Recalling all the times he showed off around Clara, trying to get her attention. All the times she laughed at his crazy jokes. And knowing all the time that she'd shared Georgie with me. He doesn't know about the night-times. He doesn't know everything. But he knows *enough*. It's the hurt in his eyes I can't stand. He liked her. He *really* liked her.

'It's just that—'

'I can see how it is.' He cuts me off. He's still stroking Georgie very gently, the bird leaning his head into Jake's hand as if he can feel how much care there is in his touch. Everything is at odds. 'I'm not fucking stupid.'

'Look, I like you, Jake, and . . .' Clara reaches forward to touch him and I want to tell her to stop, that she'll only make things worse. He's burning up inside. We've made him feel like a complete cock, and there's no taking that back with something that sounds like pity. I want the ground to swallow me. I want to be in the cave. I want to be anywhere but here.

'Just shut up.' He sounds weary. That scares me more than if he was shouting. 'Now go and wait outside. Both of you. You don't want to see this.'

'What are you going to do, Jake?' Tears are stinging my eyes. I sound like a whining child. Younger than Will. Everything is beyond my control. 'Don't take it out on Georgie. Why don't you just hit me or something instead?'

He rounds on me then, snarling, 'You think I'm going to take it out on some sick fucking bird? Who the fuck do you think I am? Who the fuck do you think *you* are? You don't fucking know me.' His hands are still so gentle on Georgie, but his words spit out like shards of glass. 'I'm going to do what you should have done. I'm going to put him out of his misery. Now. *Fuck*. *Off*.'

He's trembling. It's anger and upset and shame, all bound up into a terrible rage. Clara's crying and she leans forward and strokes Georgie's head. He doesn't even look up. Jake's right, of course. We've been kidding ourselves. He was never going to get better.

'Come on,' I mutter and take Clara's hand, pulling her up to her feet. Jake doesn't look at us. My head swims and my ears buzz. I can barely swallow. We don't look back as we walk away, but once outside, Clara collapses, sobbing, into my chest. I don't say anything, just hold her tight as she squeezes me back. We cling to each other like we have nowhere else to go. And maybe we don't.

I've no idea how long it is before Jake opens the door and comes out. Probably no more than a minute but it feels like longer. I'm filled with the memory of Georgie's little heart beating fast under my fingers. I remember how Clara wanted to set him free.

When I take the box from Jake and look down, Georgie's gone. There's just an empty dead thing in his place, still and silent, with its head at an odd angle.

'Bury him if you want,' Jake says and then heads downstairs. I watch him go. Clara is still crying for Georgie but suddenly I'm more worried about Jake. This isn't over. Not even nearly.

'Are we still playing or what?' Will is on the first landing as we come by. 'What's going on? Why's Jake stormed off?' He sees Clara's blotchy face and looks puzzled. 'Why's Clara crying?'

'Just shut up, Will,' I mutter, pushing past him. 'Not now.' Eleanor will tell him anyway. By teatime everyone's going to know.

The rain is like ice. There's no wind and it falls on us in sheets as we dig a small hole in the wet ground with our bare hands. Clara's hair is slick and flat against her face as we claw the earth away, mud sinking under our fingernails. We're both shivering in the biting cold but I don't actually feel it. I know it's there, I know I'm wet and freezing, but somehow that doesn't touch me on the inside.

I take Georgie out of the box and place him carefully into the wet earth, still wrapped in my hoodie. It's stupid, but I don't want him to be cold in the ground, even though the heat has already vanished from his small body. He ate the worms and now the worms will eat him. The thought comes from nowhere and it makes me shudder slightly.

'Goodbye, Georgie,' Clara says, her words deadened by the rain. Water runs over her face and drips from her nose. I can't tell if she's crying. 'I'm sorry you didn't fly away.' We gently cover him over, as if he can still feel something, and then stare at the bare patch of ground. The rain patters out a dire funeral beat in the trees. Otherwise it's silent. Suddenly I'm thinking about Ellory and Henry and the rest. Alone and cold in the earth somewhere. Or maybe they burn us. I can't decide which is worse, which I'd prefer, and then I remember that they're nothing now and they feel nothing and the ball in my stomach flares in a way it hasn't since Clara first kissed me.

'Feed the trees well, little friend,' Clara says. 'Reach the sunlight.'

I look at her then. Her lips are pale with cold and her freckles bright against her white skin. It's a beautiful, comforting thing she just said. A lifeboat on the ocean of dread. My heart squeezes and my stomach untangles. I know right there and then that I love her. Right down in the middle of me.

There's no time to change before the gong goes so we arrive at tea dripping wet and muddy, marking out our separation from the rest. The nurses say nothing as I collect my plate of shepherd's pie and peas. This isn't *before*. What's the point of them telling us to dry off or get warm? Why worry about a Defective catching the flu? Even though it's clear from the way eyes follow us that the story of the bird has spread, I don't look back at Clara as we head to our different tables. I don't look at Jake's table, either, although I hear their sniggers as I go by. I keep my eyes straight ahead.

'So,' I can see Will trying to make sense of it all as he speaks, 'when did you find the bird?'

'Clara found it.' I push a forkful of food in my mouth and force myself to chew. It's hot at least, warming me even though I'm not hungry at all. 'She told me about it the other day. No big deal.'

'When?' Louis is equally curious. I can see them trying to put the timeline together. Figuring out when it could possibly have happened.

'Can't remember exactly. Maybe when I was sleeping one afternoon.' It sounds like a good lie. Louis and Will learned early on not to nag me while I slept. They nod, but I don't think they're buying it. Not Louis, anyway. He's too clever. His brain is like a computer.

'Why you?' Tom is sullen, head down over his food. When he looks at me, his dislike is obvious. I guess he'd half-expected to lose Clara to Jake. I'm a curveball in his disappointment. 'Seems weird. You never speak to her.'

'We speak sometimes.' I shrug, trying to look casual. 'Maybe I was just there.'

'I think she fancies you,' Will says suddenly, an impish grin on his small face. 'I think you fancy her, too. Why would you keep it a secret otherwise?' I glower at him over my fork, but that just makes his smile wider. He wriggles in his seat. 'Have you snogged her? Is she your girlfriend?'

Tom stares at me, half-wanting the answer and half-not wanting to know.

'Oh, fuck off,' I mumble.

'Must be,' Louis says. 'Jake's flipping out. He's kicked the God Squad off his table.'

I look across to the Dorm 7 group. He's right. There's only Jake, Albi and Daniel, talking and laughing together, Daniel sending snide glances back towards us. Towards me. Ashley, Harriet, Joe and a few of the others have moved and filled an empty table at the other end of the room near where Clara and Eleanor are.

'What's he going to do to us, Toby?' Louis asks. 'It's been all right these past few days. All of us mucking around together.' I can see he's nervous and I know why. Jake won't like that he showed weakness. He's got his image to protect. It's all he *does* have.

'We'll have to wait and see,' I mutter. I feel bad for them. I don't want them to get in trouble or be scared. Mainly I feel bad because *everyone* knows. I don't want it to break anything. I don't want it to break me and Clara.

'We should get Clara and Eleanor to come and sit with us from now on.' Will is matter-of-fact as he shoves bread and butter into his mouth. 'Seems stupid to sit apart if she's your girlfriend. She's cool, anyway. So's Eleanor. Isn't she, Louis?'

Louis nods. 'For a girl.'

'Jake won't like that,' Tom says.

'Jake already doesn't like it, so what's the difference?'

Sometimes I wonder if Will is smarter than he looks.

*

They took their lunch out to the slope that led down to the tennis courts and sat cross-legged on it. Technically, all lunch had to be eaten in the dining hall, but it was hot and stuffy in the heatwave and Toby's sandwiches were soggy enough already. Not that he was particularly hungry. Jonesy had bought chips at break and they'd made rolls from them with the bread from his mum's sandwiches. He cracked open a Coke, swigged a load down and then let out a long belch.

Jonesy laughed. 'Yeah, that's going to get you into McKendrick's knickers.'

'Oh, fuck off.' Toby grinned.

'So what time's this party we're going to, then?'

'Dunno. About eight, I think.' He looked down through the ring pull to the fizzing liquid. He hadn't told Jonesy he didn't want him to come yet. It wasn't that he didn't want him there, but Julie hadn't invited him, so it wasn't like he could take him, was it? He told himself that to feel better, but deep down he was just worried that with Jonesy along he'd have no chance of fitting in. Or of getting any time alone with Julie. Together, they were just a pair of Year 11 twats, but on his own he had half a chance of at least pretending to be something else. Still, it made him feel a bit shit.

'It's going to be so cool. You can have Julie, I'll have her mate.' Jonesy lay back on the grass and grinned. 'I've heard she blows anyone.'

'Yeah, right, like she's going to blow you. You'd have to drug her first and I'm not sure a blowjob's going to work when she's unconscious.'

They laughed again as Jonesy called him a dick. It was a good day, despite the bollocking he'd got for not doing his History essay. He didn't want to spoil it. The sun was shining and tomorrow there was a very good chance he'd get to snog Julie McKendrick. Maybe do even more than that. The sun was bright and full of hope above him. He'd tell Jonesy tomorrow. By text or something. He'd say Julie'd told him he couldn't bring anyone.

'Maybe this is it, Tobes,' Jonesy said. 'Maybe this is when we finally get cool.' He sounded so content it made Toby feel bad. Maybe he should take him. They were best friends, after all. If it all went tits-up with Julie – he took a moment to smile at his own play on words – then he was going to need Jonesy. Maybe he shouldn't be so fucking shallow about it. But still, the thought of walking into that party with Jonesy grinning like some excited kid made him squirm with embarrassment.

The football came out of the blue, the sudden thump as it hit Jonesy jolting them out of their daydreams. To be more accurate, the ball hit Jonesy's can, sending it spraying sticky-sweet lemonade all over Jonesy's shirt and face.

'What fucker did that?' Jonesy was up on his

feet in a moment, pissed off and scanning the field for Year 8s. 'Who the fuck did that?'

Toby clambered to his feet as the spilled drink spread across the grass. He squinted into the sunlight at the group coming towards them. They were tall.

'Who are you calling a fucker?'

Billy. It was Billy from Year 13. Of course it was. Toby's heart sank as Jonesy visibly shrivelled.

'Sorry, Bill, I didn't realise—'

'Don't call me Bill. No one calls me Bill.'

'Come on, Jonesy,' Toby muttered, gathering up their stuff. 'Let's—' But he didn't finish the sentence. Let's go, he'd been about to say. Let's run the fuck away. But then he saw her. Julie McKendrick was there, part of Billy's entourage. And she was watching him.

'You spilled his drink, man. It went all over him. Let's just call it quits.' He didn't know where the words came from. Jonesy stared at him in disbelief. Some of the sixth-formers were virtually adults. Not Billy. Billy might be big but he hadn't done much growing up. He'd been mean as a kid and he was mean now he was nearly done with school. Billy lived for moments like this.

'Who asked you?'

Toby looked at Billy and then glanced beyond him to Julie McKendrick. How badly could Billy hurt him? He didn't want to know the answer to that. But neither could he face the shame of walking away like a coward in front of Julie. And on top of everything else, he was hot and bothered and Billy ought to be too old for this kind of shit.

'I'm just saying don't be an arsehole. Just take your ball and leave us alone.'

Billy laughed at that; a short, surprised bark that came from deep in his thick chest, and Jonesy was looking at Toby wide-eyed as if he was a stranger.

'And who the fuck are you?' Billy stepped in closer.

'Why don't we go back inside?' Julie said. 'It's too hot out here anyway.' She shuffled from foot to foot, awkward. It was clear she had no faith in Toby doing well against Billy. From inside his fear, Toby figured she had a point.

'Look, I don't see why—' His breath was coming fast as Billy squared up ready to push him over, and then, like a miracle, a whistle blew.

'Oi! You boys! Whatever you're about to do, change your minds.' Mr Mason, Head of PE, was striding towards them. 'And get your lunch off the grass.'

Jonesy was already hurrying away. 'Come on, Tobes. Let's go.'

Toby held Billy's gaze for a moment longer.

'Fuck off, you little runt.'

Toby tried to keep his pace steady as he walked

away but his legs were shaking. Julie smiled and winked at him as he passed her. His legs shook a bit harder after that.

THIRTEEN

I undo the ball of my bedpost and carefully pull out the scrunched-up wrap of toilet paper and add tonight's pill to the collection inside. In the beginning, each one was a small victory, but now there are so many I can't help thinking that my time will run out soon. Which of us will go next? I screw the tatty paper up again and stuff it back inside my bedpost. I've got more urgent things to think about than my impending death – which, if I'm honest, even in my most terrified moments is still abstract. We're all stuck in our own Henry moment of *I think there's been a mistake*, me included. Until the sanatorium, anyway. Or until I feel a strange ache or pain and wonder if it's just something normal or if it's suddenly *my turn*, and I lie in the bath and run through my checks with my heart racing. Most of the time that terrifying nothingness is still something that's going to happen to the others. Not to me. Never to me or Clara. We don't belong here. We're going to get away.

I find her in the playroom – neither of us is hungry tonight – and we kneel on the old sofa and stare out at the endless rain. The house feels vaster without Georgie in it. He'd become part of our routine and now he's gone. Clara's face is tight, fraught with worry. I'm not used to seeing her like that.

'You and Eleanor can come and sit with us if you want. You know, in the dining room. Will suggested it. I think it's a good idea.' I sound upbeat and I feel it. For once, I'm the carefree one. Will was right. What's the point of cowering and pretending nothing's changed? Why waste our time ignoring each other just because of what other people want?

'What about Jake?' She bites her bottom lip.

'He's mad already. So what if he gets a bit madder?' I grin at her. 'Why should we care what he thinks anyway? He's not your dad. These are *our* lives. Why should we be unhappy to make him happy?'

'Maybe it's my fault. Maybe I led him on.'

'Why would you say that?' A sharp knife twists inside me. 'You never kissed him or anything, did you?' I still sometimes think about that date night in the playroom, even though I know it's stupid.

'Of course not. But I knew he liked me. I just thought he'd taken the hint.'

'Then it's not your fault. And he'll get over it.' I made a silent wish for a new van to arrive with a selection of hot girls for Jake to take his pick from. It would be easier for him to move on if there were some distractions. Tom, too.

'It feels strange that people know, doesn't it?' she says softly. 'Do you think it will change us?'

My heart drops then. 'Why would it? Anyway, they don't know the half of it, do they? They know about Georgie. They know we like each other. They don't know about any of this.' I look around at the gloom we do our best living in.

'You might be different now. With people watching. You might be embarrassed about it. I know what boys are like.'

This is what she's looking so stressed about? She's worried how I'll behave? I stare at her, dumbfounded, until eventually she turns to look at me, her mermaid hair trailing and twisting down her shoulders.

'I love you, Clara.' The words tingle right through me and the final dust of Julie McKendrick's ghost is blown away in their vibration. She was never real, just a fantasy, a childish crush. 'I'll never love anyone like this. I never could. Not out there. Not *before*. Not ever, no matter what the future holds.'

'You mean that?' she whispers eventually.

I nod. I do mean it. I mean every word. Doesn't stop me from feeling a bit of a twat for saying it out loud, though.

After a moment, she grins and wraps her arms around my neck. 'Well, that's all right, then. What can Jake really do about it, anyway?'

*

She doesn't say anything about Jake scrawling 'SLUT' in felt-tip on the girls' bathroom mirror upstairs, but Eleanor tells Will and Louis and of course they tell me. They spent an hour scrubbing it off before the nurses could see it. On the surface, in the three days that have passed since he found out, you wouldn't think Jake gave a shit about me and Clara – he still swaggers around like he always has, laughing and joking with his dorm, and he doesn't look over to our table at mealtimes or acknowledge us in any way – but the whole house crackles with the electricity of his anger. It's because he feels stupid. We all know that. And stupid is the most dangerous way for someone like Jake to feel. I wonder if he's lied to Daniel and Albi about him and Clara. I bet he made shit up about what he'd done with her, and now they know it isn't true. Not that they'd say anything, but it's there all the same.

It's not so bad for me and Clara because we have each other, and most of our time is spent daydreaming together and planning our nights, but for the rest the new atmosphere in the house is horrible. A dividing line has been drawn and if you're not on Jake's side of it, then it's not pleasant. Dorm 7 don't let Tom in the music room any more, even though he's been jamming with them in the evenings until now. The younger kids don't go in the playroom so much, just in case they say or do the wrong thing if Jake's in there, even though they're nothing to do with our dorm war. Louis and Will make themselves a den in one of the empty dorms, but every time they leave it, it ends up trashed. The only people not affected are the God Squad, but no one really counts them any more. We don't even pay attention to Ashley at bedtime. We talk around him as if he isn't there and he's given up trying to join in.

After lunch, Clara wants to play cards and so I've gone to look for some. I can hear the music, loud and off-beat, coming from the music room and I know it's safe to go into the playroom. Me and Jake have become like magnetic opposites over the past three days. We veer in different directions from each other. I wish he'd just punch me and then this would be over. But he can't – that would get Matron's attention – and in this quiet war we're waging, it'd break the unspoken rules.

Apparently everyone's heard the band practising because small groups are dotted around the playroom, talking or reading or playing board games. Will and Louis are sitting in a corner, staring dolefully into a cardboard box.

'What's up?' I say.

'Nothing.' Louis hurries to close the lid and Will leans forwards to block my view. He's too slow, though, and I see the rough edge of a broken board.

'Show me.'

'It doesn't matter, Toby, really it doesn't.' Will's

face, full of hurt, belies his words. I take the box and look inside. The chessboard has been broken. The pieces are smashed, and so is their collection of conkers. Pages of Will's book are torn up.

'I don't like reading that much. Eleanor can tell me the rest of the story. And we'll just make a new chessboard in the art room, won't we, Louis? There's cardboard in there.'

'Yeah, and I was bored of conkers, anyway.'

I'm still staring into the box, something bubbling in the pit of my stomach. I can hear my breath coming fast.

'Don't do anything stupid, Toby.' Will is nervous. 'It's not worth it.'

'They're in the music room, right?' My face is on fire. I keep looking at that box. A chessboard, a book and some conkers. Stuff that was important to Louis and Will. They'd obviously hidden it all away hoping Jake and his wankers wouldn't find it. What gave them the right to destroy this shit? What had Will or Louis done to provoke him to take away whatever pathetic stuff they've found to make their lives more bearable? Who the fuck were Dorm 7 anyway?

'What are you going to do, Toby?' Louis asks.

It comes to me in a flash. It's stupid and childish and brilliant.

'Come on,' I say.

They glance at each other and shrug and then are on their feet.

Louis grins. 'We going to get even?'

'I don't think we should—' Will picks at his fingernails.

'What, we should keep on letting them wreck your stuff?'

'I don't have any more stuff.' He says it plaintively, and as he does the truth of what Dorm 7 have done sinks in. His small face hardens. 'They broke my stuff.'

'Then let's go.'

I take them to our dorm where we get our water cups and fill them from the bathroom, right to the brim.

'What are we doing?' Will whispers. I don't know why he's whispering. No one's around to hear us.

'Wait and see.' We hold the cups carefully and head towards Dorm 7. I can't hear the music room from here and the house is still as I lead the way. My heart races. I feel good. I should have done this days ago.

'Careful, dumbass.' Louis giggles behind me. 'You nearly spilled that all over me.'

'Sorry,' Will whispers. 'I've got pins and needles in my leg. Must have sat on it funny.'

'Quickly,' I say, opening the door. The four beds are neatly made and the dorm is tidy, just how Matron likes it. We all lead double lives here. The one where we do all we can to be invisible to Matron and the one where we try to be ourselves. Ever since

Henry, Jake's stopped playing to the crowd in front of Matron.

I pull back Jake's blankets and top sheet and pour the water right in the middle of the mattress. Will gasps.

'Oh, shit.' Louis is breathless.

'Do theirs,' I say. 'Quickly. Then make the beds tidy again.' I'm already stretching the top sheet down on Jake's, folding the end nice and even over the blanket and tucking in one side, just like we've learned to do every morning. 'They won't know until they get into bed, and then what can they do? Complain?' I know they won't. They'll have to live with the damp until the next laundry day. If the nurses think we're fighting they'll sedate us more heavily – or worse. Me and Clara might have to be careful tonight, though. I don't know how strong the sleeping pills are. Maybe Dorm 7 will be restless.

'Oh, man, they're going to hate us,' Louis says, but he's laughing.

By the time we come back downstairs, we're all feeling good, snickering and whispering and buzzing about what we've done. As we pass the music room, Will's grin is so wide I think his face is going to split. 'Dorm Four totally rule,' he says. It feels like we're back at school.

'Just try and act normal,' I say. 'We don't want them sussing anything's up until bedtime.'

'They're going to freak.' Louis is almost jumping up and down. I don't think he's ever done anything like this in his serious, studied life. I don't imagine there were a lot of Jakes in Louis' *before*.

'Yeah, they will. But let's worry about that later.'

'I'm not worried.' Will's chest is puffed up. 'It will be worth it.'

I grin then, buoyed by their excitement. 'Yeah, it will.' Jake can bring it, for all I care. I no longer give a fuck. He shouldn't have messed with Louis and Will's things. End of.

Louis and Will head into the art room where Ashley and Harriet are making a fresh batch of posters only the converted few will read and enthusiastically start hunting for stuff to make their new chessboard. I go to the playroom to find some cards. When I get back upstairs, Clara has fallen asleep on her bed. I watch her for a while, surprised at how content I feel, and then go to my own dorm. I could use a nap, too. My bed is warm and dry. I can't wait to tell Clara what we've done.

The Dorm 7 boys do sleep through the night, but when Clara and me, almost crying with laughter, look in from the doorway, they're all curled up on top of their covers, arms hugging their knees to try and keep in whatever warmth they have. Daniel's fat arse hangs half-out of his pyjama bottoms.

'I'd like to find a flower and stick it between

those fat cheeks,' Clara whispers.

I almost feel sorry for the four of them, and then I remember the smashed chess pieces and Will's face and the fact Jake called Clara a slut. Joe might be being punished for something he hasn't done, but if we'd left his bed dry then Jake would only have taken it. This isn't going to kill them anyway. Joe can turn to his god to keep him warm. We leave them there, cold and uncovered, and head off into our night.

They come into breakfast virtually growling, sending dagger glares our way. We pretend not to notice but Will and Louis giggle constantly.

'What's going on?' Tom says, frowning.

'Jake wrecked our stuff and we got even,' Will pipes up before I can stop him. He's bursting with pride. He and Louis are looking at me like I'm some sort of hero, all awe and admiration. The Jake of Dorm 4.

'Nothing, really,' Clara says. 'Nothing with lasting damage, anyway.'

'How come no one told me?' Tom is disgruntled.

'Spur-of-the-moment thing.' I get up and head to the food station for some toast. Jake sees me and does the same. I can feel everyone watching. My nerves jangle but I'm ready for this. We're destined to have a confrontation so we might as well get it out of the way. I'm still buzzing over what we did but I don't feel invincible like Will and Louis. I also know there'll be repercussions, and if anyone's taking them, it needs to be me.

'I suppose you think that was fucking funny,' Jake says under his breath, standing close to me. I pick up two slices of white. They're cold and a bit soggy but I don't mind. Ashley is on the other side of me, scooping up some dry scrambled egg. He must be able to hear us, but he keeps his eyes on the food.

'Yeah, I do.' I smile at Jake, making sure I'm facing the rest of the room so everyone can see I'm unafraid. It's not entirely true but the others don't need to know that. Anyway, the nurses are here. He can't touch me now. 'Me and Clara didn't do anything wrong. And whatever we did wasn't Will and Louis' fault. You need to get over it.' A small part of me hopes he'll listen to reason.

'You need to shut your fucking mouth.' His jaw is so tight I'm surprised he can even get the words out. 'Playroom. After lunch. No marks on the face.'

So we're going to fight after all. 'I'll check my schedule. I might have a date. You know, now that I have a girlfriend and everything.' I wink at him and his fingers clench hard against his plate. I really shouldn't wind him up any more. Even in a straight fight I've got no chance against Jake, and I have a feeling he won't play straight.

'This isn't about her,' he says. And I believe him.

It isn't any more. It's about everything we've been repressing since we arrived here. It's about all the anger and frustration and fear. For the first time in my life I think a fight might be good for me, even if I know I'm going to lose.

'I'll be there,' I say casually as I head back to my table. 'Wouldn't miss it.'

Even the God Squad have been watching and Ashley's eyes follow me all the way to my seat.

The morning passes slowly. I veer between overconfidence and wondering what the fuck I've done. It's like I'm back on the grass walking away from Billy in Year 13 but this time no van is coming to steal me away before I get the shit kicked out of me. I spend most of the lesson time staring out of the window but the teachers don't seem to care. They're all in good moods for some reason. By 'good moods' I mean they manage a smile and look just as distracted as me. Tom slips me a note saying he'll be my backup. It makes me feel better. Like maybe he's forgiven me a bit for Clara, but I'm also guessing he doesn't trust Jake, either.

I start to worry that Jake's going to shank me or something but tell myself I'm overthinking. He'll just give me a thorough kicking. Knock me down and then no doubt let Albi and fat Daniel get the boot in too, for revenge. I don't come out the winner in any of the scenarios that run through my mind.

The best I can see in my future is some broken ribs. The worst, being stabbed in the liver with broken glass or something and me bleeding to death on the playroom floor.

My biggest real fear is that I'll cry. I have no idea how it feels to get beaten up. The last physical fight I had was when I was twelve, and most of that was just shoving, flailing and slapping. Jake has been to reform school. He's going to be a fucking expert in pain.

I think about the chessboard and the book and the conkers and wonder how such a collection of shit got me into this mess. I wonder if being kicked repeatedly in the gut – because I know I'm not going to stay on my feet for long – could activate my Defectiveness. That's what makes the worms in my stomach wriggle the most. But there's no backing out now. I wouldn't be able to face Clara or Will or Louis again. Or even fucking Ashley, for that matter.

My palms sweat until lunchtime. I try to stay cool and casual but as the morning ticks away my nerves steadily increase until I feel sick. I've always been the joker in the pack. I'm not the kid who got the girls or started fights. Even in those last days when I thought my luck was finally turning with Julie McKendrick and the party, I ended up in Defective jail instead.

I decide that if I can at least land one punch on Jake somewhere then I won't feel too bad. That and not crying. Not crying is imperative. I manage a relatively good impression of external calm through lunch, even though I only push my food around my plate rather than eating it. Throwing up would be nearly as bad as crying – although maybe I could throw up *in* Jake's face. That would end the fight pretty quickly.

'You don't have to do it, you know,' Clara whispers to me. 'Fighting's stupid.' I can see she's worried. Her eyes keep darting across to the Dorm 7 table where Jake is eating normally and Daniel keeps squirming around in his chair and sniggering at me. His eyes are alive with delight and I'm tempted to go over there and punch him in his fat head. Daniel isn't Jake, and he never will be.

'Sometimes it's better to just walk away. Who gives a shit about Jake, anyway?'

I want to tell her that it's not even about Jake. I'm suddenly understanding what *being* Jake must feel like. Having others expect things from you. This isn't about Jake. It's about Tom and Louis and Will. I can't disappoint them. What would it do to Louis and Will if they lost their faith in me? Also, maybe Clara wouldn't care if I backed down, but I'd always wonder. We haven't done *it* yet, but if we do I'm going to be terrified enough of getting it all wrong without wondering if she's thinking I'm a coward, too. And why would she want to run away with someone who can't stand up for himself? Or her? Yeah, I feel sick, but I feel sicker at the thought of *not* fighting Jake.

It's only as I leave the dining room that everything goes awry.

'Toby? Louis?'

Matron's waiting for us in the hallway. Clara and Eleanor have gone ahead and Will and Tom are still eating. We freeze at the shock of hearing her speak our names. Her face is bland and smooth, her sharp eyes watching us with absolutely no expression. How hard does someone have to practise to look so devoid of anything *real*? Me and Louis look at each other. I see my fear reflected in his pale face. Jake no longer exists.

'My office, please.' She opens the door and we shuffle inside, my heart in my throat. I have never been so terrified as in that moment of hearing her say my name aloud. Louis is glued to my side, cringing into me. His fingers brush mine and for an awful moment I think he's going to hold my hand. As we cross the threshold I think that might not feel so bad. What does she want? Does she know about the nights? But if so, why is Louis here and not Clara?

The door clicks shut and I swallow hard. The light seems bright and there's a throbbing in my ears. The nurse – the one who spoke to us – is waiting inside. She's got a syringe out. I think of the sanatorium. Is that where we're going?

'Nothing to worry about,' she says.

'I'll do the talking, Nurse.' Matron's voice is calm, empty, but the nurse drops her eyes anyway.

'We need to redo your blood tests,' Matron says. 'Roll up your sleeves, please.'

I go into autopilot and do as I'm told, my fingers clumsy. My heart is racing. *Nothing to worry about.* That's what the nurse said. Maybe they just didn't read right? I scan through my memories of school but can't remember anyone ever having to have a retest before. Maybe their equipment isn't as sophisticated here. Louis sniffs beside me and I can see him shaking.

'It's fine,' I say. 'This happened to some kids in my school once.' I grin at him, forcing myself to relax. 'At least it's us, not Will. Needles don't bother us.'

He's looking at me as if I have all the answers. He wants to believe my lie. I want to believe my lie too. 'You want to go first?' He nods and the nurse taps the inside of his pale forearm to try and find a vein.

Matron has sat down behind her large wooden desk, already working on some papers as if we don't exist. It's a strange room. Old-fashioned like the rest of the house, but more cluttered than I'm used to seeing now. There's a sofa behind us and a small table with a kettle and some mugs, a sugar bowl and a jug of milk. A couple of bland landscape paintings hang against the wallpaper above a large old-style photocopying machine. There's no computer or even telephone that I can see.

The desk, covered with stacks of paper, dominates the room, and the wall next to it has a pinboard with several rotas tacked on, but I can't make out what they say from where I'm standing. Next to that is a small rack with various keys hanging from it. I can hear my breath and Matron's scratching pen as I realise that this is the hub of the house. Everything important is kept in here.

'Your arm,' the nurse says softly, and my fear brings my attention back to the blood test, but part of my mind is racing to mine and Clara's plan. I bet the schedule for the boat is on that wall. I flinch with the needle prick and watch my blood escape. A retest. The ball in my stomach flares until I feel light-headed and sick. My skin is clammy. Despite what I've said to Louis, I can't help but think it means only one thing. Our time is running out.

If me and Clara are going to run away, we might have to do it soon.

We stand in the hallway afterwards and watch the nurse head to the lift with our samples. I presume she's taking them to the top floor – the sanatorium. I don't want to think about it. I want to think about the boat, not the blood tests. How I can get back into Matron's study and find out when it's coming again. How me and Clara can get the fuck off this crappy island.

'I don't think we should tell the others about this,' I say quietly. 'I mean, it's just a retest and doesn't mean anything, but you know what people are like. They didn't see her call our names. No point in telling them.'

Louis nods. His face has darkened slightly with fear again. He knows exactly what I mean. He knows how we've looked at the kids who've got sick: curious, expectant, victorious. He doesn't want to be looked at like that and neither do I. My heart is racing as if time is speeding up inside me. I breathe deeply. I want it to slow down. I'm not ready for this. I don't think anyone is ever ready for this. I'm suddenly very afraid but also, weirdly, very angry. This isn't fair. None of it.

Jake is waiting for me in the playroom.

I stride down the corridor and see a small, chattering group huddled outside the door.

'He won't let us in, Toby,' Will says, bubbling with nervous excitement. 'He's in there with Albi.' I'm surprised Jake doesn't want an audience, but maybe he's worried about what's going to be said between the punches. He's lost enough face over Clara – although I want to point out to him that making me fight him isn't exactly going to give the others the impression that he doesn't give a shit.

'I'll take Tom in then.' Tom nods at me and there's no arguments. Will and Louis aren't backup material. Daniel leans against the wall further away from the door, scowling slightly, annoyed at being kicked out of the action. I feel a bit sorry for him. He needs to realise he's never going to be cool and then maybe he'll stop being such a little shit.

'You okay?' Clara grabs my hand.

'I'm good.' I'm burning inside. All my fear of what Jake might do to me evaporated in Matron's study. 'Just keep an eye on Daniel. Don't let him pick on Will or Louis.' She nods. After a second, she smiles and then leans up and kisses me. Her tongue slides into my mouth and everyone sees it. Will giggles, Louis does a poor attempt at a wolf whistle and Eleanor blushes.

'Ugly slut,' Daniel says.

'Fat pig,' Will counters. I laugh at that. It's sudden and unexpected: Will is no longer a scared little kid. Daniel glowers, weighing up whether it's worth trying to fight Will, but he's outnumbered. And anyway, under all his bullying and snide remarks I'm sure he was more picked on *before* than any of us. He's probably more used to running away than fighting back.

I'm ready. I want this done. I push the door open and go in. The chairs and tables have been shoved to the sides to clear a space in the centre of the room and Albi is perched on a stack of them in the corner by the window. He's closed the curtains. Looks overcautious to me. I've never seen the nurses or teachers go out into the garden and the weather's shit today.

Out of the corner of my eye I see Tom find a vantage point but my focus is on Jake, dominating the empty floor. His jaw is tight and his whole body is taut and tense, ready to go.

'Remember, no marks on the fac—'

I don't give him time to finish. I let all the rage and terror flaring up from my stomach rush to my fists and launch myself at him with a howl, pulling one arm back and punching him hard on the cheek. Fuck his no-marks-on-the-face rule. Fuck all the rules.

He reels backwards, one hand clutching at his bleeding mouth, his eyes wide with surprise. My knuckles throb. 'What the fuck? I said no—'

I crouch and run towards him, barrelling into his torso and taking him to the ground. We fall hard and all the air bursts out of him in a gasp as he takes my weight. We roll around on the floor, trying to get the better of each other, and the room spins. Jake's bigger and more powerful than me, but he doesn't have my anger – not right now. My hand is under his chin pushing his head back as I grunt and growl like an animal.

I glimpse Tom and Albi now standing together, looking down at us, shocked. My scalp stings as Jake grabs a handful of my hair and I let go of his face and grab some of his. This fight is a mess. We're too full of pent-up emotions to think.

'What are you so fucking scared of?' I hiss as we wrestle, all arms and legs and missed punches and wayward kicks. My jaw is clenched so tight I think my teeth might shatter. I land a soft punch into his stomach as he kicks me hard only an inch or so away from my balls.

'Are you fucking mad?' he says as he wriggles away from me. His lip isn't cut too badly but it's already swelling up and the exertion is making it bleed like a bastard all over his T-shirt, the floor and me as he spits his bloody words into my face.

'What is your fucking problem?' I snarl.

We've only been fighting for a couple of minutes but he's breathing hard and so am I, sweat sticking my clothes to me. This isn't like the movies. We're knackered already.

We stare at each other while we let the air rip hot from our lungs. My arms tremble and ache. I'm slowly cooling down, my anger burned away. Once he's got over his shock he'll pummel me into the ground. And now that I've broken the rules, he won't hold back. I'm tired and I don't want to fight any more. I haul myself to my feet and Jake does the same.

'I'm sorry about Clara and Georgie,' I say. 'I'm sorry you think we made you look like a dick. It wasn't on purpose.'

'You don't know what I think.' He's smarting.

I shrug.

'Whatever. You shouldn't have taken it out on Will and Louis. That was a shitty thing to do. So I think what we did back was fair. Your sheets dried out. Their stuff is still wrecked. You win.' I pause for a breath and lean against a table. 'Why don't we just call a truce? Before things get out of hand.' My chest aches as I speak. Muscles all over my body are screaming at me. This fighting shit is hard.

He stares at me. Albi and Tom's eyes move from me to Jake to me and then back to Jake again.

'Maybe he's got a point, man,' Albi says quietly. 'This could go crazy if it carries on.'

He doesn't need to elaborate. The invisible threat of Matron hangs like a pall in the room.

'Just stay out of my way,' Jake says, eventually. I nod. My shoulders slump as the tension vanishes and I turn and walk away.

'Oh, but Toby—'

I turn back and his fist comes out of nowhere, smacking me right on my cheekbone. For a minute I don't even feel it, just an intense shuddering that runs right down my spine and into my feet. My vision goes black, a night sky swirling with colourful stars. My neck whips back and I stagger, unsteady, my hip banging into the record player table. I stand there, gasping, and wait for the world to right itself.

'Fuck.' My face is going numb and the word is thick on my tongue.

'*Now* we have a truce,' Jake says. He nods at Albi and they walk out. I'm still reeling, but I force my legs to move under me. If me and Tom stay in here, then I look like the loser. I'm going out *alongside* Jake.

FOURTEEN

The night is bright and clear and so bitterly cold that, even with thick sweaters on, we take our blankets with us over the wall. I've got two pairs of socks on and Clara's wearing leggings under her jeans, and we still gasp as the freezing air makes us cough. If we're making out tonight, it won't be until we get back to the house, and although I think about it a lot, I don't mind waiting. After the blood test I just want to leave the house behind and feel free. In some ways I don't even mind my throbbing face and slowly closing eye. It hurts like a bitch, but at least I know I'm alive. I'm determined not to be dragged back down into constant dread after that blood test. It might be nothing. *Nothing to worry about*, that's what the nurse had said. Even if she was bullshitting, I'm clinging to it. For now I feel fine. I always feel fine with Clara. It's like she's in a bubble where none of this touches her and she's let me share it.

The blankets slow us down a bit, but once we're

on the beach we run into the cave and laugh, happy to be out of the cutting sea breeze laced with shards of ice.

'Fuck, I've never known it so cold!' she says as we settle down on the rocks that have become our night-time bench. 'This weather is mental.'

She's right. The rain isn't unusual but I don't remember ever experiencing this kind of cold. It's not English weather. Not these days. Not in our lifetimes.

We get the food out of our pockets before wrapping the blankets around our shoulders. They don't make that much difference, to be honest, but I feel cosier even though my ears are stinging. Clara chatters about the fight, telling me how cool the others all think I was to do it, but I'm only half-listening. I just like being with her listening to the steady sound of the sea and her voice like music floating on it.

'I still can't believe you punched him in the face,' she says, putting the lit candle down by our feet behind the protection of a sea-worn stone. 'I wish I'd seen it.'

'I figured it was the only way I stood a chance.' She's impressed and it feels good. In fact, everyone in the house has looked at me a bit differently since the fight. I stood my ground with Jake. He's still top dog but it's not the same any more. Thankfully, the only people who didn't appear to give a shit about our bruises were the nurses. I guess they don't care. We're dying anyway. We had a fight and sorted shit out. What's the point of giving us trouble for it? At least, I'm hoping that's the case. Maybe they know my blood is fucking up and so it's not worth punishing me. Maybe, maybe, maybe.

'I knew he wouldn't beat you up. I knew you'd fight back.'

'I just hope it's done now. It's been fucking horrible the last few days.'

'How's your eye?'

I shrug. 'Sore. I can't see out of it properly. Bet I look like a special.'

She pulls me down and kisses my battered face. Even though her lips are soft against my tight, swollen skin, I flinch a bit.

'I think it's pretty sexy.' She laughs before shivering and huddling closer.

I like when she says stuff like that, and I slide one hand under her blanket and around her waist. Even though I'm freezing, just touching her gives me a semi. I can't help it. I wonder how girls manage to switch the sex stuff on and off. How do they control it?

'How many more nights until the boat, do you think?' she says. 'I can't wait to be somewhere hot. I want to be a warm-ocean mermaid, not an icy-sea one.'

'Can't be too long. We should practise with that little boat one night. When it's not so cold. Make sure it'll hold us.'

I want to tell her about Matron's office and how I think we might be able to find out when the boat is coming, but I can't. That would mean either telling her about the blood tests or lying about why I was in there, and I don't want to do either. If I tell her, she'll worry and that will make me worry. I want things to stay just as they are. I don't want her to be looking at me and searching for symptoms. I just want her to think I'm cool and hot. I almost laugh at that. Cool and hot. In reality I'm probably a perfect mix of that – somewhere around lukewarm.

We've just finished our sandwiches when suddenly Clara's spine stiffens slightly.

'What?' I say, nervous. Has she heard something? Is there someone on the beach?

Without speaking, she drops the tinfoil sandwich wrapping, gets to her feet and moves to stand in the mouth of the cave. 'What is that?'

I don't know what she's talking about and so I join her, my legs stiff and cold.

'Look,' she breathes. 'The sky.'

And then I see it. Across the horizon, a little above the sea – a strip of green dances like fire against the night sky. It's bright, almost luminous in places, a flame that darts and licks the darkness along the whole edge of the Earth, wispy trails bursting from it and reaching upwards.

Without saying a word we take each other's

hands and walk out across the shingle, down to the water's edge.

'It's beautiful.' My whisper is carried away on the rustle of the water but it doesn't matter. She knows it's beautiful. It's so beautiful it makes my chest tighten. We tilt our heads back, oblivious to the cold. The rough blanket against my neck feels too earthy for something so ethereal.

I don't know how long we stand there, holding hands and staring upwards, eyes wide and mouths open. A second strip of green appears above the first, and then from the edges of that, purple, bright and incandescent, leaks out to the rim of the universe like ink seeping across paper. The stars peek here and there through the wash of moving colours as if they, too, are fascinated. It must be at least half an hour before we even look at each other, we're so rapt with the wonder of it.

'It's magical,' Clara says.

And it is. All the magic and mystery and delight of the universe are there for only us to see. I squeeze her hand tighter. The colours are starting to thin, melting back into the ordinary night. The show is coming to an end. I feel elated, savouring every last twist of green as it vanishes until suddenly we are back in the darkness with only starlight reflecting on the glittering black sea.

'How can anyone be afraid with that much brilliance in the world?' Clara says softly, still looking at the sky. 'Nature is perfect. Why be scared of it?'

It is only then, as I see the sadness in her face, that I realise Clara has moments of dread, too. That so much of her joy of life comes from her fear of death. Perhaps she doesn't wallow in it like I do, but it's there, somewhere under the surface.

'A mermaids' rave,' I say.

'What?' She looks at me, her eyes bright, the shadow of darkness gone as fast as it came.

'Somewhere under the water the mermaids are celebrating something brilliant. That's what changed the sky. Magical fireworks for mermaids.'

She grins and I know she likes it.

'I'm fucking freezing,' I say as I try and move my feet, which are now blocks of ice in my trainers. My socks feel damp. The sea has crept up on us. It'll be getting lighter soon.

'Me, too. Let's head back.' We collect the candle from the cave and stroll up to the road, arms and blankets around each other making us stumble and giggle here and there. Her head bumps into mine and I wince.

'I think some of the mermaids' magic hit your face,' she says. 'Your eye's gone the same colours.'

It's only when we're back in the house and have crept upstairs that she turns and looks at me for a long moment. 'That was so special,' she says. 'Wasn't it?'

I nod. I'm not good at talking about stuff like

this, but I know what she means.

'Everything's so special. We should remember that.'

She reaches up and kisses me. I wonder if this means we're going to do 'it' soon. I know I shouldn't be thinking about that after what we saw on the beach – I know she's meaning it in a spiritual way – but at the same time I can't help it. I really badly want to do it with her. Even if I fuck it up. Especially now, after the retest. There are more mysteries in the world than the one we just saw in the sky.

She kisses me harder, pushes one of my willing hands up under her sweatshirt, and for the first time, her hand rubs against the front of my jeans. I think I'm going to explode. She breaks away after a moment, smiling. We're both panting a little. My vision's as cloudy as it was after Jake punched me, but this time it's not my face throbbing.

'It's getting light,' she says. We're out of time for tonight. She kisses me again, but it's short and sweet.

'Goodnight, Mermaid King,' she whispers. And then she's running up to her dorm and lost in the darkness.

'Maybe we're all going upstairs,' Tom says. He's lying on his bed, hands under his head and legs crossed, staring up at the ceiling. 'Maybe that's it.'

I glance at Louis who's fiddling with his

washbag, and we share a moment of wary fear. The sanatorium has become more real to us since we were hauled into Matron's study. Even with Clara and the Northern Lights and the cave and our escape plan, I've had some quiet moments when I've wanted to throw up just thinking about it. As far as I know, no one else has been retested, unless they have and they're just not saying either. But I don't think so. Two people can maybe keep a secret but any more than that and we'd have heard something. Someone would talk. So maybe it is just me and Louis and there must be something wrong with us no matter what that nurse said. People always say *there's nothing to worry about* whether there is or isn't.

'I wouldn't mind that so much,' Will says. 'We'd all be together. I don't think I'd be so afraid if we were all together.' He looks even younger tonight, his face all pinched with worry. 'It's the being all on my own that freaks me out.' He pauses. 'I wish they'd let our mums visit.'

'Can we stop talking about it?' I feign boredom but my heart is racing and my skin clammy. *I hear it makes your eyes bleed*. I wish Will could just keep his mouth shut sometimes.

'You should come to church,' Ashley says. His eyes dart up at Will from where he's folding his jumper and jeans on his chair. 'You're never alone with God.'

Will stares at him, dumbfounded, and then

after a moment bursts into a giggle. 'I'm not *that* afraid.' I laugh then and me, Tom and Louis all exchange looks that send Ashley back into his shell of invisibility. Most of the time we all pretend he's not there and it works best for everyone.

'My feet just won't warm up,' Will mutters to himself. 'I'm going to sleep in my socks. They should give us extra blankets in this weather. Maybe I'll find that nice nurse and ask her for some tomorrow.'

'It's weird, isn't it?' Louis gets into bed. 'I never knew it got this cold in the north.'

I'm not cold, but then I've probably grown more used to it from going out at night with Clara. However chilly the house gets, it can't match the sheet of ice that cuts in from the sea in the dark.

'I still want to know where they've gone,' Tom says. 'What are we supposed to do in the mornings now?'

The teachers left after lunch. We were sent to our dorms and through the glass we watched them climb into a series of windowless vans, clutching one holdall each. They were chatting and laughing and it made my heart hurt. They were getting out. Returning to whatever their *befores* were. They didn't even glance back at the house as they climbed into the waiting vehicles. Matron said nothing about it at tea even though the whole room was whispering quietly about what it might *mean*, as she patrolled up and down the line of tables. My fight with Jake was forgotten. The only thing that mattered was figuring out why the teachers had gone.

'I think a lot of the nurses left, too,' Louis says, his tone reflective. 'There weren't that many teachers. I think some of them were nurses in their own clothes.'

I can't imagine the nurses having their own clothes. In my head they've come out of some factory somewhere in their starched uniforms, clocks ticking where their hearts should be, moulded faces impassive. Not human at all. Except maybe the one who spoke to us.

I try and zone it out of my thinking. I concentrate on Clara and how she touched me last night. It doesn't take much concentration, to be honest. Clara buzzes around inside my head all day in one way or another. If I'm not crapping myself about the sanatorium, then I'm thinking about her. Even when I *am* shitting it, I'm still thinking about her. Will she go out with Jake when I'm gone? I can't imagine her with anyone else. I can't imagine me with anyone else. I can't imagine the house without her.

It's the young nurse who comes to give us our vitamins. She's the only one I can imagine as a real person rather than just a nurse, but since the retest she makes me feel uncomfortable. As she bustles in and passes around the small paper cups of pills,

I'm sure there's pity in the smile she gives Louis and then me. I don't meet her eyes. I'm scared of what I might see there. I want it to be dark. I want to be with Clara. I slip the pill between my lip and gum and swallow the water. I'm thankful when she moves on.

'Why have the teachers gone?' Will blurts out as he takes his from her tray. 'They all left. Is something bad going to happen?'

Even Tom sits up to stare at him. We never talk to the nurses. Will looks so forlorn and I realise how worried he is. How much the dread's gripped him.

'Of course not,' the nurse says, her tone kind. 'There's just bad weather coming and they're changing shifts. New teachers are on their way. They're leaving a bit early in case the storm hits and they can't get home. A lot of the nurses have gone, too.' She smiles, warm and soft, and ruffles Will's hair. 'The new ones'll be here in a couple of days. Think of it as half-term or something.'

'Why didn't you go?' Will asks.

'I didn't want to. Now you settle down and go to sleep.'

In that moment, she's all our mums. Warm, caring, making everything better. She doesn't say any more, but once she's turned the light out I know I'm not the only one looking at the place where she'd stood with a kind of wonder. In the gloom I can see Will touching his hair where her hand has been. Such a small thing. So important.

We lie there in the dark and say nothing.

'I want to see Harriet's painting,' Clara says. We're in the playroom and I'm browsing the records. We're not going over the wall tonight – it's too cold and I've told her what the nurse said about a storm maybe coming. We went out to Georgie's grave and talked to him for a few minutes, but even though there's no wind the air was like ice, hurting my lungs as I breathed. We've been back in the house for half an hour but I'm still shivering.

'The one in the church?' I say. 'But that's right by the nurses' wing.'

'They're asleep. Anyway, most of them have left. Who knows, there might be more of us than them at the moment. We could have a revolution. Take over the house!' She smiles.

'Yeah, and then be ruled by King Jake.' I say.

'Okay, maybe not.' She's been curled up on the sofa and uncoils and is on her feet in one smooth movement. She fascinates me. Everything about her is mysterious. Her body, her mind, the shape of her hand in mine. How can girls be so similar and yet so different?

'Come on, let's go and look. Eleanor says it's beautiful. Harriet's been working on it all day.'

The house creaks and settles around us as we

creep hand in hand up the stairs. I've started to think of the night-time house as our friend. So much has happened since Ellory that I've almost forgotten the sound of the lift. The house is like an old galleon and at night we're the only crew. I like it better thinking of it that way. When I was a kid, a place like this would have scared the crap out of me at night, but now I know there are no such thing as ghosts. If ever a place should have ghosts it's the Death House. While the monsters in the attic do come out at night, they're very human ones. Ghosts might actually be reassuring. They'd at least offer the hope of something *after*.

My hackles rise as soon as we open the door to the church. I don't want to be in here. It's too close to the nurses and I'm sure I can almost smell Ashley's smugness in the cold air. There are more chairs than when we first came in here, and instead of being laid out in straight lines they've been moved into semi-circles curving around the desk that's supposed to be an altar.

There are posters on the walls and my heart lurches when I see what's written on the coloured paper – the names of those who've gone to the sanatorium. My stomach goes into my mouth as I read them. All the handwriting is different. These weren't done by Ashley or Harriet.

'Look at this shit,' I whisper.

Henry.
He loved science fiction and computer games.
He had a rabbit called Mason.
He missed his mum.

The lines of writing are slanted upwards in a tiny scrawl and there's a bad drawing of a rabbit in the corner. Beneath that:

The Lord is now his shepherd, he shall not want.

And then:

Ellory.
The best brother anyone could have.
County athlete. Always smiling.
Told jokes like a rock star.

Then:

Always remembered, never forgotten.

There were more, kids' names that rang bells in my memory from those first few days but who I'd never really known. *Eric, Julian, Mac and Christopher.* Each with a small part of their story underneath, carefully recorded by surviving members of their dorms.

'It's like gravestones without their ages.' What's the point of remembering? Why remind ourselves of the reason we're here?

'Age doesn't matter,' Clara murmurs. 'That's just numbers.'

The candle we stole has been replaced by several others and Clara lights them all. The flickering yellow flames make shadows in which the names of the dead dance. I suddenly feel terribly sad and I'm angry at Ashley all over again.

'Look.' Clara takes my hand. There are three windows in this room, but the one which dominates is the high arched one in the centre of the wall. Standing side by side, we look up at it. I don't know what I was expecting. Jesus on a cross, I suppose. Something like that, anyway. The bright thick paint swirls on the glass and shines in the candlelight and I imagine it glows in the day time.

'Isn't it beautiful?' she breathes.

The sky is blue and a huge sun shines down. A house sits in the background but the foreground is dominated by small images of children, smiling and holding hands in the sunshine. They're bathed in it, faces full of joy. Underneath, in charcoal grey, is printed *God's children are never alone. We are family.*

'It's stupid,' I say. It *is* beautiful but it's not real. No one could see the house that way. 'Everyone's alone. Everyone's afraid. None of this saved any of those names on the wall. I don't remember anyone trying to help Henry or Ellory.'

'*We're* not alone,' Clara says. 'And I like that they're remembering them. Someone should.'

She's still looking up at the painted window.

'You're not starting to believe in any of this shit, are you?' I ask.

'No.' She shakes her head and smiles, wistful. 'Not for a second. But it doesn't bother me that they do. If it stops them being so afraid then where's the harm? We have each other. Everyone needs something.'

'I'd take my chances on my own.'

'I feel like I've spent all my life on my own. Trying to be something for other people. To not let them down.' She looks at me. 'I'm glad I came here,' she says. 'I'd never have met you otherwise. Or learned about the mermaids and seen the lights.'

'You don't mean that.' I half-laugh. She can't mean it. I can't even imagine thinking like that, however much I love her.

'We're going to run away and live on a hot sunny beach and smile through our remaining days. Sure as hell beats what my parents had planned for me. Marry a young Black Suit. Push out some babies. Become like my poor unhappy mother.'

'A boat must have come today for the teachers. We missed it.' I'm trying to imagine not knowing Clara. I can't. It physically hurts me. I can't imagine her and me not together, but at the same time I can't bring myself to be glad I'm here. I hate my fear of the nothingness. At least I'm not like Ashley. I don't pretend I'm not afraid.

'It didn't bring supplies, though. That one will still have to come back.'

She's right. I think of Matron's study. 'I might have a way of finding out when.'

'Really?' Her eyes shine. She might be glad she met me, but she doesn't want to be here, crushed by the weight of the sanatorium above us, any more than I do.

'Maybe. Let me figure it out.'

'You keeping secrets from me?' She leans in, flirting. My sudden excitement is countered by the knife-twist of the blood retest. I kiss her instead of answering, the candles glittering like stars around us. We kiss for a long time before she breaks away.

'What?' I say.

'We're in a church.'

'We're in a room.' My head is spinning and my whole body aches. Just one touch from her and I'm on fire. 'I don't think we can be punished by a made-up God for kissing in a room.'

'That's not what I meant, dumbass.' She kisses me again.

'What, then?'

'We're in a church. Let's get married.'

I laugh aloud. 'There's no vicar and you're not sixteen yet.'

'Age doesn't matter,' she says again. 'Not any more.' She's serious now. 'And it's beautiful in here.'

I look around. If I forget about Ashley, then I suppose it is. I think about Henry and Ellory and the rest. Lives gone. We're here now. We're alive.

'Till death do us part,' I mutter.

'No,' she says, smiling and shaking her head. 'For ever. You and me.'

For ever. I remember life before Clara like a dream. Julie McKendrick and Billy. Being brought to the house. It's all shaded grey before Clara. There is grey in the past and darkness in the future, but right now everything is bright.

'Clara, will you marry me?'

My heart races.

Her freckles crease as she smiles again. 'Yes.'

'I don't have a ring.'

'We don't need one. It's not that kind of marriage. We can buy a cheap silver ring from a trinket seller on a beach in India.'

'Is that where we're going?'

'Why not? The world's our oyster.'

'So, how do we do this?' I feel clumsy. Hot. I'm not good with words out loud. What am I supposed to say for a marriage vow? I can't put what I feel into words. Not ones that would work.

She picks up two blankets and spreads them out on the floor. 'We're not going to do it like that.' Bright-red spots flush on her cheeks. 'I thought we could do it nature's way.' She turns her head and I can see she's as nervous as me. Embarrassed.

'Oh,' I croak. Every vein in my body is hammering with blood. I can't swallow.

'Unless you don't want to? I mean—'

'I want to.' Terrified as I am, I'm sure about that.

'I don't want to die not having done it,' she whispers, stepping closer. We're both trembling so much I'm sure the candle flames waver. 'And it has to be you. It has to be special.' She looks at me then, my mermaid girl, and my heart explodes. I feel like all the crazy colours we saw in the sky are inside me. I'm excited and afraid and I'm standing on the edge of an abyss and about to tumble deep into the unknown.

'Did it hurt?' I ask afterwards, when we're lying on the blankets, our arms around each other. Her skin is so soft against mine.

'No. I didn't think it would. I wasn't scared.' She kisses my chest. I'm still reeling from the whole experience. Everything looks different. We're now people who've 'done it'. It feels weird. Not life-changing weird like I always thought it would, but as if I'm more grown-up. We're not kids any more. We've transformed. Us but not us.

'Was it okay?'

Her question throws me. She's asking what I've been trying not to. It was quick and she had to guide me while my head raged at me about staying hard and wondering what the fuck I was supposed to do to make it work for her, so I know it wasn't brilliant, but at the same time it was the most amazingly strange thing I've ever done.

'Okay? It was better than okay, it was amazing.' I pause. 'And we'll know what we're doing next time.'

She giggles and then sighs. 'I feel different.'

'Me, too.'

'Good, isn't it?'

'Yes.'

I watch the candles, nearly burned out now, as they smile light on us and the gravestones of the dead.

'I love you, Toby,' she murmurs.

'I love you, too, Clara.' I love her so much I think my heart will break.

Finally, we get up. Giggling and kissing, we pull our night clothes back on and fold up the blankets before putting out the candles one by one. I don't want to leave her. I don't want this night to be done.

'Look!' she gasps suddenly. 'Look outside.' I do and I can't quite believe my eyes.

We stand by the plain glass and stare out in wonder, the sunshine in the painted window forgotten. White flakes tumble from the sky, a swirl of them.

'It's snow,' she says. 'Real snow.'

'But it never snows in England.' My brain can't make sense of it. 'Not any more.'

'Not for over a hundred years. That's what

they said at school.' Her voice is barely more than a whisper and she holds my hand tight. 'Isn't it wonderful? Like a wedding present from nature.'

I can't speak. We stand there in the dark, watching the world outside change. The snow is silent, not like the rain, drifting to the ground instead of hammering it. Curious, not angry. Flakes brush the window and cling there for a second before dissolving. It has been a week of wonderful things and the joy of it all makes me want to cry even though I'm sixteen and I don't know what I'd actually be crying about, but I want to all the same.

'This is going to make everything better,' Clara says. 'I just know it is.'

FIFTEEN

The snowball hits me right in the cheek, stinging me hard and making my bruise rage back into life.

'Sorry!' Clara shouts, but then laughs as I shriek like a girl. My hands are freezing – I've put socks on as mittens and they're already soaked through, but I don't care.

The garden is full of life and noise and so much laughter. Clara was right. The snow is making everything better. It did from the moment the gong woke the house.

It was Louis who saw it first as he stretched and yawned by his bed. Even as fast as his brain is, all he managed to do was point and say, 'Look!' over and over until everyone woke up enough to see what the fuss was about. We'd heard screeches of excitement coming from the other dorms by then. I wasn't surprised. The blizzard hadn't stopped until just after dawn and the snow now lay thick on the ground, small flurries falling here and there still adding to it.

Will, who had been complaining about his cold feet since last night, now stood in silent awe by the glass, his face full of hope and delight and disbelief. In that instant he wasn't thinking about his mum or whether it made your eyes bleed or how to play chess or anything else in this new life. He was ten years old again. Just an ordinary boy. I grinned so wide watching him that I thought my face would split.

'It's Narnia,' he breathed, eventually. 'Narnia's in the garden.'

There were only two nurses at breakfast – Louis was right about them, most must have gone with the teachers – but their eyes sparkled even if they didn't smile. The dining room had an energy I'd never felt in the house. Not even on that first day. That had been electric nervousness. This was sheer excitement. Nobody here had ever seen snow, not the nurses, none of us, not even Matron. If Clara hadn't – and her dad was a Black Suit and they got to travel abroad more easily – then sure as shit no one here had. It bubbled out of every one of us. All except Matron. She was as neutral – as dead – as she always was when she stood in the doorway and told us that once we were finished eating we could play in the snow if we wished. There were extra coats and sweaters in the playroom to take our pick from. There was no kindness in her words. I think she'd just decided it was easier to let us go out in the snow than try to keep us in, especially with so few nurses in the house.

I'd watched Matron as everyone else yelped and whistled and crammed the last bits of toast in their mouths, waiting for her eyes to fall on me or Louis, but they didn't. Maybe that's a good thing. Maybe there *isn't* anything to worry about. I'm determined not to think about the retest. Not today. Not after last night with Clara and now the snow. Everything is too good.

We look ridiculous, bundled up in clothes that mostly don't fit, but nobody cares. Not even Jake. The snow crunches as our feet dig into it. A foot or more must have fallen overnight and everything is bright white. We are a picture from a Christmas card, children spread across a snowy landscape. At least three snowmen are being built – Louis, Will and Eleanor are trying to break twigs from the trees to make arms for the barrel body they've constructed.

'Not that one!' Clara says and races to help them. 'That one further up. The end looks like a hand! I can reach it!'

As I wait for her to come back, I let the cold, crisp, snowy air burn my lungs and I look around me. Tom and a small group of boys are trying unsuccessfully to make an igloo over by the swings but it keeps collapsing, and snowballs zip through the air in all directions as kids of all ages from all the dorms playfully attack each other. Even Daniel shrieks with laughter as he gets hit by some cross-fire from a ginger boy in dorm 8, and then he giggles so hard that dimples come out on his fat cheeks.

Ashley is just standing and staring at it all with a blissful smile on his face. That is, until Harriet creeps up behind him and shoves a handful of snow down the back of his neck and he jumps almost out of his skin with the shock.

She laughs merrily as he turns to chase her. Her face shines and I realise she's not plain at all. She's one of those girls who would, in a few years' time if she had them, suddenly become a beauty. She just hasn't grown into her face yet. I also realise that me and Clara aren't the only ones in love in the house. I don't know if Ashley can even see it, but I can. Harriet's shining because of *him*.

'At least we got this day.'

I didn't notice Louis coming alongside me and his quiet words make me jump. 'You know, if our tests are bad . . .' His breath is a stream of cold mist. 'At least we got to see the snow.'

'*All* our tests are bad, Louis,' I say. 'This one just didn't read properly. Nothing to worry about, that's what that nurse said, remember? She doesn't look like a liar to me. And I feel fine, don't you?'

'I think so.' He looks down at the snow. 'I just keep thinking about it.'

'Then stop. You'll go fucking mad.' I don't want to think about it. I don't want to think about losing all this beauty or leaving Clara behind. 'We're here now. That's all that matters.' I can't quite get my head around the idea that all this could carry on without me.

He nods, but he's obviously not convinced. I wonder if the dread is worse for him, because he's so clever, but I don't think it can be. I think we're all pretty equal in the dread, we just show it differently. I withdrew from them all, Jake got more arrogant and Ashley found the church to hide behind and pretend he isn't scared. But he's just kidding himself. If his eyes started bleeding, I bet he'd cry like Henry did.

'We should play Narnia.' Will has followed Louis over, puppy-like. 'Clara could be the queen.'

'We're too old for shit like that,' I say. 'You and Eleanor play it if you want.' When I look at Will and Louis for too long I feel bad about me and Clara planning to run away on the boat. I worry about them. It will upset them. I know it will. I'll have abandoned them. We can't take more people, though, and that's that. I'm not their parent. At least they have each other.

Will shrugs and sniffs. 'I can't finish the snowman. Two of my fingers are numb.' He holds up his small hands, now red and raw. 'Here,' Louis says. He pulls a spare pair of socks from his coat pocket. They're thick and woollen. 'Put those on and warm up.'

'It's great, isn't it? The snow?' Will grins, pushing his hands into the feet. 'Isn't it great?'

'Yep, it really is,' Louis agrees.

'Hey, Toby!' I stop smiling and look across the garden. It's Jake. 'Dorm Seven against Dorm Four snowball fight?'

The garden stills for a moment as Jake's deeper voice cuts across the excited noises of everyone else and the strange snow silence takes hold as they all pause to see how this will play out. Louis and Will both glance at me, nervous, but I smile. Jake's giving me an olive branch and I'm going to take it. 'We'll smash you!' I call back.

'I'll go on their team!' Clara bounces across the snow, all energy and joy.

'Okay, bring it on!'

It turns into a free-for-all with everyone joining in. By the time the gong goes for lunch we all know exactly how it feels to get snow in your eyes and ears and nose and our skin stings and tingles and we've laughed so hard we've cried. We're not divided into dorms any more, suspicious of each other. There are no unspoken boundaries. It's too brilliant a day for that. It's not just the best day we've had in the house. I think it's one of the best days any of us has had *ever*.

It's after lunch when Jake comes to us with his plan. He pulls me, Clara and Tom into a corner near the playroom. The house is quiet. Everyone is changing into whatever dry clothes they can find to go back outside again, but he still has Albi on lookout at one end of the corridor and Daniel at the other. I feel like we're in one of those old prison films.

'I'm thinking of breaking into one of the teachers' rooms later. The old bloke who always stank of fags.' His voice is low. 'See if there's any booze and stuff. We can have a party before bed.'

'When?' I say. My heart is racing. 'And how? If you wreck the door they'll know we've done it.'

'Not a problem. This house is old, man. The internal locks will be easy.' He looks at Clara. 'If you've got a couple of hairpins.'

'Harriet does. I can bring you one of hers.'

'Two. I need two.' Clara nods.

'You really know how to do that shit?' I say. 'Did you learn it in reform school?'

He rolls his eyes. 'Before then. It's a fuck tonne easier than breaking into cars and I can do that, too.'

I don't know whether he's lying about the cars, but I figure we'll never find out so I take his word for it.

'So? You in?' he asks. 'I'm thinking your dorm and mine – none of the Jesus freaks, though.' He glances sideways. 'And Clara. No one else. And if anyone else hears about it, I'll kick your head in.'

'We won't tell,' Clara says. We know how to keep secrets better than Jake could ever guess.

'I'll need lookouts while I do it. You watch Matron's office, Toby. She's always in there for a couple of hours after tea. I'll need you to let me know if she comes out. We can set up a whistle system.'

'Sure.' I wonder for a minute if this is an elaborate joke he's playing on us, but I decide against it. He's too earnest. Plus we need the truce. The house is shit enough without fighting each other. I think about the boat schedule in Matron's office. 'Will you show me how to pick the locks?'

'Why do you want to know?' His eyes narrow slightly.

'I just think it's a cool thing to be able to do, that's all,' I say. 'I always wanted to know how people do that shit.'

'Maybe,' he says. 'After.'

I don't push it. I don't want him to know it's important.

I don't tell Will and Louis until just before the plan goes into action. They probably wouldn't have told anyone but their faces aren't great at hiding excitement. Clara takes them off upstairs and I go to my position in the hall just around the corner from Matron's office door. She can't come out without crossing my line of sight.

I take an old *Beano* Annual from the library, a relic from the years when snow was normal in England, and sit on a cushion from the playroom floor, leaning against the long radiator. I flick through yellowed pages but don't really read. There's a boy with a crazy dog who always gets in trouble and a posh kid in a bow tie. The heat at my back after all the cold excitement of the morning makes me drowsy and I'm fighting to keep my eyes open when footsteps come down the stairs. I sit up, sharply alert, and see the nurse – *our* nurse, as I've started to think of her – heading to Matron's office. She's clutching a piece of paper and the glimpse I get of her face shows none of her normal kindness. Her jaw looks clenched, her eyes determined.

Just out of sight, she knocks loudly on the office door and my heart races. She starts speaking as soon as the door opens.

'I've got the results – they're the same as before. We really need to talk about what to do.'

Matron mutters something and they both disappear inside. I'm not dozing any more. The results she's talking about have to be mine and Louis'. What's going on with us? What might they have to *do*? I lean my head back against the wall and for a moment just want to cry as the ball of dread grows and presses into my bladder and all my insides cringe.

I can hear voices through the wall and press my ear against it. I'd be less afraid if I just *knew* what was going on. That's what I tell myself, anyway.

Matron's voice is a mumble. I can't imagine her

ever shouting, but the nurse is getting heated. She's braver than she looks. How could anyone ever get angry face-to-face with Matron? I concentrate harder and make out occasional phrases.

They need to be told.

But something must be done. What are you going to do about it?

If you don't, I will.

More calm murmurings from Matron between her outbursts, a trickle of water on fire, and slowly the nurse's voice drops again. The door clicks.

I push myself into the wall as she comes out and heads back up the stairs, without the paper she had on the way in. I don't want her to see me. I don't want her to see my dread. I want to melt into the wall and never be found.

A few moments later, a quiet whistle drifts down to me. Jake's done it. *Good*, I think as I stand, leaving the book and cushion behind, *because what I really need is to get drunk and forget about everything.* I glance out of the window. It's started snowing again. I try to find some joy in it.

It's not a great haul, to be honest – three bottles of wine and two cigarettes – but it's better than nothing and between eight of us, it's plenty. Will looks nervous. He's probably never had more than a sip of beer at Christmas, and I doubt Louis' life *before* contained any nights necking cheap cider in a park somewhere. We'll be drinking most of their share. It feels like treasure as we sit in a circle on pillows in a room a little further down from where we kept Georgie. It's colder here and I wonder if they turn the heating off in the unused parts of the house.

'You watch the door first, Dan,' Jake says, pouring a measure of white wine into our plastic water cups. 'Ten minutes each, yeah?'

'No problemo.' Daniel hauls himself to his feet, huffing a little at moving his weight. He's just happy to be here. He'd probably smear himself with shit if Jake asked him to. Jake and Albi are the closest things to friends he has, and they're not really his friends.

Jake holds his cup up. 'Fuck this shit,' he toasts.

Tom laughs. 'Yeah, fuck this shit.' We all raise our plastic glasses and drink.

'To the snow! To Narnia!' Will blurts out as his nose crinkles at the taste, and we all stare at him.

Albi laughs but there's no meanness in it. 'Yeah,' he says. 'To the snow, little brother. To the snow.'

Within ten minutes, we've all got a buzz on, even Jake. It doesn't take much. None of us has been near a drink for weeks and even before that probably only Jake drank regularly. Tom takes over from Daniel at the door, loitering half-in and half-out, but we're pretty safe. No one comes down here. We tell jokes and begin to relax as the wine takes hold. I put my arm round Clara and she leans into me, kissing my cheek, after which Daniel starts singing, 'Toby and Clara sitting in a tree, K. I. S. S. I. N. G . . .' And then Louis joins in and then the rest until Tom shushes us from the doorway.

'None of that soppy shit in here,' Jake says, and although there's a twinge of jealousy in his tone, he's doing his best to get past it. Clara straightens up and I pull my arm back. From the corner of my eye I see Louis catching Will's cup as it threatens to spill and I smile.

'Pissed already?'

'I've never had wine before,' Will says and takes a big swallow. More laughter.

'Are we going to smoke those cigarettes?' Clara asks.

'Won't the nurses smell them?' I ask.

'Not if we open the window and lean out. And close the door.' She's on her feet. 'Will's never had wine, I've never had a cigarette. None of us had ever seen snow before.' She glances at me – a secret look that's just ours. 'It's been a couple of days of first things.' I think about how it felt being inside her – weird and wonderful all at the same time. I can't wait for it to be night again.

'I don't want one,' Louis says, pushing his glasses up his nose. 'They're really bad for you.'

Jake is at the window, pushing the old wooden frame up, an unlit cigarette dangling from his mouth. He turns and stares.

'Are you shitting serious?' He looks from Louis to me.

'I have to live with this,' I say.

'But they give you cancer,' Louis insists. 'Everyone knows that.'

The rest of us exchange amused glances.

'You gotta be messing with us,' Albi says. 'For real?'

'I don't see the point of making things worse, that's all.' Louis sips his wine, a picture of reasonableness, and it's so ridiculously comical that we all burst out laughing, the kind that comes from the belly that you just can't stop.

'What?' Louis says. He looks so confused, it just makes it worse. Tom is wheezing. Clara's half-taking a drink when the laughter overcomes her and she snorts into her wine and sets us all off again.

'Don't see the point of making things worse?' Jake finally says through his giggles. 'Shit, man, that is classic.'

'Don't want to make things worse,' Tom repeats. He's trying to get the words out between fits of laughter and his voice is so high-pitched it doesn't even sound like him. 'Hi, I live in the Death House, but no, no smoking for me. Don't see the point of making things worse.' The end of the sentence is barely more than a blur of sobs and squeezed-out sounds as Tom loses it again.

Finally, Louis cracks, the ridiculousness of his

position dawning on him, and the giggles take him, too. We're all lost then.

My stomach and face ache from it, my bruised eye throbbing hard, and even though I know it's crazy – the eight of us, a little bit drunk, laughing until we hurt at the fact that we're in the Death House – and even with the thought of the nurse and Matron talking about me and Louis, I still can't stop laughing. Everything seems funny. All of it.

I don't even like cigarettes but I'm going to fucking smoke one today.

I have a few puffs but the smoke makes my head spin and after a couple of goes that scorch my lungs, I avoid inhaling. Clara's trying valiantly but coughs every time she breathes in. We're like the lame kids around the back of the science labs at school. In the end, we just hand it back to Jake. He and Tom smoke the rest.

Once the wine is finished, it's only an hour or so before bedtime and Albi heads downstairs to play his sax and 'get his mellow on' as he puts it. Clara and Tom go to listen and the younger kids head off to the dorms.

'Show me how to do the locks,' I say, when it's just me and Jake left.

We hide the bottles behind an old wardrobe where we figure it will be weeks at least until they're found, if ever, and then make our way to the teachers' quarters. My head is buzzing and I still feel a bit queasy from the cigarette smoke. It clings to me like bad aftershave but I try to focus as Jake tells me how to hold the two hairpins and wiggle them against the mechanism inside. Eventually I hear a click. I turn the handle and the door opens. My heart lifts. Jake grins. 'See? Pretty easy, huh?'

For a second I glimpse a cosy little bedsit, a throw over the sofa, TV in the corner, all so *normal* and homely, and then we close the door again.

'They're harder to relock.'

He's right. By the time I get it done, my fingers are aching and I've used every swear word I know at least twice. But I manage it. I knew I would. I have to. I think of Matron's office downstairs and pray she has the same kind of lock.

'We'd better get back,' Jake says. 'Wash the fags away before the nurses come round.'

'Hey,' I say, when we reach the stairs. 'Thanks for this.' I don't know quite what I'm trying to say. His face doesn't look as bad as my eye does, but his lip is fatter and I can see where I split it. 'You know, after everything.'

He shrugs. 'Let's just leave it, yeah?'

'Sure.'

We'll be gone soon, I want to say. *We'll be out of your face for ever.* But I don't. Even with Jake it feels like a bit of a betrayal now. In a lot of ways we are all in this shit together even though we all feel so very alone.

*

I come out of the bathroom, washed and smelling of soap and toothpaste but still hazy from wine, and find Louis waiting for me in the hallway in his pyjamas and slippers.

'What's up?'

His face is drawn tight in a frown. 'Will.'

'What about him?' I hope to shit he hasn't thrown up in the dorm. What will we clean it up with?

'Do you think he's all right?'

'He's just drunk.'

'No, not that. The other stuff.' He picks at his fingers.

'What other stuff?' We need to get to the dorm. The nurses will be coming round soon.

'He's clumsy all of a sudden.' He's not looking at me, but down at the floor. 'It's weird.'

'He seems okay to me.' I'm pretty sure he is, anyway. My head is so full of Clara, the boat and the retests that I haven't really been paying attention. 'I think you're being paranoid.'

'What about you?' He looks at me now. 'You okay?'

I nod. 'I think so.'

'Me, too.'

'So let's go to bed.' I feel uncomfortable now, the overhead conversation wriggling like maggots in my mind. *Something must be done. If you don't, I will.*

SIXTEEN

I fall asleep quickly, despite myself. It's been a long day of snow and wine on top of so many days of surviving on three or four hours, and although I'm determined to stay awake and see Clara, I go out like a light.

I wake up with a start. The dorm is dark and still, the combination of wine and sleeping pills having sent the others into a deep sleep that will probably leave them fuzzy in the morning. My mouth is dry and my lungs are raw from my few attempts to smoke. I need a drink of water. I have no idea what time it is, but the night has a thick texture that tells my gut it's safe. The nurses are in bed. It's mine and Clara's time.

I get water from the bathroom and between that and the cold air I wake up a bit. I creep to Clara's dorm and find her fast asleep, curled up on her side, knees tucked under her chin, hair spread out over the pillow behind her as if the sea wind is in her face even as she sleeps. I almost shake her and then think better of it. She's so still and her breathing so even I know she's way down deep in her rest. I don't want to disturb her. She probably needs it. I watch her for a minute and decide to go back to my own bed. I don't want to steal food and go and look at the sky through the playroom window on my own any more. Those days are done. The nights are mine *and* Clara's and I'll just feel lonely and maudlin without her.

I'm between the landings when I hear it. For a moment, I don't know what it is. My body does – my heart races and I shiver with sudden fear before I freeze where I stand – but my mind takes a minute to catch up. It's the groan and wheeze of the lift coming to life. I'm not expecting it. Who are they coming for?

Me. Me and Louis. The retest.

I almost throw up. I can't think of anyone else who's sick. Not sick enough for the Angels of Death to come and wheel them away. I have the crazy thought that I should rush back to my dorm and pretend to be asleep because I'll get in trouble if I'm not there when they come for me, and then I have to stifle a terrified giggle at how stupid that is. There is no trouble that compares with the trouble I'm in now. I should run. Head out into the garden and over the wall and hide on the island somewhere they won't find me. Or take my chances in that rowing boat.

My bare feet are cold on the wooden floor and I'm only wearing thin pyjamas, but I'm still thinking about trying to escape through the snow. If I fight the nurses and make enough noise could I wake Clara up? I'm filled with a fresh dread. I can't imagine not seeing Clara again. I can't imagine her waking up to find me erased from the house. I hate that we won't have even said a proper last goodbye, just an ordinary *goodnight* and *see you later*. I can't even exactly remember how she looked at that moment. I didn't know it would be the last time I'd see her. I didn't absorb it. I want to turn the clock back. I want to stop the clock completely. To steal some more time. I want more time.

I'm so busy panicking as I stand pressed against the wall, light-headed with anxiety and clammy with fear, that I don't realise the lift has stopped and it's not on my floor. It's only when I hear the shuffle of feet above that a surreal relief floods through me, hard and fast, making me shake. It's not me. They haven't come for me. Not tonight. Not yet.

I can't hear the wheels even though the night is so silent there's a hum in my ears. The nurses must be headed far down one of the corridors. I'm confused. Most of the dorms in use are near the central stairwell. So where are they going?

Away from the windows the night is like a black sea and I creep up the stairs through it, treading carefully to avoid waking the wood and making it creak with surprise at my weight. My heart thumps too loudly as I drop into a crouch and peer around the last bannister. I can't see anyone, but my straining ears hear a door click somewhere far away along the disappeared corridor. The church and the nurses' quarters are down there, nothing else. Why would they be going to the nurses' rooms?

As the whispering of shoes grows louder, I slide down a few stairs and press myself into them, my bones unhappy against the hard edges. They won't look down, that's all I can hope, but I have to see. It's not one of our beds that goes by but rather a gurney with silent, well-oiled wheels. There are two Angels of Death, one normal nurse and one solid, recognisable figure – Matron. Automatically, just at the sight of her, I slide silently down one step further. Matron isn't like the nurses. Matron can see everything. I crane my neck to try and get a glimpse of the still figure they're wheeling to the lift. It's a woman. Strands of fine ginger hair hang over the side like gossamer from a spider's web.

It's a good book. My grandmother used to read it to me when I was little.

It's nothing to worry about.

If you don't, I will.

I stare in disbelief and feel sick all over again. I don't want to see any more.

'I think she took an overdose of sleeping pills,' Matron says.

'I found her.' It's the ordinary nurse who's with them. She looks shocked and sounds young. Almost like a real person.

'I just don't understand why,' she says.

'Her psych evaluation must have been inaccurate.' Matron's voice is soft but still devoid of any real emotion. 'She's been behaving slightly erratically for a few days. I had hoped she'd go home with the rest.' The lift doors slide open and they wheel the gurney inside.

'I'll contact the Ministry and tell them what's happened,' Matron says as she steps inside. 'You go to bed. There's nothing more any of us can do now.'

I catch a glimpse of her face before the machinery grinds into life again. Cool. Determined. Empty. The dead beating heart of the beast that is the sanatorium.

I wait until the nurse has headed off to her quarters then run back downstairs and into my dorm, curling into a ball like Clara, but mine is tight and angry and scared. The lift falls silent and I squeeze my eyes shut, willing myself to sleep. It won't come, though. My mouth tastes of metal and my stomach is greasy. The good nurse has gone to the sanatorium. This is to do with me and Louis, I know it. The test results. Her argument with Matron. Did she drug her at bedtime? Put the pills in her hot chocolate? A glass of wine? Matron's staged it somehow, but why? Too many terrified thoughts race around my brain, flaring up from the ball in my stomach. This isn't like *us* being taken away. We're Defectives. Whatever they do to us doesn't matter – not really. This is different. The nurse was healthy. *Normal*. She's gone to the sanatorium, and no one ever comes back from the sanatorium. I think about her, trying to remember her face. I think of the posters on the walls of the church, the ones with the names on. She won't even get that.

I know I won't see her again. I know that however quietly Matron is doing this, it's still murder. We come here to die. The nurses don't. I can almost feel the call of Matron's office below me. I hope that when I get in there I can find the nurse's name. Not to put on the church wall, though. That might as well be dust on a breeze. Within a year or so there won't be anyone left who remembers those names anyway. Outside is different. I want the nurse's name for when I get out of here with Clara. I want to scream it to the world in a letter to every newspaper. I want her family to know. We can't all be unimportant and forgotten. We just can't.

I wonder what they're doing to her upstairs. Pumping her stomach or letting her die? I wonder if she was already dead on the trolley. I think about Henry and Ellory and all the others and me and Louis and Will and Tom and Jake and Clara, and I think about how I love them all a little bit. Even the kids I don't speak to. I think about the lift. The silence of the night. The aloneness of it all.

I start to cry and I can't stop.

The first year they went to Cornwall that Toby could remember, he was five. They didn't go to the overcrowded resorts with the high-rise hotels and busy beaches, but instead to a cottage in an old village a little further inland. It must have cost his mum and dad a fortune but they never said. They had cream teas and swam in the pool and explored the small rocky cove a short drive away, which wasn't deserted but avoided being crammed like sardines on the sand with everyone else trying to get the best of their two weeks of summer freedom. His parents laughed and looked for crabs and paddled with him along the surf's edge. The first time they took him out in it, he cried. He'd blown the bright orange rubber armbands up so tight that they squeezed hard against his skin when he pulled them on, but they still didn't feel like enough. Not against the enormity of the sea.

This wasn't like the pool. The sea scared him. It was so vast, so endless beyond the horizon, and he couldn't imagine something that went on and on for ever like the water did. When he was in the pool, he was scared of drowning if he didn't paddle and splash hard enough, even with his armbands on. In the sea, he was scared that it would pull him away and he'd be left floating in the middle of that expanse of dark water, alone for ever.

His parents laughed and splashed and he got used to it, but it wasn't until he was about ten that he really relaxed in the sea. He liked his mother's tales of mermaids and mysterious magic living in its depths, but he never quite believed them. He loved the pull of the tide and the cool of the water, but sometimes he looked out at the emptiness of it all and wondered how terrible it would be to drown and be lost in all that water. To be gone and forever alone in its depths.

SEVENTEEN

'Sorry I fell asleep,' Clara whispers as we go in for the breakfast. 'I couldn't help it.'

'It's okay, I did, too.' I try to be normal but everything looks different today: bright and sharp. Hyperreal. I don't want to tell anyone about the nurse, especially not Clara. The nurse leads to the retest and I can't talk about that, either. I love Clara but I'm now keeping two secrets from her. I wonder if she keeps secrets from me. I wonder if we all have secrets we never share.

There's no sign of Matron and the two nurses at the food station keep their expressions neutral even though Matron must have told them what's happened. I get a plate of eggs and bacon I don't want and go back to the table. Luckily, everyone else from our dorm looks vague, too.

'My head hurts.' Will is pale and his eyes are dull. 'And I ache everywhere.'

Tom snorts out a giggle. 'Hangover,' he says.

'Well, if this is how drinking makes people

feel, I don't get why they do it.'

Louis doesn't say anything but his eyes dart nervously my way. I don't look at him. I don't have time for his paranoia. Will has a hangover, but Matron murdered our nurse in the night. The sentence is on a loop in my head but still it feels surreal. Nothing is certain any more. It feels like the solid walls of the house are closing in and suffocating me.

'The snow's still there,' Will says. 'We can finish our snowman. Can we, Louis?'

Louis nods.

'Have any of you been in the church?' Ashley stands over us and the words come out in a tumble like a held-in breath. We all look at each other. Ashley still sleeps in our dorm but we don't ever speak any more.

'Why?' Tom again. He's doing the talking today. Probably a good thing. Once me and Clara are gone he'll have to be the boss of Dorm 4.

'Have you?' Ashley repeats.

'No,' I say. 'Why the fuck would we want to go in your stupid church?' I can see each poster clearly in my head but now my imagination has put another on the wall, one with no name and just *She was kind so Matron killed her* written on it.

'Some stuff has been tampered with.' He's defensive but also awkward. He's like a middle-aged man. Who says 'tampered with', anyway? It's like something Matron would say. *A cupboard in the playroom has been tampered with*. Matron fills my head.

'It wasn't us,' Louis says. 'We haven't been in there.'

I can feel Clara's eyes on me. It's the candles. He knows someone's been using them. We need to be more careful. Everywhere I look I feel trapped. I need to get into Matron's office soon and find out when the boat's coming but at the same time I'm terrified of actually doing it. Maybe there's an alarm. Maybe she sleeps in there. I imagine opening the door and finding her sitting behind her desk, waiting in the gloom, perfectly still, with a large syringe in her hand. I think if she smiles at me I'll see a row of ragged sharp teeth and then she'll yawn wide and I'll be sucked into the endless darkness.

'Let's go outside,' Clara says, breaking the spell of my imagination so suddenly I almost jump. 'I feel really good today.'

'I want this headache to go away,' Will says, chewing listlessly on a piece of toast.

In the garden, I face away from the house and the top-floor windows that feel like eyes staring down at me. Clara wants to climb the tree and I go with her. The exertion is good and despite everything, despite all the madness of the night before, I laugh with her as I clumsily swing my legs up and get tangled in twigs. The snow is still magical and the sky is clear blue overhead, the air crisp and cold all the way to the moon. We knock inches of snow from the branches as we climb with numb fingers and tingling skin, and finally we come to rest on thick wood, separate seats on either side of the trunk.

I'm out of breath and hot and Clara's face shines as she peers round at me. Her branch is a little in front of mine and I'm in awe as she tilts her head back in the bright wintry sunshine. I'm clinging on for dear life. It didn't look so high when we started but now I'm almost afraid even to glance down, sure that I'll fall if I do.

'Isn't it lovely?'

I look out over the horizon. 'I can see the mainland,' I say. Through the distant haze I glimpse brown against the blue. 'Just.'

'Not long till we'll be there.' She smiles. 'The boat has to come back soon.'

We sit in silence as beneath us the others play.

'Don't you worry about leaving them behind?' I say, eventually. 'Harriet and Eleanor?'

'A little.' Her smile fades. 'But staying here won't change anything.'

She's right, of course. And people are tougher than I think. Everyone is caught up in their own dread – their own longing to survive.

'Maybe we'll give them hope,' she says. 'We'll be like legends. The two who got away. Even the kids who come after will hear about us.'

'We could change things when we get out. Help the others.'

'Part of us will always be here,' she says, snapping off a sharp, thick twig from above. 'Right here in this tree. Look.'

I twist round to see, gripping the trunk tight, and my stomach lurches slightly as my eyes drop down for a second to the white ground so far below. Clara laughs.

'You scared you're going to fall?'

'Maybe a bit.' I grin. My fear is obvious in my tense body, but this is a good fear, one built from adrenaline and excitement. A normal fear rather than dread.

'See, I told you the future isn't certain. You're not going to die from Defectiveness, or from drinking too much on a hot beach somewhere. You're probably going to fall out of this tree trying to get down and break your neck.' She's scratching at the trunk with her twig.

'That's very reassuring. Thanks.'

'But you'll be immortalised . . .' She pauses to scratch harder. 'Right here.'

I crane to see what she's doing, which is difficult because I don't want to relinquish my grip on the trunk and my neck aches with the strain. But when I see it I smile. An off-kilter heart roughly carved into the skin of the tree and inside it

T&C
4EVA

'Trees live for hundreds of years,' she says softly. 'Other kids who climb up here will see this and remember that two escaped. And then one day, maybe in a hundred years' time, this will just be an ordinary house again, and normal kids will climb up and wonder who T and C were. Isn't that a crazy thought?'

I try and imagine a hundred years from now. Everyone alive now will be gone. It will be all new people rushing around and thinking they're important. My head spins a bit. Even here, in the Death House, after what I saw last night, I still can't imagine the world going on without me in it. I envy the tree.

After lunch Clara pulls me upstairs. 'I want to go to bed,' she says, and for a minute I think she's tired, but then she closes the dorm door and puts a chair under the handle and I realise what she means. After the events of the past night, the fact that we've had sex has become like a dream, something from a world before, but as I stand there, my legs suddenly shaking, the wonder of it comes flooding back to me and I know I need it, I need *her*, to wipe all this shit out of my head for just a little while.

We're more confident now and we take more time. We do it twice and the second time I don't even have that edge of terror that I'm doing it all wrong. It's not like in the films I've seen or the stuff I watched on the computer. We're clumsier. We don't speak. We don't do some of those things they do, but at the same time it's more amazing than any of that. It's like a whole new world for us to explore. Her skin is hotter than I remember. She's a whole universe that I don't quite understand and I can't look at her naked body enough and the small sighs she makes and the way she moves make me want to explode. It's like all the talking we could ever do. It's like really knowing each other entirely. It's love. That's what it is.

We're lying on her bed afterwards, our clothes pulled back on, just in case, when there's a knock at the door.

'Toby? You in there?' The handle rattles and gets stuck on the chair wedged under it. 'Toby? Toby? Please come out.'

It's Louis and he sounds upset.

'Hang on.' We tidy up our clothes and Clara hurriedly pulls the sheets and blankets straight as I go to the door.

'What is it?'

Louis doesn't even glance at the messy bed or notice Clara's hair is half-out of her ponytail. His bottom lip wobbles and he's shuffling, anxious.

'It's Will. Something's wrong. You have to come.'

Clara is beside me and we look at each other, the magic of moments ago vanished, eaten up by dread. We go without saying a word.

Will is in the bathroom, sitting on the rim of the white tub. His eyes are red and although he's not crying, he has been and is still on the edge of it. He sniffs, loud and thick, and looks up at us.

I can see the problem straight away. The front of his jeans are wet, dark stains running down the legs. He's pissed himself.

'We came inside because he couldn't pick the snow up properly,' Louis says. 'And then this happened.'

'I couldn't feel it,' Will whines, a small, worried puppy-sound. 'I couldn't feel the snow and then I couldn't feel this happening. Not till my legs got wet.' The tears are coming again. He looks up at me. 'I'm scared, Toby.'

Clara sits on the cool ceramic and puts her arm around him, hushing him gently, and we let him cry himself out.

'What are we going to do, Toby?' Louis whispers. 'We can't let the nurses know.'

My head is burning with fire ants as I take it in. I was sure it would be me or Louis next. We had the retest. Whatever is happening to Will, we have to protect him for as long as possible. 'We'll rinse them out and put them on a radiator. Say they got soaked in the snow. But we have to get him into some other trousers and then go back outside and try to play. Make it look good. Normal. Just in case someone saw something. Even if only for half an hour or so, then come in and play chess or something.'

Louis nods. 'He's going to be okay, though?'

'Sure,' I say, loud enough for Will to hear. 'It's just the snow. He's not used to it. Maybe he's allergic to it.'

'Yeah, that must be it.' Louis looks relieved but there are still dark shadows behind his eyes. It must be tough having a brain that big. You can't ever ignore the logic of something, however hard you try.

'Do you think that's it?' Will says. He's younger. Sweeter. His face is suddenly full of hope. 'Can people be allergic to snow?'

'Don't see why not,' Clara says. 'Or perhaps it's the wine. Now come on, stand up. Let's get you out of these.'

She smiles gently at him and he does as he's told. He's ten going on five this afternoon and Clara's the closest thing he has to a mum. I hope he doesn't ask after the nice nurse. I don't think I can lie that well.

It's only when we peel his jeans away that we see the streaks of pink in the piss that's run down his legs. Will starts to cry again then, and I sponge his legs and tell him it's nothing while Clara washes his jeans out in the tub and Louis runs to get fresh trousers. Will's facing away and doesn't see the red that comes out of them, but Clara's expression is troubled and Louis is trembling and all around us the house looms large once again.

'It'll be all right,' Clara tells Will once he's dressed again. 'Don't worry.'

'I don't want the nurses to take me. Do you think they watch us *change* before they kill us? Do you think the changing hurts?' His voice is hollow, and he swallows between the words. I don't know if it's the result of his fear or his active Defectiveness. 'I don't want my eyes to bleed. I want my mum.'

'It happened to me once,' Louis suddenly says, loud and defiant. 'That blood-in-the-wee thing. It was just an infection.'

He's lying, I know he is, but he's determined to convince himself.

'Now come on, stop being a baby and let's go and finish our snowman.' He grabs Will's hand and drags him off, talking constantly as they head downstairs. I don't know who I feel most sorry for out of the two of them – the one who's going or the one who's being left behind. I feel sick. It's too much to think about after last night. I don't want to be awake when they take Will.

After a moment, Clara bursts into tears and, as we stand hugging in the bathroom, squeezing each other tight, so do I.

*

Tom notices at teatime. Will's struggling with his cutlery, gripping his fork ham-fisted in order to scoop some food into his mouth. Not that any of us is eating much.

'What the fuck's up?' he says. 'You sick?' We glare at him.

'It's nothing,' Clara says. 'He'll be fine.'

Tom looks at me and I can see he's pretty sure Will won't be fine and finds confirmation of that in my face. Eleanor's eyes dart around the table trying to find some truth between the kids and the 'grown-ups'. None of us can wait for tea to finish. Louis talks all the way through it, chattering about the snowman and asking Eleanor questions about the Narnia book that Jake destroyed until she says she'll tell them the rest of the story later. My jaw aches with the tension and I've got a headache from crying. I want it to be night. I want to climb over that wall and run and run and run until I collapse.

Worst of all is that I can see the glances coming from the other tables. We've learned to be like sharks scenting blood. The Dorm 4 table is now a curiosity. It's like we're all tainted. Will's clumsiness and weepiness have been noted and now the grotesque show has begun. How long will it take? When will the nurses notice? *Thank fuck it's him not me*. This is how Jake must have felt when Ellory got sick, but we're different in

Dorm 4. We won't abandon our own. We're better than that and Will is still one of us.

At bedtime Ashley asks Will if he wants to come to the church the next day and this makes Will cry all over again, his thin shoulders slumped in his pyjamas, hitching as he sobs.

'Shut the fuck up,' Tom snarls. 'He's fine.'

'I'm not talking about his health,' Ashley says. 'But he's upset and afraid. The church might help, that's all I'm saying. It might help calm him down.'

Louis' in the bathroom and I'm lying on my bed with no energy for the fight, but Tom is full of pent-up anger.

'You're just a patronising prick. You're a bug feeding on all this shit with your smug hymns and your stupid prayers and walking around as if you're Jesus and if you don't shut the fuck up I am going to break so many of your teeth you'll wish they'd already taken you to the sanatorium. You're a cockroach. A nothing.' As he rants, he towers over Ashley who shrinks back. It's the first time I've seen him look nervous and I enjoy it.

'I'm just trying to help,' Ashley says, cowed. 'That's all.'

'Just shut up,' Will says wearily. 'All of you, just shut up. My head hurts.'

He cries before he falls asleep and we can all hear the small, scared sobs coming from under his blankets. The sound makes my eyes sting and my stomach churn. I want to make things better but I can't, and I hate that I want it to stop so I can stop thinking about the same fate that's waiting for me in the not-too-distant future. In the end, Louis gets out of his bed and crawls in with Will, whispering to him, telling him a story to distract him.

I can't wait for their sleeping pills to kick in. I need peace and I need Clara.

The snow had started to thaw in the afternoon but the temperature's dropped and now it's turning to hard ice, but still we climb over the wall. We have to. We go as quickly as we can down to the small harbour where we creep silently out onto the jetty. We don't talk much but we hold hands tightly. We're both trying to leave the house behind but we can't. I know she's thinking about Will because I am, too. About Will and the nurse and Matron and the solid knowledge that everything has changed. We're trying to concentrate on our escape. Maybe we can't run from what's inside us, but we can sure as shit run from here.

We don't laugh and all my muscles are tight as we carefully lower ourselves into the small rowing boat – practice to see if it will carry us. The wood creaks but holds and it's like sitting on planks of ice. Clara looks around, back to where the supply boat will dock one night soon.

'If we untie the rowing boat, we should be able

to paddle it over there,' she says quietly. 'With our hands if we have to.'

I sniff. 'And then climb aboard the supply ship and get away.'

'Yes. If there's a way up the side. Otherwise we'll just have to take our chances from the jetty while the truck is up at the house.'

'I can't wait,' I say. I'm shivering, my teeth rattling in my head. Around us the black sea looks like thick oil and the wind cutting across it is harsh. I want the warm, friendly ocean we've talked about so much. 'Get me some hairpins and I'll break into Matron's office tomorrow night. Maybe she has the rota for the truck in there.' It's only a small bend in the truth. We're sitting opposite each other to balance the fragile, weary vessel, but I just want to wrap my arms around her. She looks up at the sky.

'I wish the lights would come again.'

There's a thin pink haze on the horizon but that's all. I don't look at it for long – it makes me think of the streaks down Will's legs. Will, the nurse and Matron.

'I keep thinking about the pills,' I say as we sit in the quiet. 'Do you think maybe there's something in them? To make it happen quicker?'

She looks at me. She's not shivering at all and I wonder how she can be warm. But then I wonder a lot about Clara, the mystery, the mermaid queen.

'You think so?' Her voice is higher – hopeful.

She worries just the same as me, but she's better at hiding it.

'I don't know. Just wondered.' After the nurse I wouldn't be surprised by anything Matron did, and dark as the thought that the pills are making us go Defective more quickly is, it's also a good thought. For us anyway. We haven't been taking the pills. Maybe we have years ahead of us, not months.

'When was the last time a Defective actually changed?' she asks.

'I dunno. Hundred years ago? Eighty maybe?' I have no idea. A long time, anyway. They had the tests when my grandmother was a kid, so it was before that. There were more Defectives back then.

'I don't even know what we're supposed to turn into. Someone at school had an old horror film about them, from before they were banned. I didn't watch it, though.'

I look out over the inky water. 'It's not good, whatever it is. We wouldn't be ourselves any more.'

'Maybe we should find an isolated island of our own. Just in case. I don't want to hurt anyone. And we should have a gun. So when one of us starts to change, the other can take care of it.'

'Are you saying you're planning to kill me?' I try and make a joke of it. I don't want to think about the throwback genes in our blood.

She smiles softly, light and shadow in the night. 'I'd kill myself afterwards. Straight away.'

'Me, too,' I say. I'm not sure if I mean it, though. I love Clara. I can't imagine not being with her. But I can't imagine the endless nothing, either. I wonder if part of the reason I hate Ashley so much is that I can't share in his fantasy of life-ever-after.

'We'll go into the earth.' she says. 'And then our atoms will race around the world together, completely free.'

It's a nice thought, but it's still not enough to ease my dread. I want to be me. I want to be me for ever and I know I'll fight tooth and nail to keep my life as long as possible. I'm not sure I could put a gun against my head and pull the trigger. I hate that, because I love Clara with all my heart and I don't want to feel weak. I don't want my fear to overrule my feelings for her.

She sniffs. 'I thought the snow would make everything better.'

'It did for a day or so. The first day was a good day. A brilliant day.'

'Poor Will,' she says.

After a while we climb back up to the jetty and talk about all the things we're going to do and what we'll eat and wear and live on when we get away, but tonight it feels hollow. Will is always with us. I feel like I have him at one shoulder and the nurse at the other. We go back to the house and make out for a while in the kitchen, but our touches are desperate – driven by a need to confirm that we're still alive, and it's tinged with sadness. Her skin is hot against my cold flesh, though, and it feels good. Clara cries a bit afterwards and I don't have anything comforting to say to her. It's shit. It's all shit. Everything is shit apart from us. Tomorrow night I'm going to find out when that boat is coming.

EIGHTEEN

I don't think I'm going to sleep but I crash hard for the few hours before we have to get up and don't even hear the gong. Tom has to shake me awake. Outside the sun is bright and everything glistens as the snow and ice melt. It's a beautiful day and I stare at it as I get dressed. Eventually, however, I have to turn around.

Louis is helping Will with his clothes and it's clear things have deteriorated overnight. His legs wobble underneath him. He looks thinner. His eyes are sunk into his face and they scream fear.

'We're going to have to help him to breakfast,' Louis says, looking at me. I wish they didn't always look at me. I love Will but I don't want to be near him right now.

'Sure.'

'I'm fine.' Will is trying to do up his shoes but his fingers aren't cooperating. Louis crouches and does the second one for him. 'It's nothing. I'm fine.'

He looks at us then, first Tom, then me and

finally Louis, desperately seeking reassurance. Only Louis gives it, fixing a grin onto his face.

'I know, but you've got a bug and we don't want the nurses prodding and poking you when there's still some snow out there to play with, and we haven't finished our chess game.'

I can't bear to look at them. It makes me ache too much.

At breakfast I have to fight not to shuffle my chair away from them. I know now why the other dorms have all done it before. It's not callousness; it's just too painful to watch up close. This isn't *our* Will. Our Will eats too much and sees the best in everything. Our Will still thinks they're going to let our parents write to us.

'I don't want my eyes to bleed.'

It's the only thing he says as we force ourselves to eat. He's staring down at his toast, his shoulders slumped. The words are soft and empty. They scare me more than anything else.

It's a long, horrible day of rising tension that feels like it's going to make every sinew in my body snap. I wish the new teachers were here so at least a few hours would be taken up with lessons. We go out into the garden and although the sun is shining the air is still cold. Louis and Eleanor try to keep Will engaged and I think neither of them really believes it's Will's turn yet. They're choosing not to see it and in some ways that makes it all worse. It means there's three of them to worry about.

'You all right?' Jake has strolled over and sat down alongside me on the other swing. I think about the bets me and Louis had on Joe being next. Joe and Daniel are kicking a ball around in the slush. They both look perfectly healthy.

I nod. 'I guess we couldn't keep up our lucky streak for ever.'

He doesn't say any more, which is a relief. Whatever peace we've made, that's all changed now. He's not one of us at the moment. This is a Dorm 4 thing and we're closing ranks.

Will coughs up blood in the afternoon and that's when we all – even Louis and Eleanor – know it's over. All we're doing is waiting now. It's a bright-red patch in the melting snow and me and Clara quickly mush it over with our feet. Will grabs my hand, holding on like a much younger child would as he stares mournfully at the ground.

'I don't want to go to the sanatorium. Not on my own.' He's crying again. 'I just want to go home. Will you ask them if I can go home? Don't let them take me up there. Please don't.'

We lead him inside to rinse the blood from his mouth and then up to the dorm, shutting even Louis and Eleanor out. He begs us not to leave him and we promise we won't. Eventually he falls asleep while

Clara and I sit and watch him as the minutes tick away and his breath hitches. He's fading in front of us. Not fast enough to escape the dread, but fading all the same. We hold hands and her warm fingers are tight against mine.

'He can't go to the sanatorium,' she says, eventually. 'We can't let that happen. He's so scared of it. He's so young.'

'Maybe they won't take him tonight. I don't think they've noticed yet.' We are far more aware of the changes in each other than the nurses. Or perhaps they just *know* when it's the right time. We don't really have a clue what they do up there. Maybe they let it go further before they finish us to see what happens or do experiments. Use our bodies to try and find a way to eradicate it entirely. Not that it makes any difference. It's death either way in one form or another.

'We should give him a last adventure. A brilliant night,' she says. 'We should take him to the cave. He'll think it's wonderful.' She sounds sad but her words run deeper. There's something else in them, something I don't quite understand.

'He wouldn't be afraid there,' she says. 'I don't want him to be afraid.'

I look at her then. I look at her for a long time figuring out what she means, and then we make our plans. When Will's eyes finally open and he starts crying again, low, quiet sobs, I know it's the right thing to do. I hope it's the right thing.

*

I don't need to wake him up when the house is silent. He's awake and ready. As soon as we told him we had a secret to share and not to take his vitamin or tell anyone – not even Louis – his mood had lifted slightly, some of the old sparkle returning to his eyes. He'd grinned at us over tea as we helped him in, and even Louis looked relieved. He was hoping Will was getting better like Joe had. Maybe it was just a nasty bug after all.

'Where are we going?' Will whispers.

'It's a special surprise.' I help him with his shoes and let him lean on me as we go downstairs, the floorboards staying quiet for us. I'm going to have to carry him some of the way, I think.

'Is this why you sleep all day? Are you awake all night?'

'Sometimes.'

'Why didn't you tell us?' In the gloom he's so pale. 'About the pills.' He sounds hurt. 'Why did you keep it a secret?'

'I dunno. Scared I'd get caught if everyone knew.' It's the truth as it stands now. I can't tell him that at first I just wanted to be free of them all, and the house, for a while. 'I didn't tell anyone. Not even Clara. She made her mind up not to take them all by herself.'

He nods and sniffs. I assume he's fine with that. Will doesn't bear grudges. He thinks the best of people.

Clara is waiting at the bottom of the stairs with two flasks tucked into her bag and a blanket slung over her shoulder. Will grins at her as I help him down the last few steps. She hands me two of Harriet's thick, sensible hairpins.

'We'll need the back gate key,' she whispers. 'I'll take Will – maybe we'll make some sandwiches?' She smiles at him before looking back to me. 'We'll see you in the kitchen. You sure the key's in there?'

I nod. I've told her that I overheard one of the nurses talking about the key rack once. It's a lie, but I couldn't tell her I'd seen all the keys hanging on the wall when I had my blood retested. I can't tell her any of that.

I'm left alone staring at Matron's office door and after a deep breath I poke the wires in like Jake taught me and try to stop my hands trembling. Sweat makes my fingertips slippery, but I concentrate hard and after a few near misses, I hear the clicks. There's no going back now. I open the door hesitantly, half-expecting an alarm to sound and lights to flash, but there's nothing. Just still silence and my own ragged breathing.

I look into the gloom, terrified I'm going to see the dark shape of Matron sitting behind her desk, all sharp teeth and monstrous shining eyes, but the chair is empty. It's just an ordinary room. After quietly closing the door, I creep across and flick on the desk light, squinting in the brightness before hurrying to the key rack and searching the labels for the right one. It's an old key, long and silver with a looped circle at the end as if it should lead to some magical place or open a treasure box. It's cold in my hand and my head buzzes and I feel sick just looking at it. When I bring it back everything will have changed.

I put it in my pocket and quickly scan the rotas on the wall but can't see anything about the boat, and for a moment I panic, my eyes running over names and times that don't really make any sense to me, and then I glance at the wall calendar. My heart races as I fix on one word, carefully written in blue marker in the box of Thursday the tenth – *Delivery*.

Realisation dawns on me that I have no idea what day it is. I look for a reference point, my mind racing, and then I see it. '*Teachers*'. The day the teachers left. I count forward from there. It's Saturday today. Tomorrow more teachers arrive, according to the calendar, and the boat comes one week tonight. My heart races again. The boat is coming sooner than we thought. After tonight I'm going to want to be as far away from here as possible. Somewhere we can put all of this behind us.

I turn and reach for the desk-lamp switch again and then I see it. A sheet of paper with my name and Louis' on it, typed in capitals. My hands shake as I pick it up, scanning the writing there, trying to make sense of the medical jargon filling the page.

Only when I reach the final short paragraph do I understand. I read it three times, staring at the words and half-expecting them to change as I read. I can't breathe. I don't know how to feel. I can't actually believe what I'm seeing.

Clara and Will and the cave and the key are waiting for me, so I take the sheet and photocopy it, flinching at the delay as the machine warms up, and then at the noise, and finally I put the original back where I found it. The copy is warm as I hastily fold and pocket it. My brain screams too many thoughts at me. Me and Clara. Me and Louis. All the others. The boat. Escape. I want to sit down and get my breath back but there's no time. Not yet.

Tonight first, I think as I switch off the light and fumble my way back out into the hallway in the dark. The paper in my pocket hasn't changed that. I have to get through tonight first.

They're ready and by the kitchen window, Will so small even in his thick jumper and coat. Clara has put two pairs of socks on his hands to keep them warm. His eyes are shining, though, as we help him carefully out into the frosty air. The clear sky has made for a cold night, but he doesn't appear to mind. He gasps as we open the gate which thankfully doesn't squeak or squeal half as much as I'd expected it to, and seeing his joy reminds me of the sense of freedom I felt the first time me and Clara climbed the wall. How alive I felt, for the first time since arriving at the house.

It's a slow journey down to the beach. Will's walk is barely more than a shuffle and every few metres one of his legs buckles a bit, but he's determined to keep going without a piggyback.

'The sea!' he says as we stand at the top of the jagged path, the wind beating at our faces. 'Look at it!'

'Beautiful, isn't it?' Clara smiles. The dark surface winks and sparkles at us with reflected starlight. Will nods, his face glowing with his grin. He's forgotten the blood. He's forgotten what's happening. He's totally in the moment of this adventure.

'Come on,' I say. 'There's more.' We carefully pick our way down, going slowly even though me and Clara know the way so well we could run with our eyes shut and still be safe. We guide Will, telling him where to put his feet and where to avoid, but holding him tightly enough that we know he's not going to fall.

He's panting by the time we reach the shingle and there's a horrible liquid rattle in his breathing but he doesn't appear to notice. I'm glad we brought him out tonight. The nurses will come for him tomorrow, I'm sure of it.

'The wind is crazy!' he calls at me, his eyes streaming. My nose is running and I nod back and we laugh at how insane it is to be battered and pushed this way and that by Mother Nature.

'Let's get to the cave.'

It feels a little like home now, this rocky secret room that has been just mine and Clara's, and as she lights the stub of the candle, I sit Will down on the rocks by the entrance and wrap the blanket around his shoulders. I can see in his face that he's a little overwhelmed by it all. In awe. It makes me proud, even though the cave really isn't ours at all.

'What do you do down here all night?' Will asks. 'Look at the sea?'

Clara glances at me and her mouth twitches. Will's so young he doesn't even think about us making out. Not in any real way. That's all part of a future he's been robbed of.

'Just stuff,' she says, unwrapping his sandwiches. They're small triangles and she's cut the crusts off to make them easier for him to eat. They look like something from a posh tea party. Probably the sort that featured a lot in Clara's *before*. 'We talk. We look at the sea. Toby tells me about the mermaids.'

'What mermaids?' He takes a small nibble from the edge of the bread but struggles to chew it.

'They live in the depths of the sea,' Clara says. 'And sometimes they come up to the water's edge to imagine what it's like to be human and walk on the land. Only at night, though. They stay so they can watch the sunrise and then the tide comes in and carries them back out into the water.' Will stares at her. Her voice is soft and beautiful. I'm afraid that

I might cry while watching them. I can't let that happen. I don't remember crying much *before*. Not since I was a little kid. I think it's the report on me and Louis that's making me want to cry the most. It's unlocked something inside me. My brain and heart are stretching in too many directions on this dark night. My throat aches and tightens. I force myself to eat, my jaw chewing on cold bread that only makes my mouth drier. I want something to drink but it isn't time for that yet.

'This is a mermaid's cave,' Clara continues, one arm round Will, 'and you're sitting on a mermaid's seat.'

'Mermaid's aren't real.' He's smiling, though. He shrugs. 'But it's a nice story.'

'Oh, they *so* are. And you know what?'

'What?'

It's then that I see it. The first glow of green on the horizon as it licks upwards in neon strands. My eyes widen and my food and my tears are forgotten. The lights are coming back. It's perfect. It couldn't be more perfect. We wanted to give Will a brilliant night and the sky is our ally, offering us this gift.

'They have these fantastic parties down on the seabed. They drink mermaid wine from conch shells.'

'Clara, look,' I cut in. 'It's happening again.'

The green is being joined by a wash of pink and yellow spreading up from the horizon and into the night sky. It's like looking into the universe. For a moment, I nearly forget the paper in my pocket that changes everything, forget that Will is dying, forget what me and Clara have planned. We're absorbed in the colours swirling over us, so beautiful.

Will's mouth falls open as he stares. I can see half-chewed bread mushed up in it. I can't see in the dark if there's blood there, too. I don't want to know. It doesn't matter any more.

'What *is* that?' he whispers. I pull him up and we move to the mouth of the cave. Clara gets the flasks from her bag and joins us.

'Mermaid magic,' I say. 'They're having a ball down there. A celebration.' I don't know if he's listening and it doesn't matter. We stand in silence, Will propped up between us on his unstable legs. His body jerks occasionally but he doesn't notice. He's lost in the colours. For a while we all are. Time has stopped.

'It's the most beautiful thing I've ever seen,' he says, eventually. 'Like a whole other world just for us. Like we're in Narnia or something.'

'See?' Clara says. 'Mermaids are real. Magic is real. Maybe even Narnia is real.'

'It's so brilliant. So, so brilliant.'

As Will keeps looking up, mesmerised, Clara glances at me. My stomach drops.

'I'm cold,' I say, trying not to let the words wobble. 'Did you make coffee?'

'Sure, here.' She hands me the flask. I open it and

make myself sip some. A tiny mouthful at first until I get the bitter bite and know I've got the right one.

'I made you some hot chocolate, Will. Do you want it?'

'Yes, please.' He looks at her and grins, wide and happy. Carefree. He is having the best night, I tell myself, but still it feels as if the lights overhead darken on me. Clara's hands are shaking as she unscrews the top and I help Will wrap his clumsily mittened hands around the flask. He tilts it to his mouth. I wonder if he'll notice. Clara keeps a hold on the base in case he drops it and I can see that her hands are still shaking.

My heart aches with a ferocity that surprises me. I love Will. Not the way I love Clara, but he's like a little brother. In the house everything is different. We need each other and he's the first of our dorm to go. I think of the letter in my pocket and wish I hadn't found it tonight.

'Drink it up,' I say softly. 'It'll keep you warm.'

Will takes another long sip, a chocolate moustache staining his mouth.

'Thanks for this, Toby,' he says. Love shines in his eyes and my heart breaks. 'It's been ace.'

We don't say anything after that. He drinks the hot chocolate and I force my coffee down, sharing the flask with Clara, and we stare at the sky, although I know that me and Clara aren't really looking at the lights any more. Even if we wanted to, we couldn't see them properly through the haze of silent, blurring tears.

After a while the flask slips from his hand and he slumps to a dead weight between us. We sit back down on the rocks at the mouth of the cave and I make sure he's facing where the lights are dancing merrily across the sky. I keep him close and warm, his body leaning into mine. His eyes are closed and his head lolls but he's still breathing, slow and uneven, but breathing all the same, and I want this brilliant night to last for ever for him. I want him to be looking up at the dazzling sky. If not for ever, then for as long as he can.

It's longer than I expect until his breathing finally stops. It slows first, growing shallower, and then finally there just isn't another one. His body sinks into me almost, suddenly heavier and hollow all at once. I don't realise how closely I've been listening to those tiny breaths until they stop.

I think I might be sick as the world swims. Clara lets her tears free in hitches and gasps of breath, and I wipe the chocolate carefully off Will's lips with the sleeve of my coat. He's not going to look mucky when they find him. I won't have that.

We stay there a while longer, me and Clara with our arms round Will's shoulders, neither of us wanting to let him go even though he's already left us behind. Clara's fingers touch mine.

'It was the right thing, wasn't it?' she whispers.

I can hear the fear in her voice. The enormity of what we've done. I think about it a long time before answering.

'Yes,' I say, and I mean it. 'A terrible thing, but the right thing.'

My bedpost is empty of pills now. We collected them all, Clara's and mine, while Will slept that afternoon, and we decided what we were going to do. I wonder if perhaps I had subconsciously been saving them for me, when my turn came to face the sanatorium. I don't think so. I'd be like all the others – just becoming sicker and sicker and hoping there'd been some mistake. It feels strange now, with Will dead beside me and the piece of paper folded in my pocket. I can't tell Clara about it. I can never tell Clara about it. Another link in the chain of secrets. But I love her. I love her with everything I am, especially now, especially after this thing we've done. I don't want anything to spoil that. I want her to stay as close to me as I am to her. I don't want her to see me differently.

'We should go,' I say, when the lights start to fade. She nods and gathers our things as I scoop Will up in my arms. He's heavier than I expected. I don't mind, though. Carrying him back to the house is a privilege, an honour. It's also a penance. It's my due for the choice Clara and I made. I have to pay it.

I'm sweating hard by the time we come in through the back gate. My clothes stick to me and my arms are trembling. My back screams at me to drop Will, but I hold him tight and safe until we reach the big oak tree and I lower him down as gently as I can so he's sitting up against it. He slumps to one side and we straighten him against the trunk, tucking the empty chocolate flask in beside him to wedge him upright. The tree is strong and supports him well and suddenly I can't hold my own tears back any longer. Clara gets the blanket and tucks it around him, and when she's done we watch him for a moment, Clara's arms around me as I sob. Eventually, she pulls me back.

I don't want to leave him out here alone but morning is coming. I should take his body up to his bed and make it look as if he died there, but even though that would be safer and look less suspicious, I don't want to. I want Matron to think Will had a final moment of defiance. That he came out here by himself to die in the shelter of the tree and out in the open air free from the house. It's a small rebellion but I want them to respect Will in his death, even begrudgingly.

'Good night, Will,' I whisper as my eyes blur. 'Sleep well.'

Clara takes my hand then and leads me inside where she tidies up as I replace the key and then relock Matron's study door. I don't struggle with the hairpins and it's easy. My hands aren't shaking any more. I just feel tired, right down deep in my bones, not from the effort of carrying Will – his weight was nothing compared to this knowledge, this *deed* we have to carry with us.

But it was the right thing, I tell myself, as me and Clara curl up on a bed in one of the empty dorms and cry into each other's hot faces until our stomachs hurt and we're empty and exhausted. It was the kindest thing. I couldn't let him die alone in the sanatorium. I just couldn't.

He could still taste the sticky, sweet Coke as he came up the path to the house and paused to look at the van pulled up beside it. His mum must have workmen in or something. Maybe she was finally getting the shower looked at to stop it randomly running cold every few minutes. His schoolbag was heavy with homework he had no real intention of doing that weekend and he rummaged in his pockets for his keys. Maybe he'd get the books out and stare at them for a bit, but mainly he'd be thinking about the party on Saturday and the best way to impress Julie McKendrick without looking like a complete twat. And how to deal with Jonesy. He was going to see him tonight and by then he had to decide whether to bring him along or not. He didn't want to – not really – but just imagining how Jonesy would look when he told him made his stomach twist a bit. And also, in the very likely possibility that it turned out Julie didn't fancy him at all, he didn't want to blow his friendship with Jonesy. It was tricky. Being a teenager was fucking tricky.

He didn't hear the van door opening behind him. He just wanted to get inside where it was cool and find something cold in the fridge to wash away the warm sweetness clinging to his mouth. He hoped his mum had bought more juice.

It was only when he was in the hallway and had thrown his schoolbag down by the line of shoes that he knew something was badly wrong. He could hear crying, a deep, awful sound that it took him a moment to realise was coming from his mum. He still didn't put it together, though – the van outside, the test, the crying. His first thought was of his dad. The long drive to work. A mangled car. His heart thumped.

'Mum?' He wandered towards the kitchen, a slight rush in his pace. He didn't reach the door before she launched out.

'Run, Toby. Run, please run . . .' Arms pulled her back and he just stared, uncomprehending. Were they being burgled? What was going on? A man was holding his mother, talking to her calmly as she raged at Toby to run. Another was carrying some of his clothes. Jeans, T-shirt, trainers.

'You can change in the van,' he said. Toby didn't really hear the words. All he heard was his mother's terrible, desperate, snotty crying, begging them not to take him, not to take her baby, there must have been some mistake.

She was screaming how much she loved him, that she would always love him, when they led him like a meek lamb to the van sitting in the sunshine. It was only when he stared inside it that the truth hit him and he started screaming for her to help him.

NINETEEN

It's quiet in the dorm when we wake up. Will's bed is gone. I try to look as shocked as the others, but I had lain in bed, my eyes squeezed shut and trying to breathe slowly while my heart raced, when they came in and took it and his possessions away to be rumbled upstairs in the lift. The nurses had sounded frantic and surprised, whispering among themselves. It was a bittersweet small victory. I wonder which one of them had looked out of the window and seen Will sitting against the tree. I hope it was Matron. They didn't have a lot of time to work in and they had rushed here and there along the corridors. But by the time the others woke up, everything was normal. Well, as normal as anything can be when one of your group has vanished in the night.

'Poor Will,' Ashley says eventually. 'I thought he had at least another day.'

Louis stares at the empty space for a long time and then bursts into ragged sobs. I go to comfort him but he pushes me away. 'Leave me alone.' He sounds like a wounded animal, angry and hurt. 'Don't touch me. Leave me alone.' He glares at me and I back off. I wasn't expecting this. Louis has always looked up to me. Tom glances over and shrugs. It's grief. That's all it is.

'Well, I'm here if you need me,' I mutter. I feel close to Louis. We share a secret, even if he doesn't know it yet. I can feel the paper burning into my skin through my jeans pocket. 'Let's talk later,' I say to him as we go down to breakfast. He doesn't even acknowledge me, and as we sit at our table he takes a seat at the end by himself and eats robotically.

Clara looks pale and when Eleanor sees Will isn't there she bursts into tears. Everyone is looking at us. I feel like they're looking directly through me. It's horrible. I feel sick. I feel a million miles from the cave but I try and fix on Will's expression of wonder as he drank the hot chocolate. The rest will never know it but what me and Clara did was a good thing. I cling to that, a small piece of driftwood in the darkness. Only a week more, I think. One week and then we'll be free. Even with everything else going on, that gives me a quiet sense of relief. Me and Clara on an adventure. A warm beach. Carefree and laughing. I glance at Louis as guilt stabs me. This is like Jonesy and the party. Do I take him with us or not? My eyes are gritty with tiredness. I'll think about it later. Talk to him when he's feeling better.

It's not long before Ashley has posters up declaring there'll be a memorial service for Will that evening. I don't know why he bothers with the notices. It would be just as easy to go round and tell everyone. It all feels so self-important and I wonder what Will would make of it. I can't remember if Will got as annoyed by the church as I do. I don't think he gave it much thought. I realise there's so much about Will I'll never know.

Clara is off somewhere looking after Eleanor but I don't mind. I need some time to myself as the house settles back into shape and papers over the Will-shaped hole. As I wander through the house it feels a little like the first days, although now I find I'm storing things to memory even though I don't really want to remember any of it when we leave. It's strange, this home-but-not-home, this place of lost things.

Louis is in the art room with Harriet. He's got a large sheet of yellow paper in front of him and his tongue almost touches his nose as he carefully sketches out letters in pencil. Beside him is a tub of thick-tipped coloured pens. He's doing something for the wall in Ashley's room. Another gravestone. I want to tell him to paint a wash of green and pink across it like the night sky but I can't. In the end I hide from it all and head back to the dorm to sleep until lunchtime.

*

In the afternoon, we watch the new teachers and nurses arriving from the dorm window. Even Louis, although he doesn't speak and just stares. We're all subdued. They look stern and efficient and don't speak to each other as they carry their small suitcases up the stairs, their feet crunching on the dying snow. There's no sea of crisp white now, just dirty grey lumps clinging to the gravel. In the garden the grass is showing through again. The snowmen look lost and I want to go and kick them to pieces rather than watch them melt slowly into nothing, forgotten and abandoned. They don't look soft and friendly any more, but icy and misshapen as if they hate us for bringing them to life and then leaving them behind. We adjusted to the snow too quickly. It couldn't hold our attention for long. We've learned to accept bigger things than unusual weather.

Clara and I are together in her dorm after tea when we hear feet going quietly past. Eleanor pokes her head through the doorway. 'Are you coming?' she asks. 'Will's service? Lots of us are going. And Tom and Louis. Joe, too.'

'Maybe,' Clara says. 'In a minute.' Eleanor nods and vanishes.

'Tom and Louis don't even believe in God,' I say. I sound more bitter than I mean to. Tom hates the church. Why would he go? What do they think Ashley is capable of? Making them all better again? We might be lepers but he's not Jesus, and all that stuff is shit anyway.

'It's not about God,' Clara says, playing with my fingers. 'It's about Will. Saying goodbye.'

'We already did that.'

'Maybe we should go anyway,' she says. 'For the others.'

I look into her eyes and imagine how the warm ocean will match their colour. 'They'll have to get used to us not being around sometime. Only a week to go.'

She smiles then. Her first proper smile of the day, all white teeth against her freckled skin. 'I can't wait.'

'We have to take our pills tonight,' I say. 'And tomorrow. Just in case.' We left the hot-chocolate flask with Will so if they test it they'll think maybe he hadn't been taking his pills and then when he got sick took them all at once, but they'll want to make sure no one else is up at night. They might test all of us, so we need the pills in our systems. I don't trust Matron. I think of the letter in my pocket and wish the boat was coming sooner. I don't know when she might act against me or Louis like she did against the nurse, but I know she will. This is why she got rid of our nurse. Then again, she doesn't have to hurry with us. We're not going anywhere. Not as far as she knows, anyway. I need to talk to Clara about taking Louis with us. I know I do.

Clara nods. 'I'll miss our nights.' She leans forward and kisses me. 'But soon we'll have them all to ourselves without needing to creep around.' She cuddles into me then and it's the best feeling in the world. We lie there for a while and then the saxophone cuts through the air, the soulful sound drifting along the corridors and filling the stairwells. It's as if the house itself is singing – old blues from the warm southern states so far away. It's coming from the church, I know it is. Even Albi's there. I wish Will could have known.

Clara sits up and looks at me and she doesn't have to say anything. We should be there. Of all people, we should be there. To say goodbye to Will *and* to the house.

'Okay. Let's go.'

We see the glow of the candles warming the gloomy chill before we reach the door. The shadows sway to the music. Clara leads the way and I follow nervously inside. I'm surprised by the number of people, but I don't see Jake. I'm weirdly pleased about that. Jake is many things but he calls bullshit when he sees it. I suspect I've broken some kind of trust by being here, but at the same time I feel like the whole room is full of Will. As if he's in the air around us already. Ashley, at the front of the semicircles of chairs, looks over at us and smiles. I can't decide if it's friendly or victorious and decide to ignore it. This isn't about Ashley.

In the corner, Albi finishes the long, last note of his piece, and as it fades over us, Ashley nods towards Louis. 'You wanted to say something?'

Louis is small in the gathering but his eyes burn as he stares at me. 'Not with them here. I don't want them here.'

My throat tightens. Clara looks from me to Louis, confused. I can see the panic in her face. He can't know. He *can't*.

'Everyone's welcome here,' Ashley says. I want to punch him for his smugness. I'm not welcome here, even though only Louis knows it. I'm a cuckoo in this nest and so is Louis.

'Not them. They can fuck off.' He spits the words out. I have never seen him like this.

'We'll go,' Clara says, awkward.

It's too late.

'You've spoiled it now. You stay. I'll fuck off. I don't need this place anyway.' Louis throws down the small piece of paper he's holding, sweaty where it's been folded in his hand, and storms out past us, bashing into me as he goes. His face is a ball of unrecognisable rage, every muscle tight, contracting against his skull.

'I'll go after him,' I whisper. 'You stay.' Clara's bottom lip is trembling but she nods. Ashley is saying something about singing a hymn. He's feeling the crackling electricity of the broken calm as much as I am. My stomach churns as I leave them and follow the echo of stomping feet on the stairs.

I find him in the bathroom – the same one we washed Will's blood-streaked legs down in. For a moment I see Will sitting there, a shadow of himself, and then I sit rebelliously upon him. He vanishes, of course. He's not really there. He's nothing now. He no longer exists.

I look at Louis. He's sitting on the toilet seat and looks up at me with such dread that I want to throw up. What does he think I'm going to do to him?

'He told me,' he says. His whole body is shaking with fear and anger and dry, red-eyed upset, and it's all my fault. 'Did you think he wouldn't tell me? I was his best friend.'

'What did he say?'

'An adventure.' He's so bitter I can feel the sharp edges on every word. 'You and Clara told him not to take his vitamins and then you were going to have an adventure.'

'They're not vitamins.' I'm so tired. I can't fight him.

'I know. I've known for ages.' He looks at me as if I'm an idiot. 'I just don't want to be awake. Why would you want to have more time to think?'

I say nothing. I remember how big his brain is and what a burden that must be. Of course he'd want the peace of sleep. After a while, the anger slips off him and he sobs – hot, wet tears dredged up from his soul. 'You killed him, Toby. You took him out in the night and killed him. How could you do that?'

'I didn't want him to be scared.' I can barely hear my own words. They're wisps of breath I don't want to say aloud. 'I didn't want him to go to the sanatorium.'

'He trusted you. *I* trusted you. I thought you'd bring him back. I watched from the window when you put him up against the tree. Even then I didn't get it. I was so stupid.'

'He wasn't afraid. He was happy.' I think of Jake and the gentle way he stroked Georgie's feathers and then broke his neck. 'We were . . .' I stumble over the words. Everything feels shaky. What were we doing? 'We were trying to be kind. I didn't want him to be scared.' The second time I say it, it sounds even lamer. My face is flushed and my palms sweat. 'We wanted to give him an amazing night. Something brilliant. Something to make it better. We didn't want him to go to the sanatorium.' The words are coming in a rush of confession, as if by telling it, all the weight of Will's dead body will ease from my chest.

'I get that.' He sighs. 'I'm not stupid.'

It comes like a curveball and I frown. I don't understand. He looks at me like you'd look at a thick kid who keeps missing the obvious answer. His eyes fill with tears again and his shoulders shake.

'I should have *been* there. You should have taken me, too.' His words are a hurt-puppy whine but they carve up my guts like blades.

'I didn't think . . . I . . .' I don't know what to say. I didn't trust you? I thought you'd tell? Neither of those were true. We just didn't think. Not beyond our own bubble of worrying about Will. We didn't consider what it would do to Louis. I want to turn back the clock. I want to make it better.

'I didn't get to say goodbye.' Snot hangs from his nose but he doesn't wipe it away. 'I had to go to the stupid church to say goodbye and now that's ruined, too. I should have been there. I was his *best* friend, Toby.' He stares at me with such intensity I wonder if time actually *will* start rolling backwards so I can make it better. 'Not you. Not Clara. *Me*.'

'I'm sorry.' It's all I've got and it's as lame as it sounds. 'I'm so sorry.'

Finally he pulls off a couple of sheets of the thin cheap toilet paper beside him and loudly blows his nose. 'Yeah. Yeah, I bet you are. But that doesn't count for shit.' He stands up, composing himself. 'I never want you to speak to me again. I'm never going to speak to you again. You got it?'

'But I need to talk to you about something,' I start. 'I have to. It's important.'

'Oh, fuck off, Toby,' he says, opening the door. 'Just fuck off and *die*.'

I sit there for a while after he leaves, perching on the side of the bath like Will did, and I cry like a baby. I cry for all of us. I cry because I don't know how to feel any more. I cry because I feel too much. I try to cry it all out, but I can't. It's a lead weight inside me.

I wait until I'm done and then I wait a few minutes longer. I don't want anyone to know I've been crying. I wash my face in cold water. The red around my eyes from my tears disguises the last embers of my bruise. I let the shivers cool my overheated body. Louis will calm down. I know him. He will. I hope he will. I have to be able to trust him if I'm going to share mine and Clara's plans with him. And I can't leave without telling him. I wonder if he'll tell Matron out of spite. I can't imagine it, but then nor could I imagine Louis ever telling me to fuck off and die before. No one says that here. Fuck off and die. It carries too much weight. Bad karma.

Jake is walking up the stairs with Daniel when I come out. I hope my face is back to normal. Jake is one thing, but the idea of a little snide fat fuck like Daniel knowing I'd been upset would finish me off. We nod at each other, awkward. We're still in the post-Will weird. The bed and possessions have gone but until Ashley stops with his stupid memorial service nothing is going to settle. And even when they do for the others, I'll still have

Louis to contend with and my own guilt. Maybe if I can make it better with Louis then one day my guilt will eventually fade. I don't want to have the ghost of Will with me for ever. I don't think I could live like that. I want to leave him behind. I *have* to leave him behind.

'Does he know?' Clara asks me, scared, after the memorial is finally done. I nod. 'Is he going to tell?'

'I don't think so.' She looks so worried. She's thinking about the boat, too. We're so close to getting away. 'We should have taken him with us,' I say softly. 'He should have been there. That's what's upset him.'

She looks relieved after that and I realise she's feeling guilty, too. We may have done a necessary thing but it was also a terrible one and I can't decide which side weighs heaviest. But if Louis wanted to be there and Louis is a genius then surely it was right? I remember the awful slump in Will's body as he died. That will never leave me. I try to think of his face as he stared up at the lights in wonder. The weight of him was so earthy but his expression in those last minutes was so ethereal. Dark and light. Horror and beauty. Everything is extremes. I just want to sleep and get this day over with.

'So, what's up with you two, then?' Tom asks when Louis goes to brush his teeth.

'Nothing.' I shrug.

'Doesn't look like nothing.'

'He's just upset.'

'Yeah, but why is he upset with *you*?'

'He'll get over it.' I don't answer the question, instead turning away and getting into bed. When the nurse brings our pills round I swallow mine quite happily. I think Louis does, too. Neither of us wants to be alone with our thoughts.

TWENTY

Over the next few days life does settle down. The snow finally melts away and the sun returns with its familiar warmth. After breakfast we go for lessons with our new teachers, who are uniformly dour and dull which makes me wonder if maybe the last lot had to leave because Matron disapproved of their smoking and drinking and whatever else they got up to in their wing of the house, and it wasn't really a half-term at all. I wade diligently through the comprehension books and sums but I have half an eye on the brightness outside, and despite my inability to shake Will's ghost away, my stomach fizzes with excitement at the prospect of being far away from here.

I imagine Clara running along a beach in cut-off denim shorts, laughing and pushing me into the sea. In my head she's as wild and free as she was born to be. I think of how uncomfortable and awkward I was *before*. How I behaved around Julie McKendrick. Clara's changed me. The house has changed me, too, but Clara mainly. I wouldn't have gone over the wall without her. I'd still be moping around in the gloom full of dread and lost hope. I wouldn't have come up with a plan to leave. I wouldn't have thought about the boat. It's all Clara. Without Clara I would never have found the report on Matron's desk.

I've read the paper I copied so many times now that I've slowly started to believe it. It fills my head more than even Will does. It excites me and scares me. Matron did what she did to the nurse in the night because of it. I try not to think the word *murder* because that in turn makes me think of Will – *Thanks for this, Toby* – and that makes my heart and stomach hurt. I wonder if Matron is waiting to see if there's any fallout from that before she comes for me and Louis. The paper, and what is printed so factually there, is dangerous. This much I know.

Louis continues to withdraw into himself. He doesn't look at me or talk to me. If he needs something passed to him at the table, he asks someone else. In lessons his head is down and he appears focused but I don't believe he's really concentrating as he scribbles out his answers. Louis doesn't need to. His brain works so fast he can think about a hundred things at once. In the afternoons he plays chess against himself or goes and sits on the swings. He mutters quietly to no one in particular.

Occasionally I think I should go and speak to

him, but every time I chicken out. I put it off. I know I have to tell him what's on the paper but I'm scared of what he might do. He's not himself. I want him to be Louis again but I'm not sure I know who Louis is without Will. He's never talked much about friends before the house, or if he has, he only told Will about them and Will is gone.

Clara and I withdraw in our own way, too. We don't hang out with the others any more and they stop asking us to. We go to the library and look at atlases and encyclopaedias and think about ways to sneak onto trade ships to start our adventures. We only have to get to France and after that it should all be easy, or at least Clara makes it sound that way.

After three nights we stop taking the pills again. Clara says she doesn't like missing out on the time and although I'm wary I go along with her. She winks and laughs and tells me I'm her serious side and she's my crazy. Her mood has lifted since Will. There's a nervous energy around her as the boat night draws closer.

She's right, as usual. I lie awake for a long time before finally plucking up the courage to creep out and find her. I watch Louis for a moment but I'm pretty sure he's asleep. I pull his blankets up a bit to cover his arms. The sun might be back during the day but the house is still cool at night.

We don't go out – even Clara thinks that might be too risky – instead picking a room between both our dorms to curl up in just in case we hear movement and have to get back fast. The added danger is almost exciting and it's not long until she's kissing me hard and pulling me down over her.

'I love you, I love you, I love you,' she whispers over and over as our faces draw close. Her breath is warm and I kiss her some more. She makes everything better. Afterwards, as we lie there, smiling and breathless, my head spins with the amazing brilliance of what we've just done and I feel relaxed and happy for the first time since *that* night. I wonder what Jonesy would make of this. Me, in love with a beautiful girl who loves me back, and who I have sex with and who I'm good at having sex with after those first awkward times. Jonesy seems like a kid to me now, just like Julie McKendrick has faded to nothing.

I trace my finger down Clara's smooth skin and hope Jonesy is okay. He doesn't have a lot of other friends. Jonesy and Louis merge a little in my head and then Clara flinches and I lean forward. There's a big bruise across her hip.

'What did you do?' I ask, leaning down to kiss it.

'Walked into something like an idiot. It's fine.'

It blooms like a black rose across her pale skin. 'Must've been hard.' I smile up at her. 'Try walking, not running.'

'Sorry, Dad.'

I pull a face. 'That's not weird at all.'

I think about my mum and dad and whether I

should call them when we get away. How much would it freak them out? Maybe when we're safe I will. Maybe later. Home doesn't feel like home any more.

'I think Will would be okay with what we did,' she says as we stare at the ceiling and imagine the night stars twinkling over us above a sandy beach. 'I really do.'

I let her speak and don't say anything. I'm realising that it's less about whether Will would be fine with it than whether we can be fine with it, but I don't want to make her think about that too hard. It's enough that I am.

'It's what I'd want someone to do,' she continues, her voice soft and serious. 'If they knew the sanatorium was coming for me.'

I kind of envy how she's made her peace with it so quickly. I think she's like the lights in the sky – all bright and fascinating and in the moment. I'm the slump in weight – earthy, dark and heavy.

'What we have to do now is live every minute. Make it all count. That's how we'll honour Will. We have to be *happy*.'

'I am happy.' It's the truth. I'm full of secrets I can't share but in this moment I'm happy. 'You make me happy.'

'Even here?' she asks.

'Yes.'

She twirls a strand of her hair and thinks for a

moment. 'I can't imagine not knowing you. I can't imagine being in my old life and never meeting you.'

'Me neither.' It's true. Time has gone funny here. I feel like I've known her for ever and everything before was a dream.

'It's like fate, isn't it?' she says, soft and sweet. 'You and me, both Defectives. Like we were meant to find each other here.'

'Maybe.'

'No maybe about it.' She slaps my head playfully and then sighs. 'You stop me being scared.'

My heart tugs so hard at that. I can never imagine Clara being afraid. I kiss her again and she's warm and vulnerable and soft. I want to look after her.

'Together for ever?' she says.

'Together for ever,' I agree. I think of the paper in my pocket and a bit of me breaks inside, forcing me to grin to hide it. 'I married you, didn't I?'

'Never leave me?'

'Never leave you.'

'At least we won't get old and ugly,' she says. 'You won't end up bald and fat like my dad. We won't become complacent with each other. Our love won't fade.'

'You could never be ugly.' I smile. 'And our love could never fade. Fate, remember?'

She wraps her arms around my neck and holds on tight. 'I can't wait to get out of here,' she breathes into my skin. 'I can't wait.'

TWENTY-ONE

This time, when the vans come, there are seven. As we did last time, we crane our heads at the dorm window to see the new kids climb out, one from each van. I've been so caught up in my own excitement about leaving that I somehow didn't expect any more to arrive. But the house is its own world and it keeps turning.

'I wonder if we'll get one,' Tom says. He doesn't look pleased by the thought of an interloper in our midst and I almost smile, remembering how we felt the same way about him not so long ago.

'Maybe there'll be some more girls,' I chip in. I kind of hope there'll be someone for him or Jake to make up for me stealing Clara away, even though it doesn't really work like that. Me and Clara are meant to be. I can't imagine anyone else feeling the way we do. But a couple of girls for them to make out with would be good. I don't really share any of the excitement, though. I'm too busy hoping that none of these new kids fuck up mine and Clara's plans. They'd better all take their pills. I can't wait to leave and every moment spent in the house weighs on me with the fear of something going wrong.

Louis is at the window as well, but after a moment he drifts away and sits cross-legged on his bed. The tatty home-made chess board is laid out and he moves one of the black cardboard pieces and then mutters something, letting out a strange little laugh. It's unsettling.

'Do you have to talk to yourself like that?' Tom asks. 'It's fucking weird.'

Louis looks up at him, eyes wide and surprised. 'I'm not talking to myself.'

'Yeah, you are.'

'No, I'm not.'

'So who are you talking to, then?'

Louis smiles. It's almost his old smile. Almost, but not quite. 'Will, of course,' he says. 'I'm talking to Will.'

He goes back to his game as we stare at him, and after a long moment, Tom sucks his teeth in disgust. 'This place is fucking crazy,' he mumbles.

None of us really talks after that. Bored at the window, I go and lie on my bed. I wonder if Louis is doing it on purpose to drive me crazy. To not let me forget. In some ways I hope that's the reason. It sure as shit beats the alternative that Louis, the genius, is cracking up. That he can handle being Defective, and the house, but not the loss of his friend. I can live with him hating me, but if I'm going tell him our plans I need him not to be barking mad. The time ticks by and we hear footsteps outside but no new arrival comes into Dorm 4. I think we all heave a sigh of relief. We've got enough shit going on in here without fresh blood.

At tea, Jake preens and talks loudly amidst the excited chattering. There are two new boys at the Dorm 7 table and he's setting out his stall as top dog of the house. I barely look at the new faces and I don't ask what their names are. There's a buzz in the air with so many fresh faces here and I feel like a new day is beginning, but I don't belong in it any more.

'No girls,' Tom grumbles into his apple crumble and custard. Louis hasn't even looked up throughout the meal. He's stuck in the old days, too.

As far as we can tell, all the new kids take their vitamins and in the hush of the night, me and Clara walk around the dorms, ghosts haunting the sleeping house, and look at them. None of them so much as twitches. I think maybe they've upped the dose of whatever it is since what happened with Will. In Dorm 9 one new boy's face is still wet, as if he's been crying in his sleep. I can't remember if I cried. I know Will did. Maybe Ashley, too. It's hard to remember those first nights now. We're all so much tougher than we used to be.

'I told you it was fate,' Clara whispers as we hold

hands and creep down to the playroom. 'Only you and me awake in the night.'

'Do you want to go to the cave?' I ask. It's crazy but I want to say goodbye to that rocky shelter before we leave. It's mine and Clara's place, the good and the bad.

'I just want to dance,' she says. 'Let's stay in.' It's not that cold tonight but she's properly dressed rather than just in her nightshirt, so her answer throws me. She's wearing jeans and socks and a long baggy jumper, when normally she likes the freedom of the air around her legs. She digs out a record and plugs the headphones in.

'You wear them,' I say. 'I want to be able to hear if someone comes.'

'Always so sensible, Tobes.' She leans up and kisses me and then she's swaying in my arms. 'Pretend we're on the beach,' she whispers as she closes her eyes. 'It's midnight and the bonfire is going and some old guy is playing guitar and we're dancing.'

'We won't have to pretend much longer.' She can't hear me. The music that's just a tinny hum to me fills her head. I move with her as best I can, but dancing always makes me feel like a twat. My arms and legs never do what they're supposed to and I can't match her natural rhythm. She's lost in it and doesn't mind. Her mouth is half-open and I kiss her, breaking the moment. I can't help it when her body is pressed so close to mine. My hand reaches under her top and she winces and pulls back, tugging the headphones away from her ears.

'Let's not do that. Let's wait until we're away before we do it again.'

'Okay.' I feel even more awkward now, like I've done something wrong, and it must show because she holds my face in her hands and kisses me again.

'Is that all right? Do you mind?'

'Of course not.' I try and smile but my mouth is like drying glue. I do mind a bit. I can't help it. Aside from the wanting to – and I kind of always *want* to, so that probably doesn't count – I feel like she's rejecting me and sudden doubt hits me hard. Has she gone off me? Is she just waiting until we're free to dump me? But what about all that fate stuff? She can't have fallen out of love with me, can she?

'Let's just dance then,' she whispers and pulls the headphones back on. 'I love to dance.' Her eyes close and she pulls me close and my head is filled with blackness at the idea that she might not want me any more. Even if I'm just being stupid right now, in this moment, I feel sick at the thought of her ever dancing with anyone else.

We go back to bed earlier than normal, Clara saying we need to preserve our energy for our adventures, but she kisses me and hugs me and tells me she loves me and I feel a bit better.

'Together for ever,' I say, trying not to sound too

desperate, as she leaves me for her dorm. She looks back over her shoulder and grins wide. 'Together for ever, Mermaid King.'

I'm happy again.

TWENTY-TWO

'Why didn't you wake me up?' Clara hisses at me as we go into breakfast. It's the last morning before the boat. I'm electric with contained excitement and her anger takes me off guard. Her face is tight and her lips thin as she glares at me. She's never been like this with me before and again I feel that darkness of fear – that she's finally realised I'm a twat.

'I'm sorry. I figured you were tired. I figured with, you know, tonight, it was better to leave you to sleep.' I don't want her to be annoyed at me. I have to ask her about bringing Louis and that will probably freak her out enough. I'm not sure what I'll do if she says no. I'll have to bring him anyway and deal with it afterwards. That's if he wants to come. Telling him is taking a risk but I don't have a choice. Not if I want to live with myself.

'It was our last night,' she says, and I can see she's hurt. 'It was important.'

'I'm sorry.' I sound lame. I feel lame. I want to tell her that I nearly woke her up. That I wanted to go to the cave. That there were things I wanted to do together to say goodbye to the house as well. I've hated it here, but lots of me and Clara are wrapped up in these walls too. Brilliant stuff's happened, too. I want to tell her that part of me was actually angry at her for falling asleep on such an important night. That in the end I just watched her sleep for a bit and then went through my old routine of getting some food before sitting in the playroom and staring at the sky. I felt lonely without her, even though it was good to have some thinking time to myself. To say my own goodbyes. I've been here longer than her, and I had another *before* to say goodbye to. Not the real *before* of our old lives, but the *before Clara* of the house. I can't bring myself to say any of that, though. I don't want us to fight. We can't get the night back now. 'I just thought . . . you know . . . that you were tired.'

She sighs a bit and her shoulders are still stiff as we sit down, but I squeeze her hand under the table and she squeezes back. I can't imagine her staying mad for long. She's too full of the moment for that.

'I'm sorry,' I whisper again.

'I know,' she says. 'You've said it three times now.'

'I won't do it again.' I smile and wink. The last night is gone. I can't believe that this time tomorrow we'll be fleeing across the mainland. I'm not worried about the boat. We'll find somewhere to hide. In the lifeboat, maybe. I saw that in a film once and it worked for them. Our fate doesn't lie in this house.

There's ten minutes after breakfast before lessons. I find her coming out of the downstairs toilets and pull her into the music room on the same draughty corridor.

'What is it?' Her eyes are wide. She looks pale and worried. She must be itching to get away, too. I take a deep breath. This isn't going to be the last difficult conversation of the day and I'm shit with words when I have to be serious.

'It's Louis.'

'What about him?'

My heart thumps. 'I think we should take him with us. I mean, not all the way, not to the beach and stuff, but I think we should get him out of here. He's not himself. Not after Will. If we go, too . . .' It's all coming out in a garbled rush of excuses that are anything but the truth. 'I'm worried he'll crack up completely.'

'Sure,' she says. 'Sure, that's a good idea.'

'I really want it to be just us, but I can't leave him, I really can't.' I'm so sure I'm going to have to persuade her that my brain can't compute her words fast enough to stop my own.

'I said it's fine.' She squeezes my arm. 'In fact, I think it's a great idea.' She reaches up and kisses me, butterfly wings on my lips. 'It really is.'

'You're sure?' I expected at least some questions.

We haven't talked about taking anyone else, not even little Eleanor.

She nods and smiles, and then is out through the door. I wonder if I'm ever going to really understand her. But still, it's a weight lifted. And I haven't really had to lie. All the reasons I gave were true even if they weren't *the truth*. I'll leave talking to Louis until later.

It's a strange day. My whole life in the house I've been wishing for time to slow down and yet now I'm wishing it forward. I can barely sit still in my lessons and my thighs itch against the wooden chair. It's a clear, sunny day and I hope the weather holds for tonight. Everything is about tonight. I try and concentrate on the comprehension questions but the words swim a little. All I know is that everything's going to shit for Ralph and Piggy on their island and that's not going to happen to us. I scribble down some crap answers anyway. I don't want to do anything that will draw attention to me and it doesn't matter if my answers are wrong. No one's going to mark them.

Even though it feels to me like the hours aren't moving at all, we finally crawl to lunch and I force myself to eat some shepherd's pie. Clara only manages a few mouthfuls before declaring she's not hungry and disappearing off with Eleanor. I don't mind. Eleanor will miss her, especially after Will.

I feel bad about that. As I eat Tom talks about the new kids and one who can't stop crying, but I don't listen. Jake is in his element and the two new boys in Dorm 7 are already picking up some of his cockiness. Daniel is back to being bottom dog in that group. I watch it all but don't really see it. My ears hum. This is our last lunch here. It's all so surreal.

I'm in the playroom staring out of the window at the garden when Jake comes over. Clara is up in the branches of the tree, staring out at the sea. Her fingers stroke the bark of the trunk, and although I can't see exactly, I know she's touching the place where she carved our initials, and my heart floods warmth through me. It's a beautiful day. Everything is bright.

'You've noticed, too, then,' Jake says.

I look at him. 'What?' I keep expecting someone to *know* what we're planning, even though I know that's crazy.

'Preacher boy.' He nods out through the window. 'He's getting sick. Joe says he stinks.'

Only then do I notice Ashley sitting on one of the swings.

'That'll make you two down.' He grins, smug. The new kids have invigorated him. He's back to old Jake, the pack animal, all about winning. Whatever feelings he has about the house, he's locked them away again. I hope it lasts for him. 'We're only one.'

'He's not gone yet.'

Jack laughs at that and then walks away. I don't care that he thinks he's somehow victorious. I'm not even in the game. I never have been, really. I look out at Ashley and for the first time I just see a skinny boy rather than a smug twat. Jake might have laughed, but if Ashley really is sick then that worries me. It's so fast after Will. I think about Matron and the pills and the new kids. Maybe she likes to keep the numbers manageable.

Ashley looks lonely on the swings. Maybe I should go outside. He's Dorm 4, after all.

'You feeling okay?' It's a stupid question. Even with the light breeze that dances across the grass I can smell him. Rotten milk. He must have scrubbed hard in the bathroom to hide that from us. A smell is bad. A smell is something the nurses will notice fast. His Bible is on his knees as he rocks the swing backwards and forwards.

'Not too bad,' he says. His eyes dart up to the windows at the top of the house. The sanatorium. He's scared. With his God or not, I know he's scared. Everyone here's scared, and he's no different.

'I hope they still come,' he says, quietly.

I frown, confused. 'Who?'

'The people who come to the church. And I hope I don't let them down. I don't want to be like Henry.'

He looks at me then. 'Why are you even asking?'

I think of all the ways I've cut him down since I arrived here. And for what? He's never hurt me. Not really. 'You're Dorm Four,' is all I can say. I want to say I'm sorry but I don't know how. 'You won't be like Henry.'

I'm breathing shallow and I hope he doesn't notice. It's coming for him fast if this stink is anything to go by. He couldn't have smelled this bad in the night – it would have filled the whole room by the time we got up. Will went quickly and now Ashley's going the same way. I think of the vitamins again. Matron doesn't see us as people, I'm certain, because Matron is not a normal person. I'm not sure she's a person at all. We're like stock in a shop and now she has new stock, it's time to get rid of the some of the old. After what she did to our nurse, I can easily believe her capable of hurrying our Defectiveness along.

'Everyone's always laughed at me,' he continues, his eyes on the ground. 'My dad was a preacher. A great one. People really *listened* to him. But he terrified them.' He pauses and sniffs. 'I never really got why it had to be about fear, you know? There's enough to be scared of. I always thought it was about love. Even though the kids at school would laugh at me and kick my stuff around and call me names, I always tried to keep Jesus in my heart.'

I cringe a bit, I can't help it, but I think that's me, not him. I just can't buy into all that crap, no matter how afraid I've been. I prefer Clara and the atoms and racing around the world like that.

'It didn't surprise me when I turned out Defective. I was always going to be. I never fitted in, anyway.' Now he's started speaking he can't stop. I can see Clara's legs swinging in the tree and wish I was up there with her.

'When they came for me, my mum was upstairs somewhere and wouldn't even say goodbye. My dad was there, though. He looked almost pleased. How sick is that? He gave me my Bible and told me to stop crying and go and bring the Lord's word to the wretched abominations.' He chokes a bit and swallows hard. 'He called me an abomination.' He looks over at me. 'Do you think it's wrong to hate your own father?'

'He sounds like a bit of a cock, to be honest.' I can still hear my mum screaming for me and I bet my dad has never forgiven himself for not being home when the van came. I think about the lies I told when I got here, the terrible stories I made up about my parents, trying to make myself sound tough, and I'm flooded with shame.

'Yeah.' Ashley half-smiles and he looks so ordinary. 'I guess he was. But I got my own back. I haven't scared anyone. And I haven't lost my faith. I've done it my own way.'

'Yeah, you have. You still are.' I'm trying to find something good to say.

'I hope I don't let them down,' he says. 'I don't want them to see me afraid.'

He doesn't say any more, and I can't think of anything that will make him feel better. I feel a bit shit. I'm sure Ashley could still irritate the crap out of me with his next breath, but right now I just feel sorry for him. He's lost in his own world now, and after a moment I get up and leave him to it. I'm glad I'm not going to have to wake up and see his missing bed. Maybe when me and Louis are gone they'll let Tom move into Dorm 7.

I wander over to the other side of the garden. The light, crisp breeze drops and the sun is warm on my back. Even after hearing Ashley's dread I still enjoy it. It relaxes my tight muscles. It makes me think of the letter I carry with me everywhere. I stop in front of Georgie's grave and behind me leaves and branches rustle as Clara climbs back down and comes to join me. This is one goodbye we'll do together. I can still feel the rapid beat of his pulse against my fingers. The soft warmth of his feathers. His dark eyes watching both of us.

'I really wanted him to fly away,' Clara says. She looks so sad and her slim fingers entwine in mine.

'We'll fly away for him,' I say. 'For all of them.'

She nods, head down, her thick hair falling over her face.

'I'll meet you in the kitchen tonight?' I say. 'I haven't talked to Louis yet – figured I'd do it before bed. I don't want him giving it away somehow.' I'm suddenly excited again.

'Come and get me from the dorm when you're ready,' she says. She smiles at me then. She's different today. Quieter. Reflective. I guess we're both finding it weird saying our goodbyes. 'I love you, Toby.'

'I love you more.'

'Not possible.'

'I think I might vom if we keep going.'

She laughs aloud at that and the sound is beautiful in the sunlight. I don't remember ever being this happy.

TWENTY-THREE

'I need to talk to you.' People are drifting up to their dorms after the film has finished and I grab Louis on the stairs. Tom is already complaining about the smell in our room now that Ashley is down from church and I can't blame him. It's creeping into the corridor like a bad fart. I hope some of Ashley's flock turned up for him, but I know that at least Harriet will have been there. We've all formed our bonds in here, whether we wanted to or not, and I'm glad of that. It's what life is all about, really. Love. Ashley's right about that.

Louis pulls his arm free.

'Fuck off.' He tries to push past me. 'I keep telling you to fuck off. Stop talking to me.'

'It's about the retest.'

He stops then and looks at me warily.

'What about it?'

'I've got something to show you. But not here.'

He chews his bottom lip, fighting between his hatred of me and wanting to know. 'Okay.' He storms towards the nearest bathroom and I follow, my heart racing. I close the door and then pull out the folded paper. I don't say anything, but hand it to him to read.

He stares at it for a long time, his brow furrowing and then relaxing and then furrowing again. It's a lot to take in. When you've lived with the fear for so long it almost becomes your friend. The future was the one thing we thought was certain. Eventually, he looks up.

'Where did you get this?'

'Matron's office.'

He looks down again. He's shaking. 'But . . . But I don't understand. Why hasn't she said anything?' He looks at me. 'Why are we still here?'

'You know that nurse? The one Will liked? She talked about his book?'

He flinches at the mention of Will. 'What about her?'

'She wanted to do something for us. And then Matron had her taken to the sanatorium.'

'What?' His eyes widen. 'How do you know that?'

'I just know.' I'm growing impatient even though I've had days to get used to the letter and Louis' only had minutes. 'I *saw* her do it.'

Realisation dawns on him. 'What's she going to do to us?'

'It doesn't matter.' I sit on the edge of the bath, refusing to see Will's ghost there. I think Will would approve of this anyway. 'We're getting out.'

'She'll send us to the sanatorium.' Louis' eyes shine with horror.

'She won't have time. Listen to me – I have a plan.' I shake his arm. 'We're going to get out.' Finally, he focuses on me, on what I'm actually saying.

'Out where?'

'There's a boat coming to the island tonight – it brings all the food and stuff for the house. Me and Clara will be on it when it leaves. We've got it all planned.' I make it sound more organised than it is, and I wonder if we'd included Louis sooner whether he'd have something cleverer figured out. 'You must come with us.'

'Does Clara know about this?' He looks down at the letter again.

'No.' I squirm a bit inside at the secret but try to sound casual. 'I'll tell her later. But you have to come with us. You know you do.'

He just stares at me for a long moment, the clockwork of his brain ticking over. His fingers are tighter on the paper. 'Just leave?'

'Yes. Tonight. Don't take your pill. Pretend to sleep. Then we'll go in the lull before they get up for the delivery.'

'An adventure,' he says softly. 'Just like you said to Will.'

I lean forward and grab his hands tight. 'Not like that. That was different. You know it was. Will was sick.' I stare at him. 'You have to come, Louis. You *have* to.'

'Why?' He pulls his hands away, leaving the paper in mine. He's still so angry with me that I can see him fucking this up for himself. Maybe for all of us. 'So you can feel better about Will?'

'No,' I say, and for once the right words come. 'Because Will would want you to.'

He cries again then, huge sobs that wrack his chest. It's not just Will this time, it's everything. It's the letter. It's me, it's life, Matron, the nurse, all of it. I want to put my arm around him but I don't. He needs to get this out of his system and I can't do that for him. Suddenly, he looks so very young.

'They always do a last round to check we're asleep so you'll have to pretend to be until then. Don't even whisper to me. After that we need to move fast and quietly. I don't know if Matron will stay up to wait for the delivery. So wear your trainers. And something warm. Okay?'

He nods through his snot.

'And don't say anything to anyone. Please.'

He almost smiles. 'Who am I going to tell?'

With that, I leave him to it. Every vein in my body thumps and pounds as I head to the dorm to get my washbag so I can brush my teeth. We're going to do it. We're actually going to do it.

*

Tom has opened a window and it's cold but the smell still creeps into every corner of the room, and even when I press my face into my sheets it's strong and sweet, as if something rotten has soaked into the cotton. The nurse's face crinkles slightly when she comes around with the pills, and Ashley's misfortune is mine and Louis' good luck because she doesn't really watch whether we swallow properly or not. She's trying to decide which one of us is the source of the stink. It doesn't take long.

No one complains when Ashley prays tonight, muttering beside his bed. I don't believe in his God but I send silent good wishes out there for him anyway. It can't do any harm even if it's not going to do any good. As the lights flick off, I think of Clara in her bed, waiting just like me and Louis are. I tingle with excitement and nerves. *Please don't let anything go wrong*, I beg, of fate or nature or simple luck. *Please let this work*.

We lie there in silence as Tom and Ashley sink into sleep and squeeze our eyes shut when the nurses do their final rounds. I wait until I sense the almost imperceptible shift in the fabric of the house that signals the slump into relaxed quiet. The nurses have shuffled away to their quarters. The children are all asleep. I leave it a little longer, always so cautious. Clara is probably sitting on her bed ready to go, foot tapping impatiently on the floor.

Not a creature was stirring, not even a mouse.

I don't know where the rhyme comes from but it's loud in my head as I push my covers off. The mice are escaping. Or maybe we're rats fleeing a sinking ship. Whatever. We're getting out of here. My heart is in my throat as I tap Louis' shoulder. He's up in a moment and we silently pull on our clothes. He doesn't look at me, but his face is tight and determined. I imagine mine is the same.

'You ready?' I whisper when he's pulled his trainers on. He nods. I take one last glance at Tom and Ashley and then leave Dorm 4 for the last time. I feel a twinge of something sad inside, but then I turn away, letting my excitement take over. No more looking back. The future is waiting for us. My heart races, part nerves but mainly pure exhilaration.

The corridor is cool and dark but the floorboards are kind and don't creak as we head for Clara's dorm. The wood has been our quiet ally in the night and it's stupid but I wish them a silent farewell. I can't see any lights on anywhere and everything is still. Matron's office is the only room we have to worry about. I dread walking into the kitchen and finding her there, or her office door flying open and her catching us as we pass. But those fears can wait. First we have to get Clara. She'll make me braver. She always does.

We stay silent as we creep towards the girls' dorm, Louis staying close to me like a small child next to a parent. I carefully open the door already grinning expectantly, eager to see her face glowing and ready to go. I'm so excited about the future that it takes me a moment to see the obvious flaw in the present moment.

Clara isn't in the room. My grin fades, confused, into a frown. Has she gone down already? Did I mishear what she said? As I stand, fixed to the spot, Louis pushes past me to her neatly made bed.

'Toby,' he whispers. 'Over here.' He takes a folded piece of paper from the mattress and holds it up. 'It's got your name on it.'

I open it, and whatever I'm expecting, it's not what I read there.

Dear Toby,
I've tried to think of a thousand ways to say this that are better or easier but I just keep coming up blank. I don't even want to write it down but I have to. I can't bring myself to say it out loud, and definitely not to you.
I can't come with you.
I wish with all my heart that I could, but I can't. It wouldn't be fair, not on you, or on anyone one else out there in the big, beautiful wide world.
I've got sick and I can't pretend it's not happening any more.
I'm sorry I didn't say goodbye but that would have hurt too much. I can't even write this without crying, so I hope you

*understand. There's so many things I want to
say to you but it would take me a lifetime (ha!
Sometimes you have to see the funny side)
to write them all down, and none of them
would be good enough, so all I'll say is this.*

*I love you very, very, very much with all
my heart. Thank you for making me so so
happy. I wouldn't change anything.*

*Go and find the sunshine, Mermaid King.
I'll always be with you. I'll be in the waves
and the water and the sea breeze.*

I love you.

Clara.

I stare at it for a long moment, unable to take
it in. How can she not be coming? Where has she
gone? I think of her strange mood of the past two
days. How much she's been sleeping. How upset she
was that I hadn't woken her on our last night. How
fine she was with me asking to bring Louis. Now I
know why. She knew then she wasn't coming. She
had her own secret. *I've got sick and I can't pretend
it's not happening any more.* I see the words, but
I still can't take them in. It's wrong. It has to be. I
think of the bruise on her hip. The way she flinched
when I touched her and didn't want to have sex
until we'd escaped. How she got dressed instead
of wearing her nightshirt. The world is unsteady
under my feet and my blood has run cold.

'Is she sick?' Louis asks. He's licking his lips, his nervous tic.

'No,' I say, automatically, and crumple the paper into my pocket. A balance with the letter in my other. Yin and yang. I want to throw up.

'Come on,' I whisper, 'let's find her.' We can't go without her. We just can't. This was all her idea. I don't think about Louis' question. Ashley's sick, not Clara. She's made a mistake, that's all. We start searching the empty dorms. She's not in any of them. She's not in the playroom. I don't know where she is.

Finally we creep past Matron's room, although the thin strip of orange coming from under the door doesn't scare me this time. I don't care if she's awake. None of that matters. I only care about finding Clara. She's not in the kitchen, either. She's gone.

I feel sick. My heart races. The boat will be coming soon and I don't know what to do.

'Are we going, Toby?' Louis looks worried. I've built up his hopes and now I might smash them. Louis can't go without me – he doesn't know where the house and the jetty are. But can I really go without Clara? And without even saying goodbye? Could I take Louis off to the distant sunshine? Louis is the cleverest person I've ever met. If anyone can find money and get across borders, he can. Louis deserves that life. I stare at the back door in the gloom for a long moment while I weigh it all up.

'Yes,' I say suddenly. 'Yes, we're going.' My decision made, I immediately feel better and we move fast. Within minutes we're climbing onto the bins and over the gate. It's dark and although the sky is clear, the moonlight only falls in pools on the road. We pause for a moment and I stare back at the house with mixed emotions. I will never see it or anyone inside it again. The windows glint dark like birds' eyes and I'm sure the house is nodding me forward. A house is a home, and if it has a soul or atoms or whatever, then it's built to protect. The house wants us to be free, I'm sure of it. I think of the initials carved in the tree whose branches rustle slightly in the night breeze. I hope the tree lives a long, long time.

'Toby?' Louis whispers.

He breaks the moment and I take his hand like I used to hold Clara's, although this time it's me leading, me being the confident one. Our breath is ragged by the time we round the corner and head down towards the water.

There's a light on upstairs in the house and I signal Louis to be quiet as we creep past. There's no sign of the boat yet, so we still have time. I'm flooded with relief. I lead him to the edge of the jetty.

'What now, Toby?'

Louis looks like a kid beside me, his coat zipped up to his chin and his face slightly shell-shocked. He's had a lot to take in. He's got more to come.

He'll have to grow up fast, but he can do it. I'm sure of it. It's time to set him free.

'The rowing boat.' We hunch over to stay as low as possible in case whoever lives in the house peers out and sees us as we trot halfway along the creaking wood. I peer over the side and see it rocking there, tied to the post. The sea looks cold around it. I try not to think about that. 'Get in.'

He does as he's told and I crouch down at the jetty's edge and peer at him below. 'When the boat comes, paddle around to the back of it and climb on. Hide in the lifeboat if there is one. If not, just find an out-of-the-way corner and stay there.'

'What do you mean?' He frowns, confused. 'Why are you telling me what to do?'

'For someone so clever, you can be fucking thick sometimes.' I smile as I fumble in my pocket for the letter with our test results on it. I give it to him. 'Do something with this. Copy it and send it to the newspapers. You're the smartest person I've ever known – you'll work something out.'

'But you're coming, too.'

'No, Louis.' I shake my head. 'I'm not.'

'But Toby—' He looks like he's going to cry and that makes my throat tighten and my nose itch, but I tough it out.

'Don't go home. Or even write to your family. Not at first. It won't be safe.'

'But—'

'Have you got all that? Tell me you've got all that.'

He stares at me. 'I've got it,' he says softly.

'You have to make this work for all of us, Louis. This life business. Will you do that?' I'm biting back my own tears now. He nods.

'And I'm sorry, Louis, I'm sorry about Will. I'm sorry about everything.'

'I'm sorry I got mad.' He reaches up and grabs at my hand. He squeezes it so tight I don't think he'll ever let me go. 'Please come with me.'

I carefully pull my hand away before I can change my mind and jump in there with him. 'I can't, Louis. I just can't.'

I grin then, wide and easy, and I'm surprised how natural it is. The last embers of the ball of dread in my stomach blow away in the breeze. I am as free as a bird. The master of my own destiny. 'Be lucky, Louis. And don't be a total nerd all your life.'

He smiles back at me and for a second everything is perfect.

'Goodbye, Louis,' I say.

'Goodbye, Toby.'

And then I'm running as fast as I can away from the jetty and the house and back to the road. I know where I have to go. I have to go home.

TWENTY-FOUR

I see the tiny flicker of the candle as I run along the beach, the wet sand and shingle crunching under my feet. The sea rustles as it laps against the land and I'm sure it's applauding me. I'm breathless when I reach the mouth of the cave.

'You didn't wake me,' I say, grinning. 'It's our last night and you didn't wake me.'

'Toby?' Clara stares up at me. She'd been lost in thought but now stares, utterly aghast. 'What are you doing? You should be waiting for the boat. Go back to the boat.' She stands, angry and upset. 'You can't be here!'

'Louis' there,' I say. 'And I *can* be here. I belong here.'

'But you can't . . . I don't want you here—'

I wrap my arms around her and kiss her, forcing her to be quiet, and I don't care that she tastes funny, sick; she's Clara and I love her. She's me and I'm her. We can't be parted.

'I want to be here,' I say.

'I'm sorry,' she says. Her anger has gone, but she sounds sad.

'What for?'

She steps back and lifts up her top. Her whole body is covered in black patches. The bruise I saw on her hip must have been the start. Now her pale skin has all but vanished.

I lean forward and gently kiss her belly button. I don't care that she kept her sickness a secret from me. I think of the secret I'm keeping from her. The letter now in Louis' pocket. The last paragraph. The last line:

> *Testing concludes that neither of these patients carries the Defective gene and their original results must have been contaminated samples. They are both healthy, normal subjects.*

Some secrets are better kept than shared. It doesn't matter now anyway. I've made my choice. I've chosen Clara.

'I'm not going back to the house,' she says simply. 'I won't go to the sanatorium.'

'I know. I figured that out.' I sit on the rocks and she sits beside me. 'I'm not going back to the house, either.'

'But if you leave now you could still catch the boat,' she says. 'There's time.'

I smile and shake my head. I'm not going with Louis. Nor am I going back to the house. I'm staying right here, by her side, where I belong.

'I figure I'll just sit right here with you.' I'm controlling my own destiny, and my fate is with her. It always has been.

'But you don't understand—' she starts.

'Yes, I do.' I push a strand of her beautiful hair from her eyes. 'Together for ever,' I say.

There should be so much weight in those words, but they're light as snowflakes on my tongue. I think maybe the right words always are.

Her eyes widen slightly and I see a range of emotions flicker in them. Surprise, fear, and then finally, as my meaning dawns on her, a bright joy of relief. Happiness. She smiles back.

'You're going to stay with me?'

'Together for ever,' I repeat, and wink at her. My heart is so full of love there's no room for the dark ball in the pit of my stomach any more.

'Together for ever,' she says and leans into my shoulder.

In the distance I hear the first thrum of boat engines, almost ghostly, but there all the same. Good. We got the date right.

'I think Louis will make it,' I say, sniffing in the breeze and staring out at the water. He's clever. And he won't want to let me down. He'll make it.

'I hope so,' Clara says, and I know she means it.

There's no bitterness in her voice, no envy.

She's fiddling with something in her hands and I peer at it. It looks like a strip of black leather with prongs at the corners. I smile again. The smiles comes easily now the dread is gone.

'Where did you find that?'

'Just outside the cave. It's weird, isn't it?'

'My mum showed me one on a beach once. It's called a mermaid's purse.' I kiss her head. 'A mermaid purse for a Mermaid Queen.'

'No shit!' She grins wide and lets out a tinkling laugh that the cave holds on to, echoing it back to us as if the rocky walls are joining in.

'Yes shit.'

We look out over the water for a while, arms around each other and her head on my shoulder. There are no bright lights in the sky tonight but it's beautiful all the same. I think the water will be cold when it comes.

'It's been brilliant, hasn't it?' she murmurs.

'Yes,' I say. 'Yes, it has.'

She sniffs and we kiss again, and just enjoy each other's quiet company. We don't say a lot. There isn't a lot left to say. The house is gone. *Before* is gone. *After* is gone. There's only us and the cave and now. But we have burned brightly, me and Clara, and that's all that matters. We just sit and wait for dawn to break and the curious waves to creep towards the cave. I wonder how long the cave will hold us before the tide stakes its claim and we slip into the depths like mermaids. I don't mind much either way, as long as we're together.

After a while, the candle splutters out.

'My mum wasn't a bitch,' I say eventually when my legs are numb with cold. There's no beach left outside the cave entrance and soon there'll be no way back to the cliff path. If there's a last moment to change my mind, this is it, but I don't. I don't even consider it. I just want to unsay my lie to someone. It's suddenly important. 'I don't know why I said she was.'

'Good,' Clara says. 'That's a good thing.'

She wraps her arms around my neck and kisses me some more. We don't stop kissing, not even when the cold water laps at our jeans and makes us gasp and shiver. We breathe each other in for as long as we can. I fill my hands with her warm, wild hair, relishing the thick texture. Her mouth is soft and I can feel all her love mingling with mine. She laughs for a moment, our faces close. Her teeth are white and bright. Her freckles sit like stars on her face.

'I love you, Toby,' she whispers through chattering teeth as the sea rises around us.

'I love you too, Clara,' I whisper back.

I'm smiling although tears sting my eyes. I hold her tight and kiss her some more. I'm going to keep on kissing her for as long as I can. I don't think about the black forever darkness of the water. I think about mermaids. I think about the boat. I hope Louis has got away. I hope he lives a long and fantastic life. I hope he finds someone he can be as perfectly happy with as Clara has made me. I think about all the atoms racing around the world, all the people who have ever been, now in the trees and the waves and the wind. I think about our initials carved in the old oak's bark that will be there for hundreds of years. Mainly, as the sea pulls at us and my heart races and we cling to each other, I think about Clara and me and how lucky we were to find each other and how brilliant life has been. How brilliant she is. How brilliant love is.

We hold on to each other even as the waves close over our heads. As my final breath burns in my lungs, I keep my lips pressed to hers while her mermaid hair streams like seaweed around us.

I am not afraid.

THE END

ACKNOWLEDGEMENTS

Thanks once again to Gillian Redfearn and the whole team at Gollancz for all their support with this book, and of course my lovely agent Veronique Baxter. A special thanks also to Lee Thompson who has to put up with all my writery struggles and knows that most of them can be solved with a good whinge and a glass of wine and some chocolate. He is the best.

ABOUT THE AUTHOR

Sarah Pinborough is a critically acclaimed horror, thriller and YA author. She has written for *New Tricks* on the BBC and has an original horror film in development. Sarah won the British Fantasy Award for Best Novella with *Beauty* in 2013, Best Short Story in 2009, and has three times been shortlisted for Best Novel. She has also been shortlisted for a World Fantasy Award.

www.sarahpinborough.com

TALES FROM THE KINGDOMS

by Sarah Pinborough

In Sarah Pinborough's wicked retellings of
three classic fairy tales, nothing is quite as you
remember it...

POISON
A wicked Snow White tale

CHARM
A wicked Cinderella tale

BEAUTY
A wicked Sleeping Beauty tale

For more fantastic fiction, author events, exclusive
excerpts, competitions, limited editions and more

VISIT OUR WEBSITE
titanbooks.com

LIKE US ON FACEBOOK
facebook.com/titanbooks

FOLLOW US ON TWITTER
@TitanBooks

FOLLOW US ON INSTAGRAM
instagram.com/titan_books

EMAIL US
readerfeedback@titanemail.com